The yellowbacks... classics of popular fiction

The yellowjackets or yellowbacks were a great series of bestselling adventure and crime thrillers that had its origins in the mid to late 19th century following on from the 'penny dreadfuls'. They virtually began the mass market revolution of the early 20th century with a clear standard format and imprint/series livery (what would today be called branding). Hodder & Stoughton published the yellowjackets in two main series with series run dates of: 1923-1939 and later 1949-1957.

As the tagline ('where thrillers really began') on the back cover implies, the imprint and series focused on thrillers that were the bestsellers of their time. This current reissue or retro revival if you will, brings back many of these masterpieces, now classics in their own way and extends it further by including key titles from that period that were either great crime or thriller or even general commercial fiction (including sub-genres of noir, horror, gothic, romance, westerns, etc.) influences of their time. There are some perennial favourites and many rarities either lost or not easily available being revived in the current series. Writers and characters ranged from adventure heroes like Bulldog Drummond, Allan Quatermain, Richard Hannay or the Saint through thriller grandmasters Edgar Wallace and E. Phillips Oppenheim, crime and mystery maestros like Patricia Wentworth, GK Chesterton, Agatha Christie and the Detection club, to western and swashbucklers like Zane Grey, Max Brand, Captain Blood and even romance or general fiction classics like Hermina Black, Denise Robins, Marie Corelli or Stella Morton. These were books that had storytelling at their heart and always entertained.

The yellowbacks had both hardback (with varying design elements) and paperback (which built the series look) versions with the latter still carrying the imprint 'yellowjacket'. The current reissues pay tribute to both and use an amalgam of elements from both editions while retaining the complete yellow (or 'mustard-plaster') livery with the author's name in blue beveled type with a 'simulated emboss' effect and a white outer 'outline', and the book title in black. These reissues retain the distinctive size of the original mass market paperback and follow the three main category variations—the thrillers (crime, westerns, mystery, adventure) had blue lettering for the author's name, while Romance and softer general fiction had red; and other categories like humour had green.

For more detail and a full list of titles visit https://www.hachetteindia.com/home/yellowbacks

THE ASHES TO ASHES

THE ASHES TO ASHES

Isabel Egenton Ostrander (1883–1924) was a mystery writer of the early twentieth century who used her own name and the pseudonyms 'Robert Orr Chipperfield', 'David Fox', and 'Douglas Grant'.

She was born in New York City to Thomas E. Ostrander and Harriet Elizabeth Bradbrook. Her Ostrander pedigree goes back to seventeenth-century Kingston, New York. She married songwriter Arthur Lamb in June 1907 and filed for divorce less than a year later.

Ostrander is also one of the creator the first blind detective which has become a sub-genre in detective fiction.

Her 1915 novel *At One-Thirty*, introduces her detective Damon Gaunt but there is speculation that there was an earlier short story that saw magazine publication but was lost. (Blind detective Thornley Colton appeared in some short stories in *People's Ideal Fiction Magazine* in early 1913 that weren't collected in book form until 1915, while Max Carrados by Ernest Bramah reached the periodicals in 1913, but anthologization in 1914. In no case is bibliography complete for periodicals, and either might be the first, though Max Carrados was the first in book publication).

In the 1920s, Ostrander was notable enough that Agatha Christie parodied her in her Tommy and Tuppence anthology, *Partners in Crime*. Tommy and Tuppence can be seen to be modelling their detective skills after Ostrander's characters, McCarty and Riordan.

THE
ASHES TO
ASHES

Isabel Ostrander

hachette

The Ashes to Ashes
First serialized in *All-Story Weekly*, in 1919; and published
in book form by: R. M. McBride and Co., New York 1919.

This Hodder Yellowback edition © Hachette India 2023
(Registered Name: Hachette Book Publishing India Pvt. Ltd.)
An Hachette UK Company www.hachetteindia.com

1

All rights reserved. No part of the publication may be reproduced, stored in a retrieval system (including but not limited to computers, disks, external drives, electronic or digital devices, e-readers, websites), or transmitted in any form or by any means (including but not limited to cyclostyling, photocopying, docutech or other reprographic reproductions, mechanical, recording, electronic, digital versions) without the prior written permission of the publisher, nor be otherwise circulated in any form of binding or cover other than that in which it is published and without a similar condition being imposed on the subsequent purchaser.

The texts in these editions in most cases have been reprinted as is, with minimal editorial changes and by and large no bowdlerizing for political correctness; though in some editions, a few words and phrases considered archaic, or those considered offensive now, along with archaic punctuation may have been modified in places to make the text more accessible to today's readers. The narratives, language, beliefs, social mores and/or cultural depictions, in these volumes are a reflection of their times and must be viewed as such. They may also contain certain cultural, racial and gender prejudices and stereotypes that may be outdated or clearly wrong then and wrong today; but their removal would be tantamount to claiming these prejudices never existed. The Publisher does not endorse or support those depictions or stereotypes; and these books have been made available for a discerning audience that will read it for entertainment value and a chronicle/record of popular fiction of past times.

Cover design by Priya Singh adapted from the original classic yellowjacket by
Hodder & Stoughton.

Cover illustration by Ishan Trivedi.

Series note: Some of the books in the series (unless otherwise credited) may have cover or inside illustrations from the original yellowbacks or early editions, and while full restoration has been attempted, some images may be grainy or faded due to the condition of the original material. The end notes or bonus material or blurb details may have been sourced from the public domain or free use publications such as Wikipedia and attribution is hereby made also allowing similar free use reproduction from here. Sources requiring further specific attribution may write in and further detailing and/or corrections shall be made in subsequent printings/editions.

Reprint specifications may be subject to change including but not limited to
finishes, paper, colour sections.

ISBN: 978-93-5731-048-2

Hachette Book Publishing India Pvt. Ltd.
4th & 5th Floors, Corporate Centre,
Plot No. 94, Sector 44, Gurugram - 122 003, India

Typeset in Electra LT STD 10/12.5 pt by Manipal Technologies Limited, Manipal

Printed and bound in India by Manipal Technologies Limited, Manipal

CONTENTS

I	The Lie	1
II	The Trap	12
III	The Blow	23
IV	The Long Night	38
V	When Morning Dawned	50
VI	The Verdict	61
VII	The Letter	72
VIII	The Truth	83
IX	The Escape	94
X	A Chance Meeting	105
XI	Luck	117
XII	Mirage	129
XIII	The Black Bag	141
XIV	In His Hands	152
XV	Ashes to Ashes	165
XVI	The Second Vigil	176
XVII	Missing	185
XVIII	The Girl in the Watch Case	199
XIX	Found	212
XX	Marked	224
XXI	The Unconsidered Trifle	237
XXII	At the Club	249
XXIII	The Scourge of Memory	262
XXIV	If George Knew	273
XV	The Final Test	284
XVI	The Key	293
XXVII	In the Library	303
XXVIII	Just a Moment Please	316

I

THE LIE

"Well, that's the situation." Wendle Foulkes' keen old eyes narrowed as they gazed into the turbulent ones of his client across the wide desk. "This last batch of securities is absolutely all that you have left of your inheritance from your father. Leave them alone where they are and you are sure of three thousand a year for yourself and for Leila after you."

Norman Storm struck the desk impatiently, and his lean, aristocratic face darkened.

"Three thousand a year! It wouldn't cover the running expenses of the car and our country club bills alone!" he exclaimed. "I tell you, Foulkes, this investment is a sure thing; it will pay over thirty per cent in dividends in less than four years. I have straight inside information on it—"

"So you had on all the other impulsive, ill-judged ventures that have wiped out your capital, Norman." The attorney sighed wearily. "I don't want to rub it in, but do you realize that you have squandered nearly four hundred thousand dollars in the past ten years on wildcat schemes and speculations? You've come to the end now; think it over. Your salary with the Mammoth Trust Company is fifteen thousand a year—on eighteen you and your wife ought to be living fairly comfortably. I grant you that three thousand income per anum isn't much to leave Leila in the event of your death, but it is better than the risk of utter insolvency, and she's been spending her own money pretty fast lately."

"It is hers, to do with as she pleases!" Storm retorted sulkily and then flushed as the school-boyishness of his own attitude was borne in upon his consciousness. "You cannot make big money unless you take a chance. I've been unlucky, that's all. My father made all his in Wall Street, and his father before him—"

"In solid investments, not speculations; and they were on the inside themselves. They had the capital to take a gambler's chance and the acumen to play the game." Foulkes rose and laid his hand paternally upon the younger man's shoulder. "Forgive me, my boy, but you haven't the temperament, the knowledge of when to stop and the strength to do it. Of course, this money is yours unreservedly; you may have it if you want to risk this last venture, but it will take some time for me to convert the securities into cash. Remember, you have reached the bottom of the basket; I only want you to stop and consider, and not to jeopardize the last few thousand you have in the world."

Outside in the bright May sunshine once more, Storm shouldered his way through the noon-tide throng on the busy pavement with scant ceremony, his resentment hot against the man he had just left. Confound old Foulkes! Why didn't he keep his smug counsels for those who came sniveling to him for them? As if he, an official of a huge and noted corporation, were a mere lad once more, to be lectured for over-spending his allowance!

The fact that the position he held with the trust company entailed no financial responsibility and was practically an honorary one, granted him solely because of his father's former connection with that institution, was a point which did not present itself to his mind. He was occupied in closing his mental eyes to the truth of the lawyer's arraignment, bolstering his defiance with excuses for the repeated fiascos of his past ventures, and the secret knowledge that Foulkes had read him aright only added fuel to the flames.

Still inwardly seething, he crossed Broadway and plunged into another narrow, crowded cross-street lined by towering office buildings whose walls rose like cliffs on either side. From the tallest of these, an imposing structure of white stone which reared a shaft high above its neighbors, a woman emerged and mingled with the hurrying host before him. She was not a toiler of the financial district; that was evident from the costly simplicity of the smart little toque upon her shining golden hair and the correct lines of her severely tailored costume. She was undeniably pretty with the delicate, tender irregularity of feature which just escapes actual beauty; yet it was not that which caused Norman Storm to halt and drove from him all thought of the late interview.

It was his wife. Leila! What possible errand could have brought her to the city and to this portion of it? Surely an unexpected one, for she had not told him of any such intention; indeed, to his knowledge she had never before invaded the precincts of finance, and he could conceive of no possible reason for her presence there.

As he paused, momentarily petrified with astonishment, a stout little man upon the opposite curb also caught sight of the young woman's hurrying figure, and he, too, stopped in surprise, a smile lighting his plain, commonplace features. Then, as though drawn by a magnet, his pale, rather faded blue eyes traveled straight to where Norman Storm stood, the surprise deepened, and with a half-audible exclamation he started across the street toward him; but a long double line of drays and motor trucks barred his way.

Meanwhile Leila had vanished utterly in the crowd, and Storm realizing the futility of an attempt to overtake her, dismissed the matter from his thoughts with a shrug. She would tell him of her errand, of course, on his return home; and a conference of importance awaited his immediate presence at the office of the trust company.

The conference developed complications which delayed him until long after the closing hour, forcing him to forego an engagement with Millard for a round of golf at the country club. He likewise missed his accustomed train bearing the club car out to Greenlea and was compelled to herd in with commuters bound for the less exclusive suburban communities on the line.

Storm was not a snob, but the atmosphere of petty clerking and its attendant interests grated upon his tired, highly strung sensibilities; the unsatisfactory interview of the morning with Foulkes returned to exasperate him further and he was in no very genial frame of mind when he alighted at the station.

But Barker was on hand promptly with the smart little car which consumed such an incredible amount of gasolene, and the air of the soft spring twilight was infinitely grateful after the smoke and stuffiness of the train. As they drove swiftly past the rolling lawns of one spacious landscape garden after another, each burgeoning with its colorful promise of the blossoming year, his taut nerves relaxed, and he settled back in contented ease. What if he had been unlucky in past speculations, if old Foulkes did consider him an unstable weakling? Leila believed in him, and she was his, all his!

The glimmer of white upon the veranda half-hidden in the trees resolved itself into a slender, fairy-like figure, and as he alighted from the car and mounted the steps she caught his hands in the eager, childish way which was one of her chief charms.

"Oh, Norman, how late you are! Poor dear, did they keep him at that wretched old office and make him miss his golf?" She lifted her face for his evening kiss, and her soft, blue eyes glowed with a deep, warm light. "George is here; I mean, he 'phoned from the Millards'. He's coming over for dinner."

"That's the reason for the debut of the new white gown, eh?" Storm laughed. "By Jove, I believe I ought to be jealous of old George! When a man's wife and his best friend—"

"Don't!" There was a quick note almost of distress in Leila's tones. "I don't like to hear you joke that way about him, dear. He seems so lonely, standing just outside of life, somehow. He hasn't anything of this!"

She waved her little hands in a comprehensive gesture as if to take in the whole atmosphere of the home, and her husband laughed carelessly once more.

"It's his own fault, then. Don't waste any sympathy on him on that score, Leila. George is a confirmed old bachelor; he would run a mile from a suggestion of domesticity." At the door he turned. "Oh, I say dear—"

But Leila was already down the steps and had started across the lawn, at the farther side of which Storm discerned a short stout commonplace figure approaching; and turning once more he hastened to his room to change.

George Holworthy, two years his senior, had been a classmate of Storm's at the university twenty years before, and the companionship—rather a habit of association than a friendship—which had grown up between the undisciplined, high-spirited boy and his duller, more phlegmatic comrade had proved a lasting one despite the wide dissimilarity in their natures. Storm was too fastidious, Holworthy too seriously inclined, for dissipation to have attracted either of them, but while the former had drifted, plunging recklessly from one speculation to another, the latter had plodded slowly, steadily ahead until at forty-two he had amassed a comfortable fortune and attained a position of established recognition among his business associates.

An hour later, as they sat drinking their after-dinner coffee on the veranda, Leila's words returned to his mind, and Storm found himself eying his guest in half-disparaging appraisal. Good, stupid old George! How stodgy and middle-aged he was getting to be! His hair was noticeably thin on top and peppered with gray and he looked like anything but an assured, successful man of affairs as he lounged, round-shouldered, in his chair, his mild eyes blinking nearsightedly at Leila, who sat on the veranda steps cradling one chiffon clad knee between her clasped hands.

George looked every day of fifty. Now, if he would only patronize a smart tailor, join a gymnasium and work some of that adipose tissue off, he wouldn't be half bad-looking. Unconsciously Norman Storm squared his shoulders and drew his slim, lithe form erect in his chair. Then his muscles tightened convulsively and he sat with every nerve tense, for a snatch of the disjointed conversation had penetrated his abstraction and its import stunned him.

"You weren't in town today, then?" The question, seemingly a repetition of some statement of Leila's, came stammeringly from Holworthy's lips.

"Oh, dear, no!" Her laugh tinkled out upon the soft air. "I haven't been in perfect ages! It doesn't attract me now that spring is here."

Not in town! But he had seen her himself! Sheer surprise held Storm silent for a moment.

When he spoke his voice sounded strange to his own ears.

"Where were you all day, Leila? What did you do with yourself?"

"I—I lunched out at the Ferndale Inn with Julie Brewster." Her tone was low, and she did not turn her head toward him as she replied, adding hurriedly: "George, when are you going to give up those stuffy rooms of yours in town and take a bungalow out here? You can keep bachelor hall just as well; lots of nice men are doing it..."

Through the desultory talk which followed, Storm sat as if in a trance. If the blue tailored frock and hat with its saucy quill had not been familiar to him in every line, he could still not have mistaken that glimpse of her profile, the carriage of her head, the coil of shining, spun-gold hair. Ferndale Inn was twenty miles away, a good sixty from town, and inaccessible save by motor; she could not possibly have reached there in time for luncheon, for it was after twelve when she had passed him on that crowded, downtown street. She had told a deliberate falsehood; but why?

"I think if you don't mind, George, I'll say good night." Leila rose at last, her white gown shimmering in the darkness. "I feel a bit tired and headachey—"

"Not faint, Leila?" Holworthy spoke in quick solicitude.

"One of my old attacks you mean?" She laughed lightly. "Indeed, no! I haven't had one in ever so long. It is nothing that a good, early sleep won't put right. I suppose it is no use to ask you to stay overnight, George?"

He shook his head.

"Must be at the office early tomorrow. I'll catch the ten-forty train to town. Good night, Leila. Sleep well."

"Good night." She touched her husband's cheek softly with her finger-tips as she passed him, and he felt that they were icy cold. "Put on your coat if you go to the station with George, dear; these early Spring nights are deceptive."

Deceptive! And she, who had never lied to him before in the ten years of their married life, was going to her rest with a falsehood between them! Storm felt as if someone had struck him suddenly, unfairly between the eyes. The fact in itself was a staggering one, but a score of questions beat upon his brain. Why, if she wished to conceal her errand to town, had she not been content merely to deny her presence there? Why drag in the Ferndale Inn and Julie Brewster?

As if his thoughts had in some way communicated themselves to his companion, the latter asked suddenly:

"What sort of a place is this Ferndale Inn, Norman?" '

"Oh, the usual thing. Imitation Arcadia at exorbitant prices. Why?"

"Oh, I've heard things." The tip of Holworthy's cigar described a glowing arc as he gestured vaguely. "I guess it is quiet enough; Leila wouldn't see anything wrong there in a million years unless she happened to run into some of her own set in an indiscreet hour. I'm informed that it is quite a rendezvous for those who are misunderstood at their own firesides."

"George, you're getting to be a scandal-monger!" Storm laughed shortly, his thoughts still centered on his problem. "The Inn is under new management this season, and anyway you needn't take a crack at our set out here. They're up-to-date, a bit unconventional, perhaps, but never step out of bounds. The trouble with you, old man, is that you're old-fashioned and narrow; you don't get about enough—"

"I get about enough to hear things!" Holworthy retorted with unusual acerbity. "Your crowd here at Greenlea is no different from any other small community of normal people thrown together intimately under the abnormal conditions created by too much money and not enough to do. I don't mean you two, but look around you. This Julie Brewster of whom Leila spoke just now; she is Dick Brewster's wife, isn't she? I don't discuss women as a rule, but she's going it rather strong with young Mattison. Dick's not a fool; he'll either blow up some day or find somebody's else wife to listen to his tale of woe and hand out the sympathy. That is merely a case in point."

"And just before your arrival, Leila was bemoaning the fact that you'd missed domestic happiness!"

"Was she? Well, there are different kinds of happiness in this world, you know; perhaps I've found mine in just looking on." He rose. "I'll get on down to the station now, old man. No, don't rout out Barker; I'd rather walk."

"I'll stroll down with you, then." Storm paused to light a cigarette, then followed his guest down the veranda steps. He shrank from facing Leila again that night; he would wait until the morning, and perhaps later she would explain. Perhaps the explanation of her prevarication lay in the fact of George's presence; whatever her errand, she might not have cared to discuss it before him. As this solution presented itself to his mind Storm grasped at it eagerly. That was it, of course! What a fool he had been to worry, to doubt her! He could have laughed aloud in sheer relief.

"This is a great little place you have out here, Norman." Holworthy halted at the gate to glance back at the house outlined in the moonlight. "I don't wonder you're proud of it. The grounds are perfect, too; that little corner there, where the hill dips down and the trout stream runs through, couldn't have been laid out better if you had planned it."

"It wouldn't be a little corner if that old rascal Jaffray would sell me that stretch of land which cuts into mine, confound him!" Storm plunged with renewed zest into a topic ever rankling with him. "I've tried everything to force his hand, but the scoundrel hangs on to it through nothing in the world but blasted perversity! I tell you, George, it spoils the whole place for me sometimes, and I feel like selling out!"

"Leave all this after the years you and Leila have put in beautifying it because you can't have an extra bit that belongs to someone else?" Holworthy shook his head. "Don't be a fool, Norman! If you can only get another head gardener as good as MacWhirter was—"

"I'll have MacWhirter himself back in a month," Storm interrupted. "Didn't Leila tell you? She saw him yesterday at the Base Hospital. He has lost a leg, but he'll stump around as well as ever on an artificial one, and if he had to be wheeled about in a chair Leila wouldn't hear of not having him back. She is the most loyal little soul in the world."

"Of course she is!" Holworthy assented hastily. "You're the luckiest man living, Norman, and she is the best of women!"

He paused abruptly, and when he spoke again there was an odd, constrained note in his usually placid tones.

"How about the South American investment? I wish you wouldn't go into it—"

"So, evidently, does Foulkes!" Storm retorted. "I had it out with him today, and the old pettifogger talked as though I were the original Jonah; told me to my face that I had no head for business—"

"Well, he's right on that," remarked the other, with the candor of long association. "This South American thing isn't sound; I've looked into it, and I know. The big fellows would have taken hold of it long ago if it had been worth while. You certainly cannot afford to take a chance where they won't."

The discussion which ensued lasted until the station was reached and Holworthy, with a final wave of his hand, disappeared into the smoker of the train which was just pulling out.

Storm had had rather the better of the argument, as usual, for the other's slower mind was not sufficiently agile to grasp his brilliant but shallow points and turn them against him, and he started homeward in high good humor. How peaceful and still everything lay under the pale shimmering haze of moonlight! Leila would be fast asleep by now. What a child she was at heart, in spite of her twentyeight years! How she had hesitated, even over that little white lie that she had been to Ferndale Inn with Julie Brewster, and how stupid he had been to force it by questioning her before George!

The house as he approached it lay cloaked in darkness amid the shadow of the trees save only the subdued ray of light which shone out from the hall door, which in the custom of Greenlea he had left ajar. His footsteps made no sound on the soft, springing turf of the lawn, but when he reached the veranda the sharp, insistent shrill of the telephone came to his ears.

As he started forward it ceased abruptly, and to his amazement he heard Leila's voice in a murmur of hushed inquiry. The murmur was prolonged, and after a moment he slipped into the hall and stood motionless, unconscious of his act, listening with every nerve strained to the words which issued from the library.

"It is a frightful risk, dear!... I know, I've had to fib about it already to him... No, of course he doesn't, but what if others... Yes, but he has only gone to the station with George Holworthy; he'll be back any minute, and then what can I say?... Of course I will, I promised, but you must be mad!... Yes, in ten minutes."

Storm heard the receiver click and had only time to shrink back into the embrasure of the window when Leila emerged from the library, still clad in her dinner gown, and passing him swiftly, seized a long, dark cloak from the rack and sped noiselessly out of the door.

Storm's breath caught harshly in his throat, and he took an impetuous step or two after her. Then he halted, and with head erect and clenched hands he turned and mounted the stairs.

II

THE TRAP

'Didn't you sleep well, dear? You look dreadfully tired." Leila's eyes fluttered upward to meet her husband's across the breakfast table and then lowered as she added hesitatingly: "I—I didn't hear you come in last night."

"No?" Storm gazed at her in studied deliberation as he responded. "I did not wish to disturb you."

She looked as fresh and sparkling as the morning, and the sudden wild-rose color which flooded her cheeks beneath his scrutiny heightened the charm of the picture she made; yet it sent a surge of hot resentment to his heart. Her solicitude was not for him, but in fear lest he had discovered her absence on that nocturnal errand!

He wondered at himself, at his stoic outward calm as he accepted his cup of coffee from her hands. Every fiber of him cried out to seize her hand and wring the truth from her lips, but the pride which had held him back from following her on the previous night still dominated him after sleepless hours of nerve-racking doubt. He would make sure of the truth without whining for explanations or dogging her footsteps.

Leila glanced at him furtively more than once as he forced himself to eat, then left her own breakfast almost untasted and turned with a sigh to the little pile of letters beside her plate.

As' she scanned them Storm saw her expression change, and she thrust one of the envelopes hastily beneath the rest; but not before his eyes had caught two words of the superscription upon the upper left hand corner.

"Leicester Building." That was the name of the skyscraper from which he had seen her emerge on the previous day! His hands clenched and he thrust back his chair with a harsh, grating noise as he rose.

"I must go. I am late," he muttered thickly.

"But Norman, dear, Barker hasn't brought the car around yet." Leila, too, rose from her chair and with a quick movement thrust the tell-tale letter into her belt.

"No matter, I'll walk." He turned to the door with a blind instinct of flight before he betrayed himself. If his suspicions were after all capable of an explanation other than the one his jealous fury presented he would not play the fool. But he must know!

"Will you be home early this afternoon?" Leila bent to rearrange the daffodils in a low glass bowl as she spoke, and her face was averted from him. "Early enough for your golf, I mean?"

"No, I shan't be out here until late. Don't wait dinner for me." A swift thought came to him, and he added deliberately: "There is to be a special meeting at the club in town; I'll try to catch the midnight train, but in the event that I decide to stay over, I'll 'phone, of course."

She followed him out upon the veranda for his customary farewell kiss, but to his relief he spied a familiar runabout halting at the gate and escaped from her with a wave of his hand.

"There's Millard! I'll ride down with him. Goodbye."

Millard was a golf enthusiast, and his detailed description of the previous day's game lasted throughout the interval at the station, but it fell upon deaf ears.

Storm's thoughts were in a turmoil. At one moment he felt that he could no longer endure the strain of the attitude he had assumed; that he must stop the train, rush back to his wife and demand from her the truth. At the next, his pride once more came uppermost; his pride, and the underlying doubt that his worst suspicions were actually founded on fact, which made him fear to render himself ridiculous in her eyes. It was true that she had lied about her presence in the city on the previous day, but she had gone openly to an office building at broad noon and left it alone. She had received a letter from someone in that building which she tried to keep from his observation, but her expression when she picked it up, although furtive, had not been guilty; rather, it had been full of pleased expectancy, as quickly masked. That visit, that letter might be simply explained, but the telephone call which he had overheard, the errand that had caused her, his wife, to steal from her house at midnight like a thief—!

There could be no other construction than the obvious one! He recalled her cool, unruffled assurance at the breakfast table, her charming air of solicitude at his own haggard appearance, and his blood boiled with rage. Did she think to deceive him, to keep him indefinitely in the state of fatuous complacency in which he had pitied other husbands? Was he to be spoken of, for instance, as George Holworthy had spoken of Dick Brewster the night before?

With the thought Storm glanced about him at his neighbors in the club car. If what he suspected were true, did any of them know already? Were any of them pitying him with that careless, half-contemptuous pity reserved for the deceived? He detected no sign of it, but the idea was like a knife turned in a wound, and he hurried from them as soon as the train drew in to the city station.

There he found himself mechanically making his way toward the Leicester Building, with no very clear impression of what he meant to do on arrival. Among its myriad offices, representing scores of varied financial and commercial activities, he could scarcely hope to obtain a clue to the purpose of his wife's visit; and yet the place drew him like a magnet.

Within the entrance he halted before the huge directory board with its rows of names alphabetically arranged; halted, and then stood as though transfixed. Midway down the first column a single name had leaped out to him, and its staring letters of white upon the black background seemed to dance mockingly before his vision.

"Brewster, Richard E. Insurance Broker."

Dick Brewster! The husband of that light-headed, irresponsible little Julie, the very man to whom his thoughts had turned in the train not a half-hour since! The man of whom George Holworthy had spoken—and what was it that George had said?

"She's going it rather strong with young Mattison. Dick's not a fool; he'll either blow up some day or find somebody's else wife to sympathize—" Was that the solution? Could old George, obtuse as he was, have divined the truth and been trying in his stupid, blundering fashion, to warn him? Could it actually be that the woman who bore his name, who belonged to him, his property, had dared to flout his possession of her, to supplant him with another, to make of him a byword, a thing of pitying contempt?

How long he stood there before the directory he never afterward knew. He came dimly to realize at last that in the passing crowd which brushed by him more than one turned to stare curiously at him; and, turning, he stumbled blindly toward the elevator. Alighting at Brewster's floor, he made his way to the number which had been indicated opposite the name upon the board below, and, wrenching open the door, he strode into the office.

A languid stenographer looked up from behind her typewriter.

"Mr Brewster won't be in town today. Do you want to leave any message?"

"No. I'll call again," Storm muttered. "Not—not in town today, you say?"

"He 'phoned just now from his country place; he'll be in tomorrow. Did you have an appointment with him?"

Storm shook his head, and, ignoring the card and pencil which the girl laid suggestively before him, he turned to the door.

"I'll call up tomorrow."

The elevator whirled him down to the street level once more, and as he made his way from the building his senses gradually cleared.

What an escape! That was his first thought. Had Brewster been there, in his uncontrollable rage he must have betrayed himself, given the other an opportunity to gloat over him! His fastidious soul writhed from the thought of a vulgar, sordid scene; yet the one thing in all his domineering life which he had been unable to master was his own temper, and he knew and secretly feared it. After all, suppose his wife had called at Brewster's office, that it was Brewster who had telephoned to her, Brewster whom she had gone at midnight to meet? Suppose the worst were true, these were all the facts he held with which to confront them; they could explain them away with some shallow lie and laugh in his very face! He must master himself, must bide his time until they should have played into his hands.

He strode on abruptly, heedless of the direction, shouldering from his path those who crowded in against him, unconscious of aught save the struggle which was taking place within him.

That it should have been Dick Brewster, of all men! Brewster, with his dapper little mustache and weak, effeminate face! Yet he was goodlooking, damn him, and attractive to women; younger, too, almost as young as Leila herself. Was that what George had meant when he spoke of people being thrown together intimately with too much money and not enough to do? Had he been trying to excuse them on the score of propinquity? When Storm in his own easy, complacent sophistry had twitted the other with being old-fashioned, George had asserted, with what seemed now to have added significance, that he went about enough to "hear things". So this was what he had been driving at!

And Leila herself? At thought of her Storm felt his rage rising again in an overwhelming wave. Her tenderness, the years of their happiness, their love, were blotted out in the swift fury which consumed him at this affront to his pride, his dominance. Her beauty, her charm in which he had reveled almost as a personal attribute to himself, seemed all at once hideous, baleful to him. As her smiling face rose up before his memory he could have struck it down with his bare hands. If this despicable thing were true—!

He fought back the thought, succeeded at last in forcing a measure of calmness and dragged himself to his own office, where the interminable hours wore to a close. Then he went to a club; not that which he usually frequented when in town where the small-talk of his friends would madden him, but to an older, more sedate affair, a remnant of an earlier aristocracy to a membership in which his birth had automatically elected him. There he ordered a solitary meal and afterward sat in the somber, silent library with his eyes fixed upon the solemn clock. He had said that he would take the midnight train...

Leila, after an equally solitary dinner had ensconced herself in her own dainty library at home that she might be near the telephone, should he call as he had tentatively suggested doing. No summons came, however, and it was after ten o'clock when a step sounded upon the veranda, and she sprang up, thrusting between the leaves of her book the letter over which she had been exulting; a letter which bore the superscription of the Leicester Building.

It was not her husband who stood before her when she opened the door. She paused, and then from the gloom of the veranda a voice spoke reassuringly:

"It is I, Mrs Storm; Dick Brewster. I hope you and Norman will pardon the lateness of this call, but I must see you, if you will grant me a few minutes." His quiet, pleasantly modulated voice seemed oddly shaken, and a quick constraint fell also upon Leila's manner, but she held the door wide.

"Come in, of course, Mr Brewster. My husband is not at home yet, and I am waiting up for him. You—you wanted to see him?"

"No. That is, I wished especially to see you."

He followed her into the library and took the chair she indicated, while she seated herself in her own once more and regarded him with an air of grave, troubled inquiry. His face was pale, and beneath the glow of the lamp she saw that it was working as though with some strong emotion, although he strove to remain calm.

"Mrs Storm, I want to ask you a personal question, and I hope you will not be offended. I should not have intruded at this hour, I should not have come to you at all, if your reply had not been vital to me. Will you tell me where you were yesterday?"

Leila laughed lightly but with an unmistakable note of confusion.

"That is a very simple question, Mr Brewster. I was with Julie. We motored out to the Ferndale Inn—"

"Alone, Mrs Storm?"

"Alone, of course. We went with Julie's new roadster." She paused, and then the words came in a little rush. "We didn't start out with any—any definite object, but it was such a beautiful day and it grew late, almost noon before we knew it, and we found ourselves further from home than we had realized, so we 'phoned back—at least, I did—"

"Where did you 'phone from?"

"From the Inn, when we decided to stop there for lunch. But really, Mr Brewster, I cannot quite understand—"

"I will explain in a moment. Tell me, was anyone there at the Inn whom you knew?"

Leila hesitated, biting her lips.

"The—the Featherstones—"

"Did you see them, Mrs Storm?"

"No, I—I had gone to the dressing-room to rearrange my hair, and when I rejoined Julie she told me they had just left."

"I see." Brewster nodded slowly. "Will you answer one more question, please? How did you reach home?"

"Why, the way we came, of course, in Julie's car." Leila's voice trembled slightly and her eyes wavered.

"*You* did not, Mrs Storm." His tone was gently deferential, but there was a note of finality in it which she could not combat.

"Not all the way," she amended hurriedly. "Julie dropped me at the house of some friends of mine over on Harper's Ridge, and they brought me home later."

He shook his head.

'You did not leave the Ferndale Inn with Julie."

"Mr Brewster!" Leila rose. "I have listened to you and I have answered your questions very patiently, but now I must ask you to excuse me. You have no right to question me, my conduct is no concern of yours—"

"Except where it touches upon my wife's." Her guest, too, had risen, and although he spoke quietly his voice quivered. "Your story is substantially the same as hers, but you both ignored one detail—that the Featherstones might have caught a glimpse of her companion and that others might have seen them both leave the Inn. Please believe, Mrs Storm, that I am not attempting to censure you. Your loyalty to my wife, your effort to shield her is very praiseworthy from the standpoint of friendship, but there is something holier than that which has been violated."

"Oh, not that!" Leila cried. "Julie hasn't done anything really wrong! You must believe that, Mr Brewster! Oh, I warned her not to go, that it was foolishly indiscreet!"

"Yet she went." Brewster's lips twisted in a wry smile. "I only came here to learn the truth beyond possibility of a mistake. I won't detain you any longer."

He bowed and turned to the door, but Leila sprang forward and caught his arm.

"Oh, what are you going to do?"

Brewster drew himself up, and his slight, dapper figure assumed a sudden dignity it had not borne before.

"I am going to turn her out of my house! To send her to this puppy, Mattison, whom she loves!"

"She doesn't! Mr Brewster, you must listen to me, you shall! You are on the point of making a terrible mistake, a mistake that will wreck both your lives!" Leila pleaded frantically. "Julie is not in love with Ted Mattison! It is only a flirtation; that luncheon yesterday was the merest escapade—"

"Like the other luncheons and motor trips and tetes-a-tete which have made her the talk of Greenlea for weeks past, while I was supposed to be blind and deaf and dumb?" Brewster shook off his hostess' detaining hand. "I have reached the end now—"

"But she hasn't. Will you drive her to it? She is young, only a girl, and irresponsible, but she is innocent now of any actual wrong. What if she is infatuated for the moment with Ted Mattison? It isn't love, I know that, and you—oh, I have no right to say it, but you have come to me and I cannot let you go without opening your eyes to the truth! You have neglected her for your new business, left her alone and lonely, forced her to seek companionship elsewhere. You are at least equally to blame for the situation, and now, instead of driving her from you for a mere indiscretion, now when she needs you most, you owe it to her and to yourself to win her back; not *take* her back patronizingly, forgiving and magnifying her fault, but win her, regain the love you have almost lost!" Leila paused and added softly: "You love her, and she cares for you in her heart. She is only deeply hurt at your neglect, and I think she began this affair with Ted in a childish effort just to pay you back. She is only waiting a word to turn to you again. Will you speak that word? You have your great chance now, tonight, for happiness or misery, to save her or to drive her to despair. Will you let this chance pass you by forever?"

There was a pause, and then Brewster turned away, his head bowed.

"I love her, God knows!" he groaned. "You may be right about neglect; I never thought of that, I was only working for her! If I could only believe that there was still a chance—! But I have heard and seen too much, things have gone too far—"

"They haven't. You must believe me!" Leila followed him a step or two and then halted. "Julie has been foolish, but no more. You admit that you still love her; then go home and tell her so. Tell her every day, over and over, until she believes *you* again, and realizes that her happiness lies with you."

Brewster turned once more, his head held high, and the tears glistened unashamed in his eyes.

"I will, Mrs Storm! You can never know what you have done for me, for us both! I came here tonight the most miserable of men, but you have shown me the way to happiness again."

Leila gave him both her hands with a glad little cry.

"Oh, I knew that you would understand, that you would see! I have done nothing, it is you yourself—"

"You have made me the happiest man in the world! I shall always remember my hour here tonight with you, and if ever doubt comes to me again, if my faith wavers, I shall think of what you have given me!"

He bent reverently and kissed her hands, and she bowed her head, the happy tears glistening in her own eyes.

Neither of them were aware of the soft opening and closing of the front door, neither saw the figure which halted for a moment in the doorway behind them, in time to catch the last speech which fell from Brewster's lips and witness the salutation which concluded it; neither of them heard the muffled, almost noiseless footsteps as the figure withdrew as silently as it had come and disappeared in the further recesses of the house.

III

THE BLOW

In his little den at the rear of the house Storm closed the door softly before, with shaking fingers, he sought the chain of the low light upon his desk. Then, dropping into a chair beside it, he raised clenched fists to his head as though to beat out the hideous confirmation which drummed at his brain.

It was true! His wife had betrayed him. That soft, pliant, docile thing of pink and white flesh which in his fatuous idolatry he had believed imbued with the soul of loyalty had slipped airily from his grasp, given herself, her love to another! — Love! What did she know of love or loyalty? This creature whom he had honored had dragged, was dragging his name in the dust, setting him aside as an unimportant factor, a mere dispenser of bounty to be cajoled and tolerated for his generosity, his protection, while she indulged her desires for fresh admiration, new conquests!

Curiously enough, his enmity was not active against the man he believed to be his rival. Brewster, for the moment, was a secondary consideration in his eyes; had it not been he it would have been another. The woman was to blame!

How blind she must think him! How easily she had fallen into the first simple trap he had laid for her feet! How in her fancied security, she must be laughing at him! The little acts of wifely forethought and service, evidences of which surrounded him even there in his sanctum, were but as particles of sand thrown in his eyes! His humidor freshly filled, his golf sticks of last year cleaned and laid out across the table that he might choose which ones to take to the country club for the opening of the new season!—Faugh! Did she hope by such puerile trivialities as these to prolong his unquestioning faith in her.

Against his will, the past came thronging to his mind in ever-changing scenes which he strove in vain to shut out. That summer at Bar Harbor, the moonlit nights, the little, golden-haired maid just out of school... How fast and furious his wooing had been! The dim, rustling, crowded church, the Easter lilies which banked the altar—God! he could smell their cloying fragrance now!—that radiant, fairy-like white figure moving slowly toward him down the aisle...

Storm groaned, and involuntarily covered his eyes as other pictures formed before his mental vision. Their honeymoon at the Hot Springs, that brilliant first season in town, and then her sudden illness and the dark weeks during which he had feared that she would be taken from him and he had crouched in impotent supplication before the door he might not enter. Than that exultant moment when he learned that his prayers had been answered, that she would live; poor fool, what thanks he had given!

Her convalescence had seemed to draw them more closely, tenderly together even than before; and pitilessly, mockingly his thoughts ranged through the quiet, happy years which had followed in the planning and beautifying of their home; this home which she had desecrated!

Brewster's words rang in his ears. "You have made me the happiest man in the world! I shall always remember my hour here tonight with you—" And then that adoring salutation, that impassioned kissing of her hands!

Checking the harsh laugh which rose to his lips and unable longer to contain himself, Storm sprang up and paced the floor. Brewster's happiness would be of short-duration; his hour was over! Softly, under his breath, Storm began to curse them both with horrible, meaningless curses; blood surged to his temples, pounded in his ears. A lurid red mist rose before his eyes, blinding him so that he staggered, stumbling against the furniture in his path. He, Norman Storm, had been flouted, betrayed; and by that smiling, lying, corrupt creature there beneath his roof whom he had trusted, idolized!

All at once through the roaring in his ears he heard his name called in wondering accents and turned. The door had opened, and Leila stood before him; a pale and trembling Leila, with wide, apprehensive eyes.

"Norman! When did you come in? Why do you look at me so strangely? What has happened?"

The mist cleared before him, the leaping blood was stilled as though a cold hand had tightened about his temples, and in a voice of dangerous calm he replied: "A great deal has happened. For one thing, I have found you out, my dear!"

"'Found me out?'" she repeated advancing toward him in sheer wonderment. "Norman, what do you mean?"

"I returned home somewhat earlier than you expected, did I not?" He smiled, but the light in his eyes grew steely. "A trite, time-worn trick of the deceived husband, I admit, but it served! You thought yourself secure, didn't you? Or perhaps you gave no thought whatever to my possible intrusion; you fancied you had sufficiently pulled the wool over my eyes to blind me indefinitely?"

"Deceived husband!" Her voice had sunk to a whisper of incredulous horror. "You cannot know what you are saying, Norman. You must be mad!"

"On the contrary, I have never known a saner moment. My madness lay in trusting you as I have all these years, loving you with an idolatry which could conceive of no wrong."

"But I—I have done no wrong—"

"Don't lie now!" he cried harshly. "Can't you realize that it will avail you nothing, that it did not deceive me even yesterday? And tonight I come home and find your lover here beneath my roof thanking you for the happiest hour of his life!"

"My—!" Leila shuddered and drew herself up abruptly. "Norman, you go too far! The construction you have placed on Mr Brewster's visit here tonight would be ridiculous, ludicrous under the circumstances if it were not so hideous, so unspeakably vile! I will leave you until you come to your senses."

She turned, but he sprang before her and locking the door dropped the key into his pocket.

"You will stay here! I'm through with evasions. We're going to have this out between us here now. You went to the Ferndale Inn with Julie Brewster yesterday, didn't you?"

Leila eyed him steadily for a moment, then her eyelids drooped and she moistened her lips nervously.

"I have told you—"

"A lie! You were not at the Ferndale Inn yesterday, you were in New York, in the Leicester Building, in that rat Brewster's office!"

"Brewster's, office!" she repeated. Then comprehension dawned, and she smiled sadly with infinite reproach. "Norman, you will regret that accusation bitterly when you learn the truth."

"I know it now." His tones shook, but a strange, tense calm had settled upon his seething brain, and even as he voiced his accusations a monstrous resolve was forming within him. "You received a letter from there this morning which you tried to hide from me. Couldn't your poor, pitiful, complacent mind conceive that a mere child would have seen through your evasions and shallow subterfuges?"

THE BLOW

"Stop! Stop!" She retreated from him with her hands over her ears as if to shut out the sound of his voice. "I tell you, you are mad! I can explain—"

"It's too late for that." His tone had steadied, and a hint of his dawning, implacable purpose glinted in his eyes. "You called him 'mad' last night, too, over the telephone, yet you called him 'dear' also, and when he held you to your promise you stole out of my house to meet him in the darkness, like a thief. You did not know that I stood listening, close enough to have touched you as you passed!"

"This is infamous!" Leila turned upon the hearth rug and faced him, her head proudly erect to meet the menace in his eyes. "You were eavesdropping, spying upon me in your insane, unfounded jealousy and suspicion! Why did you not follow me as well? Then you would have learned the truth for yourself!"

"It was not necessary. It was sheer accident that I came upon you at the telephone, but I did not have to dog your footsteps to learn the truth. My judgment was better than yours; I knew that you would walk into the first trap I set for you, that you would give yourself into my hands. And you have!"

"You will unlock that door and permit me to go now, if you please." The quiet dignity of her tone was filled with cold contempt. "You are beside yourself; I will not listen a moment longer to your wild accusations, your insults! I have offered to explain, but you said it was too late. Take care that you do not make it forever too late!"

Storm read disdain in the defiance of her eyes, mockery in the faint curl of her lips, and his swift resolve crystallized.

"It is you who have made it too late! Take that damnable smile from your lips, do you hear?" As he advanced toward her his outflung hand touched something smooth and hard, and closed upon it. "I tell you I've caught you, I've found you out! You've had your hour, you and the man for whom you deceived me! I'll settle with him later, but now you'll pay! — Damn you, stop smiling!"

Blindly in the sudden unleashing of his rage he struck, and the small, colorless face with its tantalizing, disdainful curl of the lips vanished as though the red swirling mist which rose again before him had closed over it and blotted it out.

No sound reached him at first but the drumming of the pulse in his ears and his hoarse, sobbing breath as he stood swaying, tearing with one free hand at the collar which seemed tightening about his throat. Then gradually for the second time the lurid haze lifted, and as the space before him cleared a great trembling seized him.

"Stop smiling! Stop smiling! Stop smiling!"

What queer, grating whisper was that which repeated the words endlessly over and over in unison with the throbbing in his brain? Dimly he became aware that it issued from his own lips and moved his hands up from his throat to still the sound.

His other hand still grasped the smooth, hard object upon which it had closed in that moment of vengeance, and now he gazed down stupidly upon it. It was a driver, one of that collection of golf clubs from the table, and upon its glittering, rounded, hardwood knob was a smudge of red...

His wavering gaze traveled on and downward. Then it fastened upon something which lay at his feet, and slowly his face stiffened and grew leaden.

It was Leila, huddled and still, with one side of her forehead blotted out in a crushed, oozing mass of crimson.

The driver dropped with a soft thud from his relaxed hand, and he knelt, lifting the limp body which sagged so horribly, with such unexpected weight. Shaking as he was, he managed to raise it to a half sitting posture, the shoulders supported against his knee; but as, mechanically, he whispered her name, the head rolled back, its jaw hanging grotesquely; and from between the half-crossed lids her eyes stared dully back at him in a cold, fixed, basilisk gaze.

As confirmation came to him, the body slipped from his nerveless grasp and with a soft, silken rustle rolled over and fell face downward, settling into the hearth rug with the dishevelled golden head against the fender.

He had killed her! He meant to do it, of course; he had been conscious of that resolve before she defied him, while she had stood there vainly striving to maintain her attitude of injured innocence; but now he realized that it must have been his unacknowledged intention from the moment suspicion changed to conviction. The stupendous fact, however, and the consequences which it portended, held him suddenly at bay.

He had committed murder, and he would be called upon to pay the penalty! It was not death he feared—how easily it had been meted out, there in that little room!—but the dragging, infernal machinery of legalizing his punishment; the trial, the publicity, the hideous disgrace, the sordidness of the whole wretched proceeding!

No tinge of grief or remorse colored his thoughts. She had wronged him, had richly deserved what had come to her. That dead thing lying there had become simply a menace to his own life, and the immediate future in all its horrors ranged before his mental vision. The discovery, the arrest, the stark headlines in the papers—Wall Street, the Trust Company, the clubs, all his world ringing with it! Then the legal battle, long drawn out, the sentence, the weeks of tortured waiting in an ignominious cell and at last the end, hideous, inevitable!

How life-like she looked, lying there, lying there with no hint of the tell-tale wound visible! She might almost have fainted and slipped from that huge armchair behind her with her head against the fender...

Why could she not have fallen so tonight? The thought seared across his brain like a flash of lightning, and Storm drew his breath in sharply. He was safe, so far! No one knew of what had taken place in that room; no one knew yet that he had even returned to the house. Brewster had not seen him, and Brewster was the only living person who could suspect a motive for the crime.

A motive? But what was he thinking? There would be no question of motive, for there would be no suggestion of crime. Since childhood Leila had been a victim of *petit mal*, that mild form of catalepsy which, while it baffles cure, yet is in itself not harmful; a moment of faintness, of unconsciousness followed by slight weakness, that was all. Everyone knew of these attacks of hers; George Holworthy had referred to that tendency only last night when she had complained of feeling not quite herself. The chance that she might injure herself in falling when the fainting spell came was the sole danger attached to her old malady. That danger was what must seem to have overtaken her tonight!

Storm rose weakly, his eyes averted from the thing lying there upon the floor, and strove with all his mental force to collect himself. She had come here to his den and seated herself in that chair to await his return. Faintness had overcome her, and she had fallen forward, striking her temple there on the heavy brass knob on the corner of the fender. That was the solution, that was what the world must think, must believe without question.

And he? What must be his part in this drama which he was staging? Not an active one; caution whispered to him to keep as much in the background as would be consistent. He must remember to eliminate this hour wholly from his calculations; this hour and the events which had led up to it He knew nothing of her visit to the Leicester Building in town; of the telephone summons, her secret nocturnal meeting with Brewster, the letter she had tried to conceal or the fellow's visit there that evening. Only by erasing from his future train of thought all such memories could he hope to succeed in conducting himself down to the smallest detail as though all had been as usual between them.

In the ordinary course of events, on returning as late as this and finding the house dark—for the single low light in the den far at the rear of the house would not be calculated to attract his attention—he would have concluded that Leila had long since gone to bed, and would himself retire without disturbing her. In the early morning the housemaid would discover what lay in the den and raise the alarm.

He would then have only to play the role of the dazed, grief-stricken husband, and none—not even Brewster—would suspect. There would be the formality of a medical examination, the funeral, the conventional condolences, and soon their little world would forget.

What was that! Was there a stir, a vibration from somewhere in the house above? A cold sweat broke out at every pore, and fear gripped him, but he flung it off and tiptoed to the door, turning the knob and striving to open it. Then he remembered, and taking the key from his pocket unlocked the door and pulled it toward him inch by inch. Except for the pin-point of light from the lamp on the newel post at the foot of the staircase, the house was in absolute darkness, and his straining ears detected no repetition of that sound, if sound there had been.

Closing the door at length, Storm set himself resolutely to the task which remained before him. At his feet lay the driver where he had dropped it when the full realization of his act swept over him. There had been a smudge upon it—God! had it marked the rug?

Before he touched it, however, he went to the window, assured himself that no aperture between its heavy curtains would permit a ray of stronger light to be visible from within, and then switched on the wall brackets, flooding the room with a dazzling radiance.

Next he examined the driver itself. The blow had been delivered with the rounded knob, and to the sinister clot of red upon it there adhered a single golden hair which glinted accusingly in the light. Storm plucked it off with trembling fingers and approaching the hearth coiled it over the knob on the corner of the fender, close to that shining, inert head.

Then with his handkerchief he wiped the driver carefully, polishing it until even to his super-critical eye it appeared immaculate once more, and replaced it among the others on the table.

Shudderingly, he glanced down at the square of linen crushed in his hand, and as his fingers slowly opened a hideous crimson stain appeared. It seemed to his horrified gaze to be growing, spreading, and he felt an almost irresistible impulse to cast it wildly from him. Her blood! Her life-blood, still warm and red and all but pulsing as it had come from her veins!

To his distorted imagination it seemed to be still a part of her, and alive, clinging to his hand in futile, mute appeal. It must be obliterated, must cease to be! That inert body could not accuse him; the driver lay in spotless seeming innocence among its fellows; even that single golden hair which might have proved his undoing had been made to serve as a link in the circumstantial chain he was forging; but this most damning evidence of all remained! He must rid himself of it at once, must destroy it utterly! But how?

The stout linen would not tear easily, and even though he ripped it apart the torn strips would still bear their revealing stains; if he took it to his room and washed it there would be no place where he could hang it to dry without Agnes finding it, and she would think such a proceeding strange. Moreover every instinct within him shrank from the thought of pocketing the gruesome thing and clamored for its destruction.

Dared he burn it? What if the betraying odor lingered in the room? To start a blaze in the fireplace which had been swept clean for the coming summer was not to be thought of, yet burning was the only means left to him.

His roving glance fell upon the desk. There lay the sealing wax, tray and spirit lamp with which it had been his pride to stamp the Storm coat of arms upon his letters. In an instant he had touched a match to the tiny wick, and a flame, narrow and curling like a bluish, tinseled ribbon, sprang into being.

He waited until it had steadied, and then at arm's length he dipped a corner of the handkerchief into the flame and held it there. God, how it smoked! The linen charred slowly at the edges as the blue tongue of fire licked it hungrily, and a pungent odor permeated his nostrils, but no answering flame appeared. Would it never catch?

At last a tiny dart of red shot out and ran around the border, and Storm snuffed out the wick and held the handkerchief over the little bronze tray. Slowly, creepingly the tiny flame ate into the linen, and flakes of fine light ash drifted down into the receptacle beneath. The sinister stains still stood out glaringly in the curling smoke, and as though possessed of a very demon the flame eluded them, skirting about them in sheer mockery. Would even the elements defy him in his plan?

Then the crimson turned to brown, and a darker curl of smoke arose, while a strange, acrid odor mingled with the dry smell of burning linen. Her blood was being consumed there before him, just as her body would later be consumed by the earth in which it would lie! A thought of the ancient human sacrifice came to him, and he trembled anew. This bloodstained rag, this symbol of her living body, was being offered on the altar of his self-preservation!

The flakes were dropping now like sifting, gray-white down, and the handkerchief was a mere wisp. Slowly the brown stains crumbled and disappeared and the smoke lightened, but that dreadful, sinister odor still lingered. Thread by thread the linen was consumed, but Storm held the last shred until the diminished flame seared his fingers, then dropped it into the tray and stood watching it with somber eyes until the lingering flame died and only the little heap of ashes remained.

Gone! That hideous, accusing stain had been swept into nothingness, obliterated by the breath of clean fire. Only that unclean odor still prevailed, and the contents of the tray must be disposed of. If the room were subjected to a minute examination and the ashes analyzed, all that he had done would go for naught. If he could scatter them, sow them to the winds —

Storm listened. The night breeze was rising, blowing briskly, strongly about the house. Without, the flower garden and broad lawns with a border of hedge and clustering trees screened him from his neighbors. With a quick gesture he switched off the lights and tiptoed to the window, thrusting back the curtains and opening it wide. The fresh, sweet, blossom-laden air rushed in upon him, and he breathed it in great gulps before he turned and felt his way to the desk.

Picking up the little bronze tray he turned to the window and stood for a moment gazing out. Under the pale glow of the rising moon, Leila's flowers which she had tended with such loving care lay sleeping tranquilly, their small myriad faces glistening beneath a spangled veil of dew. She had brought them into being, and now her ashes, these ashes which held a part of her, were to fertilize and give them renewed, life!

He thrust the thought from him in a paroxysm of physical revulsion, and as a gust of wind swept about the house he cast the contents of the tray far into the air. It seemed to him that he could see the ashes, swirling like a faint, driven mist before him, settling lingeringly among the flowers, and he stared half-fearfully as though anticipating that a phantom would rise from them; but the sudden gust of wind died, and the garden slept on, unconcerned.

The tray, swept clean of the last flake, shimmered faintly in his hand, and he replaced it on the desk. Then, seizing the window curtains, he waved them about until even his overstimulated senses could detect no lingering whiff of smoke. Closing the windows at last, he drew the curtains as carefully as before and switched on the lights.

The first thing that met his blinking gaze was the burnt match with which he had lighted the spirit lamp, and he thrust it into his pocket as he bent to examine the desk top. No single flake of ash remained to bear witness against him, and with a sigh he turned to the work yet before him.

He had marked the exact spot upon the rug where the impromptu weapon had rested; but here, too, a prolonged scrutiny revealed no slightest trace, and he arose from his knees with a sigh of relief.

After all, he was not preparing for a rigid police inquiry; only the most casual inspection would be given the room, with the cause of death so self-evidently manifested, yet the slightest overlooked clue would bring crashing down upon him the whole circumstantial structure he was so painstakingly erecting.

Was that armchair in the exact position from which the body would have fallen?

He studied it, moved it an inch or two, and then turned his attention to the body itself. The wound was upon the right temple, and, shuddering, he raised the head and rested it upon the corner of the fender. It settled back upon the rug once more as he released it, but he saw to his satisfaction that the knob of brass was no longer bright; a smear of crimson marred its surface, and a loosened strand of her hair trailed over the fender into the hearth.

As Storm stepped backward to regard his handiwork something metallic grated against his heel. A gold hairpin! He picked it up meditatively. Had Leila really fallen forward that pin, jarred from her head by the force of the impact, would have shot across the fender; he reached over and dropped it upon the hearth.

No flaw remained now in the scene he had arranged, and with its consummation a traitorous wave of horror rose within him, an hysterical desire almost of panic to flee from that silent, sinister room. He switched off the wall brackets, and approached the desk. His hat and gloves were all that remained to indicate his presence, and he caught them up and reached out to extinguish the low reading lamp before remembrance stayed his hand.

The housemaid must find the lamp still burning brightly in the morning when she came to set the room to rights. Was his nerve failing him that he should have almost overlooked so vital a detail? The horror was mounting now, but he forced himself to a final, searching survey; his hideous task was accomplished!

A few hurried, cautious steps, a moment of hesitation, and he stood at last outside the door. He felt an overmastering impulse to close it, to seal that room and its gruesome contents away from the living world, but he reminded himself sternly that it would not be a logical move. Leila, awaiting his coming, would have left the door ajar that she might hear him. He reached behind him and drew it close to its casing until only a narrow line of light cleaved the darkness with dimmed radiance; then, repressing a mad desire to run, he tiptoed noiselessly down the hall.

At the foot of the stairs he paused and glanced back. Only the faintest lightening of the shadows betrayed what lay beyond, and extinguishing the lamp upon the newel post he crept up to his room.

From Leila's empty dressing-room adjoining, the yawning blackness seemed to rush out menacingly to envelop him, but he shut it away with the closing door and, moving to his window, flung it wide.

Soft moonlight everywhere, silvering the treetops and shimmering upon the trout stream beyond. Moonlight and the whispering night winds and the peace and hush of a sleeping world.

It was over! He had done his utmost to forestall any possible doubt or suspicion, had nullified every clue, had set the scene for the farce which would start with the rising curtain of dawn and felt confident that he was prepared at all points to meet the issue.

But what of the hours that lay between, the long night before him?

IV

THE LONG NIGHT

Storm turned from the window with a sudden realization that his task, instead of having been finished, had only begun. If he were to keep up this farce it would not be enough to attempt to obliterate from his memory the hour which had just passed; he must live from this moment as though it had never been. He must remember that, tempted by the beauty of the spring night, he had not come directly home by way of the short cut, but had chosen the winding path which skirted the club grounds and the lake. That would account for the time that had elapsed since the arrival and departure of the train.

He had only just come in, and finding the house dark had proceeded at once up here to his room. He would suppose Leila to be asleep in there, behind that closed door, and he would therefore move about softly, so as not to waken her. Every nerve shrank in revolt from the thought of retiring, of courting sleep and the nightmares which might arise from his subconsciousness to haunt him, yet he must proceed in all things as though this were but a usual homecoming.

He must at least prepare for bed. He reached for the pendant chain of the reading lamp and then paused. The servants' rooms were directly above; what if the bright square of light shining from his open window awoke one of them and she came downstairs? The next minute he was cursing himself beneath his breath. Was his light not often going as late as this, or later, and had he ever before paused to think or care whether it disturbed the servants or not? Tonight must be as all other nights! Why could he not bear that in mind?

Nevertheless, he crossed to the window once more and closed the shutters; that concession, at least, was not an unusual precaution, for an early night moth or two, lured by the prematurely warm weather, had already made its appearance. Then he turned on the light resolutely and started to undress. The suit he was wearing was of dark blue serge with a white pin-head stripe, and as he divested himself of it a new thought sprang up to his mind. Suppose it, too, bore traces—? That head with its shattered, gaping wound had rested against his knee...

Seizing the garments he moved close to the bed-stand, and beneath the powerful rays of the lamp he examined every thread with straining eyes. No stain was visible; even his shirt cuffs by a miracle had escaped contact, and with a sigh of relief he plunged his hands in the various pockets to remove his keys and small change.

The first object his fingers touched was the burnt match with which he had ignited the spirit lamp, and impatiently he filliped it out of the window.

Everything was there in his pockets which he normally carried except his handkerchief. That was gone, reduced to ashes and flung to the winds of the night; but it would not have been had his homecoming been as he must pretend even to himself.

Storm frowned. He would in all likelihood never wear that suit again; even if it were not for the fact that mourning garb alone must be his for many months to come, he could still never look upon it again, remembering...

He thrust that thought violently aside and continued with his reasoning. Agnes always went through the pockets of the clothes he had worn during the week for stray handkerchiefs when she was collecting the laundry. Would she note that he had used one less than usual?

It was not so much the fear of that, however, as the mental urge to play up to his part, to make all things seem as though that hour in the den had never been, that prompted Storm to go to his dresser and take a fresh handkerchief from the drawer. Without effeminacy, his fastidious taste inclined toward a dash of delicate scent, and several varieties stood before him.

Testatively he lifted a bottle of rose toilet water, but the first whiff of fragrance made him replace it with a shudder. It brought back too vividly the remembrance of that garden below where the opening buds were even now scattered with filmy ashes. The lilac water he also thrust aside—Leila had met him at the gate only a week before with her arms filled with white lilac, and as she stood there, her head looming fair and golden above them, he had thought her very like a picture of the Annunciation...

Finally he sprayed a few drops of eau de Cologne on the handkerchief and stuffed it in the pocket of his coat lying across the chair. Then, clad in his pajamas, he glanced at the clock on the mantel.

Half-past twelve! It would be half-past six in the ordinary course of events when Agnes would descend to dust the first floor and set the breakfast table. Six hours to wait! Three hundred and sixty slow, dragging minutes! How could he ever live through them? How did the condemned spend the last hours before the end? He had read, marveling, that some hardy criminals slept unconcernedly, some raved, some prayed...

God, why did such hideous thoughts intrude themselves now? He would never stand in their shoes, no breath of suspicion would ever approach him; he had laid his plans too well, had fortified himself against any contingency which might arise. The scene had been perfectly staged with not a detail missing to break the continuity of the version of what had occurred which must impress itself upon those who would view it.

Crossing the room, he seated himself on the side of the bed and lighted a cigarette. He could keep the light going a little longer without occasioning remark should one of the maids wake up, for he had often read until past one. He must not overdo it, though; he must not overdo anything. That would be the one great danger; he must hold himself impervious against self-betrayal.

He smoked cigarette after cigarette until a single stroke tinkled from the little clock, and, rousing himself from his reverie, Storm reached over and extinguished the lamp. The darkness seemed sinister, overwhelming, but as his eyes gradually accustomed themselves to it he saw pale, silvery moonbeams creeping in between the slats of the shutters, lying in shimmering bars across the floor and lightening the gloom with a faint, almost spiritual effulgence. The stillness of the night, too, was all at once broken by a myriad sounds which had not penetrated his consciousness before: strange creaks and groans in the walls as though something invisible were abroad, sibilant whispers in the chimney and the liquid, monotonous tap of water dripping from the faucet in the bathroom. Outside, the wind blew gustily, and somewhere about the house a loose shutter banged with a dismal, hollow sound.

What a hideous thing night was! There was something about it which loosened a fellow's thoughts, freed them from his stern control and let them wander where they would, unrestrained. Only one other such vigil had Storm kept: that of the crisis in Leila's desperate illness after their marriage. Every hour of it was branded on his brain, every detail arose again to attack his senses: the pungent, penetrating odor of carbolic, that strange, high voice which babbled and was still, the white-clad nurse, gravely non-commital, shutting the door behind which he might not pass, the taste of his own blood as he caught his lip between his teeth to keep back the groan of utter despair.

The night then had seemed interminable, but in the end had come the glorious promise that she would live! Now the dawn would bring only tidings of death, but he would not call her back again if he could; would not undo what he had done even if it lay in his power. His Leila had never existed; the pedestal was empty, that was all!

Gad, if only he could smoke! His nerves shrieked for the solace of nicotine, but he dared not light another cigarette. The smoke curling up from his opened window to that of one of the maids upstairs would tell her, should she also be awake, that her master was keeping vigil there in the darkness alone. She would think nothing of it now, perhaps, but later when the discovery was made she might wonder. He must manage, somehow, to get through the night without even the slight comfort that he craved!

With a whirring of soft wings, some tiny creature of the night came and beat upon the shutter, and Storm started violently. The bars of moonlight had traveled a barely perceptible inch or two across the floor, and from the distance there came the crowning note of desolation: the long-drawn, mournful howling of a dog.

Storm shivered. An old superstition which his Irish nurse had instilled into his mind in the nursery days swept over him. A dog's howl was the sign of death! *How could the beast know?* In all that sleeping countryside, there was one who shared his vigil, one who raised his voice in warning and lament!

Storm rose and, tiptoeing to the window, opened the shutters wide and fastened them noiselessly back against the house wall while he strained his eyes in the direction from which the dismal baying of the dog rose once more. Was it nearer now? Could it be that the beast, led by some instinct more subtle and unerring than man could fathom, had picked up the scent—the scent of the drifting ashes? Bridget had told him that a dog could sense the presence of death though it were miles away and would come to cry the news of it. What if the creature were to appear suddenly there between the trees and leap across the lawn to crouch beneath the curtained window of the den downstairs and howl its dread message?

The next minute Storm's tense attitude relaxed. What a fool he was to be stirred by the idle superstition of an old-wives' tale! His nerves must be going back on him, what with that accursed howling and the shifting shadows of the moonlight which were worse than utter darkness could be. Would it never end?

As if in answer the mellow chime of the clock sounded upon his ears. It must be three o'clock at least, possibly four—! He waited breathlessly. A second note pealed forth softly to die away in a vibrating echo, and then silence. Only two o'clock! Nearly five hours more! God, could he endure it and keep his sanity? Doyle's gruesome story of Lady Sannox came to his mind. Would he be found in the morning as the great physician had been after the night of horror, a gibbering idiot trying to thrust both feet into one leg of his trousers and babbling meaninglessly? Lady Sannox had been unfaithful, too, but it was the lover, not the husband, who paid!

He forced the hideous picture from his thoughts and turned for one final glance at the garden below. How still everything was! The howling of the dog had ceased, and the wind had died down to a mere rustling, whispering breeze. The moonlight, too, was paling, and beneath its waning radiance the garden still slumbered undisturbed as it had when he cast the ashes forth upon the air. From these ashes would spring the phoenix, not of love, but of murder; of hatred, vengeance and the lust to kill! What had he not loosed upon the world!

He covered his eyes as if to shut out the scene of false peace, of menacing, brooding calm before the crimson dawn; and staggering back to the bed, he sank down upon it once more. The touch of the smooth, cool linen beneath his fevered hand steadied him and brought a moment of tranquility to his reeling senses, but he could not stretch himself out upon it. The space beside him where Leila had so often lain was blank and empty, yet oddly her presence seemed near. He could almost hear her light tap upon the connecting door, almost see it open and her slender, white-clad form appear with the two heavy ropes of golden hair falling over her shoulders. She would come to him swiftly, tenderly, and he would take her in his arms and hold her close...

But no tapping came upon the door, no form appeared, his arms were empty! Great God, why could he not forget!

The clock struck three, the moonlight faded and vanished, swallowed up in the darkest hour which comes before the dawn, and still Storm crouched there at the bed's foot sunk in a reverie of retrospection.

In just such another springtime as this they had gone upon their honeymoon. The awe and ecstasy of those days like a half-forgotten fragrance stole again over his spirit and thrilled him anew. How wonderful she had been, how wondrously sweet her shy confidences, her little outbursts of tenderness, her bewitching, bewildering changes of mood! How he reveled in each new phase of her nature as it revealed itself to him; how he had worshipped her, gloried in the possession of her! In the golden years that followed, the first ecstasy had not faded; it had but stabilized, deepened into a steady glow of unquestioning devotion, and the honeymoon had never really ended until this hour!

Impotently he struck his forehead with his clenched fist. Why must he go on thinking, thinking! The past was dead, buried beyond hope of resurrection! Why must it come trooping back to rob him of his strength and lull him to forgetfulness of the immediate future and the crisis which impended? The night had been years long! Would it never come to an end? Would this hideous darkness envelop him forever?

Four o'clock! Thank God, he had missed an hour! Only two more now, or three at the most, and then the cry of alarm would come winging up from below and the curtain would rise!

A chill dampness as of the grave itself stole in at the window, and Storm shivered although he was bathed in sweat. His pulse slowed and weakness descended upon him, while a swift, unnerving fear laid its clammy hands upon his throat.

He fought it off desperately. This was the dreaded hour before the dawn, the hour of lowered vitality when life's guard is down and death stalks in upon those awaiting it, those whose time has come and who slip out into the unknown quietly, peacefully. But for those who are hurled into it suddenly, hideously, by shot or stab or crashing blow—!

He dropped his wretched head upon his hands. This was madness! He must not succumb to it, he must marshal his resources, steady his brain, gather strength for the coming of day!

Slowly, almost imperceptibly, the darkness was changing from black to gray. The eastern sky was unbroken, but a mist which could rather be felt than seen was rising from the darker shadows, and the wind had been succeeded by a dead calm. A hushed expectancy seemed to brood over the world, and Storm waited, too, dreading yet longing for the end of this prolonged suspense.

The clock ticked with maddening precision, and he tried to count the minutes, to keep his traitorous thoughts from wandering into dangerous, forbidden channels. His weakness had fallen from him, his pulse quickened and a mounting excitement drove from him all thought of fear. He would be ready when the time came to meet the issue. But would the time ever come?

There were faint gray streaks in the sky now, the shadows had sharpened and suddenly, piercingly, a cock crew. Storm welcomed the strident sound with uplifted head and squared shoulders. The dawn was coming at last!

He turned, crossed his arms on the foot of the bed and, resting his chin upon them, stared out through the open window at the lightening sky.

Five liquid, mellow notes sounded from the mantel, and he smiled grimly. One hour more and he could begin to listen for the maid's step upon the stair! His nerves were tingling in anticipation, and without urging his thoughts leaped ahead. He must be ready when the cry came, but not too obviously prepared. Surprise must come before alarm, consternation before a show of grief. The maid her- she must lead him to her discovery. His face and manner must reveal no slightest inkling of his knowledge of the truth.

Both of the servants were undeniably stupid. He had anathematized them many a time for their crass density and ignorance, but now he blessed it. They would suspect nothing, would seize upon any explanation of the tragedy which was subtly planted in their shallow brains and make it their own.

Of the outsiders, Carr must be called in first. He was a country practitioner of the old-fashioned sort who had been established there when Greenlea was known as Whigham's Corners, and croup and gout with their intermediate ills had been the range of his experience. He, too, could be counted upon to see only what was placed before him, and the details of the aftermath could safely be left in his hands.

A score of vague, anticipatory visions passed through Storm's brain. How shocked the crowd out here would be; *and* old George! He was probably fast asleep now, filling the air with contented snores. What would he say and do when the early edition of the evening papers brought the tidings to him? Storm thanked heaven that neither he nor Leila had relatives to come flocking with tears and questions and advice. He would be free at least from prying eyes beneath his own roof after the official medical inquiry had been concluded.

Gray turned to rose in the eastern sky, the mist lifted, and the world showed delicately green beneath it. The lone cock's crowing had been augmented by a chorus, and the birds stirred and twittered in the trees. All life was waking to greet the new day, but Leila...

What time was it? Storm rose weakly and tottered to the mantel. The clock's face was plainly visible in the half-light, and he drew his breath sharply. Five minutes to six!

The pink glow deepened to crimson, and the sun in a blaze of glory peeped over the low-lying hills, but Storm did not see the spectacle for which he had waited through interminable tortured hours. He had caught a glimpse of his reflection in the mirror and stood gazing in incredulous dismay at the face which gazed back at him. Could it be his own with that sickly, bluish pallor, unshaven jaw, and haunted, sunken eyes which stared from dark-rimmed sockets?

Great heavens, if he appeared like that before even the servants his guilt would be patent to all the world! — But would it? The maids would surely be too agitated to note him in the shock of the discovery; and later, when the doctor came, horror and natural grief would account for the change in his appearance. His night of vigil had provided him with that which would perhaps be an asset rather than a danger.

What was that? He whirled about and stood listening. The floors and ceilings were thick, and no ordinary sound could penetrate from above; but had he not heard a step upon the stair? He waited in an intensity of strained attention, for several moments. The silence within the house remained unbroken.

With a sigh he glanced back at the clock. It must have struck the hour while he stood glaring at the apparition the mirror had revealed, for now the hands pointed to a quarter after six. Could it be that perverse fate would ordain that the maids should oversleep this day of all days and prolong his agony?

Then his glance fell upon the bed. Its pillows were smooth and untouched, its covers creased but not tumbled about. The veriest child could see that it had not been slept in, the most casual glance would reveal the secret of his night-long vigil!

In three strides he had reached it and thrown back the covers, pommeling the pillows and crumpling the sheets. What a narrow escape! He paused, breathless, when his task was completed and gazed fearfully about him for other overlooked evidence.

His light had been burning until one o'clock. Hastily he picked up a book at random from those on the table and opening it laid it face downward upon the bed-stand. The stubs and ashes of the cigarettes he had smoked would occasion no remark; and the most painstakingly minute scrutiny failed to reveal any other incongruity in the room.

While he paused anew a sound came to his ears about which there could be no doubt; cautious but naturally heavy footsteps were descending the stairs from above. His heart leaped, and the blood raced in his veins, but he stood motionless as the steps passed his door and descended again.

It would come now, the cry for which he had waited! He held his breath until his ear-drums seemed bursting, and the minutes lengthened, but still the summons did not come. What could the girl be doing? Would she set all the other rooms to rights before approaching the den, or did she mean to shirk it altogether? Surely that streak of artificial light burning in the daytime must catch her eye as she passed along the hall! Was she gossiping with the milkman, idling on the porch? The suspense was unbearable!

He had borne with it through the long watches of the night, but now he could contain himself no longer. Every nerve was strained to the breaking point, and his nails bit into the flesh of his clenched hands. Was this agony to be stretched out interminably?

And then it came at last! A piercing, prolonged scream rang suddenly through the quiet house, to break and rise again, echoing back from the very walls.

Storm dropped his head in his hands, and an answering cry of unconscious blasphemy trembled on his lips.

"Thank God!"

V

WHEN MORNING DAWNED

While Storm hesitated, relaxed in that moment of utter abandon to relief, it came again; a wild shriek mounting from below in a high feminine voice and dying away in a quivering wail!

The long awaited discovery had come; now he must play his part. One false move!—But he put that resolutely from his thoughts as he flung his dressing gown about him and started for the door.

"What is it? What has happened?" He was leaning over the stair-rail now, and his voice, although subdued, held just the proper note of sharp inquiry. Even as he spoke he heard a heavy foot along the hall above and was conscious of the cook's head peering down affrightedly.

"Oh, Mr Storm, sir! Mr Storm!"

Agnes, the housemaid, sped along the lower hall and collapsed at the foot of the stairs.

"Well, what is it?" Storm demanded peremptorily, but still in that subdued tone. "Burglars here in the night? Don't you know better than to scream like that? You'll frighten Mrs Storm"

He paused, and the girl's shocked wail arose once more.

"Mrs Storm! She's down here, sir, in the den. Oh, come quick!"

"Down—!"

The word died in Storm's throat, and still conscious of the cook's eyes he turned, dashed open the door of his wife's empty room, uttered a loud ejaculation and then plunged down the stairs.

"I thought she was asleep in her room!" he exclaimed. "Where—?"

"In the den, sir!" Agnes scrambled to her feet and stood clinging to the newel post as Storm passed her and rushed down the hall. "Oh, may God have mercy—!"

He heard a startled cry from above and lumbering feet hastily descended the stairs as he burst into the den and then stopped short. Leila's body was lying face upward now upon the rug, her waxen features clamped in the rigidity of marble, a hideous brown clot enmeshing the soft gold of her hair and smeared across her forehead.

The cry of horror which burst from Storm's lips was not all simulation, for anticipated as it was, the sight brought a sickening qualm to him. He had conquered it the next moment, however, and crossing to the body knelt and forced himself to touch it, to raise it until it rested against his knee just as he had done the moment the blow was struck. It was cold and stiff, the neck rigid, the eyes half open and unwinking in their stare.

As the trembling servants appeared in the doorway he laid the body gently back upon the rug and, rising, dashed his hand across his eyes. He remembered that gesture; he had often seen a favorite tragedian use it upon the stage.

"She is dead!" Horror, grief unutterable rang in his tones, and the maids began to sob hysterically.

Without seeming to note their presence Storm staggered past them to the telephone in the library.

"Greenlea 42... Dr Carr, please... Doctor, this is Storm, Norman Storm. For God's sake get over here as quickly as you can!... No, I can't go into details, but it's a matter of life and death!... All right, hurry, man!"

For a moment he sat there hunched over the silent instrument while the sweat poured in rivulets down his face. So far, so good. His shaking nerves were aiding him in the role he was playing, but he must not let them get the upper hand.

The early morning sun streamed in at the long French windows which opened on the veranda, and the twitter and chirp of birds came to him from the lawn outside, mingling with the muffled wail from the rear. He must go back. God! If only it were all over!

Agnes had collapsed again in a little heap in the den doorway, but Ellen, the cook, knelt by the body, crooning pitifully over it as Storm reentered. She made a grotesque figure clad only in the blanket which she had thrown over her voluminous nightgown, her iron-gray hair screwed back in a tight knob and tears streaming down her round, honest face.

"Oh, sir!" She looked up, her eyes tragic with horror. "Who in the world did it, sir?"

Storm started. A suspicion of murder already, and from the source which he had least anticipated! If stupid, unimaginative Ellen had leaped to such a conclusion could he hope after all that the truth would not reveal itself to Dr Carr and the authorities? He moistened his lips with his tongue and stammered:

"She—she must have fallen—one of those fainting spells. It looks as though she had struck her head on the fender, there." He added quickly, "When I came home late I supposed Mrs Storm was asleep in her room and did not disturb her. How did she come to be here?"

"Must have been waiting up for you, sir." Agnes lifted her head from her hands. "The mistress didn't expect you home for dinner, and I served her on the little table out on the veranda. She was sitting out there still when Ellen and me went to bed, along about nine. I asked her should I wait to lock up or see if you wanted a bit of cold supper, sir, but she said no, that she would attend to it herself. If only I'd known one of those attacks was coming on I wouldn't have left her for a minute! I'll never forgive myself! But the mistress seemed all right, as ever she was in her life, and I was that tired—"

Storm eyed her steadily:

"You would have heard Mrs Storm had she called for help?"

"I don't know, sir." The girl twisted her hands. "I'm a pretty heavy sleeper, and I never heard a thing during the night. I'll never forget the turn it gave me when I came down this morning and found the light still on and her lying there on the floor—"

"God rest her soul!" Ellen ejaculated piously. "Sure we wouldn't have heard, away up there on the top floor at the back, unless she'd screamed fit to wake the dead. I'd had a full day's ironing, and I was asleep the minute my head touched the pillow. The first I knew was when Agnes here let that yell out of her awhile back. The best lady ever I worked for and the kindest I She must have been took sudden to fall over like that!"

Storm drew a breath of relief. It was evident that they were telling the truth and that neither of them was aware of Brewster's visit on the previous night, nor had an inkling of its aftermath. He sank into a chair and buried his face in his hands, the better to think. He must get rid of them some way; their chatter and lamentations were driving him mad!

"'Tis God's will, sir," Ellen ventured, in a hesitating effort at consolation, though the tears still coursed unchecked down her cheeks. "Couldn't we move her, sir? 'Tis terrible to leave her lying here, poor lady—"

"Not until the doctor comes." Storm's tones were hoarse and muffled. "Please go away, both of you. I want to be alone. Mind you say not a word of what has happened to the milkman or anyone else who may come to the door until the doctor has taken charge. We should have all the neighbors about our ears."

"We won't breathe a word." Agnes scrambled to her feet. "You'll ring, sir, if you want anything? A cup of coffee, now—?"

"Nothing!" Storm waved aside the suggestion with a shudder of disgust. "I only wish to be alone."

When the maids had withdrawn and their sobs were cut off by the closing of the pantry door, Storm's hands dropped to his knees. They had accepted his suggestion of the cause of death without question, but would it be safe for him to volunteer that theory as a foregone conclusion to the keener mind of the doctor? He knew the strength of first impressions; were the circumstantial proofs of accidental death obvious enough to preclude all suspicion of foul play? The evidence which had seemed so impregnable to him when he first conceived it crumbled before the wave of torturing doubt that assailed him. He did not find it as easy as he had planned to put behind him forever his secret knowledge of the truth. What would his thought processes have been had he indeed believed his wife to be sleeping safe in her room and come down to find her lying dead here?

The whirr of a light-running motor outside galvanized Storm into action, and he sprang up from his chair and hurried down the hall, flinging the front door wide just as the doctor mounted the veranda steps. A fine, grizzled stubble adorned the latter's usually clean-shaven jaw, and his light ulster was buttoned close up about his neck as though to conceal deficiencies in his hastily donned attire.

"What is it, old man?" he began genially, and then at sight of the other's face he paused abruptly.

"Come."

Without another word Storm turned and led the way to the den, and the physician followed in silence. At the door the former, with a gesture, stepped aside, and Dr Carr's glance fell upon the body.

Stifling an exclamation he advanced and made a brief, deft examination. Then, shaken from his professional calm, he rose.

"There—is nothing I can do," he announced jerkily. "She has been dead for several hours—seven or eight, at least. Good God, Storm, what does this mean?"

The gaze of the physician was filled with blank amazement and horror, but to the other man it seemed sternly accusing, and he stammered brokenly:

"I don't know! She must have been here all night like this, while I thought her safe in bed and asleep! It is horrible! Horrible!"

He hid his face in his hands to shut out those keen eyes bent upon him, and Dr Carr advanced and forced him gently down into a chair.

"Here, man, don't give way now! Pull yourself together! Do you mean that you only just discovered—?"

"A minute before I telephoned to you. It was the housemaid who found Leila like this when she came down to dust around, and her screams awakened me." Storm paused. A detailed explanation would look too much like an attempt at an alibi; he must wait for the other to drag the facts from him. "Oh, why didn't I speak, why didn't I look in her room when I came home last night! But I was afraid of disturbing her—"

He paused, and Dr Carr asked quickly:

"You returned late and thought she had retired?"

"Yes. It was after eleven—I took the ten o'clock train from town—and when I got here the house was all dark and silent, and Leila's bedroom and dressing-room doors were closed." Storm's hands dropped to the arms of his chair, and he stared straight ahead of him as he added deliberately: "I went to bed as quietly as I could so as not to waken her, for she hadn't been well; she was threatened with one of these fainting attacks the night before last. I should never have left her! But you know how it has been, Doctor; you never could tell when they were coming on, and she had never done any real harm to herself before—"

"'Fainting attacks?'" the doctor repeated sharply. He wheeled and approached the body once more and Storm watched him with bated breath. "The right temple bone has been crushed in, as if with some heavy, blunt instrument!"

"That knob on the corner of the fender—" Storm felt his way carefully. "It—it's all covered with blood! She must have fallen—"

The doctor glanced at it and then turned swiftly to him.

"Look here, Storm, have you questioned the servants? What do they know of this?"

"Nothing. I've been too nearly crazed to question them coherently, but from what I gathered they went to bed early and left her sitting out on the veranda, and the housemaid said something about Leila having told her that she would wait up for me. Think of it, Doctor! She must have come in here—"

"Hold on a minute. Was the body lying just like this, face upturned, when you saw it first?"

Storm nodded.

"Yes. I rushed to her and started to lift her up, but when I saw that—that she was dead—"

He bowed his head on his breast as if unable to continue, but he saw the physician measure with a swift eye the distance from the chair to the body, and then stoop to examine the fender again. Storm's knuckles whitened as he gripped the chair-arms in an agony of suspense. Would his implied suggestion bear fruit? Had he too palpably ignored the other's intimation that a blow had been struck? Would it have been more natural for him to have presupposed violence, murder, as the physician obviously had done? It was too late now for him to question the wisdom of his course; he could brace himself for the next step in the ghastly farce.

"Has anyone touched the body?" Dr Carr spoke with professional brusqueness.

"Yes; when I came back here after telephoning to you both the servants were in the room, and Ellen was bending over my poor wife—I can't speak of it, Doctor; I can't realize it! I feel as if I should go mad! Leila—"

"I know, old man, but we've got to get at the bottom of this thing. Try to collect yourself and think back. You said you were awakened by the housemaid's screams when she discovered the body. Do you know if she touched it before you got down here?"

Storm shook his head.

"I never asked." He kept his eyes lowered carefully to hide a glint of triumph. When Carr discovered that Agnes had found the body lying face down, the case he had manufactured would be complete. "I wish you—you'd talk to them, Doctor. I—I can't, just now. I'm all in!"

"I will. Don't think about them." *Dr* Carr glanced at the low light on the desk which still glowed brazenly in the gloom of the curtained room. "Who turned on that light instead of drawing aside the curtains?"

"It must have been on all night. Agnes said that was the first thing she noticed when she got to the door here; that the light was still going. Then she saw the body—" he halted again and added in studied ingenuousness: "I might have observed it when I came home last night, I suppose, but it is scarcely perceptible from the front hall, and finding it all dark there except for the lamp on the newel post which Leila always leaves lighted for me, I went straight upstairs. It never occurred to me that she would be waiting up for me, and in here, although she has done so occasionally. I was pretty tired. My God, Doctor, if

I had seen the light and come in here, I might have been able to save her! There might have been something I could do—!"

"No, Storm, no one could have done anything for her. Death was instantaneous. You heard nothing after you went upstairs? No sound of a fall, or disturbance of any kind?"

"Nothing." Storm started from his chair. "It couldn't have happened after I retired! Surely, if Leila had been alive when I entered the house she would have heard me! The servants sleep like logs, but I waken at the slightest sound. I would have known—!"

"That's so. Of course, you would, old man." Dr Carr's tone was soothingly compassionate. "You'd better go upstairs now and put on some clothes; you haven't even slippers on your feet. I'll have a word with the servants while you're gone—"

"But Leila!" Storm forced his shrinking eyes to turn yearningly toward the still form. "I can't bear to leave her lying like that! Ellen wanted to lift her to the couch, but I thought we'd better wait until you came—"

"Why?" The doctor shot the question at him, and Storm, realizing his slip, swiftly countered:

"I didn't know what to think! I tell you, Doctor, when I first came in and saw her it looked almost like murder! My brain isn't clear yet from the shock of it, although when I saw the blood on the fender, of course, I knew she must have fallen, and then I remembered her condition—those fainting spells, and all that. There isn't a soul in the world who would harm a hair of Leila's head!" He threw up his hands with an impotent gesture. "I felt dazed, helpless! I had to depend on you, and I wanted you to see everything just as it was."

"You can rely on me, old man!" The doctor patted his arm and led him to the door. "We must not move her yet, however. Under the circumstances we'll have to notify the authorities, merely as a matter of form, and they may want to investigate for themselves. I'll call them up and then come and give you something to steady your nerves. You're bearing up splendidly, but we can't have you going to pieces until the formalities have been concluded. Is there anyone you would like me to send for; any member of the family, or friend?"

"Yes!" Storm exclaimed in a sudden flash of inspiration. "Get old George for me, will you, Doctor? George Holworthy, you know; 0328 Stuyvesant. Tell him to come out here on the first train, that I need him. Don't—don't go into details, but make him understand that it's serious, desperate! I'm not a weakling, I won't break down, but I'd feel stronger if George were here. We've been friends for years."

"I know; I'll get him." Dr Carr drew out his handkerchief and mopped his forehead. "Get into some clothes now. I'll be right with you."

"I would rather stay here with Leila, alone with her—" Storm murmured mendaciously. "I won't touch her, Doctor ; let me stay!"

"No." The physician transferred the key to the outside of the door and locked it decisively as he spoke. "It wouldn't do you any good, Storm. You've got to brace up. You have put this affair in my hands now, and I order you to pull yourself together. Get upstairs and take a cold shower and then I'll give you a sedative."

With a last glance at the closed door, Storm stumbled to the stairs and mounted, lurching against the banisters as though overcome by weakness; but in reality his brain was seething with the thought of the danger yet ahead.

He closed the door of his room softly behind him, and then paused. What if Carr's sympathetic, friendly manner had been assumed to cloak a suspicion of the truth? The physician had seemed to accept his theory, but he had not committed himself. Suppose he were following, tiptoeing up the stairs now to peer in at the keyhole—!

The thought was madness, yet Storm turned instinctively. The key of his door had been mislaid long ago and never replaced, but a heavy lounging robe hung from a peg on the center panel. Catching a fold of it he drew it back over the door-knob so that it trailed before the lock like a curtain, thick and impenetrable. His bathroom had no entrance leading to the hall, and the only other door—that opening on Leila's dressing-room was protected by a cretonne portière.

He realized that he had no need for secrecy, there was nothing to be done now which all the world might not safely see—and yet an insane desire came to him to conceal himself from all eyes. He must have a moment of respite from the role he was playing, a moment of peace and calmness to gird himself anew for what the immediate future might hold.

Did Carr accept the situation at its face value? The man whom in the night he had half-scorn fully dismissed from his mind as a simple country practitioner now appeared in a vastly different light. For the moment he held in his hands Storm's immunity from suspicion, and the latter's disquietude increased.

There was his step upon the stair! What would his face reveal?

With a quick revulsion of feeling, Storm sprang to the door and opened it.

The smile with which the benign physician greeted him removed all lingering doubt.

"Not taken your shower? Come, Storm, this won't do! I've 'phoned, and the coroner's assistant is on his way over from the county seat." He held out a small glass, and the other took it mechanically. "Drink this and pull yourself together, for there are some trying hours ahead."

VI

THE VERDICT

"You were right, unquestionably, Storm," Dr Carr announced twenty minutes later as the other joined him in the library. "I don't mind admitting that my thoughts—my sensations, rather—when first I saw the body were identical with what yours had been, but there's only one possible conclusion. Mrs Storm must have been seated in that big chair by the hearth when she felt suddenly faint; and in trying to rise, she must have fallen forward, striking her forehead with crushing force against that solid brass knob on the fender. Agnes tells me that she found her mistress lying face downward against it, and thinking she had merely fainted, turned the body over. It was only when she saw the wound that she screamed. Of one thing you may be sure; Mrs Storm didn't suffer. She never knew what struck her. Death came instantly."

Storm sank into a chair, his twitching face turned from the light. If Carr only knew!

"I must try to think that!" he murmured. "Did you get George Holworthy on the 'phone, Doctor?"

"Yes. He is on his way out here by now. Agnes gave me some coffee, and I told her to bring a tray for you.—No protests!" as Storm made a gesture of repugnance. "You are under my orders, remember, and you've got to keep going."

Storm drank the coffee obediently enough when it came, conscious of a craving for its stimulus. The first and most hazardous milestone was passed; Dr Carr had fallen for his game, had been completely hoodwinked by the circumstantial evidence he had arranged. He had won an unconscious yet powerful ally, and the way seemed clear before him, but the glow of elation was past.

While the physician droned on in a soothing monotone, seeking for words of consolation to assuage the grief of his patient and neighbor, the humming of a high-powered car reached their ears as it turned in at the gate and ploughed up the driveway, and Storm sank back.

"That is the coroner's man now." Dr Carr strode to the window. "Oh, he has sent young Daly, and the chief medical examiner is with him. That will simplify matters tremendously. I know them both, and I'll see that they don't bother you any more than is absolutely necessary."

Agnes ushered in a tall, lanky young man and his stouter, elderly companion who nodded in brisk, professional gravity.

"This is Mr Daly and Dr Bellowes, Mr Storm." Carr presented them smoothly. "Sorry to have brought you so far on a mere matter of form, gentlemen. I am prepared to issue a certificate of accidental death, but I should like to have you examine the body. This way, please; nothing has been touched."

Storm rose as the physician turned to lead the others to the den, but the young man called Daly waved him back.

"Your presence won't be necessary, Mr Storm." His tone was deferential, but there was a note of authority in it that brooked no opposition. "I will have to ask you a few questions later, but we won't trouble you now."

Storm bowed and waited until their footsteps diminished down the hall, and the door of the den closed definitely behind them. Then, with nervously clenching hands, he turned to the window. What a fool he was to harass himself with idle fears! Had not everything gone like clockwork, exactly as he had anticipated? He had been complete master of the situation so far, and he would be until the end. He must not, could not fail!

Old George would come soon, now. That had been a master stroke, that summoning of him! Besides being the natural, logical thing to have done under the circumstances, it provided a staunch, reliable buffer between himself and curious, sensation-seeking eyes. George's dense stupidity and blind affection would be in itself a safeguard, and he anticipated no difficulty in dissembling before him. What if George had suspected or even known of Leila's affair with Brewster? He would never dream that Storm himself had discovered it, much less that he had killed her.

What were the officials doing in there so long? Storm paced the floor restlessly. Surely the case was obvious enough; he couldn't have overlooked anything, after all! Why didn't they have done with it and get out of his house? He wanted time to think, a breathing space in which to prepare himself for the onslaught of neighbors and reporters when the truth came out.

As if timed to his thought, a familiar runabout which was passing halted at the gate just as it had on the previous day, and Millard, after gazing for a moment in blank amazement at the official car drawn up at the veranda steps, descended and came hurriedly up the path.

Storm saw him from the window and muttered in exasperation. To be annoyed now by that he-gossip was unthinkable! He'd soon send him about his business—!

He caught himself up suddenly. This was the moment for him to court sympathy, not brusquely repel it and awaken an antagonism which might beget dark rumor and suspicion. He hurried to the door, and when Millard puffed fussily up the steps of the veranda he found his host awaiting him with outstretched hands.

"Millard! It was good of you to stop. I hoped you would when I saw you passing."

"What's wrong, old chap? That's the Chief Medical Examiner's car, isn't it? I was afraid—" He broke off as the other raised his eyes. "Heavens, Storm, what is it?"

"My wife!" Storm bowed his head, and added brokenly: "She's dead, Millard! Died suddenly, sometime during the night."

"Mrs Storm!" Millard fell back a step, his apoplectic face paling. "What—? How? God, this is frightful! What caused it?"

"Dr Carr says it was one of her fainting spells. She must have fallen and struck her head. I—we only found her this morning."

"Terrible! I—I don't know what to say, old chap!" Millard stammered. His small, beady eyes strayed eagerly past his host into the darkened hallway, and he advanced, but Storm's figure barred the entrance. "I'm simply aghast! Poor, dear little woman! I can't believe it! You have all my sympathy, dear fellow, but words can't seem to express it just now. How—how did it happen—?"

"We don't know yet." Storm gripped the agitated little man's arm for a moment as if for support. "I can't talk of it! Carr will tell you all about it later, but I don't think he wants the news to get about until the formalities have been concluded with the coroner's men. I can depend on you—?"

"You know that, old chap!" Millard interrupted him warmly. "I say, isn't there anything that I can do? The car's right here, you know, and I'm glad to be of service—"

"Why, yes." Storm eyed him gratefully. "I've sent for George Holworthy, but he hasn't been told what has happened. He ought to be here on the next train, and it is due any minute. Would you mind running down to the station and bringing him back here, and—and break the news to him for me?"

"Certainly, dear fellow!" Millard clapped his hand to the other's shoulder. "I'll go at once, Storm. There doesn't seem to be anything a chap can say at a time like this, but I'm right here if you want me! Remember that, and try to—to bear it, some way. I'll be back in no time!"

He bustled off down the veranda steps and toward his waiting car, and Storm closed the door with a grim smile. He was well aware that Millard—who was known facetiously about the Country Club as the "town crier"—would spread the news of the tragic "accident" far and wide, and he had carefully planted in the other's mind the impression that Dr Carr was responsible for the theory of accident. He had always maintained a certain reserve with Millard, and realized that his confidence now had immeasurably flattered the little man, cementing a friendship which would prove valuable if by any chance ugly whispers arose.

Then, too, he had avoided the task of breaking the news to old George. Difficult as it had been to play his role before the tearful servants, the cautious physician and the county officials, he shrank far more from the ordeal of facing his friend with the story he had fabricated. It would be easy, of course; almost too easy. It was a battle of wits, a fair fight with others, but with slow-witted, loyal old George... He had turned back to the library when a voice speaking his name aroused him swiftly from his reverie.

"Mr Storm, I'd like to see you for a moment" It was Daly. "Don't be alarmed, please. Dr Beilowes is quite satisfied that Mrs Storm's death was accidental, but the circumstances are so unusual that as a mere matter of form I want a statement from you to file in my report. Will you tell me, please, what occurred from the time of your arrival home last evening until you summoned Dr Carr at seven o'clock this morning?"

Haltingly, as if still dazed with the shock, but with every nerve tinglingly on guard, Storm repeated his story exactly as he had told it to Dr Carr, and Daly listened attentively, punctuating it with quick nods of satisfaction, as though he were mentally checking off each detail.

At its conclusion he made no comment, but instead asked a question which brought a start of renewed apprehension to the other man.

"Do you know, Mr Storm, if your wife had any enemies? Is there anyone who will profit by her death or who had any reason for wishing her out of the way?"

"Good heavens, no!" Storm could feel the blood ebbing from his face, and his voice had grown suddenly husky. "You don't mean—?"

"I don't mean anything," Mr Daly retorted calmly. "I told you this was a mere matter of form, Mr Storm. Do you know of any enmity which your wife might have incurred?"

"None. Everyone who knew her loved her; she hadn't an enemy in the world," Storm stammered. "No one could profit by her death, and as to—to wishing her out of the way—"

"That is all right, sir. I don't want to distress you, but these facts must be clearly established." Mr Daly paused. "How long have you been married, and what was Mrs Storm's maiden name?"

"Leila Talmage. We were married ten years ago." Storm controlled his wildly leaping pulses and forced himself to reply calmly, weariedly, as though the subject caused him infinite pain. "She was an orphan, the ward of a friend of our family, and has no living relatives of whom I ever heard."

"Did she have any money of her own?" the other pursued.

"Very little. Ten or twelve thousand, I believe." Storm moistened his lips and drew himself up slightly. "My attorney, Wendle Foulkes, took charge of it for her at her request, but I have never made any inquiries concerning her expenditure of it. It was hers, to do with as she pleased."

"Then you don't know the value of her estate now?"

"No."

"Nor whether she left a will?"

"I do not, Mr Daly. My attorney can answer all such questions far better than I." Storm drew his hand once more across his eyes. Why did the fellow stare so infernally at him? "I must refer you to him. He will have to be notified, of course; I hadn't thought of that. My mind—I cannot collect myself! It is horrible that there should be even a thought of foul play in connection with my poor wife; it is almost a profanation! Her life was an open book, she was the soul of honor and goodness and charity—"

His voice broke realistically, and his inquisitor rose.

"I don't doubt you, but you will understand that we have to take every possibility into consideration in a case of this sort. The Chief will want to see you when he's through in there, but won't detain you long."

His searching gaze lowered at last, and he turned and left the room.

Storm listened to his retreating footsteps in a maze of conflicting emotion. Had that inquisition been merely the formality that the young official claimed, or had they stumbled on the truth? If Daly's efforts had been directed toward establishing a possible motive, Storm congratulated himself that he had more than held his ground. He had succeeded in placing on record a statement of absolute faith and trust in his wife, and surely his bearing as a grief- stricken husband had been seemingly sincere beyond question! If they suspected, though; if they unearthed that damnable affair of hers with Brewster, discovered that he had been in that house on the previous night and could prove that Storm himself returned before the other's departure...

The impudent chug-chug of a runabout broke in upon his troubled thought, and he turned to the hall just as the housemaid appeared on the stairs.

"Agnes, I'm going to my room. Mr Millard has just brought Mr Holworthy up from the station, I think. Send Mr Holworthy up to me, but tell Mr Millard I'll call him on the 'phone later. I can't see him now."

"Yes, sir." Agnes sniffed and lowered her red-lidded eyes. "The other gentlemen—?"

"They're still here. Let me know, please, when they want me."

She stepped aside and he passed her, mounting to his room. It was in order, and with rare tact the girl had left the door leading to Leila's apartments closed; yet as plainly as though it were open Storm could see before him every intimate detail: the little silver articles on the dressing table, the quaint old fourposter bed which had been his mother's the absurdly low chairs piled with cushions, Leila's favorite books scattered about—

A sudden dizziness seized him; the same sickening qualm which had assailed him that morning when he entered the den swept over him in an overwhelming flood. He had been keyed up since with the need of self-preservation, but now a swift reaction came, and he flung himself into a chair, his head buried in his arms outflung across the table. He had killed her, and she deserved it; she had been faithless! It was done and over with, and yet—!

Her presence seemed nearer him, the years of their love and life together rose before him, and something very like a dry, harsh sob burst from his throat.

"Norman! God, it isn't true! It can't be!"

The broken cry from the doorway fell like a dash of icy water on his rising emotion, and instantly on guard once more, Storm raised his head.

George Holworthy stood there, his homely face working grotesquely, tears starting unashamed from his faded blue eyes.

"I never dreamed—I was afraid when I got Carr's message that she was ill, but that a thing like this should have come—!"

"George!" Storm rose and their hands clasped. "I sent for you as soon as I could! I can't talk about it, I can't realize it! It is like some horrible nightmare! You won't leave me? You'll stay here and see me through?"

"I'm here, ain't I?" George gulped fiercely. "I suppose you've been badgered enough, and I won't add to it, but for God's sake tell me a little! Remember, I loved her, too!"

"I know you did, and she had a very real affection for you." Storm averted his head, for the sight of the other's genuine sorrow was unnerving.

"All I could get out of Millard was that you found her dead this morning, and that Carr said it was her old trouble, that catalepsy—*petit mal*, they call it, don't they? I never thought it could prove fatal!"

"It didn't. But she fell, striking her head—!" Storm paused eloquently. "When you see her, George, you'll understand. It's too awful, I can't—"

"But where is she? What have they done with her?" George glanced toward the closed door, and Storm shook his head.

"In the den. Agnes found her there and screamed—"

But Agnes herself appeared in the doorway, cutting his sentence short.

"If you please, Mr Storm, the gentlemen downstairs would like to speak to you."

"I'll be down." By a supreme effort he braced himself to meet the verdict. "You'll come too, George?"

George nodded and blew his nose resoundingly.

"I'm with you," he said simply, and together they descended the stairs.

Dr Bellowes met them at the library door.

"We have concluded our examination," he announced. "As my colleague, Doctor Carr, had already surmised, Mrs Storm's death was due to a fracture of the right temporal caused by a fall while suffering an attack of *petit mal*"

Storm closed his eyes, and for an instant the earth seemed to rock beneath his feet.

It was over and he had won! He had fooled them all!

"I feared it, Doctor," he remarked quietly, and congratulated himself at the calmness of his tone. "I should not have left her alone last night after the warning we had of a possible attack the day before—but I must try not to think of that now. Can't I offer you something before you start on your ride back? A cup of coffee perhaps?"

Dr Bellowes shook his head, but his eyes traveled to the humidor on the table, and Storm followed his glance.

"A cigar, then?" He opened the humidor and passed it around. "The matches are just in there—"

He lighted one, watching his hand curiously meanwhile. How steady it was! Not a tremor to reveal the excitement mounting within him. He had pulled off the greatest, grimmest scheme in the world, and yet not the flicker of an eyelash betrayed him!

Dr Bellowes blew out a cloud of smoke.

"Yes, Mr Storm," he resumed, "it was unquestionably an accident; a most unusual and unfortunate one. Unofficially, I should like to tender to you my most sincere sympathy."

"Thank you, Doctor."

Storm bowed and stood quite still as George showed them out.

If anyone had told him that such a plan could have been conceived and carried out successfully without a single hitch, he would have laughed him to scorn. He would not have believed anyone capable of such combined ingenuity and self-control, least of all himself!

The position of the body, the smear upon the brass knob of the fender, the blood-stained driver cleaned, the handkerchief and its ashes eliminated, the hair pin, the single golden hair, the light left burning—he mentally reviewed each clue in the case, recalled each step of the investigation, and realized that there had been no flaw.

It had been a supreme battle of wits, his against all the rest, and he had beaten them! He had won!

VII

THE LETTER

Despite his sense of victory the day was a long- drawn-out period of torture for Storm.

Upon the departure of Dr Carr and the officials, George Holworthy had to be told in detail the story of the night's tragic event, and its reiteration drew heavily upon the store of self-control which was left to his companion after the ordeal through which he had passed; but Storm narrated it carefully, with a critical consciousness of every effect.

"I don't know what is the matter with me!" he cried dramatically in conclusion. "I can't break down, I can't seem to feel, George! I saw her as she lay there, I tell myself that this ghastly, unbelievable thing is true, and yet it has no meaning for me! I catch myself listening for her step, waiting to hear her voice! Am I going mad?"

"It's the shock," George said quietly. "The stark horror of the thing has stunned you, Norman. You can't feel it yet, you are numb, I suppose."

He looked curiously shrunken and withered and years older as he sat hunched in his chair, his faded, red-rimmed eyes blinking fast. Storm felt a sense of impatience, almost of repugnance as he regarded him. His evident sorrow was a subtle reproach before which the other writhed. Could he endure his presence in the days which must decently elapse before the funeral? George would be useful, however, in the interim, and when it was all over he could shut himself away from everyone.

"That's why I sent for you," he observed. "I can't seem to get a grip on things, and I thought you would take charge for me and keep off the mob of sympathizers—"

"I will. I'll attend to everything, old man. There's bound to be a certain amount of publicity, you know, but I'll see the reporters myself, and fend off the neighbors. Carr will send in the undertaker, and I'll 'phone Foulkes. Is there anyone else you want me to notify?"

George did indeed prove invaluable, for Millard had spread the tidings and soon the house was besieged by horror-stricken friends of the dead woman. They came from all walks of life, from the humblest country-folk about to the most arrogant of the aristocratic colony, in mute testimony to the breadth of her kindliness and the affection she had inspired. From earliest afternoon, too, reporters began filtering in on every train, but George held them off with surprising tact and diplomacy, and by nightfall a semblance of peace had fallen upon the bereft household.

The den was restored to its normal state, the door locked, and in the dainty drawing-room across the hall from the library Leila lay as if asleep, her golden hair falling low to hide the cruel wound and all about her the early spring flowers she had loved.

Now that they were alone together, George's presence proved insufferable, and Storm, professing complete nervous exhaustion, suggested that they retire early.

George, worn out with his own emotions and the strain of the day, acquiesced in evident relief. He had dreaded a night-long vigil with his bereaved friend and rejoiced that the strange, seemingly dazed apathy which had held him in its grip was giving way to the demands of over-taxed nature.

Sleep, however, was furthest from Storm's intentions. There was work still to be done, and in secret. Foulkes had signified his intention of coming out on the first train in the morning, and it was possible that he might suggest going over Leila's papers. If that letter which she had tried to conceal the day before were found, or any other correspondence from Brewster, it might precipitate the rise of a suspicion which otherwise seemed now to be eliminated.

Leila's desk was down in the library, and waiting only until he felt assured that the occupant of the guest chamber across the hall had fallen asleep, Storm put on soft felt slippers, drew his dressing gown about him, and descended.

How still the house was! Still, yet vibrant with something unseen but palpitating as though the spirit had not wholly departed from that immobile form lying amid the blossoms, whose fragrance stole out with cloying, sinister sweetness upon the air.

Storm closed the library door noiselessly behind him, switched on the light and crossing to the little rose-wood desk stood transfixed.

A book lay upon it, and from between its leaves protruded, as if carelessly or hastily thrust there, what appeared to be the very letter he sought. "Leicester Building". The engraved letters stood out as he drew the envelope forth, but above them was a line which made him start.

"National Tool & Implement Company".

But Brewster was an insurance broker! The name had an oddly familiar ring, too. What could it mean?

With shaking fingers he drew the enclosure from the envelope and read:

Mrs Norman Storm:
Dear Madam:-

I have reconsidered my decision of this morning and am willing to sell to you the strip of land adjoining your property at the price you named, on condition that the deal be consummated with you personally. I will enter into no negotiations with your husband. If you will call at my office tomorrow, the ninth inst., with your check I will have the deed and bill of sale ready.

     Your obedient servant,
       ALPHEUS JAFFRAY

Storm crushed the letter in his hands. The trout stream! Leila had bearded their irascible neighbor in his town office and induced him to sell her the property which he himself had been unable to force or cajole the old scoundrel to relinquish! But why had she been so secretive about it? Why had she lied about her presence in town, sought to conceal the letter, striven to make a mystery where no cause for one existed?

The queries which hammered at his brain were swiftly swept aside by the one dominating fact. Her visit had not concerned Brewster, her lie had concealed no act of guilt or even indiscretion! What if—Great God! If he had made a hideous mistake—? But no! He had seen them together, she and her lover, in that very room not twenty-four hours before; had heard Brewster's impassioned words, witnessed his act of devotion! Whatever motive had prompted her secret purchase of the trout stream, it was beside the point at issue. There must be proof in her desk, proof to augment and support the evidence of his own eyes.

He tore the drawers open one after another, scattering the neat piles of correspondence, social notes, cards of invitation, receipted bills, memoranda and household accounts—his feverish fingers sought in vain among them for a single line of an intimate or sentimental nature. But then, Leila would scarcely have kept secret love letters in an open desk. Somewhere in her apartments upstairs, perhaps, she had arranged a hiding place for them.

Then a swift remembrance came to him. The secret compartment! Back of the small drawer between the pigeon-holes on the desk top was a small space to which access could be had only by pressing a hidden knob. Leila had found it by accident one day and had been almost childishly delighted with her discovery.

Storm removed the drawer, pressed the spring, and the false back slid aside revealing two packets of letters. One was bound by a bit of white satin ribbon, yellowing now and slightly frayed; the other encircled with a rubber band.

The sight of them brought a grimace of triumph to Storm's lips, but it changed quickly as he tore the ribbon from the first packet. The letters were all postmarked prior to ten years ago and were in his handwriting—his own love letters, written during the period of their engagement and before. One end of the ribbon was knotted about a dried flower; an orange blossom! It must have been from her wedding bouquet.

A strange tightness constricted his throat, and he thrust the packet hastily aside. He did not want to be reminded at this hour of the happiness, the fool's paradise in which he had lived before enlightenment came. No sentimentality about the past must be permitted to weaken his self-control now.

But the second packet, too, contained only his letters; those written since their marriage, mere notes of a most prosaic sort, some of them, sent to her during his infrequent absences from home and reminding her of trivial, everyday matters which required attention. The last, dated only a month before, concerned the reinstatement of MacWhirter, their ante-bellum gardener. Why had Leila kept every scrap of his handwriting as though she treasured it, as though it were precious to her?

For a long time he sat there staring at the scattered envelopes, the first vague, terrible stirring of doubt which had come when he read Jaffray's letter returning again to torture his spirit Then once more the scene of the previous night in that room arose in reassuring condemnation, and with a smothered oath he seized the letters and tore them viciously, the older packet with the rest, until nothing remained but a heap of infinitesimal scraps and the bit of yellowed ribbon.

He wanted them out of his sight, destroyed utterly, but where—? The fire in the kitchen range would have been banked for the night, but he could rake the coals aside. Sweeping the torn letters into a newspaper together with the ribbon, he made his way quietly to the kitchen. The range balked him at first. He strove vainly to coax a blaze from the livid coals, but with the aid of kindling wood and after much manipulation of the dampers he succeeded in producing a tiny flame. Upon this he thrust handfuls of the paper scraps, and when they caught and blazed up he thrust the ribbon deep among them.

How slowly they burned! The edges of the ribbon charred and it curled up, writhing like a living thing in agony. The flame was dying down, and Storm had turned frantically to the wood-box to pile on more fuel, when suddenly there came a grayish puff, a leaping tongue of fire, and the ribbon vanished, leaving only a heap of pale flakes against the darker, coarser ashes.

Storm scattered them and was placing an extra stick of wood upon the glowing coals to make sure that the evidences of his work would be wholly obliterated, when the utterance of his name in surprised accents made him wheel as though a blow had been dealt to him from behind.

"Norman! I thought you were in bed!" George, his short, obese figure, grotesque in an ugly striped bathrobe, stood blinking in the doorway. "What on earth are you doing down here? And what's burning? There's a funny odor—"

"Wretched green wood. No wonder the cook grumbles about this range; I thought I should never get it going!" Storm interrupted hastily. "I couldn't sleep, and wanted a cup of coffee. There was no use in disturbing the servants."

"Why didn't you call me?" demanded the other. "I could have made it for you. You look all done up, Norman. Did you take that sleeping stuff Carr left for you?"

Storm shook his head.

"It would take more than that to bring sleep to me tonight," he said.

"Well, anyway, I don't know what you are poking about in here for!" objected George. "You're a chump to try to get the range going at this hour when you've got that electric percolator in the dining-room. Here's the coffee; come on in there and I'll have it ready for you in no time!"

Storm followed him in silence, only too glad to get him away from the kitchen, and watched him as in deft bachelor fashion he manipulated the percolator.

Storm drank the coffee when it was made and then dragged George off to the library where the latter at length fell asleep upon the couch; but Storm sat huddled in his chair, dry-eyed and brooding, until the dawn.

Wendle Foulkes appeared at nine o'clock, his keen old face very solemn, and almost his first words, when his condolences were made, set at rest a question which Daly had raised on the previous day.

"You know, of course, that Leila left no will," he began. "At least, none to my knowledge, and I am certain she would have consulted me had she entertained any thought of making one. Death was farthest from her imagining, poor child! What she left is yours, of course, but we will have to comply with the law and advertise for heirs."

Storm made a gesture of wearied impatience, and the attorney went on:

"There is something I must tell you, Norman. You were not my first visitor on Monday morning. Leila had been before you; she left only a few minutes before your arrival, but she had requested me to say nothing to you of her coming."

"But why?" Storm stared.

"She came to consult me about a piece of property which she wanted to buy: that strip of land next your place here, over which you and Alpheus Jaff ray have haggled and fought for years. She had gotten in the old man's good graces somehow, and she believed that she could persuade him to sell it to her even though he was so violently antagonistic to you. I don't mind telling you frankly that I advised against it, Norman. It would have taken all that she had left of her original capital, and I knew how yours was dwindling, but she won me over." He paused and wiped his eyeglasses, clearing his throat suspiciously meanwhile. "She ordered me to keep the proposed transaction a secret from you, and I promised, but now it is only right that you should know. She left to go to Jaff ray's office, over in the Leicester Building."

George Holworthy, who was hovering in the background, drew in his breath sharply, but Storm repeated with dogged insistence:

"Why should my wife have wanted to keep such a secret from me? I cannot understand it I She told me everything—" He paused involuntarily, biting his lip. There was one other thing she had not told him, had not confessed even at the last!

"You would not have been kept in ignorance long." The attorney's tone was pitying. "Have you forgotten what day tomorrow is?"

" 'Tomorrow?' " Storm repeated blankly.

"Your birthday."

"God!" The exclamation came from George. "And the funeral!"

Storm sat as if turned to stone. It had been for him! Her secret trip to town, her innocent, pitiful subterfuges, her joy over the letter which had told her that the surprise she had planned was within her grasp! All for him!

Then a swift revulsion of feeling came. Bah! It may have been to throw more dust in his eyes, to render his confidence in her doubly assured; a sop to her own conscience, perhaps. The infinite reproach in her eyes when he had accused her there in the den, her air of conscious righteousness when she had said: "You will regret that accusation bitterly when you learn the truth—" What a consummate actress she had become!

Fate had played into his hands, though; he had witnessed her perfidy with his own eyes. Had it not been for his opportune return that night, how easily his suspicions would have been allayed! How contrite he would have been at his doubt of her, and how she and her lover would have gloated over the ease with which he had been deceived!

But the others were looking at him, amazed at his silence, and with an effort he pulled himself together.

"Her last thought was for me!" His voice shook with the irony of it, but to the two men it was an evidence of purely natural emotion. "The thought of it only makes what has come harder for me to bear! Her unselfishness, her devotion !"

"I know, boy, I know." Foulkes laid his hand for a moment on Storm's shoulder. "You must try to remember that you have been far luckier than most men; you have had ten years of such perfect happiness as falls to the lot of few of us!"

"That is true." Storm bowed his head to conceal the sneer of bitterness which rose unbidden to his lips. "I cannot realize that it has come so suddenly, so horribly to an end!"

A brief discussion of business affairs ensued, and then Wendle Foulkes took his departure. A silence had fallen between the other two which was broken at last by George.

"So that was it!" he murmured as if to himself. "That was why she invented that luncheon at the Ferndale Inn—"

THE LETTER

"What?" demanded Storm, aghast; How much did George know? "Invented what luncheon?"

"Don't you remember when I dined here with you—God! Was it only last Monday night?—and Leila told us she had lunched that day at the Ferndale Inn, when in reality she had been to the city? I repeated that remark, because I could scarcely believe my ears, but she stuck to her little fib. I did wonder at your surprise for I had seen you both in town at noon."

"You had—seen us both?" Storm repeated.

"Yes. I was going through Cortlandt Street coming out of the Leicester Building and saw you standing there staring after her as though you had seen a ghost," George explained innocently. "I started to hail you and tried to cross, but a line of traffic got in the way and when the street was clear you had disappeared. I meant to tell you that night but I didn't."

"Why, that's so! It must have been Leila, after all, whom I saw." Storm weighed each word carefully. "I wasn't sure, you know, she passed me so quickly, and when she spoke that night of having been to the Ferndale Inn I naturally concluded that I must have been mistaken; it couldn't have been she I saw. It did not occur to me for a moment that she was telling even a little white lie, for Leila has never kept anything from me in all her life, George."

He spoke with a deliberate emphasis, striving desperately to eradicate from the other's mind the thought that he had been aware of her deception. Confound the fellow! Why had he, out of all in the city, been the one to witness that unexpected meeting! His silence later was significant, too. Had he an inkling of Storm's state of mind that night?

"I see. Couldn't imagine why she should have kept her little expedition to herself, but it wasn't any affair of mine, of course." George spoke with an elaborate carelessness which did not seem wholly convincing to the critical ears of the other man. "Funny it should have deceived you, for she didn't take me in for a minute, she fibbed so—so clumsily, bless her! I thought it probably some little joke she was planning, but your approaching birthday never occurred to me. It is odd, isn't it, that we should have talked of old Jaffray and that trout stream when you walked to the station with me later?"

"Leila knew how I had set my heart upon it," Storm returned. It would do no good to revert to the topic of the lie. Reiterated explanation of his attitude would only deepen any suspicion which George might still entertain. To ignore it, to pass it by as a thing of no moment, was the only course. "Do you remember that she complained of feeling ill that night?"

George nodded.

"That was the first thing I thought of when Millard broke the news to me, after I could begin to think at all," he observed. "She must have had a warning that one of those attacks was coming on. I spoke of it to her, as you may recall, but she denied it; afraid of worrying you, I suppose. To think that it should have come the very next night when she was alone and helpless!"

Storm drew a deep breath. At least, George had no shadow of a suspicion as to the real cause of her death.

"Don't talk about it!" he implored. "I've reproached myself a hundred times with not being at hand, but how could I know?"

"Forgive me! You couldn't, of course. No one could have anticipated it. It was to be, that's all one could say, though God only knows why! You were not to blame."

He threw his arms across the other's shoulders in an affectionate, consoling clasp, and in his mild, candid eyes Storm read only pity, sorrow and an abiding trustfulness.

VIII

THE TRUTH

"I am the resurrection and the life—" The white-frocked minister's voice rose solemnly above the subdued rustlings and sighing whispers in the little vine-wreathed church, and the stirring ceased. A robin peered in curiously at one of the open windows from his perch on a maple bough and chirped inquiringly, and the scent of lilacs was wafted in from the rector's garden to mingle with the heavier fragrance of lilies and white roses heaped about the casket at the altar steps.

It was such a small casket, almost like that of a child, and fairly buried beneath the weight of the floral offerings which banked it; a varied collection of offerings, for the costliest of hot-house set pieces mingled with sheaves of home-grown blossoms, and rare orchids nestled beside humble wild violets, but each had their place.

The congregation, too, was a heterogeneous one. Rich and poor, smart and shabby, the country club colony and the villagers met in a common democracy to do honor to their dead friend.

"The Lord gave and the Lord hath taken away—" The minister went on to the end, and then the voices of a hidden choir chanted softly: "Lord, thou hast been our refuge: from one generation to another..."

In the front pew Norman Storm rested his sleek head upon his black-gloved hand, and George Holworthy beside him cleared his throat huskily. In the moment of stillness which followed the Psalm, a woman's sob rose from somewhere back in the church, the sound jangling in Storm's ears like a touch upon naked nerves.

The last act of the farce, and then peace! Peace in which to plan for the future, to gain strength with which to shut out vain, maddening memories, to meet and cope with the change which his own act had wrought in his life. But would peace come?

Everything had gone smoothly; his scheme to evade justice and preserve himself from danger had been crowned with success; but in fortifying himself against suspicion and accusation from outside, he had not thought that a more subtle enemy might arise to be faced and vanquished or forever hold him in miserable thrall.

His love for Leila had not died with her. Despite her unfaithfulness, to the thought of which he clung doggedly, he could not exorcise her gentle influence. Everything in the house spoke mutely to him of her, everywhere he turned were evidences of her care and thoughtfulness and charm. In vain he reminded himself that it was over and done with, a closed chapter never to be recalled. He was beginning to fear himself, to dread the hours of solitude ahead as much as he looked forward to them. The voice of his conscience was whispering, threatening, and he must silence it or know no peace.

George glanced furtively at him now and then as the service went on, but he gave no sign. It drew to a close at last, and still he sat there immersed in his own thoughts until a touch upon his arm roused him to a consciousness of the present. Half-way down the aisle Richard and Julie Brewster with exalted faces and hands clasped like children stood aside to let him pass, but he did not even see them, and those who pressed forward and would have spoken paused at sight of his face. Pitying shocked murmurs followed him as he and George stepped into the car, but he did not heed them, and the long ride to the cemetery progressed in silence.

The brief, simple service of committal, the clods of earth falling dully, heavily into the grave and then came the interminable drive home. George's glances were less furtive now, more openly charged with amazement. Storm had not shed a tear, had not vouchsafed an utterance of emotion throughout those solemn hours. His friends wondered how great the reaction would be from such long, pent-up grief, and as they swept into the driveway before the silent, empty house which awaited them he ventured a suggestion.

"Norman, don't you want to pack up and come and stay in town with me for a few days? The change will do you good and give you time to—to get used to things."

Storm stifled the exasperated rejoinder which rose to his lips and replied quietly:

"Thanks, old man, but I want to be here, alone. I've got to face facts sooner or later, to bring myself to a realization that she has gone, and I'm better off here."

"Well, maybe that's so," George conceded. "Country air's the best, and I'll run out now and then to cheer you up. You'll take to playing golf again after a bit—"

"Don't!" The cry was wrung from Storm's very soul. Never again would he hold a golf-stick in his hands! He could see now before him that driver with the dark stains spattered upon it, and he recoiled shuddering from the apparition, while George inwardly cursed his own tactlessness, the while wholly ignorant of how his clumsy, well-meant effort at consolation had pierced the armor of the other man's self-control.

The fickle May sunshine vanished, and before the coming of twilight a bank of heavy gray clouds formed in the west, presaging a storm. They made a pretense of dining, while the rising wind swept gustily about the house and moaned in the chimneys like a thing in pain.

Storm still preserved his stoic calm, and George's perturbation grew. It wasn't natural, wasn't like the Norman he had known from college days. The younger man had always been outwardly reserved, but such stern, almost deliberate self-repression was new to him and filled his friend with vague alarm.

"You didn't close your eyes during the night before last, and you couldn't have slept much last night, Norman, for I heard you walking the floor at all hours," he remarked. "Don't you think it would be well to call in Carr and have him look you over and give you something quieting? You'll be ill if you keep this up."

"I'm all right!" Storm responded with a touch of impatience. "Don't worry about me, George. I'll turn in early and by tomorrow I'll get a fresh grip on myself—"

"I think you've got too tight a grip on yourself as it is," George interrupted.

"What do you mean?" Storm shot the question at him almost fiercely. Was he under surveillance, his every mood and gesture subject to analysis? Why couldn't the other let him alone?

"You're not meeting this normally," replied George in all seriousness. "Hang it all, I'd rather see you violent than like this! There's something horrible about your calmness, the way you are clamping down your feelings! If you would just give way—"

"I can't," Storm protested in the first wholly honest speech which had passed his lips. "I'm all frozen up. For God's sake, don't nag me, George, because I'm about all in!" The other subsided, but Storm could feel his eyes upon him, and their mute solicitude drove him to an inward frenzy. At all costs he must get away from that insistent scrutiny! He would lock himself in his room, feign sleep, illness, anything! George had served his turn, and Storm thanked fortune that business would of necessity demand the fussy, faithful little man's presence in town the next day.

He was casting about for an excuse as they rose from the table when all at once the front door knocker sounded faintly, almost apologetically.

"I can't see anyone! I won't!" The haggard lines deepened about Storm's mouth. "In Heaven's name, can't they respect my—my grief? I'm going upstairs. George, you get rid of them. Send them away, whoever they are!"

But George did not send them away. Listening from above, Storm heard the front door open and close, heard George's low rumble, and a reply in higher but softly modulated feminine tones. Then came a masculine voice which made him grip the stair rail in sudden fury not unmixed with consternation.

Richard Brewster! It couldn't be; the fellow would not dare intrude his presence here, even though he fancied his secret unshared by any living soul! But that was unmistakably Julie's voice raised in almost tearful pleading, and then Brewster spoke again.

What had brought them here? Why didn't George get rid of them as he had been told to do? Could it be that Julie had discovered the truth of her husband's unfaithfulness, and with a woman's hysterical notion of justice had brought Brewster here to force his confession to the man he had wronged? It was evident from the sounds that reached his ears that George was showing them into the library, was taking it upon himself to disregard Storm's express commands. Damn them all! Why couldn't they let him alone?

A brief colloquy ensued, and then George mounted the stairs.

"Look here!" he began in a sepulchral whisper. "It's the Brewsters, Norman, and I think you ought to see them for a minute. There's something they want to tell you—"

"I don't want to hear it!" interrupted Storm fiercely. "Good God, man, can't you see I'm in no condition to listen to a lot of vapid condolences? I told you to send them away!"

"I would have done so, but I think you ought to let them tell you," George insisted with the meek, unyielding tenacity which the other man had always found exasperating. "Julie Brewster is terribly wrought up; she says that in justice to—to Leila's memory you must hear what she has to say."

In justice to Leila's memory! Storm gave a sudden, involuntary start. There could be no ambiguity about that phrase. With a feeling as if the world were crashing down about his ears, he thrust George unceremoniously aside and descended the stairs.

They were standing side by side on the hearth rug awaiting him, Julie in tears but with her face bravely lifted to his, Brewster meeting his eyes without a tremor.

"It is good of you to see us, Mr Storm." Julie was making an obvious effort to control her emotion. "We wouldn't have intruded, but I wanted you to know the truth; I couldn't bear the thought that the shadow of even the slightest misunderstanding should rest between you and—and Leila's memory now, especially when it was all my fault."

"'Your fault'?" Storm repeated, "Sit down, please. I don't understand—"

"We won't detain you long, old man." It was Brewster who spoke, but his words failed to pierce the tumult in the other's brain. "We felt it would comfort you as much as anything could to know that almost her last thought on earth had been for the happiness of others."

Storm's eyes had never left the woman's face, and to their mute command she responded:

"I'm not going to try your patience with a long story of my own foolishness, but I did a wicked, selfish thing in dragging poor Leila into my troubles just to save myself. She was so generous, so self-sacrificing that she did not murmur at the risk to herself, and I never realized until she—she was dead that I might have been the cause of a misunderstanding between you at the very last. It has almost killed me to think of it, and I simply had to come and tell you the truth about the whole affair!"

Storm tried to collect his reeling senses, but only one clear thought came to his rescue. These people must never know, never suspect that any trouble had arisen between him and Leila.

He steadied his voice with an effort at composure.

"I don't know what you mean, Mrs Brewster. If my poor wife was able to help you out of any difficulty—I am glad, but I know nothing of it. You speak of a risk—?"

"Yes. I have been very foolish—wilfully, blindly foolish—in the way I've acted for weeks past." She paused and then hurried on shamefacedly. "You see, I thought Dick was neglecting me, and to pay him out I've been flirting outrageously with Ted Mattison. Leila tried to influence me, but I wouldn't listen to her, and when Dick woke up to what was going on and ordered me not even to speak to Ted again I—I resented it and defied him.

"Last Monday I motored out to the Ferndale Inn for lunch alone with Ted, and some horrid, gossipy people were there who knew how I'd been trotting about. I didn't think they had caught a glimpse of Ted then, but I was sure that if they had recognized me they would put two and two together and tell Dick, and I was afraid; terribly afraid, for Dick had threatened to leave me if I disobeyed him.

"As soon as I reached home that afternoon I rushed to Leila, told her the whole thing and made her promise to say that she had been to the Inn with me. It never occurred to me that that promise would make her tell you a lie; I'm afraid I didn't think about anything except the trouble I was in and how I could manage to get out of it."

So that was it! They had come to explain about that paltry lie! Brewster dared to stand there while his wife made her trivial confession, while all the time—! A turbulent flame of rage arose in Storm's heart, but he quelled it rigorously. Caution, now! Brewster must not suspect!

"I knew that my wife had not been with you." Could that be his own voice speaking with such quiet restraint? "In fact, I had seen her myself in town at noon, although she did not know it. Please don't distress yourself further, Mrs Brewster; I know what her errand was in town and why she wished to keep it from me."

"Oh!" Julie started for a moment and then added miserably: "Leila was sure that you guessed she had fibbed to you. The very next day—the last day of her life!—she begged me to absolve her from her promise, for she said you had seemed so strange and cold to her that morning she was afraid you suspected, and it was the first time she had ever told you an untruth!"

"She must have imagined a change in my attitude," Storm said hastily. "I was preoccupied and in a hurry to get to town, but that little white lie never gave me a moment's uneasiness. I would have chaffed her about it only I did not want to spoil her surprise."

"Surprise!" Julie echoed.

"Yes. When I had seen her in town the day before she was just coming out of Alpheus Jaffray's office in the Leicester Building." He felt a measure of grim satisfaction at Brewster's uncontrollable start. "She had been there to arrange to purchase from him the trout stream which adjoins the property here and which he had refused to sell me; you know as well as the rest of the crowd what a veritable feud has existed between the old fellow and me. I learned the truth from my attorney, whom Leila had consulted previously about the transaction.

My poor wife intended it as a birthday surprise for me. My birthday is today—today!"

He turned away to hide the rage which was fast getting beyond his control at the smug, hypocritical presence of that other man, but his emotion was misread by both his companions.

"Today! How terrible for you, Storm!" began Brewster, but his wife sobbed:

"If Leila had only guessed! But that untruth made her positively wretched! Why, when I telephoned to her late that night and she came out to meet me—"

"You telephoned to her! She met you—!" The room whirled and grew black before Storm's eyes, and the woman's voice, although clear and distinct, seemed to come from far away.

"Yes. I'd had a terrible row with Dick when he came home that night, and I knew he had heard something more about Ted, though I didn't know what. I was nearly crazy, Mr Storm, and when he rushed out of the house in anger I 'phoned Leila and begged her to meet me and help me; tell me what to do! She had promised that afternoon to come to me if I needed her. You had gone to the station with Mr Holworthy when I called up, and Leila did meet me, at the edge of the golf course.

"She urged me to tell Dick everything, but I wouldn't. I might just as well have done so, though, for those horrid people had seen Ted with me at the Inn, after all, and they went straight to Dick the next day. If only I hadn't persuaded Leila to lie for me! It wasn't any use, and it made some of her last hours unhappy. I shall never forgive myself, never!—Oh, don't look at me like that, Mr Storm! I can't bear it!"

Storm had slowly risen from his chair, one hand clutching the table edge as though for support, his eye fixed in an unwavering gaze of horror at the one thing visible in the whirling vortex about him: the white face of Julie. In his dazed brain a hideous fact was taking shape and form, and his soul cowered before it.

He essayed to speak, but no sound issued from his dry lips, and Brewster stepped forward.

"Try not to blame Julie too much, old man," he begged. "You see, the poor little girl was desperate. I was as much at fault in the situation between us as she was; your dead wife showed me that and brought me to reason. The last act of her life was to save me from wrecking both mine and Julie's, and we can never be grateful enough to her memory. That is why we had to come here tonight to tell you."

Slowly Storm's gaze shifted to the other man's face, and the inexorable truth of Brewster's sincerity was forced upon his wretched consciousness. Still he could find no words, and the other continued:

"When I confronted Julie and she stuck to her story, I came here to your wife to confirm the truth of what I had heard. She was loyal to Julie, she tried to make me believe that she had accompanied her to the Inn, but she was too inherently honest to brave it out, and I practically tricked her into admitting the truth. I was going to rush home then in my jealous rage and break with Julie forever, but your wife restrained me, Storm; she convinced me that Julie hadn't done anything really wrong, anything that I could not forgive, and showed me where I, too, had been at fault in neglecting her for my business, even though it was for her that I wanted to succeed. She made me see that we could begin all over again on a firmer basis even than before, just when I thought everything was ended and the future held nothing but separation and despair.

"I can't tell you what it meant to me, that quiet talk with your wife here in this very room! It was Tuesday night, you know, and death must have come to her shortly after. I can't realize it even now, she seemed so radiant, so splendidly alive! I'll never forget what she did for me, and if I thought that—that the excitement of our interview—! I'm afraid I made rather a scene! If it hurt her, brought on that stroke, or fainting spell—!"

"No. It was a form of catalepsy, you know." A totally strange voice was speaking in a monotonous, dragging undertone. Storm did not recognize it as his own. Blind instinct alone braced him to a last effort to dissemble. "No one could predict when it was coming on or what caused it... No one was to blame."

The lie died in his throat, and all at once he began to tremble violently as if the chill of the grave itself were upon him. He caught at the table again, his whole body shaking, collapsing, and with a harsh, strangling cry the floodgates were opened at last. Sinking to his knees, he buried his face in his arms lest the guilt which consumed him be revealed, and sobbed out his anguish unrestrained. He did not feel Julie's arms about him, her tears against his cheek, nor know when her husband led her gently away. He was face to face with the warped and blackened thing which was his soul, and with that vision he descended to the nethermost depths.

IX

THE ESCAPE

When Storm came to himself he was lying on the library couch with the gray dawn seeping in at the curtained windows and George's rotund figure in the hideous striped bathrobe looming up grotesquely from an improvised bed formed of two arm-chairs.

Storm felt a vague sense of irration. What was he doing there, dressed save for his shoes and collar, instead of being in pajamas in his own bed, and why was George hanging around?

Then the mists of sleep cleared from his brain, and remembrance came. Leila was innocent, and he had killed her! True to him in every act and word and thought, yet he had flung a monstrous accusation at her, and struck her down. His Leila! He saw her again as she lay huddled at his feet, and could have cried aloud in his anguish.

If he could but take back that blow! If only it were given him to live over once more the time which had passed since he saw her on that crowded street and doubt first entered his mind! If he could only speak to her, tell her—!

Then a measure of sanity returned to him. She was dead. He had killed her. Nothing could alter that, nothing could bring her back. No reparation, no expiation would undo his mad act and restore the life that he had taken. If he himself were to live, to go on, he must put behind him all thought of the past; crush back this creeping menace of remorse which threatened to overwhelm him. Regret would avail him nothing now. He had loved the woman who had shared his life for ten years, but she was gone and the future was before him, long years in which, since he could not atone, he must school himself to forget.

At least no one would ever suspect the secret which he carried in his heart. The worst was over, he had fooled them all! But with the thought a new terror gripped him by the throat. What had he done, what had he said when the revelation of Leila's innocence swept him from his moorings of self-control? The Brewsters had been there, both of them, staring at him as though the ghost of Leila herself had risen to accuse him! George must have been hovering about somewhere, too; must have taken care of him, helped him to the couch, watched over him throughout those hours of unconsciousness, *and listened!* Great God! Had he betrayed himself?

The light was growing brighter now, bringing out the familiar shapes of the furniture against the gloom and revealing in startling clarity the tired lines in the relaxed face of his self-appointed nurse. Storm sat up and scrutinized it half fearfully. Could George sleep like that, exhausted though he well might be, if he had gained an inkling of the truth? It seemed impossible, and yet Storm felt that he must know the worst. A direct accusation, even, would be better than this suspense. The first look would tell, the first glance that passed between them.

Storm coughed, and George's eyes opened sleepily, wandered vaguely about and then as they came to bear on the upright figure on the couch, warmed with a sudden clear light of affectionate compassion.

"Norman, old boy! How do you feel? Can I get you anything?"

Storm sank back with a sigh of relief.

"No. I—a drink of water—" he mumbled and closed his eyes as George rose and padded off in his flapping slippers down the hall. There still remained the Brewsters, and his sudden collapse in their presence was enough of itself to arouse their suspicion aside from the wild words which might have issued unbidden from his lips. He must learn what had taken place!

When George returned with the glass Storm drained it and then asked weakly:

"Went to pieces, didn't I?"

"You sure did, but it was coming to you," George affirmed. "You're all right now, though, so just rest and try not to think of anything. Carr fixed you up in good shape—"

"Oh, Lord!" groaned Storm. "Carr! I didn't even know he was here! How did you get rid of the Brewsters?"

"Well, it wasn't easy!" A faint smile lighted George's tired face. "Dick's got sense enough, but that little scatterbrained wife of his wanted to stay and take care of you! It was all I could do to persuade her to go home."

"And all that while I was making an exhibition of myself before them!" Storm exclaimed bitterly.

"You were not," retorted George. "You broke down, of course, just as I knew you must, sooner or later. I hadn't been easy in my mind about you all day, and I didn't like the look on your face when you went down to the library to see them, so I stuck around, not eavesdropping, old boy, but to be at hand in case you needed me. I could hear their voices, and then you gave a kind of a cry, and I butted in.

"I found Julie fussing over you, and I motioned to her husband to get her away into the drawing-room. He came back and we put you on the couch, and that's all there is to it. I told them to stop in at Carr's and send him here."

"What did I say? I mean," Storm hastily amended, "I don't remember anything. Julie and Dick came to tell me how Leila had brought them together again when they were on the point of a separation. You remember when she told us that she had been out to the Ferndale Inn with Julie? That wasn't only to keep her visit to old Jaffray's office secret, but because she had promised Julie to lie for her. They thought I might have misunderstood, and that it would comfort me to know she had made peace between them, but instead it—it broke me up! The full realization came over me of all that I had lost, and I went off my head, I guess. Tell me what I said, George."

"Why, nothing! You just—hang it all, man, you gave way to your feelings, that's all! You didn't *say* anything," George replied uncomfortably. "When the doctor came he gave you a good stiff hypodermic, and you dropped off to sleep like a baby. You're bound to feel rocky, you know, but you're over the worst of it!"

"Poor old George!" With renewed confidence there came to Storm a twinge of compunction. "You look as though you needed the doctor yourself! You must have had a rotten night."

"Never you mind about me!" returned George gruffly. "Here! Carr said you were to take this when you woke up and not to talk too much."

Obediently Storm took the medicine and almost immediately drifted off into troubled sleep.

It was broad noon when he awakened once more with the fragrant odor of coffee in the air and George standing before him, dressed for departure.

"Sorry, old boy, but I've got to run up to town, you know. You'll be all right for a few hours, and I'll be back before night. Drink your coffee, take a cold bath and get out on the veranda in the sun. Nobody'll bother you; I've seen to that."

Storm tried faintly to protest against George's return; he didn't need any care, he would be better off alone, and the other mustn't neglect his business affairs any longer. But George was not to be swerved from his purpose, and after a few hours of solitude Storm was in a mood to welcome his return.

In his weakened state he did not find it easy to keep his truant thoughts from straying to the past, and a horror which he was unable to combat made him shun his own society.

For the next few days, while the flood of condolences still poured in, he clung to George as to an anchor; but when the last dismal conventions had been observed and the household had settled down to something like order, his old feeling of irritation against his friend returned. George's eternal pussyfooting about the house as though death yet lingered there, his lugubrious face and labored attempts at cheer and consolation became insupportable, and his host breathed a sigh of relief when he ultimately departed.

Spring advanced, and with returning strength Storm's nerves steadied; and, secure in the knowledge that his guilt was buried forever, he took up the daily round once more.

A week after the funeral, he returned to his sinecure at the offices of the Mammoth Trust Company. The neighbors, possibly because of George's forewarning, had left him considerately alone in the interim, but now as he stood on the station platform awaiting his customary train for the city, the ubiquitous Millard advanced beaming.

"By Jove, this is good, old chap! Glad you are getting back into the harness again; best thing for you!" he exclaimed. "Fine weather we're having now, and the course is in wonderful condition; never better! I'm in topping form, if I do say it myself; and I haven't missed a day."

Despite his volubility, there was an odd constraint in his manner, and Storm eyed him curiously. Could it be a latent suspicion?

"You'll be going in for the tournament?" he enquired briefly.

"Surest thing you know! Too bad you—" Millard caught himself up. "I say, though, why don't you get up early now and then and play a round or two with me before breakfast?

Nobody else out then, it would do you no end of good. How about tomorrow?"

Storm shook his head, checking the shudder which came involuntarily at the suggestion.

"Thanks, but I'm not quite up to it. I think I'll let golf alone for a while," he replied, adding hastily as he saw signs of remonstrance in the other's face, "I've got too much to do, reinvestments to make and that sort of thing."

"Of course," Millard nodded. "You'll have your hands full, but you would find that an occasional round would set you up wonderfully. Nothing like it to straighten you out and take your mind off things. Just 'phone me if you feel like it any day, old chap, and I'll join you."

The appearance of several belated fellow-commuters saved Storm from the necessity of a reply, and as they came up to greet him he eyed each in turn furtively.

They were cordial enough, but none alluded directly to his bereavement, and the same constraint was evident in their bearing that Millard had manifested. He continued to study them on the train from behind the shelter of his newspaper. Unmistakable relief had registered itself on their faces when the train came, and now a few of them were ostentatiously buried in the market reports; but for the most part, in groups of two and three, they were discussing their business affairs, and to the listener their tones seemed unnecessarily raised. Not one had ventured to take the vacant seat beside him.

Had the Brewsters spread broadcast the story of his emotional outburst in their presence, and could it have occasioned remark, started vague rumor and conjecture which might yet lead to the discovery of the truth? In vain he told himself that he was over-analytical, that these old friends shrank not from him but from dilating upon his tragic loss. To his apprehensive imagination their manner held a deeper significance than that of mere masculine inability to voice their sympathy, and with gnawing persistency the menacing possibilities rankled in his brain.

At the office, after the formal condolences of his associates, Storm slipped mechanically into the old, well-ordered routine; but here, too, he fancied that he was being eyed askance. He could at least avoid running the gauntlet of his clubs for a time without occasioning remark, but the thought of Greenlea itself and all that it held for him had become obnoxious, hideous! The return to that empty house day after day; could he endure it without going mad?

He caught the club car in a mood of surly defiance, but he had scarcely taken his accustomed place when Richard Brewster appeared and without waiting for an invitation seated himself beside him.

"Awfully glad to see you on the job again." He spoke heartily, and his beaming face corroborated his words. "We were worried about you, you know, the other night; Julie wanted to stay and take care of you, but Holworthy wouldn't hear of it. I hope you've forgiven us for intruding."

Storm eyed him watchfully, but the guileless friendliness of the younger man was patent, and the other sighed in relief.

"I understand your motive, and I thank you both for coming," he said after a moment's pause. "Sorry I lost control of myself, but I'd been keeping up for so long—"

"It was only natural," Brewster interrupted. "You'll be leaving us, I suppose, for a time anyway, as soon as you've got the estate settled. We'll miss you—"

"Leaving?" Storm stared.

"You'll go away for a—a rest, won't you? New scenes and all that sort of thing? It will be hard for you to go on here." The younger man broke off and added hastily:

"Julie was saying only this morning at breakfast that if you decided to keep the house open you would need a housekeeper, and she knows of a splendid woman, an elderly widow in reduced circumstances—"

Storm halted him with an abrupt gesture of negation.

"I haven't made any plans yet, Brewster. The maids I've got are used to my ways and capable of running things temporarily, although it will be necessary to make other arrangements, of course, if I decide to remain in Greenlea." The reply was mechanical, for his thoughts were busied with the new vista which the other's assumption had opened before his mental vision. "I am grateful to Mrs Brewster for her interest, and if I need the woman of whom she spoke I will let her know. Just now I am drifting; I haven't looked ahead."

Barker met him as usual at the station, and during the short drive home he glanced about him at the smug, familiar scene with a buoyant sense of coming escape. To get away! To cut loose now, at once, from all these prying people, the petty social intercourse, the thousand and one things which reminded him of Leila and of what he had done! The revulsion of feeling from the contentment of past years which had swept over him that day culminated with a sudden rush of hatred for it all. The house loomed before him a veritable nightmare, and the coming days had appeared each a separate ordeal from the prospect of which he shrank with unutterable loathing.

He had felt chained to the old order of things by the fear of arousing suspicion if he ran away precipitately, but the one man of whose opinion he had been most apprehensive had himself suggested the way out as the most natural course in the world.

Storm could have laughed at his uneasiness of the morning; the other fellows had been merely embarrassed, that was all, reluctant to mention his tragic bereavement, and trying with awkward constraint to bridge over the chasm. If they took it for granted, as Brewster did, that he would seek a temporary change of scene, the main obstacle was removed from his path.

It would be a simple matter to sell the house, and then the world would be before him.

On the hall table he found a letter from George Holworthy, and tore it open with an absent-minded smile. He would soon be free even from old George!

> Dear Norman, (he read):
>
> Tried to get out to see you tonight, but must meet Abbott. Had a talk with Jim Potter yesterday. The firm has ordered him to the Coast immediately and he is winding up his affairs here and wants to get rid of his apartment. Willing to rent furnished, just as it stands, cheap, until his lease is up in October. It is a bully little place up on the Drive and the stuff he has there is all a fellow would want to keep a bachelor hall. Why don't you take it off his hands and close up the house out there? Jim will take his man with him, but you can get another, and New York is the best little old summer resort in the world. Take my advice and get out of that place for a while anyway. I told Jim I'd write you, but you've got to speak quick if you want to take him up on it. Think it over.
>
> Yours,
> GEORGE

Storm folded the letter slowly. He knew Potter, knew the comfortable, even luxurious sort of place his ease-loving soul would have demanded, yet he had wished to go farther afield. The first thought of escape had entailed a vague dream of other countries—South America, perhaps, or the Far East—but now he forced himself sternly back to the realities of the situation.

Such an adventure would mean money, more ready cash than he could command at the moment. It would mean waiting until the house was sold, and burning his bridges as far as the Trust Company was concerned. Moreover, the few thousands the house would bring would not last long, and unless he connected with new business wherever he went, he had nothing to fall back upon but the beggarly three thousand a year which was left from his share of his father's estate. He must convert the capital into cash, and Foulkes had warned him that that would take time. Could he wait there, within those four walls which had witnessed what he had done?

He dined in a meditative silence, oblivious of the anxious ministrations of Agnes. The empty place opposite, the chair in its new, unaccustomed position against the wall, the silence and shadows all worked upon his mood. Potter's quarters in town would at least bear no reminders to mock and accuse him at every turn, and drag his treacherous thoughts back to a past which must be buried. He would be free, too, from Brewster and Millard and the rest of them; but on the other hand George would be constantly thrusting his society upon him.

Undecided, he wandered out to the veranda, but the vines which Leila had tended peered at him over the rail and whispered together; in the library her books, her desk, the foolish, impractical reading lamp she had bought for him all mutely recalled her vanished presence. There remained only the drawing-room, where her body had lain, the den—!

With a shudder he turned and mounted the stairs. The blank, closed door of her room stared at him, and within his own were evidences on every hand of feminine thoughtfulness and care. Her influence vibrated like a living thing, all about him, clutching him by the throat, smothering him! Anything, anywhere would be preferable to this!

It was only half-past nine. He could not go to the country club, he shrank from the society of any of his neighbors; he could neither sleep, nor read, nor find a corner which did not cry aloud of Leila! There would be other nights like this, weeks of them...

In swift rebellion he descended to the library and seized the telephone.

..."Mr Holworthy, please... That you, George?... Yes, Norman. I've got your letter and you're right. I can't stand it out here. I'll take Potter's rooms at his own price, and I want possession by Monday... All right, fix it, will you?... No, but it's got on my nerves; I can't go on, I—it's hell!"

X

A CHANCE MEETING

"Told you you'd like it here." George Holworthy crossed one pudgy knee over the other and eyed his friend's back at the window with immense satisfaction. "Old Jim certainly knows how to live, doesn't he, from percolators to night-lights? You'll be mighty comfortable here, Norman."

Storm turned slowly from his contemplation of the shadowed park below, the broad sweep of the river and twinkle of the Palisades beyond.

"It's great!" he declared briefly but with a ringing, buoyant note which had long been absent from his tones. "I tell you George, old boy, I feel like a new man already! I never knew until now how stagnant a backwater like Green-lea can make a fellow become! Same old trains, same old country-club, same old crowd of petty-minded busybodies! Lord, I don't see how I stood it all these years!"

The outburst was spontaneous, and not until he saw the look of reproachful amazement which crossed George's face did he realize that he had lowered his guard.

"You were happy," ventured George.

"Of course," Storm hastened to acquiesce. "That made all the difference. But alone—"

He shrugged and turned away lest the other read too clearly the change which had come with his escape from the scene of his crime. Significant of that change was the fact that he could think of his deed as a crime now without shrinking. After the first shock of horror and remorse had passed together with the fear of detection, a sense of triumph began to dominate him, a sort of pride in himself and his achievement. He had hoodwinked them all! He, who had fancied himself a weakling merely because luck had been against him in the past, had proved his strength, his invincibility now. Old George, sitting there so placidly, blinking at him with those good-natured, near-sighted eyes of his: how little he suspected, how little he could ever suspect of the truth! The rest of them, with their smug condolences and pity!

Gad, how easy it had been!

"What do you think of Homachi?" George's question broke in upon his self-congratulation.

"The Jap you got for me? He's an improvement on Agnes, I can tell you!" Storm opened the bronze humidor and offered it. "Smoke?—You've no idea how that girl's sniffling got on my nerves! Of course I appreciated her feelings, but hang it all, a man can't buck up and carry on with other people constantly thrusting his own sorrow at him! Homachi is a cheerful, grinning little cuss, and he certainly can make an omelette. Come up and have breakfast some Sunday morning and you'll see."

"Thanks." George spoke a trifle drily. "Glad you like him. Have you made any plans yet about the disposition of the Greenlea house?"

The constraint in his tone warned Storm that for the second time he had shown his hand too plainly, and he forced a look of pained surprise.

"Disposition of the house?" he echoed. "Heavens, no! It's closed up, of course, and I've left MacWhirter there as caretaker. It was one of Leila's last wishes, you know, to give him employment when he came out of the Base Hospital. I hadn't dreamed of disposing of it; I couldn't bear to think of strangers in her garden, under her roof, in the home she loved! If I'm glad to be out of it, it's not that I am callous, but that everything about it affects me too much, George. You ought to be able to understand. If I hug my grief I'll just simply go under, and Leila herself wouldn't want that."

"I do understand, old man." George's voice trembled now with quick sympathy, and Storm hid a smile of relief. "You're trying to be brave for her sake, and it is fine of you! Stay away from the place by all means while it makes you feel that way. You could do worse than take a lease here for yourself next year when Jim's expires."

Storm shook his head.

"I've been thinking that I'd like to take a trip somewhere, later on," he said slowly, watching the other's face through narrowed lids. "A long trip; China or South America or way up North. I could come back and start all over again—"

"But your position with the Trust Company?" George sputtered. "They couldn't put a man in your place and then oust him for you when you came back."

"I wouldn't expect them to," Storm responded. "To tell you the truth, I feel that I've been stagnating there, too. It's a sinecure and I've been content to drift along sure of the income and not taking chances, but I'm responsible for no one else now and I can afford a risk."

George rose.

"Don't do anything rash," he advised. "Fifteen thousand a year is a mighty safe little bet in these uncertain times, and you've never known what it is to get out for yourself, you know. You've got the habit of luxury—"

"And no business head? Thanks," drawled his host pleasantly. "I'm not going to make a fool of myself and kill the goose until

I find golden eggs elsewhere. That notion of a trip was just an impulse. I may get over this restless fit and settle down here permanently, after all. I like these rooms of Jim's, and town looks good to me."

Nevertheless, the next day found him in Wendle Foulkes' office facing the keen old attorney with an air of quiet command which brooked no expostulation.

"How long will it take you to convert my securities into cash?" he demanded. "When we talked about it a fortnight ago I listened to you because of my wife, but now I've only myself to consider, and I have a right to take a risk with my own if I feel inclined."

"Of course you have, my boy," Foulkes returned slowly. "I have gone beyond my province, perhaps, in trying to influence you, but I promised your father—however, I've nothing more to say. I will have the cash for you in ten days. You have exactly fifty thousand dollars, on which you've been getting six per cent; I hope you'll be able to better it."

"Thanks." Storm was conscious of an air of defeat in the old man's manner and he resented it vaguely, then shrugged. What did it matter, anyway? He would be free from this pettifogging nuisance soon enough. "About the other matter—?"

"You mean Leila's estate?" Foulkes' tone softened. "I have the papers all here for you to look over. We must advertise for claims for six months, of course—a mere formality in this case—and then what she left can be turned over to you. She had just fourteen thousand when she married you and spent eleven of it. Here are the accounts. It was a matter of pride with her to buy your Christmas and birthday presents with her own money, Norman, and I couldn't gainsay her. Two thousand went for that black pearl scarf-pin, three thousand."

"Don't!" Storm cried sharply. "I don't want to hear all that! Send the papers up to my rooms. Can't you see—?"

He stopped with a gesture of repugnance, and the attorney, ignorant of the source of the other's emotion, nodded compassionately.

"I know, my boy, but I want you to see how matters stand. There are three thousand left, of the principal, which were to have been paid to Jaffray for that land adjoining yours, and accrued interest on the constantly depleted original capital which aggregates almost as much again. Her estate, roughly speaking, will amount to between five and six thousand dollars; I'll send you the exact figures."

"I don't care about them! I'm not thinking of what she left; it isn't that." Storm rose, unable to meet the kindly gaze of the older man. "I only want to get the whole thing settled and done with. I can't bear to discuss it; these details are horrible, impossible for me to contemplate sanely just yet!"

"I quite understand, Norman, but they must be attended to, you know." Foulkes rose and held out his hand. "I'll render you an accounting in six months, and then it will be over.—About your own affairs. You have never taken the advice I volunteered with very good grace, and I shall not offer any now. I am getting old, and you are no longer a boy; you know your own mind. However, if in the future you feel the need of disinterested counsel or help you know where to come for it."

"Thank you, sir." Storm felt an odd sense of contrition. "I'm not going into that South American scheme. I shall look around before deciding definitely on what I have in mind, and I'm sorry if I have seemed to resent your interest in the past. A man can't be in leading-strings all his life, you know, and I have a good, conservative proposition now."

He had. Storm chuckled grimly to himself as he departed. Fifty thousand would carry him far away, give him a year or two of utterly care-free existence, and leave a respectable sum to start in some fresh venture. The European countries were practically bankrupt; a little cash would bring monumental return and in some continental capital he could start a new life. Just as the thought of escape from Green-lea had made his surroundings there suddenly intolerable, so now the contemplation of utter freedom and a wider vista brought with it an impatience, a longing for instant action. The lease on Potter's rooms, the trumpery five thousand from Leila's estate — these details need not deter or delay him!

Another thought did, however. It was one thing, and a perfectly natural one, under the circumstances, for him to have closed the house and moved in town; it would be quite another question were he to throw up a fifteen-thousand-a-year job, seize all the cash he could lay his hands upon and rush out of the country. No man in his sane senses would take such a step unless some more urgent and sinister motive actuated him than a mere desire for forgetfulness of grief in strange scenes and a new environment.

Forcing himself to regard it from a detached point of view, he saw the madness of that course. His imagination conjured up the blank amazement which would ensue not only among the Greenlea people, but in his town clubs, in the Trust Company. There would be hints that grief had unsettled his reason, then darker whispers still; whispers which would grow in volume until the echo of them reached him wherever he might be, at the uttermost ends of the earth. He must not spoil all now by a precipitate move; he must possess his soul in patience until a favorable opportunity presented itself. He had inserted an opening wedge in mentioning his tentative intention to George; in a few weeks he would refer to it again, speaking of it casually but frequently, as a trip with definitely planned limitations, and hinting at a sound business proposition which awaited his return. The idea must filter through the clubs and out to Greenlea, must have become an old story before he finally acted upon it, so that his going would occasion no remark.

Once away, it would be simple enough to cable his instructions regarding the sale of the house and postpone his return from time to time until the old crowd had practically forgotten him. George would remember, but old George wouldn't suspect the truth if he vanished tomorrow!

With the onus of fear lifted from him, Storm still shrank from solitude. Decency and convention precluded an immediate return to his clubs, and he desired above all things to avoid the society of those who knew him and the details of the recent tragedy. He took to satisfying his gregarious need by seeking out-of-the-way hotels and restaurants frequented for the most part by the visiting foreigners who thronged the city, where, sitting long over his coffee, he could lose himself in the study of his neighbors.

On an evening a few days after his interview with Foulkes he was seated at a table in an old-fashioned French hostelry far downtown, listening to the snatches of staccato conversation which rose above the subdued cadences of the orchestra and watching the scene brilliant with the uniforms of half a dozen nations, when to his annoyance he heard his name uttered in accents of cheery surprise.

Turning swiftly he beheld Millard, flushed and evidently slightly exhilarated, rising from the corner table where he had been seated with a sallow-faced, distinguished looking stranger in mufti.

He bowed coldly and returned with ostentatious deliberation to his entree, hoping to discourage the other's advance ; but Millard was in no mood to comprehend a rebuff.

"By Jove, old chap, delighted to find you here!" He shook Storm's reluctant hand and without invitation pulled out the opposite chair and seated himself. "That's the boy! Get around a bit and work up an interest in life. No use moping. We miss you out home, but as I told Dick Brewster, change is the thing for you, change—"

"What are you doing here?" Storm interrupted him brusquely. "Thought you were wedded to the three-forty; it's been a bully afternoon for golf."

"Business!" Millard waved a pompous hand toward the table he had just quitted. "Golf's not in it with high finance, and this is the greatest proposition you ever heard of! Hundred per cent profit in three months and safe as a church; good deal safer than the churches on the other side have been!"

He grinned expansively at his own witticism, then his face clouded dismally.

"Can't go into it, though; wife won't hear of it, and you know what it is, Storm, when a woman holds the purse strings. You know how I'm situated!"

Storm nodded. Everyone in Greenlea knew that Millard had married a rich woman and suffered the pangs of hope deferred ever since. Then he glanced up and frowned.

"Your friend is coming over," he remarked in bored impatience. "When you gestured toward him he must have taken it for an invitation."

"'S all right!" Millard responded easily. "Wonderful chap, Du Chainat. Wonderful proposition—Look here! You spoke of making some reinvestments; here's chance of a lifetime! Never heard of anything like it! Gilt-edged—"

The stranger halted by the table and Millard made as if to rise and then thought better of it.

"Storm, let me present Monsieur Maurice du Chainat. My old pal and neighbor, Mr Norman Storm."

The Frenchman bowed with courtly suavity, and Storm could do no less than proffer him a chair at the table and beckon to a waiter.

"Mentioned your little proposition, old chap," the irrepressible Millard continued, adding airily as a shade of protestation passed over Monsieur du Chainat's mobile countenance: "Oh I know it's confidential, but Storm's all right. He wants to make some reinvestments, and now's his golden opportunity!"

"Mr Millard has told me nothing of the nature of your proposition, Monsieur," Storm hastened to reassure the Frenchman. "He merely mentioned it in passing."

For a long minute, Monsieur du Chainat regarded him in courteous but unmistakable appraisal. Then a genial smile lifted the ends of his small black mustache.

"It is a confidential matter, as Monsieur Millard says, but there is nothing—how do you say?—equivocal concerning it. We of France do not make our transactions ordinarily as you do in America; we discuss, we deliberate, we wait. And yet in this affair which I have undertaken haste is, alas, of the utmost need. Time is of value; such value that I will pay twice over for three hundred thousand francs."

"You see, it's a factory in one of the devastated towns," Millard interjected eagerly. "Old feud, trying to get ahead of the other fellow. It means sixty thousand in our money, and the French government's giving him a grant of a hundred and twenty thousand in three months, but it means ruin to wait. Other man's got his capital now—"

"But, my friend, Monsieur Storm is perhaps not interested; we bore him," Monsieur du Chainat interrupted. "The letter which our consul here has given me to your great banker, Monsieur Whitmarsh, has interested him to such an extent that the affair is all but closed."

"Whitmarsh?" Storm pricked up his ears. The proposition must be good if that most astute of international financiers considered it.

"But, yes." The Frenchman shrugged deprecatingly. "It is, of course, a trifling matter to engage his attention, but I am to have a second interview with him tomorrow at three. I shall be happy to conclude my mission, for there is attached to it the sentiment as well as what you call business."

A second interview! Whitmarsh wasted no time, and this must mean a deal. Sixty thousand dollars, and doubled in three months! Storm leaned impulsively across the table.

"What is your proposition, Monsieur, if I may ask? It sounds a trifle—er, unusual."

"It is." The Frenchman smiled again. "You will understand, Monsieur Storm, that in France it is not the custom to develop a manufacturing concern until it grows too big for us and then sell out to a corporation. With us business descends from generation to generation, it becomes at once the idol and life of the family.

"My father-in-law, Henri Peronneau of Lille, has a soap factory established by his grandfather. Twenty years ago, a dishonest chemist in his employ stole the formula which rendered the Peronneau soap famous and set up a rival factory. Both, of course, were dismantled during the German occupation.

"Monsieur Peronneau has been granted a loan of six hundred thousand francs from the government, but it cannot be obtained for three months yet; meanwhile our rival has acquired more than that sum from an English house, and if his factory is the first in operation it will steal all our old trade, and Monsieur Peronneau, who is already ruined, will have no opportunity to recoup. He is in frail health from the slavery of the invasion, and his heart will be broken. Three hundred thousand francs now will enable him to compete with his rival, for his factory is in far better condition, and for that he is willing to pay the entire sum which the government will lend him.

"I admit that I have tried to obtain the amount at a sacrifice less great, but there is no time for lengthy investigation, and I have found that people even in your generous America are afraid to trust my credentials and the sponsorship of our consul. Only a man of Monsieur Whitmarsh's experience and caliber could comprehend that the affair is bona fide, that he takes no risk. *Voyez*, here is the personal letter which I have received from him."

Storm glanced over the single sheet of terse, typed sentences ending in the well-known, crabbed signature, and returned it to the Frenchman.

"I congratulate you, Monsieur. I know Whitmarsh's methods and this looks as if he intended to take you up on it"

Monsieur du Chainat flushed with pleasure.

"It is of great happiness to me," he said simply. "Almost I have despaired of my mission. At the Hotel Belterre, where I am staying, there are so many of my compatriots here also to try to borrow that they may rehabilitate themselves, and with so little success that I, too, feared failure. But Monsieur Whitmarsh is shrewd; he knows—what you say?—'a good thing,' and he makes no mistakes."

The conversation drifted into desultory topics and after a half hour Monsieur du Chainat took his leave, dragging the reluctant Millard with him. As for Storm, he sat long over his cooling coffee, and until far into the night he pondered the possibilities which this chance meeting opened before him. The difference between sixty thousand dollars and a hundred and twenty meant the difference between luxurious living and the petty economies which would try his soul; between independence for years of travel and care-free pleasure, and the necessity of knuckling down after a brief respite to uncongenial money-grubbing. It must be all right if Whitmarsh were going into it, and his letter left no room for doubt on that score.

If he, Storm, had only met the Frenchman first!

In the morning he tried to concentrate on the affairs of the Trust Company, but it was of no avail. The glittering opportunity aroused all his gambling instinct and seemed all the more alluring in that it was out of his reach. But was it? Perhaps Whitmarsh would fail, for some reason, to accept the proposition; not from lack of faith in its genuineness, for he must have looked into it with his usual caution before going so far in the negotiations; but he had been known to turn down deals of much greater magnitude at the last moment through sheer eccentricity.

If Du Chainat could offer bona fide securities and he himself could obtain a mortgage of ten thousand on the Greenlea house, he could add that to his capital and take the plunge.

At noon, Storm telephoned to the Belterre and asked for Monsieur du Chainat.

"This is Storm talking, Millard's friend," he answered. "I called up, Monsieur, to tell you that if by any chance the Whitmarsh deal falls through, I might consider your proposition myself... Yes, call me up at my rooms, 0519 Riverside, at six. Goodbye."

He hung up the receiver slowly. Suppose, after all, the man should be an impostor? He would be risking all he had in the world in the event that Whitmarsh did not take the proposition; all that stood between him and the accursed treadmill of existence here within reach of the memories which thrust out their tentacles to crush him. If that Lille soap factory were a myth—!

He reached for the receiver once more and called the French consulate. Yes, Monsieur Henri Peronneau, of Lille, was well known to them. His son-in-law, Monsieur Maurice du Chainat, was now in this country negotiating a loan to reconstruct the Peronneau factory. If Mr Storm were interested, a meeting could be arranged...

Storm turned away from the booth with sparkling eyes. If Whitmarsh refused the loan he would take a chance! Luck must be with him still; that marvelous luck which had enabled him to elude the consequences of his crime was yet running strong, At six o'clock he would know!

XI

LUCK

Promptly at six that evening the telephone in Storm's apartment shrilled, and it had scarcely ceased vibrating when he sprang to it and caught up the receiver.

He uttered a quick monosyllabic assent to some evident query, listened intently for a minute and then threw back his head in a smile of elation. The next instant he was speaking calmly, quietly.

"Too small a proposition for him to tackle, eh?" he observed. "Well, I'm not a magnate, Monsieur du Chainat, but I would like to talk it over with you. How about dining with me in an hour at the Rochefoucauld where we met last night?... Bring along your papers, and we can come back here later and go into the details... Very good, at seven."

His luck was holding! Old Whitmarsh had turned the loan down as too petty a transaction to interest him. The chance was his now, make or break! But pshaw! he couldn't lose; not if Du Chainat's securities were all right. Past failures had made him skeptical, but now fortune had changed. A hundred and twenty thousand!

He whistled exultantly as he changed from one somber suit of mourning to another, and only paused when a casual glance in the mirror brought home to him with a shock the incongruity between his expression and his attire. He threw back his shoulders defiantly.

"The past is dead!" he muttered. "Three months, and I shall be free to forget!"

Monsieur du Chainat met him in the hotel lobby and greeted him with undiminished enthusiasm.

"I am delighted, Monsieur, that you find yourself interested," he remarked, after their order had been given. "Since I telephoned to you an hour ago I have received yet another offer to take up the loan, this from an associate of Monsieur Whitmarsh, whom he must have consulted; a Monsieur Nicholas Langhorne. You perhaps have heard of him?"

Storm nodded.

"I know him," he said briefly, forbearing to add that the gentleman in question was the president of the Trust Company which he ornamented with his presence. To get ahead of old Langhorne! That would be gratification enough were the profits cut to a minimum.

"I have replied to him that the affair is already under consideration"—Monsieur du Chainat poised a fragment of hors d'oeuvre gracefully upon his fork,—"but should you not, after examining the documents I have brought, desire to close, Monsieur, I will see him tomorrow."

" 'Tomorrow!' " Storm echoed in dismay. "I should like a little longer time than that in which to decide. It may take me some days to convert my capital into cash, and there are other contingencies—"

"But Monsieur forgets that to me time is of paramount importance." The Frenchman's face had clouded. "It is for that we pay one hundred per cent interest in three months! When I have acquired the loan I do not even wait for the ship which takes me back; I cable to my *beau-pére* the money, that the work may start without an hour's delay. You comprehend, Monsieur, how urgent is our need by the extent of our sacrifice.

I shall have an inheritance from my uncle soon, and I shall aid Pere Peronneau in paying off the government loan for which he is responsible when he repays it with the debt we incur here. There is the sentiment as well as the business, as I told you last night, Monsieur. If you could but see the *beau-père—*"

He drew a simple but graphic word picture of the old manufacturer, but his listener was distrait. Could he get the fifty thousand from Foulkes at such short order, to say nothing of arranging the mortgage on the Greenlea house? Monsieur du Chainat's haste seemed plausible enough, and then there was Langhorne only too ready to snap up the prize!

By heavens, if the Frenchman's security looked good to him, he would raise the money, come what might!

And the security did look more than good when later they repaired to his rooms, and Monsieur du Chainat produced his sheaf of multitudinous documents. There were the unassailable correspondence on the letter heads of the consulate, Henri Peronneau's authorization of his son-in-law, Maurice Pierre du Chainat as his agent, duly signed and attested to by the notary of Lille, a deed formally making over to the lender of three hundred thousand francs—the space for whose name was left significantly blank—the government loan of six hundred thousand in its entirety, and lastly a formidable-appearing document of the French government itself announcing the grant of the loan.

"For further evidence of our good faith,"—Monsieur du Chainat drew a second packet of papers from his pocket,—"I have here a deed to the factory itself which can be held as security. As you can see from this photograph, Monsieur, the factory is a mere shell now, but a stout and solid shell, and the land upon which it stands is worth more than the sum we require. Our government has not asked this security of us but accepted instead some undveloped coal properties to the south. Here are the documents attesting to that and also those which prove the factory to be the property of Monsieur Peronneau, free of lien or mortgage." They talked until far into the night, and when the Frenchman at length took his departure he bore with him Storm's agreement to advance the loan.

The morning brought no breath of misgiving, save anxiety lest he should fail in his efforts to secure the cash in the space of twenty-four hours specified by Du Chainat. The Trust Company would assume the mortgage on the Green-lea house, he knew, and waive technicalities to give him the ten thousand at once, but there remained Foulkes to be managed, and if the old rascal knew that haste was imperative to the transaction he would balk it in sheer perversity.

On one point Storm was determined; he would not take Foulkes into his confidence, nor anyone.

He had a stormy session with the old attorney, adjourned at noon only to be renewed with more wordy violence an hour later; but in the end Storm emerged triumphant, with a certified check for fifty thousand dollars and Foulkes' dismal prophecies ringing in his ears. The mortgage on the house was, as he had anticipated, a simple matter to arrange, and on the following morning he handed to Monsieur du Chainat the sixty thousand dollars which were to return to him twofold.

The momentous transaction concluded, he repaired to his desk at the Trust Company, gloating over the unconscious bald head of Nicholas Langhorne. He had put one over on him, beaten that conservative financier by a matter of hours! Du Chainat had shown him Langhorne's letter, and he read between the lines the latter's eagerness to grasp the coveted opportunity which he had himself placed within Storm's reach by taking up the mortgage. How he would writhe if he knew who had forestalled him, just as he and the rest would writhe if they realized the enormity of that other affair which he had put over on all the world!

They would never learn the truth about Leila's death; that was buried forever. But he would give much to tell Langhorne how he had outwitted him, and watch the old fox's face! Perhaps he would tell him some day, the day on which his six. hundred thousand francs came and he resigned from the Trust Company!

George Holworthy found him a strange companion for the rest of the week. The faithful friend could not understand his moods, for Storm, never easily comprehended by the other's slow-moving brain, seemed all at once to develop a complexity which utterly baffled him.

Storm himself found it difficult to preserve a calm and resigned demeanor to mask his thoughts which seethed with plans for the future. When haunting memories came unbidden, he thrust them fiercely aside, smothered them beneath the exultation of having escaped the lax hands of justice.

"Upon my soul, Norman, I don't know what to make of you!" George complained one evening as they strolled up the Drive. "If you were a woman, I'd swear you were hysterical!"

Storm halted, glad of the semi-obscurity of the trees which tempered the searching street lights.

"You're crazy!" he retorted.

"No, I'm not," insisted George in serious refutation. "You're down in the dumps one minute and all excited the next. You haven't been speculating again?"

"Good Lord, no!" Storm breathed more freely. He must be careful! If old George thought his manner odd, how would it impress others? "I'm through with all that sort of thing."

"Well, I didn't know," the other said lamely. "There's a streak of recklessness in you, and when you get in one of those don't-give-a-hang moods of yours you are apt to pull off some fool stunt—"

"My dear George!" Storm's tone was pained. "I've been through enough, God knows, in the last few weeks to sober me down—"

"But it hasn't!" George persevered. "You seem hardened, defiant, just in the frame of mind to do something desperate! I tell you I've been worried about you these days."

Storm shrugged ironically.

"Sorry I can't set your mind at rest," he replied. "I don't seem to be taking what's come to me according to your notions. First, you are disappointed because I don't rant around and tear my hair, and now you accuse me of hysteria!"

"That's it; that's what I don't like!" exclaimed George. "That callousness; it isn't natural, it isn't you! You're putting it on because your trouble has made you defiant, bitter. I know you, Norman, you can't fool me; I'm only trying to help you, to keep you from doing anything you will have cause to regret."

"Don't you worry," Storm reassured him, the while his face twitched with mirth. George knew him, did he? He couldn't fool him? He checked an impulse to laugh aloud and added quietly: "I'm not in such a desperate mood as you imagine, old man; I can't seem to settle down to the new order of things just yet, that's the trouble, but I've no intention of going to the dogs, financially or any other way. I'll get a grip on myself soon."

But as the days passed Storm did not find it so easy to control himself. He had gained complete ascendancy over the faint twinges of conscience which assailed him now with less and less frequency, but with the assurance of absolute safety came a dangerous, almost insane tendency to test that safety. Although he had no desire to revisit the scene of Leila's death, and shrank from any reference to her, the subject of crime in general began to exert an inordinate fascination for him, and with it his pride in his own achievement increased.

He eagerly awaited the news of Du Chainat's arrival in France, and his occasional glimpses of President Langhorne filled him with renewed complacency. He would most assuredly tell him about getting in ahead on that little deal one of these days!

The temptation became overwhelming one morning after a brief interview with his august superior during which the latter had called him to account, courteously but firmly, for a trifling dereliction. The sting rankled, and at the door he turned, the impulse to retaliate mastering him.

"Oh, Mr Langhorne, you've heard of a man named Du Chainat, I believe?"

The president looked up in surprise at his subordinate's presumption.

"Du Chainat? Can't say I have," he responded shortly.

Storm smiled and raised his eyebrows in polite incredulity. "The agent in that little deal Whitmarsh was considering only last week; a loan for the reconstruction of a French factory—"

"I am not in Mr Whitmarsh's confidence, Mr Storm." President Langhorne darted a keen glance at the other and added: "May I ask why you assume that I know anything of this particular affair?"

"I understood that you were interested in it." Storm paused expectantly, but the president shook his head.

"Never heard of it," he asseverated. "You've been misinformed, Mr Storm. The man you mention is absolutely unknown to me."

He turned pointedly to his desk and Storm withdrew, still smiling covertly. The old fox wouldn't admit that; he had tried to get in on the game, of course, now that someone else had beaten him to it. Wait until he learned who that someone was! The joke was so good that it would keep a little longer, especially since Storm had given him something to puzzle over. He would have been a fool to give it away now; old Langhorne could make it infernally unpleasant for him around the office if he chose.

The three months stretched interminably before him, and George with dog-like fidelity seemed determined to stick close and make it as irksome as he could. God, if only he were free from them all!

Storm had left his own car locked in the garage at Greenlea, but on an impulse he hired another when his work was finished for the afternoon and had himself driven out to a shore resort for dinner. The season had not yet opened, and the place was semi-deserted, yet the isolation fitted in with his mood. George would in all probability put in an appearance at the apartment that evening, and to avoid him Storm lingered deliberately over his meal and ordered the chauffeur to take the longest way home.

He would not admit even to himself that the sudden aversion to the companionship of the man he had for so long regarded with amused, half-condescending tolerance had sprung from the fact that George unconsciously brought to his mind the aspects of his crime which he was most determined to put behind him. George was a constant reminder of the years which must be forgotten; his grief at the loss of the woman who had given him a valued friendship was a constant reproach.

How easy it had been to blind him to the truth! How easy it had been to blind everybody! Why, a man with sufficient intelligence could pull off almost anything in this world and get away with it if he had only enough nerve and self-control!

Storm was still smiling at the thought as he entered his apartment house long after ten o'clock and found George sitting patiently in the hall, his near-sighted eyes glued to a newspaper.

"I waited for you," the latter explained, happily oblivious to the coolness of the reception. "Knew you wouldn't be late, and I wanted a little talk with you."

"Come on in," Storm invited wearily, opening the door and switching on the lights. "I ran out of town for a breath of clean air.—The cigars are in the humidor; help yourself."

George settled himself comfortably in a huge leather chair and smoked in silence for a space, while Storm moved restlessly about the room.

"I came," remarked the visitor at length, "to ask you what you know about Millard's nephew. He applied to us for a job, and the only thing open is a rather responsible position."

"Don't know anything about him," snapped his host. "He held some sort of minor clerical position in Washington during the war. Weak chest and the only-son-of-his-mother stuff kept him from active service. He's a likable enough chap, plays good golf—"

George shook his head.

"Hardly material to the point," he observed. "I want to know whether he's dependable or not; conscientious and steady, not given up to these quick-rich ideas that get so many young fellows. I tell you we can't be too careful nowadays—"

Storm laughed shortly.

"My dear George, I wouldn't give you an opinion on any man's honesty. Given the incentive and the opportunity, how do we know where anyone gets off?"

"Oh, come, Norman!" George's tone was scandalized. "That's a pretty broad assertion. We're not all potential criminals!"

"No?" Storm paused to light a cigar. "Well, if we're not you must admit that the opportunities lie around thick enough. The wonder of it is that there isn't more crookedness going on!"

"The example of what happens to the fellow who has tried it is a deterrent, I imagine," George observed sententiously. "When he's caught—"

"And when *is* he caught except through his own negligence and loss of nerve?" demanded Storm, the train of thought which had occupied his mind an hour before recurring to him. "Certainly it isn't through the extraordinary ability of society at large to track him down. A man gives himself away; he is safe until he makes a mistake."

"Then every crook in the world must be a bungler, for they're all caught, sooner or later," George retorted. "The cleverest ones over-reach themselves in time.—Take this fellow Jan Martens, or whatever his real name is. To be sure, he hasn't been caught yet, but his game is up; he tried it once too often."

"Martens?" Storm repeated absently, his mind fixed upon his own argument.

"Haven't you looked at the evening papers?" asked George. "He's been working an old con. game with a new twist and getting the suckers for anything from five to fifty thousand. Worked Boston and Philadelphia before he came here and got away with a tremendous haul. They only got the goods on him today, but he had skipped. It was a clever stunt, too; he played upon a combination of sympathy and cupidity in his victims that only failed when he tackled a wise one. His line was getting loans on forged securities for rebuilding demolished property in France and Belgium—"

"What?"

Storm was not conscious that he had spoken, that he had turned and was staring at his visitor with wild eyes. He only knew that George's solid, compact figure was wavering oddly, and his voice seemed to come from far away.

"He rather upsets your theory, Norman," George continued complacently, ignorant of the effect of his disclosure. "He wasn't giving himself away, by a long shot, and his paraphernalia was certainly elaborate and imposing enough in all conscience! In Boston he posed as Jan Martens, a Belgian looking for a loan to rebuild the family chateau and giving forged Congo properties as security. It worked so well that when he came here he tried to improve on it, and over-reached himself, as I contended a few minutes ago.

"A lot of foreigners are over here now trying to negotiate perfectly legitimate loans on the same order, but with bona fide securities to offer, and he fell in with one of them who was vouched for at the French consulate here, a citizen of Lille named Du Chainat."

Storm drew a long breath.

"But this—Du Chainat is all right, you say?" he stammered. "His proposition was legitimate?"

"Absolutely. He must have taken this Martens into his confidence, shown him his papers and left them where the crook could get at them, for Martens forged a duplicate set,— they found the stacks of counterfeit government deeds and grants, both Belgian and French, in his room today together with official letter-heads from the consulates,—and then when Du Chainat returned to France he impersonated him. Du Chainat had put through his loan all right with Whitmarsh."

"When—" Storm moistened his dry lips. "When did this Du Chainat leave America?"

"Three weeks ago, according to the paper. The impostor was only exposed through a woman, too, a rich widow whom he approached yesterday with his proposition; but he didn't take into consideration the fact that she had lived abroad. As it happened, she knew the Du Chainat family in Lille, but by the time she made up her mind to risk notoriety and inform the police of the attempted swindle the bird had flown."

He paused, but Storm had heard only the first three words of his utterance. "Three weeks ago"! And only a week had passed since he handed to the bogus Du Chainat every cent he had in the world! It couldn't be true! There must be some hideous mistake!

"Here, it's all in the paper. I was reading about it while I waited for you. Want to see it?"

George picked up the newspaper from the table where he had dropped it on entering, and Storm seized it, hoping blindly, doggedly against all hope. His luck could not have deserted him! Fate would not play him such a ghastly trick now!

But the headlines stared at him in uncompromising type, and the article itself left no room for doubt. He had been despoiled of his only means of freedom! Penniless, he was chained forever to the environs of the past, to the friends who had been Leila's, the life of which she had been a part. The curse was upon him, and he might not even flee from the memories which dogged him! He was bound hand and foot, held fast!

XII

MIRAGE

Storm realized later when the dawn brought coherency of thought that it was blind instinct alone, not conscious will, which had enabled him to shield the death blow that had been given him from George Holworthy's peering eyes. The crumbling of his air castles had left him stunned, and he remembered nothing of the rest of the interview save that George had moralized interminably and in leaving at last had harked back to the Millard boy. Surely he would not have droned on of trivialities had he gleaned an inkling of the tumult in his host's brain!

Until the morning light stole in at the windows Storm paced the floor in a frenzy of consternation. He had one slender hope: that the false Du Chainat would be apprehended. If he appeared against the scoundrel or entered a complaint the resultant revelation of how easily he had been fleeced would be a bitter pill to swallow. Old Langhorne would recall that conversation of the previous day, and it would be his turn to smile, while Foulkes and George would descend upon him with galling criticism and reproach.

He could endure it all, however, if only it would mean the recovery of his money or even a portion of it! As his hope of getting away vanished, the absolute need of such escape grew in his thoughts until it assumed the proportions of an obsession. He felt as if something he could not name were tightening about him slowly but inexorably and he struggled wildly to free himself from the invisible fetters.

If he had to stay on at the trust company, suffer George's continual presence, run the daily gauntlet of mingled sympathy and curiosity of his friends, he should go mad! Other men lived down tragedies, went on in the same old rut until the end of time, but he could not.

And then all at once the truth burst upon him! If Leila had died a natural death as the world supposed; if she had been taken from him in the high tide of their love and happiness, he might have gone on with existence again in time with no thought of cutting himself adrift from the past. It was the secret knowledge of his guilt which was driving him forth, which rendered unendurable all the familiar things of his every-day life!

Yet he must endure them! Unless the bogus Du Chainat were caught there was no way out for him.

Unconscious of irony, his breast swelled with virtuous indignation at thought of the swindler and dire were the anathemas he heaped upon the departed one. He searched the papers feverishly, made what inquiries he dared without drawing undue attention to himself and haunted the Belterre grill for news, but all to no avail; and as day succeeded day he developed a savage moroseness which rebuffed even George's overtures. He would take no one into his confidence; there would be time enough for admitting that he had played the fool when the miscreant was caught. If he were not, Storm determined to accept the inevitable in silence; but day by day the obsession of flight increased. Somehow, at any price, he must get away!

The papers still played up the pseudo Du Chainat as further exploits of that wily adventurer were brought to light, and the press gleefully baited the police for their inability to discover whither he had flown. The flickering hope that he would be apprehended died slowly in Storm's breast, and the blankness of despair settled upon him.

One morning Nicholas Langhorne sent for him, and before the president spoke Storm sensed a subtle difference in his manner. The pompous official attitude seemed to have been laid aside, for once a warmly personal note crept into his voice.

"Sit down, Storm; I want to have a little talk with you." The other seated himself and waited, but Langhorne seemed in no hurry to begin. He took off his glasses, wiped them, replaced them and then sat meditatively fingering a pen. At last he threw it aside and turned abruptly to face his subordinate.

"Storm, I knew your father well. We both started here away down on the lowest rung of the ladder, and although he soon branched out into a wider, less conservative field we never allowed our friendship to flag. It was on his account that we took you, and because of his memory you were given preference over more experienced men."

He paused and Storm stiffened, but he replied warily:

"I am aware of that, Mr Langhorne. I hope that I have executed my duties—"

Langhorne waved him to silence.

"I have no complaint to make. I sent for you because my personal interest in you as the son of my old friend has caused me a certain amount of disquietude. When you came to me a fortnight ago and requested that I arrange an immediate mortgage on your suburban property I waived the usual procedure and complied at once. It was not my province to question your need or use of the money, although I knew of your previous unfortunate ventures, and I hoped that you had not again been ill-advised.

"A week later—ten days ago, to be exact—you came to me and mentioned a person named Du Chainat, whom you said had been in negotiation with Mr Whitmarsh. This Du Chainat, or rather the man impersonating him, has been exposed as a swindler on a rather large scale. I trust that you yourself did not fall a victim to him?"

Storm's eyes flashed, but he held himself rigidly in control. Bleat to this fathead and give him an opportunity to gloat? He would see him damned first!

"Hardly, Mr Langhorne." He allowed the ghost of a smile to lift the corners of his mouth. "The investment I had in mind was quite another sort."

Langhorne frowned doubtfully.

"You appeared to take it for granted that I knew this Du Chainat. May I ask what your motive was in mentioning him to me?"

Storm hesitated and then replied with seeming candor:

"Well, if you want the truth, Mr Langhorne, I—er, I believed that you yourself were one of his intended victims."

"I, sir?" The president stared.

"Yes. I met this man in the Rochefoucauld grill one night, and he worked his usual game; told me of the loan he was attempting to negotiate and said Whitmarsh had turned it down because it wasn't a big enough proposition for him. Du Chainat, as he called himself, showed me your letter, and as I had reason to distrust him I ventured to mention the matter to you, thinking that I might be of service in warning you of the whispers I had heard against him."

"My letter?" Langhorne gripped the arms of his chair. "I never wrote a letter to the man in my life!"

"When you denied having heard of him," Storm continued, unmoved by the other's expostulation, "I naturally concluded that you resented my intrusion into your private affairs, and said nothing more. The man was exposed in the evening papers that very night, as I remember."

"You saw a letter purporting to have been written by me?" the president demanded.

"I would have been willing to swear to your signature, Mr Langhorne," replied Storm.

"Forgery!" The clenched hand came down upon his desk. "That signature was forged! I'll look into this when the fellow is caught. His effrontery is astounding! What was the gist of this letter, Storm?"

"An intimation that you would advance the loan," he responded dully. There was no mistaking now the sincerity of the other's indignation. "The letter was a forgery, of course, as you say, but it was a remarkably clever one. The signature was almost identical in every detail with yours."

"I wish you had told me of this before!" The president fumed. "This may cause a vast amount of trouble. However, I am glad to be assured that you were not victimized by this person. By the way, this is not my custom—in fact it is emphatically against my rule, especially where officers of the company are concerned—but I shall be glad to make an exception in your case, Storm. I may be able to give you a little advance information, strictly confidential, you understand, on a certain investment later, if you are looking for one."

"Thank you, Mr Langhorne. I'm not thinking of making any just now." He smiled again, reading the other's motive, and added pointedly: "I have mentioned the Du Chainat letter to no one else, of course, nor shall I do so."

The president flushed but dismissed him with forced cordiality, and Storm returned to his own sanctum in a bitter mood. Even the small satisfaction of believing that Langhome, too, had fallen for the alluring proposition was denied him!

At noon, as he left the trust company building to go to the luncheon club of which he was a member, he collided with Millard.

"Hello, there! Just coming in to see you." The little man's usually apoplectic face was pale, and his small, beady eyes shifted nervously beneath Storm's gaze. "Where are you off to?"

"Lunch," replied the other briefly. Confound the little golf hound! It was he who got him into the Du Chainat affair!

"Then have it with me, do!" Millard urged. "I want to talk to you. Let's run in to Peppini's where we can be quiet."

Storm was on the point of refusal, but something in the other's manner made him change his mind.

"If you like." He turned, and Millard fell into step beside him. "How's the golf coming along?"

"Hang golf!" Millard exploded. "I've had other things on my mind, Storm, old chap! I've been in the very devil of a hole, and Mrs M.—well, you know what she is when she has got anything on me! I haven't had a minute's peace."

"What's the trouble?" Storm asked perfunctorily as they entered the little restaurant and made for a corner table. Millard did not reply until the waiter had taken their order and departed. Then he leaned confidentially across the table.

"It's all about the scoundrel, Du Chainat," he began. "You remember him; chap I introduced to you in the Rochefoucauld. By Jove, I owe you an apology for that!"

"Not at all." A hidden thought made Storm's lips curl in grim humor. "We are all of us apt to be mistaken in the people we think we know."

"That's what I say!" corroborated Millard eagerly. "How're you going to tell a crook nowadays? The fellow took me in absolutely! And now, to hear Mrs M. talk you would think I had been in league with him!"

"You tried to get her to go into one of his schemes, didn't you?" Storm asked. The other nodded gloomily.

"I did, and I shall never be permitted to hear the last of it!" he observed. "That isn't what is worrying me, though. You see, I introduced him around pretty generally, and if any of my friends fell for his graft I should feel personally responsible. There you are, for instance; that's what I wanted to see you about, Storm; I hope to the Lord that you didn't—"

"Not by a damn sight!" Storm retorted savagely. Was he to go through a repetition of the scene with Langhorne? "What do you take me for? I'm not looking to line the pockets of every adventurer that comes along."

Millard winced.

"All right, old chap, only I was anxious. You seemed interested that night."

"I was, in the man himself; he was a new type to me, but I don't mind telling you now that I didn't trust him." Storm smiled patronizingly. "I don't wonder his little proposition looked good to you. It did to me; too good. Money isn't so scarce for a legitimate deal that a man has to offer one hundred per cent profit in three months. You would have realized that yourself if you had stopped to think. The trouble with you was that the man's personality blinded you, Millard. I'll admit that he was a plausible rascal, but if anyone had been fool enough to fall for his game they deserved what was coming to them."

"I suppose so," Millard mumbled shamefacedly. "Anyhow, they've got him now."

"What!" Storm sat back in his chair.

"Fact. I've just come from Police Headquarters." Millard nodded, visibly cheered by the impression his announcement had made. "It has been established beyond a doubt that he is on board the *Alsace* en route for France. He'll be arrested the moment they reach Havre."

Storm's brain whirled, yet he strove mightily to command himself. Millard must not know, must not guess! Could it be after all that luck had not deserted him? Hope had died so utterly that he found it difficult to believe this sudden turn of fortune.

"How can they be sure?" he stammered. "There may be some mistake."

"Not a chance!" Millard, his equanimity restored, chattered on. "His movements have been traced from the moment he left the hotel until he walked up the gangplank, and they've got him dead to rights. Nervy of him to go back to France when he knew the Government was out after him, wasn't it? I suppose he banked on that; that they would never dream he would dare to return. He's under a different name, of course, and all that, but the detectives have been in wireless communication with the captain of the *Alsace* and there isn't a loophole of escape for him. He is cornered like a rat in a trap and a good job, too!"

The garrulity of his companion had given Storm time to collect himself. He must learn all that he could and yet not seem too eager. He shrugged.

"His cleverness didn't get him far, did it?" he remarked with elaborate carelessness. "Let's see; the *Alsace* sailed three days ago, if I am not mistaken."

"Four," the other corrected him. "She won't reach port for another three days, however; traveling slow, for there has been a report of some floating mines having been sighted in her path. It is just a wild rumor, of course; the sweepers gathered them in pretty thoroughly after the war. Don't know what they'll do about extraditing him, for both countries want him badly. The main thing his victims want, I imagine, is to get their money back."

In this Storm concurred heartily but in silence. After a pause he observed, still in that detached, bored tone:

"I fancy that won't be difficult, if he has it with him."

"He has," Millard affirmed. "He must have cleared more than half a million, they tell me at Headquarters, and they've proved that he didn't dispose of any of it here. Think of it! Half a million in cash! I wonder how he planned to explain it to the custom's officials on the other side?"

"He could stow it about him, I suppose," Storm responded absently. "If he had laid his plans carefully and believed himself immune from suspicion he would have no reason to anticipate a personal search. What on earth were you doing at Headquarters?"

Millard squirmed uneasily.

"We-ell, when all this racket came out about Du Chainat I felt that it was my duty to go down and tell all I knew about the fellow. In the course of justice, you know, old chap—"

"Precisely," Storm grinned. "You had rather identified yourself with him, hadn't you? I don't blame you for clearing your own skirts. It would be deucedly awkward for you if some of these people you presented him to—"

"Don't!" protested Millard. "How was I to know? He came to me with a forged letter purporting to be from Harry Wheeler, of Boston. I haven't seen Harry in years; wouldn't know his handwriting from Adam, but it looked all right. When I explained, they understood the situation immediately at Headquarters, I assure you."

"Don't 'assure' me, Millard; I know you!" Storm laughed; then his face sobered. "How is everyone out at the Country Club?"

"Fine I" Millard waxed enthusiastic at the welcome change of topic. "We've taken on some more members; a new family or two from out Summit View way, and a most attractive widow. We talk of you a lot, Storm. You can't think what a gap your poor wife's death and your leaving us has made in the community! She was a wonderful little woman! You've no idea how she is missed."

"I think I have," Storm responded quietly.

"Oh, forgive me, old chap!" Millard flushed with honest contrition. "You more than anyone else in the world must feel—but I'm glad to see that you are not taking it too hard."

Storm shot a quick glance at him. Was there a suggestion of criticism in the other's tone?

"One cannot always see," he said stiffly. "Sometimes a thing cuts too deep to show on the surface. But I can't talk about it even yet, Millard. I can't find words."

He couldn't. One thought alone was racing through his brain. His sixty thousand was safe, after all! It would be given into his hands again, and he would be free! Free from these hypocritical mouthings about a dead past, these constant reminders of the old life!

What a fool he had been to disclaim so emphatically to both Langhorne and Millard the fact that he had been victimized! How they would laugh at him when the truth came out! Well, let them! Unconsciously he squared his shoulders. He would have the last laugh, sixty thousand of them! God, what a reprieve!

The afternoon passed in a glamor of renewed hope and revived plans. No more trifling with investments for him! When once the money was safely in his possession again he would throw up his position without a day's delay and catch the first steamer that sailed, no matter for what port she cleared. Anywhere! Any war-riddled, God-forsaken corner of the globe would be heaven after this caged existence, surrounded by potential spies—and judges!

He was dimly aware that those with whom he came in contact that afternoon gazed at him curiously, but for once he was heedless of their possible criticism. The exalted mood lasted throughout his solitary dinner, and on returning to his apartments he ignored a painfully spelled message which Homachi had left requesting him to call up 'Mr Holworth' and paced the floor in utter abandonment to the joy which consumed him.

His days of slavery and imprisonment were over! Just at the moment when life had looked blackest to him and all hope was gone, the shackles were struck from him and the way lay open to a new existence. Never again would he decry his luck! His capital, which had shrunk to insignificance before the wild idea of doubling it, now loomed large before him. It meant freedom, life!

He would go to the Far East. Many changes were bound to come there, many opportunities would arise in the general upheaval of worldwide readjustment to the new order of things, and the colorful atmosphere there had always held a fascination for him. Europe would do later, but at first he would lose himself in the glamor of a new world.

He halted, drawn from his reverie by the sound of confused, raucous shouting in the street, and realized vaguely that it had been going on for some time. His apartment was on the ground floor, and he opened a window of the living-room and leaned out. The Drive seemed deserted, but on the block below he descried two retreating figures with flat white bundles beneath their arms.

Their shrill call came again to his ears.

"Wuxtry! Turr'ble disaster!... All on board!"

A train wreck, perhaps. Storm was withdrawing his head when from the second newsboy came the cry which struck terror to his heart.

"French steamer wrecked at sea! Awful loss of life!"

The *Alsace!* For a moment Storm stood as though petrified; then, turning, he dashed hatless from the apartment and out into the street. The newsboy raced toward him and he tore a paper from the grasp of the foremost, thrust some silver into his hand and made for the apartment once more. He dared not halt beneath a street lamp to read the staring headlines; he must be secure from observation behind closed doors when he learned the truth.

It might be some other ship. It must be! Fate would not hold out this promise of a reprieve to him only to snatch it away just as his fingers closed upon it!

Again in his apartment, he approached the lamp and spread the paper out with shaking fingers. There in bold black letters which seemed to dance mockingly before him he read:—

"S. S. Alsace Lost at Sea. No survivors."

He tried to read on, but the letters ran together before his eyes, and he dashed the paper to the floor. The walls of his prison closed in upon hi again, stiflingly, relentlessly! The cup had once more been dashed from his lips, and a groan of utter despair surged up from his heart while the bitterness of death settled upon him.

XIII

THE BLACK BAG

Morning found Storm with a desperate, hunted look in his eyes still pacing the floor, his heart sick within him. Why had that blundering ass, Millard, told him yesterday? Why had he been plunged in the madness of a fool's paradise for a few short hours, only to be drawn back into an existence that had become all the more unbearable by contrast?

He had contrived a sufficient measure of calmness in the late hours to read the amplification of the damning headlines. The *Alsace* was supposed to have struck one of the floating mines of which she had been warned, and to have gone down with all on board. No calls for help had been received by wireless, no survivors picked up. Another liner, westward bound, had run into a mass of wreckage on the course of the unfortunate ship; wreckage which denoted a fearful explosion and fragments of which bore the name "*A'lsace*". That was all; but it was conclusive, damning to Storm's last hope.

The morning's news had little to add save a verification of the ocean tragedy in a message radioed from a second ship which had encountered the flotsam of the wreck. It was evident beyond peradventure of a doubt that the illfated *Alsace* had been blown to atoms, and all on board must have perished instantly with her.

The article was followed by a copy of the passenger list together with brief obituaries of the more prominent of the wreck's victims, and beneath it was a terse paragraph which verified Millard's disclosures of the previous day. The notorious swindler, Jan Martens, alias Maurice du Chainat, was known to have been on board, and arrangements had been made to take him in custody upon the arrival of the ship at her destination; in fact he had been placed nominally under arrest by the captain of the *Alsace*, as the last wireless message known to have been sent out from the unfortunate ship announced. It was feared that the bulk of the money netted by his gigantic swindle had gone down with him.

Storm left his breakfast untasted, deaf to the polite concern of Homachi, and took his miserable way to the trust company. God, how he loathed it all! The very sight of his desk, familiar through long years of usage, awoke anew the spirit of senseless, futile revolt; doubly futile now since the mirage of a different future had risen again only to be blotted out.

In the bitterness of soul which surpassed anything he had known in his blackest hours, Storm forced himself to go through with the dreary round; but the close of day found him desperate, at bay. He could not go on! What was the use, anyway? What did the future hold for him now? Only memories which rose up in the silent hours to take him by the throat, from which there could be no escape while life lasted!

With the waning afternoon the sky had become overcast, and twilight brought a gentle summer rain through which Storm plodded doggedly. Food was distasteful, the thought of a restaurant was abhorrent to him in his morose mood, and yet he shrank from hours of solitude in his apartment. He was afraid of himself, afraid to think, and he longed desperately for the companionship of a fellow being; not George nor anyone connected with his life of the past ten years, but someone unconcerned in his affairs, someone with whom he could talk and forget.

He had seized upon the trivial excuse of a call at his cigarette importer's as an expedient to while away a half hour. The tobacconist's shop was just across the street from the Grand Central Station, and as Storm passed among the arrivals who swarmed out of the edifice one face in the crowd caught his eye. Little of it was visible, the collar of his light summer ulster turned up to meet it, and he tramped along beneath his umbrella without glancing to right or left.

Storm caught him impulsively by the arm.

"Jack!" he cried. "Where on earth did you drop from?"

The stranger shook him off unceremoniously.

"Your mistake, I'm afraid—" he mumbled.

"I beg your pardon." Storm stepped aside. "Sorry to have accosted you, sir. I thought that you were—yes, by Jove! You *are* Jack Horton! Don't you know me, old man?"

The stranger hesitated and then with a hearty ring in his voice which he checked instantly as he glanced cautiously about him.

"You've got me!" he exclaimed with subdued joviality. "I'm Jack, all right, and of course I know you, Norman, you old scout! I meant to pass you up, though; fact is, I've got no business to stop in town now. For the love of Pete, if you've got nothing to do, take me somewhere where we can get a bite and have a good old chin without a lot of folks giving us the once-over!"

Storm was mystified. This pal of his freshman year at college whom Providence had thrust in his path this night of all nights when he needed human companionship seemed to be in some strange predicament, but he did not stop to question. He was only too glad of the promised relief from solitude.

"Come along! I've got just the place. Lord, but it's good to see you! We'll go straight up to my own rooms. My man will have gone, but I can rustle up some grub and anything else you feel like having."

He gestured toward the line of waiting taxicabs, but Horton drew back.

"Where are you living?" he asked, with a trace of nervousness.

"Riverside Drive," Storm replied impatiently. "Come on, old man, your umbrella's leaking."

"Is there a subway station near you?"

"Yes, of course, only a block or two away. But what in the—"

"Never mind now. Let's go up that way," his friend proposed. "I'm not stuck on these taxis under the present circumstances. A lot of the fellows that drive them are crooks, and you never can tell—. Me for the subway, and don't talk too much on the way up, Norman. This is serious business."

"All right," Storm acquiesced shortly. "But let me carry that bag, won't you? You've got enough with that umbrella and brief case."

"Not on your life!" responded Horton with emphasis. I'll carry it myself. You lead the way, Norman."

Storm obeyed. He had known little of Horton in the past and nothing of how or where the years since their college days had been passed. Without having much in common, they had traveled in the same crowd during the first term at the university, and many had been the scrapes, engendered by Horton's reckless love of fun and Storm's rebellion against discipline, which they had shared.

Horton had been compelled to leave college at the end of the freshman year by his father's failure and gradually had dropped from sight of his old classmates. In the first few years he had been heard of now and then in widely different parts of the country, employed in positions of minor responsibility, but of late no news had come and Storm had forgotten him completely until this passing glimpse of his face recalled old associations.

In the subway he studied his companion furtively. Horton's figure had grown heavier with the years, his face more full but healthily tanned, while the prominent jaw and clear, steady eyes betokened added strength of character. Storm speculated on his possible circumstances; his clothes were of good quality but obviously ready-made, and the bluff heartiness of his manner suggested an association with men of a rougher caliber than Storm himself counted among his friends. Here was a man who had mastered circumstances, not permitted himself to be enslaved by them! Storm wondered what the other would do in his place. At least he would not allow penury to hold him chained to an existence which had become unendurable! Then he dismissed the idea with a shrug. Horton could never stand in his place; he would not have the cleverness to cloak murder in the guise of accident, or the quick wit and self-control to see it through. No one could have done it save Storm himself!

When they reached his station he touched Horton lightly on the arm to appraise him of the fact and was amazed at the latter's quick, defensive start. What did the man fear? His secretiveness, his evident intention at first to deny his identity: what could they portend? Could it be that Horton was a fugitive from justice? Storm smiled at the thought. Why, he himself, if the world only knew—!

But Horton's ebullient spirits bubbled over when they emerged on the street level, and a hasty glance about assured him that no other pedestrians were near.

"Lord, but it's good to be in New York again, Norman!" he exclaimed. "The old burg is the greatest little spot on God's green earth, let me tell you! The sight and sound and smell of it get into a fellow's blood. Talk about the East a-calling! It's deaf and dumb compared to the urge of little old Manhattan!"

"Feel that way about it?" Storm's lips curled as he remembered his own glowing, futile dreams of the Far East.

"You bet I do!" Horton shifted his umbrella to grasp more firmly the small black bag which he was carrying. "Do you know, Norman, there have been nights down in Mexico and up in Alaska and out on the plains when I would have given five years of my life for an hour here! Mind you, it isn't so much the bright lights—I can't afford, for more reasons than one, to cut loose as I used to—but it's what these literary cusses call 'atmosphere', I guess; there's something in life here, any phase of it, that gets under a guy's skin and makes him itch to get back!"

"Mexico? Alaska?" repeated Storm with unconscious envy. "You've been about a bit, Jack, haven't you?"

"Surest thing you know!" The other laughed, adding, as Storm halted: "This where you hang out? Oh, boy! Some class to you!"

"I took these rooms off the hands of a friend only lately," Storm replied, wincing in spite of himself at Horton's uncouth appreciation. "I have lived out of town for years."

He opened the apartment door and switched on the lights, and his companion gave a low whistle.

"Some class!" he repeated admiringly. "You must have made good, Norman."

There was an element of surprise in his tone that nettled his host.

"I'm an official of the Mammoth Trust Company, you know," he said loftily. "Let me take your coat, Jack, and just put your bag down anywhere."

Horton allowed himself to be divested of his coat and hat, but when he followed Storm into the living-room he was still carrying the black bag, which he deposited on a corner of the couch, seating himself beside it.

"Mammoth Trust, eh?" he repeated. "Your old man was a big bug there at one time, wasn't he? I remember you used to talk about it in the old days; said he was going to get you an easy berth there when you graduated. By Gad, you did fall in soft!"

Storm flushed at the imputation, although he found no words with which to deny it. What a rough boor Jack had become! He almost regretted that he had brought him home. Still, even he was better than no one.

"Cocktail?" he asked suggestively.

Horton shook his head.

"I'm off the fancy stuff," he replied. "The fact is, I'm not supposed to be touching anything at all, but I may as well take the lid off since we're going to make a night of it. Got any Scotch?"

Storm produced the bottle, siphon and two tall glasses, and went into the kitchen to crack some ice. His guest followed him to the door after a quick backward glance at his bag.

"Great little place you've got here." He glanced about him and back at his host. Then for the first time he noted the latter's mourning garb, and his eyes widened. "Look here, Norman, you—you've lost someone. Not your wife?" Storm nodded.

"You don't say! I'm confoundedly sorry, old scout!" Horton exclaimed with re&l feeling. "I knew you were married, of course; saw your wife's picture in the society papers more than once a few years ago. When you brought me here and I lamped it was a typical bachelor's diggings, I didn't like to ask questions; divorces here are thicker than flees below the border, and you never can tell. When did it happen, Norman?"

"A little over a month ago." Storm turned to the ice chest as if to cut off further questions or attempt at sympathy, but Horton was as impervious to snubs as a good-natured puppy.

"Isn't it hell?" he soliloquized. "When a fellow's happy, something rotten always happens. Beautiful woman, wasn't she? Any kids?"

"No," replied his host shortly. "Come on, let's have our drink and then we'll see what we can dig up for dinner. Homachi usually stuffs the pantry shelves pretty well."

The glasses were filled and Horton raised his, somewhat uncomfortably oppressed with the lack of fitting words. Storm forestalled him hastily.

"I don't talk much about my trouble, Jack. Let's try to forget it for tonight. This is a reunion, and I'm damn glad to have you here! Happy days!"

Horton nodded and drank deeply, drawing a long breath of satisfaction.

"That's the stuff!" he approved. "Some kick to it, all right! Do you ever see anything of the old crowd?"

"I run into one or another of them at the club now and then." Storm put down his glass. "I'll go and investigate the pantry; you must be starved."

"I could do with a little nourishment," Horton acquiesced. "Let me help you rustle the grub. You don't look as if you were much of a hand at it."

"Are you?"

Horton laughed boisterously.

"Just watch me!" he cried. "I've been roughing it for years, in one way and another; mining camps, oil leases, cattle ranches and even a tramp steamer."

"Really? You haven't told me a thing about yourself yet, Jack. The last I heard of you, you were working in a bank out in Chicago."

"Yeah!" Horton snorted disgustedly. "Nice kid-glove- and-silk-hat job; thirty bucks a week and a bum lung. — Say, where can I put this bag of mine?"

"Why, leave it here." Storm stared. "Nobody is going to walk off with it."

"Not if I know it, they're not!" returned his guest with emphasis. "I've got some mighty important stuff in here. Got any place where I can lock it up? I'd feel easier in my mind—"

' "Why, of course!" Storm threw open a closet door. "Here, keep the key yourself if it will give you any satisfaction. Now come on; I'm hungry, myself."

They found the pantry well stocked and made a hearty meal. Storm, usually an abstemious drinker, poured out a second

Scotch and under its influence grew expansive. He regaled his guest with tales of high finance, adroitly registering his own importance in the trust company and his intimacy w eh men of large affairs. It was only later when they returned again to the living-room that he became conscious of a seeming reticence on the part of his friend.

"But tell me about yourself," he demanded. "Will you smoke? Try one of these."

He offered the humidor, and Horton selected a cigar and eyed it almost reverently.

"A fifty-center!" he exclaimed. "Gee, you're hitting the high spots, all right, and I don't wonder after what you've been telling me! As to myself—well, I'm no great shakes, but I'm not kicking. I've had a pretty good time of it, by and large."

"But you said something about lung trouble." Storm lit his own cigarette and held the match to the other's cigar. "You certainly don't look it now."

"Fact, though," Horton nodded. "Good thing, too, or I would have been a pasty-faced, pretty-mannered bank clerk to this day. It was a question of living out in the open or dying in a hall room, and the West looked good to me. I started in as paymaster in a mining camp, and believe me it was some job for a tenderfoot who had never been nearer to a gun than across the footlights at a melodrama! I learned to travel heeled and be quick on the draw and a few other things; human nature generally. It's funny the fascination other's people's money has for some folks. Never felt that way myself; I guess that's why I've usually had charge of the payroll."

Storm smiled bitterly, his thoughts reverting to the pseudo Du Chainat and his own money lying now at the bottom of the sea. He had boasted of his affluence to Horton to soothe his wounded self-esteem at the latter's naive appraisement of him, but his own predicament had returned with crushing force.

Happily, Horton was aware of no lack of response on the part of the host.

"Yes, sir!" he continued. "It's no credit to me that I've run straight, but it kind of gives a fellow a damned good feeling to know that folks realize without question that he's worthy of trust. Why, right now—!" He broke off and added in a lower tone: "I'm a hell of a fellow to pin medals on myself! I ought to be miles away this minute and going fast. Couldn't resist a glimpse of the old town, though, and I reckon I can take care of myself. I thought I would just look 'round a bit and then be on my way, but you came along—"

"And you tried to pass me up!" Storm recalled the other's furtive manner. "What is the game, anyway, Jack? Where are you bound for?"

"A jumping-off place back in the Alleghanies." Horton grimaced. "Some different from your berth here, isn't it? You've got a nice mahogany roll-top, I suppose, and nothing on your mind but your hat, while I travel with my eyes peeled and my finger on the trigger. See this?"

He reached in his hip pocket and produced a blunt-nosed pistol which winked wickedly in the light.

"Good heavens! What do you carry that thing around with you for?" Storm gasped.

"Looks like business, doesn't it? Fact is, I'm pay-master now for one of the biggest coal companies in Pennsylvania, and when you've got charge of a small fortune every month and an army of Hunkies and general riff-raff know it, it's just as well to be on the look-out." He laid the weapon on the table and ground out the stub of his cigar regretfully in the ash-tray. "That was some smoke!"

"Have another," Storm invited. "I only smoke cigarettes myself, but these cigars are supposed to be pretty good, I believe."

"They are that!" his guest agreed with unction. "Lord, I don't know when I've had a feed like this, and three good hookers of Scotch and such tobacco!" He lighted a fresh cigar and sprawled back in his chair with a sigh of content. "This is certainly the life!"

"There's more Scotch—" Storm began suggestively, but Horton shook his head.

"Not for mine, thanks. I'm at peace with the world. If it weren't for that bag of mine—"

"What's in it, anyway?" Storm asked idly. "Money for your gang out there?"

"You've guessed it, son." Horton sat up suddenly. "I'll show you something that will make your eyes pop out, for all your big deals! You fellows who write checks and tear off coupons don't know what money is; it is only when you handle the actual coin in bulk that you realize what it stands for."

He crossed to the closet and unlocked it while Storm watched him, diverted in spite of himself at the other's complacency.

"Here you are!" Horton placed the bag on the table and opened it. "Have a look!"

Storm obeyed. Packets of yellow-backed bills, sheaves on sheaves of them, met his gaze, and cylinders of coins. The bag was filled to the brim with them!

"All gold!" Horton explained, pointing to the cylinders. "Some of the Hunkies won't take anything else. Do you know how much I've got here, old scout? One hundred and twelve thousand, five hundred and fifty-two dollars and eighty-four cents!"

XIV

IN HIS HANDS

In contemplation of the money Storm was stirred despite his sang-froid. Horton's psychology had been sound; it was one thing to deal in figures and quite another to view the actual cash before one.

"This is some money!" He unconsciously adopted his companion's slang. "I don't wonder you go heeled, as you call it, with that much at stake!"

"I've handled twice as much during the war, when we were speeding up production to the limit," Horton boasted as he fastened the bag and placed it on the floor at his feet. "Twice as much and then some, and never lost a cent! I'm not taking any chances, though; the constabulary down there do their part, and a wonderful lot of fellows they are, but they can't be everywhere at once. The last guy that held my job was found in a thicket by the road with his head bashed in. The birds that got him were caught, but a lot of good it did him! No, *sir*. I take mighty good care not to land in his shoes!"

A hundred and twelve thousand dollars! The figures themselves held an odd fascination for Storm, and he could not keep his eyes from straying to the bag.

"I had an experience out in Montana in the early days when I was new to the game." Horton settled back once more luxuriously into his chair. "I was only carrying five thousand then, but it looked as big as a million to me, and I don't mind telling you that I was plumb scared of the responsibility. I had a wild bit of road to cover between the town and the mine, and I jumped at every shadow. We had a rough lot out there, too; scum of the earth, even for a raw mining camp. One night four guys that we had turned off laid for me; they'd have done for me, too, only by sheer dumb luck I got the drop on them first. I held 'em there, all four of 'em, till a gang of our own men came along, but it was a narrow squeak for me! Lord, but I was one sick *hombre!*"

He chuckled reminiscently, but his host did not smile. Instead, his lips tightened and an avid gleam came into his eyes. A hundred and twelve thousand dollars! What it would mean to him! If he had Jack's opportunity—!

"There was another time down in Mexico." His guest was in the flood tide of garrulity now, all unconscious of the train of thought his innocent display had evoked. "A couple of greasers tried to stick me up, but I drilled a hole in one of them, and the other beat it for the hills. It's tame here in the East compared to those days, but there's always a chance of trouble in my game."

How ridiculously small and flimsy the black bag looked to contain such tremendous potentialities! All that Du Chainat's alluring proposition had held out, and more, was there before him in the custody of this smirking, self-assured boor! Storm felt a wave of unaccountable hatred for the other man sweeping over him. What right had Jack Horton to flaunt that money in his face? God, if it were only his!

He roused himself to realize that the other was eyeing him in a crestfallen fashion, disappointed that his narrative had seemed to make no impression, and Storm collected his vagrant thoughts.

"I envy you your experiences," he said. "The element of danger must be exhilarating. To walk out of the station, as you did tonight, and realize that if the very men who rubbed shoulders with you in the street knew what was in that bag your life might not be worth tuppence—"

"Say, look here!" Horton showed traces of alarm. "I told you in confidence, old scout! For the love of Pete, don't mention it! It would mean my job if the company heard that I had been flashing the payroll! They must never get onto it that I stopped off in town; no one must know! You'll keep it a secret that you met me?"

"Of course." Storm nodded. "You don't know how well I can keep a secret, Jack!"

"You're the only living soul who knows where I am this minute!" The other chuckled, reassured. "Not that I'll be missed for these few hours. The company don't check me up on time nor keep tabs on me; they know I'm honest, and the money is as safe in my care as though it were still in the bank."

"The only living soul who knows where I am!" The words rang in Storm's ears with the insistence of a tolling bell, and a tremondous, sinister idea was born. Nothing stood between him and the money there before his eyes, within reach of his hand, but this cocksure fathead! If he could get it away from him, secretly, without the other's knowing—But that was impossible! The fool knew his business too well to be tricked; he had learned it in the roughest, wildest parts of the country, and here they were in the midst of the crowded city, where a single outcry would bring immediate investigation. Jack Horton would guard that bag while he lived. *While he lived!*

"No one will ever learn from me that I saw you tonight," Storm said slowly. "You needn't worry about that."

Horton nodded.

"Knew I could trust you, old scout! You know, now that I'm here, though, I'm damned if I wouldn't like to telephone a certain party." He turned speculative eyes on the instrument on the desk. "She needn't know where the call came from;

I could tell her I was in Trenton or Scranton or Altoona, and she wouldn't get me in a million years. I'd kind of like to hear her voice—"

"You're crazy!" Storm interrupted in rough haste. "This wire is listed! Don't you know a call can be traced? Suppose this woman, whoever she is, thinks of something else she wants to tell you after you have rung off, and gets Central to call you back on the wire? It isn't always possible for them to do it, but they have been known to. It is nothing to me, of course, but you know how women talk; if you want her to know that you spent the evening here in town—"

"Not on your life, I don't!" ejaculated Horton. "She's all right; greatest little kid in the world, but I'm not giving anybody anything on me, especially when I'm in charge of the company's money."

Storm nodded acquiescence. No plan was as yet forming itself in his mind, but the sinister idea was becoming a resolution. He must have that money! Fate, after robbing him of his own, had replaced it twofold within his grasp. If Horton would not surrender it—and that was not worth considering—then Horton must be eliminated. He had done it once and gotten away with it; why not again? But he must feel his way carefully, he must learn just where Horton stood, what his ties were. He must know from what quarter to expect inquiries if—he tried to say it to himself calmly, but his senses reeled at the immensity of it—if Horton disappeared.

"But you haven't told me anything about yourself, Jack; only about your work. You're not married, I suppose?"

"Not me!" the other laughed, then amended: "At least, not yet. I've looked 'em all over, from Tampico to Nome and from 'Frisco to Boston, but I haven't seen one yet that I'd tie up to for keeps; except maybe this little dame I wanted to talk to just now. Prettiest little thing you ever saw in your life, Norman, and got a lot of horse sense besides. Want to see the picture?"

He pulled out his watch, snapped the case open and extended it across the table.

The face in the little photograph was undeniably pretty, but the style of coiffure was over-elaborate, and even to Storm's untrained masculine eye the gown seemed cheaply ornate; not the sort of thing that Leila or any of her set would have worn.

"Who is she?" he asked; then correcting himself hastily, "I mean, where does she come from? She is mighty pretty," he added as he snapped the watch shut and handed it back.

"You've gussed it; she's no New Yorker; comes from Pennsylvania, out Bethlehem way. Her daddy made a pot of money in steel during the war, and she's on here trying to catch up with the procession. She'll do it, too, with the old man's cash and her looks." Horton grinned fatuously. "She's strong for your Uncle Jack, all right."

What an ass he looked, blithering there about a girl while at his feet lay the price of his life! But Storm must know more.

"Then I suppose congratulations are in order?" he queried, eying his guest through narrowed lids.

"Not yet. I don't mean to brag, but I have an idea they will be as soon as I make up my mind to say the word." He paused to lay his cigar stub with the others in the tray, and Storm's eyes followed the motion as if fascinated. The mounting heap of pale gray ashes reminded him suddenly of certain ashes which he had scattered in a garden at midnight a month before. They were so like them, light and flakey, tossed by a light wind, gone forever at the twist of an arm! How easily that had been accomplished! Not only the destruction of the handkerchief, but of all other clues! How easily he had outwitted them all, and then he had been a mere amateur and handicapped by the fact that the blow had been unpremeditated; when he started to build up the circumstantial evidence of accident he had been compelled to make what use he could of conditions as they lay. Sinister but intoxicating reflections came to him. He had succeeded then; could he fail now when the opportunity was his to prepare beforehand each step of the way?

"How about your family, Jack? I haven't heard, you know, since I lost track of you." He must keep the conversation going somehow until he formed a plan.

"Haven't any." Horton shrugged. "My dad died right after his failure—you knew that?—and mother went in two years, while my kid brother was killed in France. There's no one left except an uncle in Omaha, and I cut loose from him years ago. It's too bad mother didn't live; she'd have liked 'Genie."

" 'Genie?"

"Old man Saulsbury's daughter; girl in the watch. Her own mother is dead, and she's staying here on Madison Avenue with some old widow who is long on the family tree business and short on cash. She's going to fit 'Genie out properly and put her through her paces."

"You may lose her if she gets into the social game," Storm remarked absently, his mind intent on his problem. On one thing he was determined; Horton should not leave that door with the money! Yet to kill him here was unthinkable. A phrase which the other had used in telling of his predecessor's fate returned to Storm like a flash of inspiration: *"found in a thicket by the road with his head bashed in"*—The Drive! Later it would be deserted enough; but how to get Horton out there—?

"Lose 'Genie?" Horton repeated. "Not a chance! There's no nonsense about her, I can tell you! She is only doing this to please her daddy, but she'll never get stung by the society bug. I knew her before the old man made his pile, and it hasn't changed her a mite. She'd stick to me through thick and thin, but when a fellow has led the free life I have, he isn't in too much of a hurry to settle down in double harness, even if it is silver mounted."

"There is no one else?" Storm regarded him quizzically. "For you, I mean? No other girl in the running?"

"No, sir! I never bothered much with them, anyway; been too busy. This Mid-Eastern Consolidated Coal Corporation is the biggest job I've had yet, and I'm planning to stick right with them and go on up. They know me, and once I get on the inside—!" Horton paused and reached for the humidor. "I'm eating up your cigars, old scout! Look at that pile of ashes."

"Help yourself." Storm tossed the match box across the table. "That's what they're here for. *Damn* the ashes."

"Well, it's my last." Horton glanced at his watch. "Great Scott! Eleven thirty! I ought to be changing at Altoona right now for a little jerkwater road up into the mountains!—Oh, what's the odds! It's been worth it, this powwow with you, Norman. I'll catch the twelve-forty—"

"Why? I thought you were going to stay over night!" stammered his host, aghast at this sudden hitch in his half-formulated plan. "I'm all alone here, as you see, and we can turn in any time you feel like it."

"I—I oughtn't to!" Horton hesitated, and Storm seized upon his opportunity.

"You're safer here with that bag than you would be traveling at night. You can get a train at almost any hour in the morning, and you said they didn't check up on your time." He paused, and as the other still visibly wavered he added persuasively: "Tell you what I'll do, Jack. I've got some business to attend to in Philadelphia that would require my presence there in a day or two, anyway; if you'll wait over I'll go part of the way with you tomorrow. It isn't often that two chaps who were such good pals at college meet after so many years, and we have a lot to talk over yet."

"That's so," Horton agreed. "A few hours more or less won't make any difference, I guess, and I'll be mighty glad to have your company part of the way in the morning. I'm not due back until late in the afternoon; got through my business today ahead of time. That's how I came to think of stopping off for a look at the old town."

"It would make trouble if you weren't there tomorrow, though?" Storm asked slowly. "I mean, if you should stay over with me—?"

"Trouble? Say!" Horton leaned forward impressively. "If I weren't there by six o'clock tomorrow night every wire in the east would be hot from efforts to locate me. I'm not so precious to them, but their little old hundred thousand odd—wow!"

He flickered the ashes from his cigar, and a few flakes missed the tray and fell on the shining surface of the table top. Storm watched them settle, just as those other ashes must have settled among the flowers... God, why did he have to think of that now? *'In a thicket with his head bashed in'!* There was a spot up the Drive past the viaduct where the path turned sharply, and on the other side of the low wall was a sheer drop of fifty feet or more with stout bushes clinging to it all the way down. A living man could grab them and save himself, perhaps, but a dead body, hurtled over the wall—

"You'll get there, all right." Storm forced himself to speak casually. "You're traveling light, but I can make you comfortabe for the night—"

"Comfortable?" Horton spread his legs out luxuriously. "I'm so darned comfortable right now that I wouldn't change places with a king! Lord, but it's like old times to see you again, Norman! Twenty years is a long stretch, but it seems only yesterday that we sat smoking together in your old rooms, and usually planning some devilment, too! Remember the love letters on pink paper that we sent to the old chemistry prof.— what was his name? Oh, yes, Peebles. Gad, we kept them up for weeks until he was afraid to look even the president's old maid sister in the face!"

He chuckled reminiscently, and Storm's lips twisted in a smile. *'Head bashed in!'* How could he do it? What sort of weapon—? From where he sat he could look over his guest's shoulder into the hall, and the umbrella stand was in a direct line of vision. Potter had been rather a connoisseur of canes, and among those he had left behind him in his hurried departure was a curious one with a loaded head. A tap with it would crack a skull like an egg-shell! But not if that skull were covered by a thick, soft felt hat, such as Horton wore when they met. If he could contrive to make him put on an old golf cap, on some pretext; could get him up the Drive to that lonely spot where the wall sheered down, he would have but to strike once and the bag and its precious contents would be his! He listened. Had the rain stopped? It was no longer beating against the window. He must make an excuse to look out and see.

"We certainly pulled off a few stunts in the old days!" he observed. "Don't you think it's a bit stuffy in here? Let's get some of the smoke out."

He rose and strolled to the window, trembling with inward excitement, but forcing himself to walk slowly, casually. He raised the window. The pavement was still wet and glistening, but overhead the stars winked down at him.

"Hello, it's clearing off!" he announced "We might have a stroll later, before we turn in."

"What for?" Horton asked unenthusiastically. "I've been on the jump all day. It is good enough for me right here."

"Then what do you say to a little drink?" Storm heard the footsteps of a lone pedestrian approaching, and hurriedly closing the window, pulled down the shade. Horton was seated where the light played strongly on his face, and he would be plainly visible from the street. A passer-by glancing in would think nothing strange about seeing a man sitting quietly smoking there, but he might chance to remember the face; he might recall it later when a hue and cry was raised and pictures were printed in the newspapers... "As long as you're staying on here with me tonight another little nip or two won't do you any harm. This is an occasion, you know!"

Rigidly as he held himself in control, there was a note of suppressed eagerness in his tone which the unsuspicious Horton misread.

"On with the dance!" he cried gaily. "I'm with you, old scout! Just one, though; got to have a clear head in the morning. Booze is a good thing to let alone in my business, but I know when I've had enough. Do you remember the time we got pickled in Dutch Jake's, and you wanted to go and serenade the whole faculty?"

While he chattered on serenely Storm moved in and out bringing glasses, ice and a fresh siphon. He mixed as stiff a drink as he dared for his guest, a light one for himself, and raised his glass.

"To ourselves!" he exclaimed with a reckless laugh. "That's the best toast in the world, Jack, and the most honest one. To us!"

"And our next meeting." Horton drank, nor noticed that his host set his glass down untasted while a faint shudder swept over him. "Phew! but that's a strong one! I need a little more fizz in that, old scout." He reached for the siphon. "Say, what wouldn't I give if we could all be together again, just once; the old crowd, I mean! There was Van Tries and Caldwell and Holworthy and Swain and Mc-Knight. I wonder what has become of them all!"

"Holworthy is here in town; I run into him now and then." Storm raised his glass slowly, watching the hand that held it. Steady as a die!

"That so?" Horton looked up, interested. "What is his line?"

"Real estate. He's the same old plodding George, except that he is getting fat. McKnight died in the prison camp at Rastatt and Swain went under in Wall Street and blew the top of his head off."

Horton's ruddy face sobered.

"That makes three of the old crowd gone, for Caldwell was killed in a motor smash-up," he said. "I remember reading about it in the papers. All violent deaths, too! Well, maybe we're none of us fated to die in our own beds."

Storm started nervously and glanced at him. Was there something prophetic in Horton's speech? Then he shook himself angrily. Bah! he was getting morbid. Morbid, with a hundred thousand dollars at his feet, waiting for him to stoop and pick it up!

Horton, too, stirred in his chair as though shaking off unwelcome thoughts, and added:

"*Anyway, here we* are! You're well fixed, and I'm on the road to it; that leaves only Van Tries, of our bunch. Ever hear anything from him?"

"Not since he beat it for Japan with another man's wife."

"You don't say!" Horton's eyes widened. "Well, he always was a wild one; too much money and no responsibility. I tell you, Norman, money is a comfortable thing to have, but it causes a hell of a lot of trouble in this world! Not that mine will bother me very much, but fellows like Van Tries. They don't know the value of it till it's gone, and then they're out for the count because they've never learned to do anything except spend."

His tone dropped to a monotonous drawl with a note of fatigue in it, and Storm drew a deep breath. It was nearly one o'clock. His plan was complete and there remained only to put it to the test. How quickly the inspiration had come to him! How simple it was and yet how masterly! Perhaps that first murder had sharpened his wits for this! There was no reason for waiting longer; it must be now or never! He rose.

"What do you say to a little stroll, Jack, before we hit the hay?" he asked with a studied carelessness. "Not a long one, for I know you must be tired after traveling all day; but I don't sleep very well unless I get a bit of fresh air just before I turn in."

Breathlessly he watched the other. What if Horton should suggest that he go alone? What if—?

"I'm with you." Horton rose equably. "We must be smoked up like a couple of hams."

He reached out a hand for his pistol, but Storm stopped him with a nervous laugh.

"Here! There's a Sullivan law in this town against carrying concealed weapons! You don't want that thing with you; put it in the table drawer there."

"All right." Horton opened the drawer and then hesitated. "The money! There have been hold-ups on the Drive. I've read of them—"

"Good Lord, you weren't going to cart that bag along, were you?" Storm's tone was a perfect blend of amusement and good-natured expostulation. "Why, man, we'll only be gone ten minutes, fifteen at most! Lock it up again in the closet; *no one is going to break in here!*"

Horton shook his head obstinately.

"I never leave it out of my sight when I'm on the job," he said. "You never can tell, you know, Norman."

"I suppose some sneak thief is clairvoyant enough to know that money is here tonight of all nights, in a bag in a locked closet!" Storm shrugged. "Camouflage it behind some hat boxes and things on the shelf if you like. I tell you we'll only be gone a few minutes, and the watchman is right outside."

"It's a big chance," Horton responded doubtfully. "I suppose it sounds foolish to you, but I've learned to play safe. Still, if it is only five minutes—"

He picked up the bag and started for the closet. Storm watched him stow it carefully away with a smile of triumph. The fool was taking such pains—for him! He put on his own coat and then caught up Horton's. The felt hat which the latter had worn rolled to the floor, limp and sodden.

"I say, your hat is drenched!" He could scarcely keep the note of exultation from sounding in his voice. The last obstacle removed! Everything was playing into his hands; he couldn't fail! "I told you that your umbrella leaked! Just reach up on the top shelf there and get a golf cap. There is a stack of my old ones up there, and none of my hats would fit you. There is no sense in getting a cold in the head from wearing that wet thing, and you'll have to get it reblocked before train time tomorrow. It's a mess."

"It sure is!" Horton eyed it ruefully and reaching up into the closet brought out a golf cap of thin, dark blue cloth. Storm himself locked the closet door and held out the key.

"You'll feel safer if you've got it yourself," he remarked. "Now come on."

Horton dropped the key in his vest pocket and then drew on the cap with a ludicrous grimace at his reflection in the hall mirror.

"I look like a bally yachtsman!" he commented. "I suppose I'll have to go in for golf and all the rest of it if I land in right with the Mid-Eastern Consolidated and hitch up with the little girl, eh, what?"

"You'd be a shark at it, too." Storm switched off the lights and opened the door, stepping aside for his guest to precede him. "I don't play any more, but it's a great little game."

As Horton crossed the threshold Storm's hand closed over the head of the heavy cane, and he drew it out of the stand. Then the door closed behind them.

XV

ASHES TO ASHES

The night elevator man was almost slumbering peacefully before the telephone switchboard as they traversed the hall to the vestibule, and the street itself seemed deserted, but from afar echoed the measured tread of the watchman approaching upon his rounds.

"Let's cut across to the path!" suggested Storm with a hint of nervousness in his lowered tones. "It is better walking, and you can get a really magnificent view of the river lights from a few blocks further up."

He led his companion across the driveway and bridle road to the path deeply enshrouded by trees and bordered by the low stone wall which ran along the edge of the embankment. The night was moonless, but overhead the stars shone brightly and the broad sweep of the river below them at their left was dotted with the lights of ships and barges riding at anchor or moving slowly out with the tide.

"By jingo, it's some night!" Horton thrust back his shoulders and drew in a deep breath as he strode along at the rapid, vigorous gait of one habituated to covering long distances afoot. "Glad you thought of getting a bit of air, Norman; this is great! Look at the old river down there, and the Palisades beyond!

I tell you there isn't a spot on the face of the earth that can touch little old New York!"

"I like it out here myself. Sometimes when I can't sleep I walk along this path for hours, watching the lights and the river; there is a bigness and impersonality about it that is restful." Storm spoke truly, but back of his mind was the shuddering consciousness that never again would he find peace and tranquility in this nocturnal haunt. After tonight the shadows would be peopled with ghosts, the dark river would run red and the frowning cliffs on the farther bank would echo with the doings of this hour.—What matter? He would be far away with the means to live his own life and not a trace left behind him! Unconsciously his grip tightened on the cane, and he glanced speculatively at his companion. How easy it was going to be! Just a moment of steady courage, of carefully calculated effort; one smash—and the task would be accomplished! A few more blocks, a quarter mile at most—!

"You ought to see the harbor at Yokohama," Horton remarked. "Prettiest sight in the world when a ship comes in, if you didn't have to use your nose at the same time! All the sampans come out with their strings of colored lights and I can tell you they beat our barges any day in the week for picturesqueness! You hear the coolies chanting and the samyens and samisens tinkling, and the very taste of the East is in your mouth. Oh, I'm not getting poetic from the effects of your Scotch, old scout! It's all ugly enough and dirty and mean and distorted in the daylight, but there is a witchery over it at night. Here you don't get that; there's a hard-and-fast realism about it that dispels any illusion. It is a sort of bigness, as you say, but it doesn't hit me with any *dolce-far-niente* stuff; it means bustle to me, and commerce and adventure and wealth. Gee, when I've made my pile I'd like to sit in at the window of one of those white stone fronts over there and watch my coal barges slouching along on the end of a tow line and my cranes and winches and flat-cars getting busy along the docks! Fine pipe dream for a guy whose only contact with big money is in handling other people's, eh?"

He laughed boyishly, without cynicism, and Storm clapped him on the shoulder with assumed heartiness.

"You'll get there yet, Jack! Perhaps you're on the way to it now, who knows?" Only six blocks more and then they would reach that turn in the path! The unintended double significance in his words swept over him, and he felt an insane desire to laugh aloud. "You say you are in right with this Mid-Eastern Consolidated Corporation, and your wife will have money—"

"I'm not marrying her for what her old man has got!" Horton interrupted hastily. "It may be convenient some time for her to be able to help me swing something big, but you understand I like that little girl for herself. She's a thoroughbred, if her mother did run a miner's boarding house in the old days, and she's got the pep to keep a fellow right up on his toes and make him make good on his own account. I kind of wish I had telephoned to her tonight; it'll be a couple of weeks at least before I can hit this burg again, and I'd like to have heard her voice—"

"You can 'phone in the morning," Storm suggested, his eyes intent upon the path ahead. A figure was advancing toward them out of the darkness, and midway between them a street lamp shed broad rays. They would meet the stranger directly beneath it if they kept up their present gait. Storm halted deliberately and drew out his cigarette case. "Wait half a second till I get a light. Tell you what you can do, Jack. Stop over a train in Philadelphia with me tomorrow and call the lady up from there."

Horton shook his head decisively.

"Not me! Once I get on my way in the morning I'm going to keep right on going," he declared. "I don't feel right in my mind yet about this little stop-over, but it sure has been worth it! The next time I come to town—"

The advancing figure passed under the rays of the lamp and was revealed as a blue-coated policeman swinging along idly but with a certain brisk watchfulness. Storm blew out his match and fell in step once more beside his companion.

"The next time you come, drop me a line ahead and we'll fix up a little dinner with Holworthy and any of the rest I can find lying around the club," he said suavely. "It is a good thing to get in touch with the old crowd now and then; livens a chap up and keeps him in the running."

The policeman passed with only a casual glance at the two obviously respectable citizens, and his footsteps died away behind them. Only four blocks more!

"You bet it does!" Horton assented heartily. "Why, just running into you tonight like this and having a chat over old times has given me a new lease of life! I'll like first rate to see old Holworthy and the rest again, but most of all I want you to meet my girl. She's aces high, Norman, and you'll agree with me when you know her. We'll get her to shake the old lady for an evening and come to dinner—" he paused suddenly and added: "Say, we've come further than I thought. Hadn't we better be getting back? I don't want to cut short your stroll, but that bag back there is on my mind."

"All right. Just let us go to the top of the hill here around the turn." Storm threw his cigarette away and strove to speak casually, but his throat had become all at once parched and strained, and a tremor of excitement threatened his tones. "There's a down-stream boat almost due, and I want you to see it come round the bend. I watch for it here nearly every night, and it's a sight worth seeing. I suppose you'll be taking a trip somewhere on your honeymoon?"

"Haven't got as far as that yet!" Horton protested laughingly. "Oh, the little girl knows what is in the wind, all right—trust a woman for that!—but I haven't put it up to her in so many words. I want to lay my pipes with the Mid-Eastern first and see where I'm likely to stand before I tackle her old man. He likes me fast enough, but when it comes to me horning in on the family he'll expect me to spread my cards on the table, and I have not got much to show for the last twenty years except the trust of the people I've worked for."

"That is a pretty big asset," muttered Storm, his eyes on the brow of the hill just ahead. If he could keep Horton going, keep him talking until they reached that dark stretch and then, unsuspected, fall a step or two behind—! "It is a long step of the way toward success to gain the trust of your associates."

"Sure!" the other responded with pardonable pride. "But it is not so much of an asset as an income producer to an old guy who has struggled all his life and then struck it rich all of a sudden; so rich and so easy that he figures any fellow who hasn't done the same is a dub. But I'm not worrying; I've got it pretty good out there, and two or three more trips with the payroll will about be my finish. There's going to be a big reorganization soon, and I mean to edge in then on the inside."

Storm glanced hurriedly, keenly behind him. Not a figure was in sight, no sound broke the stillness save his companion's voice and the whispering of the wind in the rows of trees along the deserted drive. On the other side of the low wall the ground dropped away into seemingly limitless space, while outward and far below the broad river waited. A few yards more, a few steps—

A sudden raucous honk blared upon the air, and over the top of the hill appeared a wildly careening motor car which bore down upon them and passed in a bedlam of screeching brakes and maudlin song.

An oath borne of his keyed-up nerves burst unbidden from Storm's lips, and Horton turned.

"Gave you a start, eh?" he remarked. "This is a nice stretch of road on which to be flirting with death like that, isn't it? Thirty miles an hour and a chance to see the scenery, that's my motto; but then as I told you I've learned to play safe."

"My nerves aren't what thy used to be," Storm admitted, listening intently. The roar of the car had diminished in the distance to a low humming whirr which seemed only to accentuate the silence. "Just at the turn of the path there ahead—I think the boat is coming. Do you see any lights on the river?"

Horton quickened his pace, peering expectantly out over the wall. He was sensible that Storm had fallen back and heard the click of his cigarette case and the rasp of a match.

"Just those bobbing down there on some tugs," he announced. "A river steamer is a pretty sight at night, isn't she? I remember—"

The words ended in a gasp as something crashed down hideously upon him from behind, and the world was blotted out. His body lurched, sagged, and slumped down in a crumpled heap against the wall.

Storm's arm sank nervelessly to his side and a sickening wave of horror swept over him. Had Horton cried out, or had he himself? It seemed to him for an instant that tumultous shouting rang in his ears, that footsteps were beating upon the pavement behind him, a myriad of lights flashing in his eyes. Then silence and darkness descended again, and a shuddering sigh escaped him. The blow had been struck, but had it been sufficiently heavy? Suppose Horton still lived! What if he survived to be found in the morning by some damnable chance and to name his assailant?

Storm bent swiftly over the body, and his groping fingers came in contact with the back of the head, only to be shrinkingly withdrawn. God, but that sturdy stick had done its work well! He had only to possess himself of the key to the closet and heave the body over the wall—

Then a swift thought brought beads of sweat out upon his brow. The cap! The maker's name and his own initials were inside; suppose he had forgotten it! With fumbling, sticky fingers he felt about on the wet pavement. Thank heaven the puddles left by the rain had not dried!

The sinister stains would be obliterated, washed away—But where was the cap? Horton had been leaning toward the wall when the blow reached him; could the cap have fallen over and down, to be found on the morrow and traced?

With wild fear clutching at his heart, Storm straightened and groped feverishly along the wall. Was this to be the end, after his scheme had worked so smoothly; was he to be betrayed by the merest detail, one of the details which he had himself worked out to insure success? He felt along to the very edge of the wall, and then a sob of relief welled up in his throat; for his fingers had closed at last upon the cap, caught by a clutching tendril of vine as it must have fallen from the head of his victim.

He stuffed it into his coat pocket and stooping once more thrust his hand beneath that crumpled body and after a moment produced the key to the closet which contained the treasure. His! One hundred and twelve thousand—

But what was that light, quick tapping like hastily running feet? Storm recoiled and turned instinctively to flee, then by a supreme effort of will stayed the wild impulse. The tapping sounded there upon the wall close at hand; it was just a dead branch of the vine whipping in the wind. What a fool he was! Where had his nerve gone?

He must finish his job and quickly. That policeman would pass shortly again upon his rounds, or if not he, some strolling night prowler might appear at any moment to stumble over the body and raise an alarm. Every minute that he lingered there increased his danger, and yet he felt a loathsome repugnance at the thought of touching Horton again.

Nerving himself desperately he slipped his arms beneath the body and gave a convulsive heave. It jerked, swayed suddenly but slumped back again, and Storm's breath came in a sobbing gasp. God, how heavy it was! Could he ever get it up to the top of the wall? The sweat poured like rain down his face, and with a mighty effort of strained and snapping muscles he lifted it from the pavement, poised it for a moment on the edge of the abyss and sent it crashing over and down.

Weak and trembling in the nausea of sickening reaction, he cowered back and listened. Would the thing ever stop rolling? The first thud and crash of underbrush was followed by a sound as of mighty beasts trampling through a forest, then a pattering hail of pebbles and then, at last, silence.

Swaying drunkenly, Storm groped for the cane, found it and turned. Every instinct impelled him to frenzied flight, to run while wind and limb retained strength to obey his will; yet beneath the shuddering terror which obsessed him he realized that he must walk slowly, casually, that no chance passer-by might connect this strolling pedestrian with the horror which lay behind.

Quivering with the effort to stay the mad impulse, he moved stiffly off down the path nor dared glance once behind him, although he could feel the gooseflesh rising upon his neck with the sensation of being watched by something supernatural, unclean! He must pass beneath the first street lamp, but in the shadows midway the block he could cross the bridle road and driveway and continue south on the sidewalk. It would not do to remain on the path; if he should encounter the policeman again, and the latter recognizing him, should question him, should question why only one returned where two had gone—

Each dragging step sent a spasm of nervous torture through his frame, but he gritted his teeth and held himself erect as he passed beneath the light, even giving a jaunty swing to the cane which seemed to gain weight with every moment that went.

Twenty yards further he turned to cut across the driveway to the sidewalk, and as he did so a sound came from behind him that stilled the blood in his veins. It was merely the hoot of the fog horn on the river, but it came to him like the long-drawn wail of a soul in pain.

A sense of utter desolation swept over him with its echo, but he rallied it with a savage defiance. In spite of everything, in spite of fate itself, had he not won? The money was his, money for a life-time of travel and ease and forgetfulness! No one could trace him, not a clue had been overlooked. What if commonplace Jack Horton with his petty affairs and affections and ambitions had been snuffed out? He had taken one chance too many, that was all, and the Mid-Eastern could well afford their loss, while to Storm the contents of that bag meant reason, life itself!

Still that odd sense of loneliness oppressed him, and in spite of his eagerness to examine and gloat over his treasure as he neared the apartment house his steps lagged. He realized all at once that he missed Horton's presence, his easy, self-centered chatter. How confidently the fellow had boasted of his 'girl' and his prospects, talked of the future as a condition already brought to pass; and then at one blow, one single muscular effort of another, he had been sent into eternity!

What an easy thing it was to take a life and to evade the consequences, if only one used a modicum of courage and caution! Murder was nothing more, after all, than the twang of a pea shooter at a bird, the tap of a butcher's hammer! A stealthy glow of elation stole over Storm's spirit, stilling the qualms which had beset him, and a heady exhilaration coursed through his veins like wine. The future was his; he was invincible!

The elevator man still slumbered in the same position as when Storm had left the house, and he let himself into his own apartment with infinite caution, closing the door noiselessly behind him. He longed to drag the bag from its hiding place and thrust his hands into its contents in a very orgy of triumphant possession, but he reminded himself sternly that an imperative task still lay before him. Ho- machi must find no traces of a visitor when he came in the morning. Then, too, there were other possible evidences to consider...

Storm switched on the lights and examined his hands and clothing with minute care. The latter bore no stains which he could discover, but upon his fingers were brownish smears which made his gorge rise, and about the thumb-nail of his left hand—the hand which had come in contact with Horton's fallen head—a thread of dull crimson had settled.

He turned to the bathroom in revolted haste when a fresh thought made him pause and grope for the pocket of his overcoat. The cap! Had the glancing but deadly blow which knocked it off to catch it by a miracle upon the vine spattered it with Horton's blood? He drew it forth and smoothed it into a semblance of shape with shaking hands. It was damp and crumpled, but no spot marred its surface or lining; the blow had been too swift and sure!

Tossing it upon the rack, Storm made for the bathroom, where he scrubbed his hands until the flesh smarted before turning his attention to the cane itself. When he had dropped it upon the path in order to raise the body it must have fallen into a puddle left by the storm, for it bore no marks save the discoloration of dampness; yet to make sure he carried it into the kitchen and held its heavy head beneath the strong bow of water from the faucet in the sink, then polished it with a rough towel until it shone. How it reminded him of that other rounded knob of wood with the sinister smudge of blood upon it and the single golden hair...

What a timorous, morbid weakling he had been that night! Afraid of his own shadow, of every move and breath! Nothing could touch him now, nothing could harm him; no one could ever know!

He replaced the cane in the umbrella-stand and was turning again toward the kitchen when his eyes fell upon the center table in the living-room. There beneath the lamp lay the bronze ash tray ringed with cigar butts and filled with ashes. Again the thought came to him of that other tray with similar contents which he had scattered to the winds. Why not these also? *Ashes to ashes.*

Those other ashes had been symbolic of his deed and vanished at a mere gesture; these were the concrete evidences of Horton's presence beneath his roof and yet might be as easily dispelled.

With a quick movement he pressed the button of the living-room switch, plunging the room in semi-gloom. Then, by the faint light which came in from the hallway, he made his way to the window and opened it. Not a soul in sight, not a sound save the rustle of the wind in the trees across the drive!

Storm caught up the tray from the table and gripping it firmly flung its contents far outward with all his strength lest any of the cigar stumps fall upon the sidewalk or in the gutter directly before him. On the instant the wind rose in a sweeping gust, and it seemed to him that he could see the gray handful spread out in a haze and swirl away into the void of night.

There stole over him once more that glow of achievement, as of some strange and pagan ritual performed, and he was closing the window when again there came the lingering, challenging, deep-throated note of a ship's fog horn upon the river. He shivered, in spite of himself, for to his distorted imagination it held no longer a wail as of a passing soul; rather, it sounded a menace and a warning, an awesome portent of doom.

XVI

THE SECOND VIGIL

With an almost physical effort Storm flung off the vague, harrowing suggestion which had laid itself upon him; and shrouding the window carefully with its curtains he turned on the lights once more, and glanced at the tall clock in the corner.

Quarter past two! Scarcely an hour had passed since he and Horton had left that room to start upon the little stroll which was to end so momentously for them both. For Horton it meant obliteration, the end of all things, but for him the beginning of a new life, a life which should begin with no memories, which should be crammed so full of color and motion and excitement that thought itself would be crowded out!

The money! He must know that it was still there even though he dared not lose himself in the joy of contemplation of it until every last trace of the visitor's presence had been removed.

He turned to the closet and halted suddenly. There on the settee before him lay Horton's felt hat, shapeless and sodden and somehow oddly pathetic. Storm put the womanish thought from him and gazed at the storm-battered object in momentary disquietude. He must get rid of it in some way, but that would resolve itself later. Now he must assure himself that the prize for which he had risked all was within his grasp,

With eager, trembling fingers he produced the key, opened the closet door and felt about on the shelf. Horton had hidden the bag well, poor confident fool! He had made sure that none but knowing hands should seek out its hidingplace.— There it was! Storm felt the grained surface of the leather, the hard, square edges of the packets which bulged its sides, and a light of exultation gleamed in his eyes. His! All his! That afternoon, a few short hours before, he had been the most miserable, hopeless of men, and now, through his courage, his resourcefulness and cunning, he had changed the face of destiny!

But he was wasting precious time in pandering now to the obsession which filled him. Storm caught the golf cap from the rack and tossed it lightly upon the closet shelf where it had rested so brief a time before, then reluctantly closed the door. Moving to the living-room once more, he collected the glasses, siphon and bottle and carried them to the kitchen where with scrupulous care he cleared away the debris of the earlier repast. As he applied himself to his unaccustomed task his thoughts raced forward to the magic years ahead, and if the lingering specter of a lonely, huddled, battered form lying somewhere out in the night intruded itself to block the vision he thrust it sternly aside.

Nothing could stop him now! The cup of forgetfulness, of hope and adventure and rejuvenation which had been held to his lips and snatched away was at last safe within his grasp, and he meant to drink of it to the full! That picture of Yokohama harbor which Horton had drawn; he should see it, too, arid soon! The bobbing lights and tinkling notes of the samisens, and taste of the East in his mouth; it should be his, all of it, until he was satiated with it and turned to other lands!

He looked about the conventional, luxurious rooms as though already they were strange to him, lost in a haze of half-forgotten memories. How soon they would be wholly forgotten, merged with those other more poignant thoughts of Greenlea in the blankness of a descending curtain! Not a memento should go with him into his new life; every thread must be clipped short on the day when he finally shook the dust of the past from his feet. And that would be soon, soon! There was nothing now to wait for, no lack of funds to hold him back. He would hang about, of course, until the little flurry of Horton's disappearance had blown over and been forgotten, and then he would set sail!

When all was in order again Storm gave a final approving glance about the kitchen and turned out the light. Homachi would note the quantity of food which had been consumed, of course, but that could be casually explained, and of Horton's hour there remained no other indication.

The gold! He could revel in it now, feel its solid, reassuring touch, know that for each separate clinking coin and crackling bill he could demand of the world full measure in all that he had thought denied to him forever! He dragged the bag from its hiding place, and dropping un-heedingly into the same chair which Horton had occupied two hours before, he opened it, working the secret spring as he had seen the other do. There it all lay before him; the few neat cylinders of gold, the many compact piles of yellow-backs! He fondled them in a strange ecstasy of possession, drunk with the knowledge of his own power. Had a glimpse of his face been vouchsafed him at the moment, he would not have recognized it as his own, so distorted was it by the passion which consumed him. Avarice had never laid its clutching fingers on him before, he had never known the rapacious hunger for wealth which assailed others; and it was not now the money itself over which he gloated, but all that it stood for, all that it would mean to him.

He had known the galling shackles of necessity which bound him to the wheel of circumstance, and now at one blow he had struck them off! He was free!

How long he crouched there he never knew, but after a time the first ecstasy passed and a measure of sanity returned. The money was his now; but he could not make instant use of his fortune, nor could he leave it in that bag. The logical thing would be to place it in the safe built into the wall of his bedroom, of which Potter had shown him the combination before he departed. The gold and banknotes would form too bulky a package to be concealed from Homachi's sharp eyes anywhere else in the apartment, and Storm repelled the thought of conveying it secretly to some safe deposit vault. He must keep it in his immediate possession, within reach of his hand.

He rose and carried the bag into the bedroom where he carefully counted out its contents upon the bed. One thousand, ten, twenty, fifty, one hundred, a hundred and twelve! He gasped at the immensity of it spread out before him! A hundred and twelve thousand dollars; and there were still some smaller gold coins and a two-dollar bill! As he lifted the bag something clinked within it, and investigating an inner pocket he discovered eight shining new dimes and four bright pennies. Five hundred and fifty-two dollars and eighty-four cents in addition to the thousands! He recalled Horton's statement of the amount, and an ironic smile curved his lips. What a methodical, cautious, conscientious protector of other people's money he had been, and how little it had availed him or them when the blow fell!

Storm opened the safe, deposited the money within it down to the last penny, and closing it slid the panel back into place. The bag remained to be disposed of, and there was Horton's hat and pistol, too, in the drawer of the livingroom table. He must get rid of them at the earliest possible moment, and in a manner which could not be traced. Of course, there was a chance that Horton's body would not be discovered until all means of identification had been obliterated; but it was so unlikely that Storm dismissed it from his thoughts. He could not afford to gamble on a favorable long shot now; he must look at this situation as squarely as he had the first desperate one of a month before, and prepare himself for every contingency.

Horton's clothing must surely contain papers revealing his identity and attesting to his connection with the MidEastern coal people. In the event that his body were found on the morrow, they would be communicated with, perhaps even before they had time to grow uneasy over the non- appearance of their paymaster. In a few hours, twelve at most, that ordinary looking bag might become the most important and sought-after article in the country, its description down to the minutest detail spread broadcast in the press.

How could he rid himself of it and of the pistol and hat as well? Gruesome accounts recurred to his mind of dismembered bodies having been wrapped in clumsy packages and dropped overboard in midstream from ferryboats. But something had always gone wrong; some sharp-eyed passenger had observed the action and marked the luckless individual for future identification, or the package itself had been recovered and the murderer traced by some such trivial detail as the wrapping or string which enclosed it. Clearly that means was not to be considered; and yet something must be done, and Storm could conceive of nothing more difficult to destroy than a stout leather bag. If he could only pack the other damning evidence—the hat and pistol—into it and ship it somewhere far away or else check it at some parcel repository—

Why not! The audacity of the thought made him gasp, and yet its feasibility instantly took hold upon his mind. If he attempted to express or send it by parcel post he would be compelled to write an address, and handwriting could be traced; but if he went to one of the great railroad terminals at the morning rush hour and checked the bag at the parcel desk he would merely be handed a numbered paper tag which could be easily destroyed, and in the hurrying crowd his identity would surely be lost. Better still, he could employ a stolid porter to check the bag for him, and it would be held for ten days or more before investigated as unclaimed.

Of course, there was the danger of his being recognized by some acquaintance in the passing throng of travelers, but it would be a simple matter to provide himself with a plausible excuse for his presence there. The bag itself was inconspicuous in appearance — Horton had seen to that! — and it bore no signs to reveal the purpose for which it had been used. The more Storm pondered, the more favorable the idea impressed him. He would have to get out in the morning without Homachi's observation and that of the elevator boy, but it could be managed. For the rest he must trust to luck until he had finally rid himself of it; it was the only possible solution.

He took the pistol from the table drawer and weighed it thoughtfully in his hand. It would not make the bag heavy enough to occasion remark, and yet it must be packed in carefully; the bag must have the outward appearance of being filled with the ordinary concomitants of travel. The hat would help, and for the rest paper would serve—

Then Storm remembered and blessed his valet's saving propensity. On an unused upper shelf in the pantry were a pile of old newspapers, some of them left from the litter of Potter's departure, but most of them painstakingly collected and preserved for some purpose known only to Homachi's Asiatic mind.

Storm procured a sheaf of them, and was on the point of wrapping up the pistol to stow it into the bag when on the front page of the topmost newspaper he saw roughly scrawled in pencil the characters, "One-A". It was the number of his apartment — the newsdealer's or house superintendent's guide for the delivery of the papers — a common practice, as he knew, all over the city, and yet it might furnish a clue.

Whipping off the outer sheets of each newspaper, he folded them and replaced them on the kitchen shelf, then crumpled the others and lined the bag with them, nesting the pistol secure from movement or jar in their depths. The hat, folded into a wad, came next, and then more paper until the bag was full. When closed it had a comfortably bulging appearance, and Storm snapped the secret spring into place and set it on the floor between the dressing table and wall where it would escape Homachi's eyes when he came to call his master in the morning.

Morning? Already a dim gray effulgence was stealing in between the curtains of the window, and Storm smiled to himself. How different was the vigil from the one of a month ago when he had sat quaking and bathed in sweat upon the foot of his bed, longing for yet dreading the coming of the dawn, waiting through tortured ages for the cry to echo up from below which would tell him that the body of his first victim had been discovered!

Now he knew that he had nothing to fear. He was master of this situation as he had been of the other, had he but realized it fully then. He extinguished all the lights except the low wall bracket at the bed's head and disrobed lazily, glorying in his steady nerve, his iron control of himself.

No compunction came to him at the thought of the night's work. Jack Horton had played so small a part in his life in the all but forgotten college days that the reminiscences had awakened no responsive chord. Hungry as he had been for human companionship in his despondency, the commonplace, cocksure stranger who spoke with the easy familiarity of an old friend had bored and slightly repelled him until he displayed his treasure. Even then he had not become a personality, but merely a wall of flesh and blood which stood between Storm and that which became in a twinkling of an eye imperative to his whole future existence.

How every circumstance had played into his hands! The remarkable coincidence of their meeting, the need of caution on Horton's part which had prevented their taking a taxicab, prevented the establishment of any clue which would lead to this apartment on the Drive! From the moment when Horton stepped from the train until sooner or later his body would be discovered up there among the bushes above the rail road track which skirted the Hudson, there would be a blank which the most astute detectives in the world could not fill in! The bag and its contents would be discovered and identified in time, of course, but the treasure which it had contained would never be traced; it would seep out gradually through the vast market places of the world in exchange for the good things of life!

Horton's easy surrender to the proffered hospitality, the fortuitous clearing away of the storm which made that nocturnal stroke possible, the accident of the rain-soaked hat which had necessitated a change to headgear that offered no protection from that blow—all these had contributed miraculously to the result; but had it not been for Storm's instant conception of the masterly scheme, his nerve and cleverness in carrying it out, his foresight in arranging for every possible contingency, the money would within a few short hours have been forever beyond his reach! Such chances come to but few men and then only once in a life-time; yet what man but he would have had the genius to grasp it!

Remorse? He choked back a laugh that rose in his throat at the very thought. What did it matter that a clod like Horton had dropped out of existence? Yet somehow Storm could not quite dispel the memory of that shrunken, inert figure slumped helplessly against the wall; he could not quite close his ears to that good-natured voice prattling of the trust reposed in him, of the love of the girl who was "aces high".

Bah! Was he getting squeamish now? One could only rise on the shoulders of another, and it had been the way of the world through countless ages that the strong, the ruthless, the resourceful should triumph! There had been something doglike about Horton's unaffected pleasure at their meeting, his unquestioning acceptance of the hospitality offered, the gusto with which he relished the unaccustomed luxuries, his openhearted affection and confidence...

Storm thumped his pillow viciously. Dogs had been kicked from the path before and would be again! There, within reach of his hand behind the panel lay the price of all that he asked of the future! A little more of George Holworthy's puttering solicitude, of Nicholas Langhorne's sleek patronage and domineering authority, a week or two still perhaps of the mask of mourning, the treadmill of the office, the dodging of hypocritical, unctuous sympathy over Leila's loss; and then freedom! Freedom at last and the wide world in which to forget it all!

XVII

MISSING

When Homachi, usually as punctual as a time-clock, arrived twenty minutes late in the morning he found his employer already risen and attired for the day. His elaborate protestations of apology were summarily cut short.

"That's all right, Homachi, only get me some coffee. I'm in a devil of a hurry this morning." Storm checked himself. "Er— I cooked a bite for myself last night and rather messed up things, but I fancy you can find enough left for breakfast."

Homachi's slant eyes widened.

"Any time you want me I stay, sir," he declared reproachfully. "I please cook dinner. Unhappy cars no run this morning, sir. I hurry coffee—"

He slipped away to the kitchen with his noiseless, catlike tread, and Storm glanced uneasily toward the corner where the bag lay. Could Homachi have seen it from where he stood in the doorway?

He gulped his coffee hastily when it was prepared, keeping the valet busy with trivial services lest he enter the bedroom. The man held his coat for him, presented his hat and stick and then stood waiting to usher him out. Confound the fellow's obsequiousness! Was he waiting purposely to spy upon him?

Inwardly fuming, Storm turned with an assumed start toward the desk in the living-room.

"Forgot those papers!" he muttered for the other's benefit, adding carelessly: "Go ahead and clear up the breakfast things, Homachi. By the way, I shall not be home until late. You may go this afternoon at the usual hour."

Homachi bowed and departed while Storm made a pretense of rummaging through the papers on the desk. How rocky his nerves were! He must pull himself together, he must be prepared to face the risk of the next hour.—That fellow was dawdling unconscionably! Would he ever clear out?

At last Storm heard the sound of running water in the kitchen and the subdued clatter of dishes. He tiptoed into the bedroom, seized the bag, and holding it under his coat made for the door.

Luck was with him! The telephone operator sat at the switchboard with his back squarely turned, and the elevator had ascended. The way was clear!

Closing the door behind him Storm walked briskly down the hall and out into the sunshine, swinging the bag casually in plain view. It seemed to him to be increasing in dimension and weight at every step, to be growing to colossal size, dragging his arm from its socket! He had purposly chosen an early rush hour when clerks and shop people would be hurrying to their work, but he felt that the eyes of every passer-by were fastened upon him, boring into the burden that he carried.

Suppose Horton had been followed on the previous night after all by some emissary of the company whose funds were in his charge? In spite of the heat of the morning, the thought brought a cold sweat out upon Storm's brow. Horton had boasted volubly of the trust reposed in him; but what if, unknown to him, the company had placed a guard or checker upon him? Surely it would not be unusual when a man was carrying sums of such magnitude in cash? Suppose the watcher had lost sight of him at the terminal the night before; was Storm running too great a risk by returning to the same station? If the fellow were hanging about and should recognize the bag—!

A thousand wild apprehensions flashed through his brain, but he fought them back resolutely. He must get rid of the bag at once, and boldness was his best course. Every moment that he retained it in his possession increased his danger, and he could not trail over the town with it in broad day. Even now the body might have been discovered and identified and messages might be humming back and forth from Pennsylvania to New York raising the alarm for the bag and its precious contents. He could not hesitate; he must go on!

The subway express train was crowded to the doors with a heterogeneous mass of the city's toilers, and Storm wedged himself on the platform of one of the rearward cars among a group of laborers and clerks, hoping fervently that he might escape recognition before he reached his destination. Remembering the loaded pistol, he guarded the bag as well as he was able from the jostling throng, his heart in his mouth at every lurch of the speeding train. He was glad that he had not thought to remove the cartridges, for he might have left fingerprints in handling the weapon; but his nervousness increased as he neared his station. Dared he trust a porter? Suppose the bag were dropped—

"Grand Central!" called the guard, and Storm braced himself. He must go through with it now; the moment had come.

He made his way out into the vast terminal and mingled with a crowd of commuters pouring through one of the gates from an arriving train. His hat, with its decorous mourning band, was pulled low over his eyes, and he averted his face, fearing every minute to feel a hand upon his shoulder and hear his name uttered by some acquaintance; but he passed on unmolested until he found himself confronted by a redcapped porter.

"Carry yo' bag, suh? Taxi, suh?"

Storm eyed the dusky, stolid countenance keenly for a moment, and then made his decision.

"No, I want the bag checked. Take it to the parcel room, will you?"

"It'll be a dime, suh," the porter announced, taking over the burden nonchalantly.

Storm produced the dime and a quarter more.

"Get me the check as quick as you can. I'm in a hurry."

The porter scurried off, intent on finishing the job and obtaining a new client, and Storm followed as well as he was able through the crowd, keeping his eyes upon the bobbing red cap ahead. He saw the porter worm his way through a queue of people waiting before a long counter, saw the bag slammed down upon it to be grasped by a hand from the other side and disappear. A cry of relief surged up from his heart, and the impulse to turn and flee before the porter could return with the check almost overmastered him, but he fought it down. No question must be raised now about the bag; the porter must have no cause to recall his appearance later.

"Here yo' is, suh. Want a taxi?"

Storm pocketed the check, shook his head and turning hurried from the station in the throng which surged out upon the sidewalk once more. It was done! No link remained to connect him with the dead paymaster except the money securely locked away in his safe, and that bit of numbered cardboard in his pocket. His apprehensions of the early morning fell from him, and he felt as though he were treading on air. Now he had only to wait until the news came out and the nine-days wonder over the murder and the missing money had subsided, and then he could start upon his journey.

On arrival at the Mammoth Trust Building he went at once to a washroom downstairs and locked himself in. Then, secure from observation, he took the parcel check from his pocket. It bore the number "39", and as he tore it in strips he wondered whether in the near future those numerals would stare out at him in scare-head type from the newspapers. Twisting the strips of thin cardboard together, he touched a match to them and watched them blaze down to a pinch of smoldering ashes in the hand-basin. He washed these away carefully, leaving no slightest smudge behind and then hurried out and up to his office. More ashes! Ashes now of the last menacing bit of evidence against himself!

A tiresome conference awaited him, and more than once during its course Storm had to take a fresh grip on himself to keep from allowing the secret elation within him to show upon his face. What would they think, what would they do—these smug-faced, pompous, eminently conventional members of society who surrounded the table—if they knew what he had done? Two murders in the space of a few short weeks, two lives wiped out in the very heart of civilization, and not a question raised against him, not a breath of suspicion! By God, he was immune, invincible! He could commit any crime on the calendar and get away with it! There wasn't a living soul clever enough to hunt him down! He was the greatest murderer of the age, the cleverest man in the world!

The madness of exultation had passed when the noon hour came, but his spirits were still dangerously high. The sedate luncheon club did not appeal to his mood and he turned into Peppini's where he had lunched with Millard only a few days before.

A voice hailed him from the corner table, and Millard himself rose with extended hand.

"Hello, old chap! I say, if you're alone won't you join me?"

To his surprise Storm found himself responding almost jovially.

"If you'll lunch with me; I see you are just starting. How is everything out at Greenlea?"

"Fine! We've got a new pro. out at the club and he's running things in fine shape; but there isn't much that he can teach us old boys, eh?" Millard lowered his voice. "I say, you have seen the papers?"

Storm started. Could it be that already—? Then he checked himself half angrily. What did Millard know of Horton?

"Papers?" he repeated vaguely.

"Yesterday. The loss of the *Alsace*. You remember I told you that Du Chainat, as he called himself, was on board."

"Oh, that!" Storm laughed loudly, so loudly that Millard stared at him in surprise. "Odd thing, wasn't it? Fancy how the people he swindled must have felt when they read that he had escaped their clutches!"

Millard looked shocked.

"Terrible thing, I call it," he said slowly. "It makes a chap believe that there is such a thing as retributive justice, after all."

"Bosh!" Storm waved his hand in contempt. "Where is the justice in the loss of six or seven hundred lives just to drown one rat of a swindler and sink all his loot with him? It was chance, that's all. I tell you, Millard, if a chap is clever enough he can get away with anything these days."

"There isn't any such clever animal!" Millard shook his head. "I tell you, after what I learned at Headquarters when I went to explain about my acquaintance with Du Chainat, I wouldn't like to pull anything in this town and hope to get away with it. We who live a normal, well-ordered, conventional existence haven't the least conception of their organization down there; it is perfect!"

Storm shrugged skeptically.

"If Du Chainat had been careful enough of the details of his getaway, I'll lay you a wager that they would never have discovered he was on board the *Alsace*. No organ- izatin can be flawless; it is the innividual, one-man system that is perfect, if that man has the mentality and courage and patience. Given such a man, I'd pit him against the whole Department any day."

"You wouldn't if you knew the inner workings of that department, their tremendous ramifications—" Millard broke off and added eagerly: "I say, would you care to run over to Headquarters with me sometime? I'll introduce you to a chap there who will show you all over the shop, and you'll be dumbfounded, as I was, at the thoroughness of their methods of investigation. It's an eye-opener, Storm! Of course, if you're not interested—"

"But I am," Storm said slowly. Millard's suggestion was at once a challenge and temptation. The authorities, all unknowing, had become his natural enemies now. To enter their stronghold voluntarily, place himself in their hands and have them exploit for his benefit the very weapons which would be turned against him if they but dreamed of what he had done! No criminal of the century, of the ages, would have dared such a move! It would be a test, a secret test of his own strength, but it would be a triumph! "I am tremendously interested, Millard. In fact, I'd like nothing better. When can you arrange it?" Storm decided to make a bold test of himself.

"Tomorrow, if you can spare an hour. Excuse me, and I'll 'phone my friend there and find out the best time to take you through." The other rose. "Funny business for two respectable, suburban golf enthusiasts like us to be poking our noses into the methods of crime detection, isn't it? It is fascinating, though, as you'll admit."

While he was gone Storm sat back in his chair, a little smile playing about his mouth. By tomorrow, Horton's body might have been found; by tomorrow, at any rate, the alarm would have been sent broadcast for him and the money which had been in his charge. To hear the affair discussed perhaps in his presence by these so-called experts; to watch the machinery in motion which was designed to reveal and crush him and to know that not in a thousand years would it attain its object, to face them all and laugh in his soul!

What a tremendous situation! He would have to guard himself carefully, more carefully than he had that morning; he had noted Millard's look of surprise at his laughter when Du Chainat was mentioned; but Millard was an egregious ass, anyway, and there had been no need of restraining his amusement. What did he care about Du Chainat now? Was he not possessed of more than the latter had stolen from him, almost as much, in fact, as he had promised? Had he not gained it in one stroke by his own adroitness and nerve? Gad, but tomorrow would bring the rarest sport in the world!

"At four o'clock!" Millard bustled back to the table. "My friend is a high official there and it means open sesame all over the place. He says there is nothing very big on now since the Du Chainat affair went to the wall; but you never can tell when a sensational case is due, you know, and you'll be interested in the workings of their system. Won't you come out to Greenlea afterward with me for dinner? We can put you up for the night—"

Storm shook his head.

"No thanks, old man. I don't feel quite up to the old surroundings just yet." He did not have to inject the tremor in his tone. In the midst of his exultant thoughts the mention of Greenlea had brought back a thrill of the old horror, a sudden vision, clearer than it had come to him for days, of Leila lying there in the den as he had struck her down. God, would the memory of it never rest? That other blow struck in the dark only a few hours before seemed less real, less vivid, than the image which had been mirrored on his brain for the month past. Was he never to be free from it?—Never, he assured himself savagely, until he had cut absolutely adrift from all such as this blundering fool Millard, who kept dragging the past back and spreading it before him! Ah, well, the time would be short now...

"I understand how you feel, of course, Storm. Forgive me." Millard nodded sympathetically. "Later on, perhaps, you'll run out for a few days?"

"Perhaps." The tremor was gone from his tones, and Storm's face was inscrutable as he took leave of his garrulous companion after arranging a meeting for the following day. His thoughts had swerved back into the old, impatient, maddening channel. How soon could he get away? How long would it be before Horton's death was established and the hue and cry for the lost money susided?

There was no link connecting him, Norman Storm, with his classmate of twenty years before. There was no reason why he, his constitution impaired by grief over the accidental death of his wife, should not resign from his position at the trust company and go in search of forgetfulness and health on a long sea voyage since, as far as the world knew, he had ample means left from his father's estate.

And yet Storm realized all at once that he could not go! He was bound even more irrevocably than by the lack of funds which yesterday had oppressed him to the environs of this latest act of his. In vain he told himself that it was mere morbid curiosity; that he didn't care, it couldn't matter to him how or when the crime was discovered. He knew in advance what the result of the investigation would be and how the furore over the disappearance of the money would die out in sheer lack of evidence upon which to continue the search. Morbid or no, there was a secret spell upon him, a secret fascination which would hold him there until the case had run its course and been relegated to the limbo of forgotten things.

In lesser degree, the same impatience which had filled him during that night-long vigil when he waited for the servant's cry to announce Leila's death now assailed him to learn of the discovery of Horton's body. He bought the early editions of the afternoon papers and scanned them eagerly, but they bore no reference to such an episode. Had the body, in its fall down that steep declivity, been arrested by the branches of some clump of underbrush, to lie concealed perhaps until autumn stripped the foliage away? The thought was unendurable, the prolonged suspense would drive him mad!

The money, too, began to worry him. Was its hiding place really secure? What if Homachi had discovered and made away with it? He tried to concentrate on the routine work of his office, but the effort was futile, and at four o'clock he closed his desk and hurried home to his rooms.

Homachi had departed for the day, and Storm pushed back the panel in the wall and opened the safe with shaking hands. There lay the neat piles of bills and roulades of gold just as he had placed them on the previous night; and the sight of them calmed his jangling nerves like a potent, soothing draught.

As he stood lost in contemplation of them there came a double ring at the bell, and he cursed softly beneath his breath as he closed the safe and pushed the panel back into place. That was George Holworthy's ring, and George was the last person he cared to see in his present mood. Perhaps if he did not reply the other would go away—

But the bell rang again, and resigning himself to the inevitable Storm opened the door.

"Hello, Norman." George's placid face broadened with a smile of assured welcome. "I stopped in at the trust company for you but they said you had left early and I was afraid you were ill. You do look rather seedy."

"Oh, I'm all right," Storm answered shortly. "Didn't sleep very well last night, that's all. Come on in."

"Suppose you come out?" suggested the other. "I've borrowed Abbott's car and we can run up the road to some quiet little joint for a bite of dinner; the air will do you good."

A sense of relief pervaded Storm. He had dreaded the thought of seeing George seated where Horton had sat last night, smoking the same cigars and piling up the ashes on the same tray. He assented readily enough to the plan, and soon they were seated in the little car with George at the wheel heading up the Drive.

"Where shall it be?" the latter asked. "The manse or Bryan's or out on the Post Road?"

Storm did not reply. They were chugging over the viaduct and around the turn where he and Horton had walked the night before. They were nearing the top of the incline where the wall sheered down—was that a crowd collecting there on the path? He strained his eyes ahead and unconsciously a muttered exclamation arose in his throat. The next moment they were upon a little group, and he saw it was comosed of a gossipping phalanx of nurse-maids with baby carriages, lingering in the last, slanting rays of the westering sun.

He sank back with a sigh, and the little car plodded on.

"What's the matter with you?" George demanded in good-natured sarcasm. "Getting deaf, or something? I asked you where you wanted to go."

"Eh?—Oh, anywhere," Storm responded absently. "As long as it isn't one of those jazz places. Don't go too far; I don't feel like a long walk home, and you are bound to strip the gears or do some fool thing."

"I like that!" the other retorted. "I only did that once to your car and then Leila—"

He paused, biting his lip, and Storm clenched his hands. He could have turned and struck the man beside him!—Leila! Greenlea! Damn them all, would they never allow him to forget, even for a moment? Wasn't there enough on his mind— with that body lying somewhere back there undiscovered and the thought of the alarm which must be even now manifesting itself out at the Mid-Eastern plant in the Alleghanies—without recalling that first hideous affair?

"I—I've learned to drive all right now," George amended hastily. "Wait till we get up to the road where I can let her out and you'll see!"

The drive thereafter was a silent one. George, dismayed by his blundering touch upon his friend's supposed grief, felt contrite and self-conscious, and Storm was buried in his own thoughts. What would George say when he read in the papers of Horton's disappearance? The two men had not been over congenial at college, for George had disapproved of the other's wild pranks, but there had been a certain camaraderie between them. Storm felt an almost irresistible impulse to speak Horton's name, to hear George talk of him. It was madness, he knew; the fellow had not been mentioned between them for years, and if he were to do so now the coincidence, in the face of the news which must soon come, would strike even George's dull perceptions. Yet as they drew up at a cosy little inn and settled themselves before a table on the vine-screened veranda, the desire persisted, dominating all other thoughts.

Wholly innocent of subtleties as he was, it seemed as though George himself had some divination of his companion's mental trend, for as he glanced about him he remarked:

"This is like old times, isn't it? Away back, I mean. Doesn't this put you in mind of that little place outside Elmhaven where we used to drive for those wonderful shore dinners in our college days?"

Storm started almost guiltily, but George chattered on:

"What was the name of it?—Oh, Bailey's! You remember it, don't you, Norman?"

"Of course," Storm responded cautiously. "We had some great old times there, didn't we?"

"Rather." A reminiscent glow came in to George's faded blue eyes. "Pretty good crowd, too. I wonder what has become of them all?"

Storm's hand trembled as he started to raise his glass to his lips, and he set it down hastily. Horton had uttered those same words only the night before! With an effort he collected himself and steadied his voice.

"Let's see," he began deliberately. "There were Swain and McKnight and Van Tries and you and I—"

He paused and George nodded.

"Swain and McKnight are gone, but you're forgetting Caldwell and Horton. I haven't heard of either of them in years, have you?"

Storm shook his head, unable to frame a word. In a quick revulsion of feeling, he wished fervently that he might change the subject, but his dry lips refused their office.

"Jack Horton was a wild fellow, but there was no real harm in him," George pursued. "Just the irresponsibility of youth, I guess. He's probably settled down somewhere now and making good."

Storm gritted his teeth. 'Making good'! He could have laughed aloud at the irony of it. God! if he could only silence George before his self-control broke down!

"You can't tell what a man will be in twenty years' time." Was that his own voice speaking so coolly, so casually? "Our old crowd has scattered all over the face of the globe.—Let's order; I'm starved."

The talk drifted off to other topics, to his unutterable relief, but contrary to his assertion Storm scarcely touched the food which was placed before him. He hoped that George would take a different route home, but shrank from suggesting it and instead lapsed into a morose silence. As they passed again that ominous spot upon which his thoughts centered, he strove to pierce the darkness, but the path was deserted and no sound came to his ears but the humming of the motor.

Sleep did not come to him until nearly dawn and he was awakened from a troubled dream by the sharp, insistent ring of the telephone.

Springing up to reply, he heard George's excited tones over the wire, and the words themselves drove all the haze of nightmare from his mind.

"Say, have you seen the papers yet? I didn't mean to wake you up, but this is the damnedest thing! One of the very fellows we were talking about last night—Jack Horton—is spread all over the front page. He has been employed of late years as paymaster for the Mid-Eastern Coal Corporation, and he is missing with a hundred thousand dollars!"

XVIII

THE GIRL IN THE WATCH CASE

Storm received the news with outward composure, feigning a natural irritation at being aroused from sleep to mask the chaos of his thoughts, and cut George off as soon as he was able to stem the tide of his volubility. Then, throwing a bathrobe about his shoulders, he stumbled to the hall door and opened it. His own morning paper lay on the mat, and even before he picked it up the staring headlines met his eye.

"$112,000 Missing. Trusted Employee Of Mid-Eastern Disappears With Huge Sum In Cash".

He shut the door and sinking into the nearest chair read on absorbedly:

"John M. Horton, pay clerk for the Mid-Eastern Consolidated Coal Corporation, disappeared on the sixth inst. with a black leather handbag in his possession containing the total sum of $112,552.84 which he had just drawn from the Mid-Eastern Trust Company's Poughkeepsie branch. He was last seen boarding a train in the latter city at four- forty P. M. for New York en route to Altoona, Pa., and the alarm was not sent out until late yesterday afternoon. Representatives of the Mid-Eastern C.C.C. who have been interviewed loyally declare their faith in the missing man and assert that he must have met with foul play. When last seen 'Jack' Horton, as he is known, wore a dark green felt hat, black overcoat, blue serge suit and low tan shoes. He is about forty years of age—"

Storm's eyes traveled on to the last line of the personal description and the few meager details added, and the paper dropped from his listless fingers. This was a contingency which he had not for seen. He had taken it for granted that the body would be discovered and identified before the Mid-Eastern people would have time to take alarm and send out tracers after the missing man.

To his mind in its warped state came no reminder of his own treachery, no thought of the hospitality betrayed, the blow struck in the dark from behind. He felt no animosity toward Horton; he had killed him because the latter stood between him and the money he coveted. It had been a necessary, even a brilliant stroke, and he felt no remorse for the dead.

But suppose Horton's body were not found? An aspersion of theft might logically follow in the course of time, but it could not harm him now, and that solution would end any local search. It might be as well, after all...

As he dressed a vague desire came over him to revisit the scene of that sudden, crafty blow. It could do no harm to stroll up along that path and just glance over the wall. No suspicion could be attached to him for that if the body were found later, and he longed to see for himself if no trace of it could be discerned from above.

Then he thrust that trend of thought from him in a wave of horror. Great heavens, was he going mad? Murderers had been known to haunt the scenes of their crimes; that was the way in which they were frequently caught! He must avoid that spot as he would the plague! Yet the vague, terrifying sensation of being drawn toward it persisted, and in sheer desperation he fled downtown earlier than was his wont and plunged feverishly into the business of the day. It had a steadying effect upon his nerves, and when noon came he had quite recovered command of himself.

George telephoned again, asking him to lunch, but he pleaded another engagement. If he had to listen to old George's theories and speculations it would madden him, and he wanted to have himself well in hand for his visit to Police Headquarters with Millard.

As the hour drew near his keen anticipation mounted. Millard had said that there was nothing very big on, but that was yesterday; the disappearance of a man with a hundred thousand dollars in his possession would be a sensation even in the manifold events of so huge a city, and he was eager to hear what view had been taken of the case by the authorities. As on the previous afternoon, he purchased the earliest editions of the evening papers; but although they contained lengthy accounts of the Mid-Eastern affair, no mention was made of the discovery of a dead man near the Drive.

Millard was bubbling with enthusiasm when they met.

"Come along!" he said gaily. "Shouldn't be surprised if we heard something about this Horton affair. You read of it, of course?"

Storm pondered. It was far from his intention to draw any possible limelight on himself, yet if his companion ran into George the latter would be sure to mention that Horton was an old friend of them both, and Millard might think it strange that he had made no reference to it.

"Yes." He nodded carelessly. "Rather a shock, too. There was a chap in our freshman class at college of that name. Holworthy thinks it may be the same fellow, but I doubt it. We lost track of him years ago, anyway."

"They'll get him," Millard asserted with conviction. "He won't get far, even with that bank-roll. I tell you, I wouldn't steal a pewter golf cup—and that's the nearest thing to temptation of that sort that I can imagine—with that organization down here after me!"

At Headquarters, while Millard searched for the official who was to be their guide, Storm gazed reflectively at the ornate brass plate let into the wall on which were inscribed the names of the former Chiefs and Commissioners. Each had held his own pet theories of the detection of crime, each had had his widely published successes, his obscure failures, and each of them in turn had passed on and out of the office. He could have faced them all just as he was about to face their successor, and he could have beaten them at their own game! Surely no other man in the world with such a secret as he carried would have had the supreme audacity to enter this building on so innocent an errand and converse calmly with the very men who would be hot upon his trail if they knew! It was immense!

Millard returned with a secretary of the Commissioner, and they were conducted through the small octagonal anteroom to the inner sanctum of the great man himself. The latter greeted them with brisk geniality, and during the brief talk which followed the introduction, Storm studied him blandly. He was a comparatively young man, not much older than Storm himself, with a pleasant, mildly intelligent face and frank, terse manner. He might have been a mere broker or bank official, courteous but pressed for time, Storm reflected contemptuously; a business man in a political job! What had he to fear from an organization with such a man at its head?

His eyes wandered to the tall glass cases which lined one wall. The shelves were filled with a miscellaneous collection of small objects; pistols and revolvers of every caliber and pattern, ugly looking bludgeons and sawed-off lengths of lead pipe swathed in frayed, stained cloth and various small phials half-filled with tablets and liquids of ominous color. As Storm stared idly at the curious collection, his eye was caught by a strangely incongruous object on one of the lower shelves. It was a pale blue satin slipper, absurdly small, inconsequentially gay and flippant among its grim neighbors, lying on its side with the narrow sole and heel turned toward him as though its wearer had kicked it carelessly aside. Then he saw that imbedded in the heel was an odd sliver of steel like a coarse needle on a strong, slender, curved wire, and he started involuntarily.

The Chatsworth case! Less than a year before, the city had resounded with the sensational death without apparent cause of the beautiful Mrs Chatsworth. Then that infinitesimal wound had been discovered upon her heel, the subtle poison traced and the secret spring in the slipper revealed. Storm remembered vaguely that the Commissioner himself was said to have taken a hand in the work of the Homicide Bureau, and that a timely suggestion of his had much to do with the solution of the affair.

The insolently gay little slipper seemed all at once more sinister than the grimmest of the weapons which flanked it, and Storm's eyes were still fastened upon it when he became aware that the Commissioner was adressing him.

"It's the wickedest of the lot, Mr Storm, isn't it? It looks strangely out of place there at the first glance—just a bit of woman's finery among those crime relics; and yet it is the most deadly weapon of them all."

Storm turned to the other in surprise. Could he have uttered his thoughts aloud?

"I—er, I didn't—" he began, but the Commissioner smiled.

"It was a simple matter to follow your trend of thought, Mr Storm. You were surprised at seeing such a thing there, naturally; then you noticed the needle on the spring and recalled the case which put the dainty, innocent little slipper in a different light to you. It was an extraordinary case, too much so for the ingenious gentleman who conceived it to have hoped for success. Its bizarre, unusual features rendered it all the more simple to solve. The casual, unpremeditated cases are the ones which give us the most trouble because as a rule they leave fewer clues. The man who plans a crime most carefully is bound to over-reach himself in some particular, but the one who picks up a weapon lying innocently or accidentally to his hand, strikes with it and lays it down again, is the man who gives us the longest run."

Storm could feel the blood ebbing from his face. Could this genial, smiling person be reading his mind, probing to the depths of the secret he guarded; or was he merely voicing his own favorite theory? At any rate, Storm realized that his previously formed opinion of the Commissioner was undergoing a swift reversal.

He murmured a polite phrase or two of interest, and the Commissioner said:

"I wish I had time to tell you the history of even a few of the things there, for each is a relic of some case celebrated in the annals of the Department. However, I suppose you gentlemen would like to have a look at the Homicide Bureau and the Bureau of Missing Persons; they are usually the most interesting departments to outsiders. My secretary will introduce you."

He took leave of them with hearty cordiality, and once outside the anteroom Storm smiled quietly to himself. The Commissioner's unique collection lacked two specimens which might have graced it: a certain golf club known as a driver, and a cane with a wickedly heavy head. But the Commissioner, astute as he was, would never miss them! His theory was all very well in its way, Storm conceded, but it did not go quite far enough. What of the man who did not over-reach himself; the man who perfected his coup in advance and left no clues whatever behind? All unconsciously the Commissioner had been lauding Storm's own achievements, and his sense of elation heightened.

"Nothing doing in the Homicide Bureau this afternoon that would interest you, I am afraid," the secretary announced.

"We'll try the Bureau of Missing Persons; there is usually something going on there."

He led them down the wide stairs and along the echoing corridor to a door at the left, and Storm saw a large room divided by a rail and subdivided again at the end by partitions forming two smaller offices. An older man with a delicate, high-bred, sensitive face came forward, and as he was presented to the Captain, Storm watched the latter's quick changes of expression with something of the contempt with which he had at first discounted the Commissioner's frank, genial manner. This man, he reflected, might have been a scholar or priest; a father confessor, but surely not an analyst of human nature; a pedant, not a person of ' quick decision and unerring action. Pah! The Captain would be a mere tool in his hands; he could deceive him, trick him, beat him at his own game as easily as he had tricked the Greenlea officials and the simple-minded, guileless community out there.

He had already beaten him! Storm smiled again at the thought. The Captain must be combing the country now for a man whose body had lain exposed more than thirty- six hours within the limits of the city, and Storm alone knew where! One word from him would set that quiet office in a furore! And this was the man who had located the supposed Du Chainat on board the *Alsace!* Du Chainat must have been more of a bungler than Storm had believed!

While the secretary was explaining the object of their visit, Millard drew Storm through the opened door of one of the inner offices and pointed out the swinging files of photographs which stood out from the wall.

"Unidentified dead!" he remarked pompously with the assurance of a privileged visitor. "Morgue cases and Potter's Field, you know, mostly derelicts. Dreadful looking lot, aren't they?"

Storm shuddered in spite of himself. The relaxed faces leering maudlinly or with jaw wide in a seeming snarl stared fixedly at him with a look of supreme sophistication, and his own eyes dropped before them. To his super-sensitized imagination they seemed to be crying mutely in a silent chorus: "We know!" Jack Horton knew, also!

"Horrible!" Storm ejaculated in answer to his companion's comment. "Millard I believe you are an inherent ghoul! You've been coming here gloating over these wretched things and regaling the country club with a nice lot of cheery anecdotes, haven't you? I'll wager half the members have taken to drink!"

Millard laughed and turned as the Captain entered.

"Not as bad as all that!" he disclaimed, adding to the official; "I suppose you're all working over time on that Horton case that the papers were full of this morning; chap who disappeared with the payroll of the Mid-Eastern coal people. My friend here knows him."

"You do?" The voice which had greeted them so gently took on in the instant a keen, knife-like edge, and the paternal, rather dreamy eyes narrowed in swift focus like the lens of a camera. Storm felt himself flush beneath the gaze, and he could have annihilated the garrulous Millard.

"To be perfectly frank, sir, I don't know." His tone was disarmingly candid. "When Mr Millard spoke of the case I mentioned the fact that there was a chap in my class at Elmhaven of that name. He only stayed for one term and I shouldn't know him now if I met him, I'm afraid. That was twenty years ago."

He smiled deprecatingly, but the steady glance of the Captain did not waver. "You haven't seen him since?"

"No." Then, realizing the inevitable question to follow, he volunteered: "The last I heard of our Jack Horton, and then most indirectly, was that he held some sort of minor position in a bank in Chicago. I'm inclined to doubt that this is the same fellow."

The Captain's face softened, and he said, with a swift return of his old genial manner:

"Twenty years can change a man, Mr Storm. It is the same Jack Horton, I am afraid. We have his record and he attended college at Elmhaven at the time you mention. But it is not certain that he absconded, you know; if it were, the case would not be up to this department. He is merely officially 'missing' as yet."

"With a hundred thousand in cash!" Millard smirked. "Not much danger of his having suffered an attack of aphasia, is there, Captain? By Jove, if I had that much money about me, I might forget my own name myself!"

The typewriters clicking behind the rail in the outer office ceased all at once as the door leading to the corridor opened slowly, and a girl appeared, hesitating on the threshold. She was an undeniably pretty little girl despite the fact that her eyes were reddened and swollen, but her light summer frock was oddly out of place in that grim setting. She peered slowly about until her eyes caught the Captain's, and rested there.

"Is this," she began in a high, strained voice, "is this the place where they find people who have disappeared?"

"We try to." The Captain's tone had mellowed and a persuasive, paternal note crept into it. "Tell me for whom you are looking."

He seated himself at his desk, motioning her to a chair beside it, and drew a blank form toward him. Millard was staring in goggle-eyed interest, and Storm stared also, but from far different motives. Where had he seen that pretty, piquant, slightly sullen face before?

As for the girl, she stood undecidedly, twisting the chain of her platinum mesh bag between her hands.

At length she burst forth half-confidentially, half-shyly:

"For—for Mr Horton! Oh, you must know who I mean! Mr John Horton, the paymaster of the Mid-Eastern Consolidated Coal Corporation. The papers say this morning that he has disappeared, but it cannot be true! I was told that if I came here—"

The girl in Horton's watch case! Storm drew a sharp, quick breath and did not need Millard's nudge to rivet his attention. The girl! He had not calculated upon her taking a possible hand in the game.

At a sign from Captain Nairn the stenographers had filed into the second of the inner offices, and to all appearance he and his client were alone.

"Who are you, my dear?" His fatherly tones showed no indication of change or added interest.

The girl hesitated again.

"I'm just a—a friend, but I felt that I had to come to you. If Jack has really disappeared, you know what terrible things will be said about him soon, since he had all that' money in his possession. If he hasn't returned to the colliery it is because something frightful must have happened to him. He must have been set upon by thieves; killed, or hurt and perhaps held prisoner somewhere! Oh, if you don't find him—!"

"Your name, please?" A note of sternness crept into the Captain's tones.

"I am Eugenia Saulsbury." A little quick color came and went in the girl's cheeks, but she held her head proudly erect.

"You reside here in New York?"

"No. I am visiting an old friend of my mother, Mrs Van Alen on Madison Avenue, but I live with my father near Bethlehem in Pennsylvania. He will be annoyed, I am afraid, that I have courted publicity in coming to you like this, but he—he thought a great deal of Jack, and I know he will back up any investigation to find him to the limit of his resources." She paused. "I—I have thought of hiring the best private detectives

I could find—I wired Daddy so—but I felt that I simply had to come to you, too! I do not believe that Jack ever reached the city."

"Why not, Miss Saulsbury?" The stern note quickened to imperative demand.

"Because if he had I am sure he would have made an attempt to communicate with me." She sank into a chair and fumbled in her bag for her handkerchief, her eyes blinded by sudden tears. "He—I—you see, we—we were very good friends! I know that he is honorable to a fault, and something dreadful must have happened if he cannot be found! You are the head of this bureau, are you not?"

"I am Captain Nairn," the official nodded gravely. "Have you any reason for thinking that he met with foul play other than the fact of his disappearance, Miss Saulsbury? Do you know of any enemies?"

"A hundred thousand dollars in cash would invite the enmity of a great many people if they knew it was in your possession, wouldn't it?" she observed, with unconscious cynicism. "Jack was always armed when he had the company's payroll in charge, but I warned him that he was too confident, too sure of his ability to protect it. You see, Captain Nairn, he would never believe any evil of anybody; that was one of the strongest traits in his character. He has had some narrow escapes before, but they were from rough characters down in the mountains. If he took that train at Poughkeepsie, as they say, he must be somewhere between there and here, and if he is not dead, he is badly hurt and unable to communicate with his friends. Please, please lose no time in finding him!"

"If what you think proves to be the case he will undoubtedly be discovered," the Captain began soothingly, but the girl interrupted, wringing her hands.

"Every hour, every minute counts, not only if he is hurt physically, but to save him from mental torture! If he is lying injured and helpless somewhere and thinking that people may consider him dishonest, he will be suffering more from that than from what may have been done to him, and the thought is driving me mad! It would be better, almost, to know the—the worst!"

The telephone shrilled once at the Captain's elbow and he picked up the receiver and listened. His face, which Storm had thought mobile, had become a mere expressionless mask. The girl was dabbing at her eyes, but her tears had ceased and her small chin came out indomitably.

Captain Nairn uttered the one word "Right!" in reply to the communication which had come to him, then hung up the receiver and turned once more to his visitor.

"Miss Saulsbury, no effort will be spared to find your friend, you may be sure of that."

"But you—you believe he hasn't taken that money, don't you? You'll find out if he has been hurt or imprisoned somewhere?" She had taken his assurance as a dismissal and, rising, held out her hand in appeal.

The Captain shook it gravely.

"We will do our best to find him, Miss Saulsbury, dead or alive."

When she had withdrawn and the clicking of her small shoes diminished in the corridor outside, Millard stepped forward.

"That was mighty interesting, Captain! Don't mind our listening! So that little lady was in love with Horton, eh? Saulsbury—from Bethlehem! She must be the daughter of 'Big Jim' Saulsbury, of International Steel! Do you think she was trying to—er, stall?"

"No." The Captain shook his head. "Her motive was honest and straightforward enough, I think. She made only one misstatement, or attempt at evasion."

"What was that?"

Storm drew closer to catch the reply.

"That she intended to put the case in the hands of private detectives; she has already done so.—At eleven o'clock this morning, to be exact. You see, gentlemen, her house has been watched since midnight and she has been under surveillance every moment. We could take no chances, and in cases of this sort we look first for the woman!"

XIX

FOUND

When, a few minutes later, they came down the steps of the building, Millard was still descanting on the infallible methods of the bureau they had just quitted; but Storm was silent, although in his heart he gave grudging assent to the eulogy. They were thorough, for a fact; he had not anticipated such extensive work on the part of the police in so short a time. The alarm sent out at sundown from Pennsylvania for the missing man, and by midnight his record known and the house in which his sweetheart lived placed under surveillance!

To Millard and himself as mere curious visitors no information had been dropped, and he had an uneasy idea that the mental reservation indicated by Captain Nairn's attitude concealed a far deeper knowledge of the case than had been given out to the press. In the latter's manner, especially when they shook hands at the moment of departure, he felt that, had the Captain chosen to speak, he might have learned something of vital importance to himself. Had the bag been already discovered at the station, and was the porter's memory for faces more keen than he had judged? Were detectives even now scouring the city for a man of his personal description?

"I'll wager that telephone message had something to do with the Horton affair," Millard remarked suddenly. "Maybe he was caught then!"

Storm roused himself from his meditations with a start.

"Why do you think that?"

"Well, you see, I've watched the Captain before," replied Millard. "You saw how quickly his expression could change when he wanted it to. By Jove, that chap should have been an actor! He put me over the jumps for a solid hour, I don't mind telling you, when I went in to explain about my acquaintance with Du Chainat, and although he did it in a perfectly courteous, kid-glove manner I felt as limp as a rag when I came out. His expression ran the gamut from bland incredulity to direct accusation, and if I had had anything to confess he would have broken me down absolutely. Those fellows at Headquarters could force a confession from the cleverest crook in Christendom!"

"And what has this to do with the telephone message today?" Storm inquired in bored disgust at his companion's garrulousness.

"Everything, my boy!" Millard retorted. "While he was talking to Big Jim's daughter just now and drawing her out, his face was alive with expression, but after he had heard the first few words which came to him over the 'phone he looked absolutely blank and wooden. He got some information right then that he did not mean to convey, or I am very much mistaken. I say, there was something rather fine, wasn't there, about that girl?"

"She was rather pretty," Storm admitted, with a shrug.

"I don't mean that!" exclaimed the other impatiently. "She was gotten up like a circus queen! I mean her attitude, her loyalty toward your friend Horton. Jolly white of her, I thought it!"

"Oh, when a woman is in love!" Storm sneered and added in cold displeasure, "Don't call Horton my friend, please. I doubt still that this fellow is the one I knew at college."

"But the Captain told you he was at Elmhaven—"

"After I had myself informed him that there was a chap of that name there; don't forget that, Millard. A mere play to the gallery." Storm laughed. "Captain Nairn is highly successful, I have no doubt, in cases of lost children and runaway girls, but I must confess I see no basis for your remarkable faith in the powers of the Department. They've failed in other cases just as they will in this."

"You wait and see!" Millard's tone was distinctly ruffled. "I've known the Commissioner's secretary for years and I'm going to get him to let me in on this case from the inside and watch how they work it. I'll bet you fifty dollars they get that man Horton!"

"And the hundred thousand?" Storm was still laughing, but there was a reckless glint in his eyes.

"*And* the hundred thousand!" Millard repeated with emphasis.

"Any time limit?"

"Oh, well, if the fellow succeeds in getting out of the country—" Millard hedged.

"Shall we say six months?—Done! Come up and dine with me at my rooms on Tuesday night, and we'll let George Holworthy hold the stakes." Storm held out his hand in a sudden volatile accession of cordiality. "Goodbye, and thanks for a most interesting afternoon, old man, really!"

After he had left Millard, however, a quick revulsion of mood came and he cursed the impulse which had led him to extend the invitation. The voluble little man bored him horribly, but he had felt an impish desire to goad him on in his laudation of the Department, and to seal the compact of the wager within a few feet of where the money lay securely hidden had seemed a great joke at the moment. It might be a wise move, at that, to keep in with Millard if the latter managed through his boasted friendship with the Commissioner's secretary to obtain any inside information on the progress of the case. He would be sure to retail it in defense of his argument, and in spite of his sense of security Storm determined to be forewarned of any possible danger.

He dined alone at an old down-town hotel which he frequented when the mood for solitude came upon him. It was a stately place with an air of faded grandeur about it, left far behind in the upward march of the city, but still retaining a remnant of its ancient patronage.

As he sat over his coffee, Storm idly studied the diners scattered about at the nearby tables. They were elderly for the most part with a solid air of conscious rectitude and well-being, and they ate with the deliberation and grave relish due to the reputation of the cuisine. A shining bald pate above a coat of magisterial black at the next table caught Storm's eye by its glistening expanse. The man was sitting back luxuriously reading a paper which he held outstretched to aid some defect of vision, and over one ample shoulder a few letters of the headline jumped out in staring type.

"—ton's Body—"

Storm caught his breath, and for a moment the page wavered and blurred before his eyes. Could it mean Horton's body? Had it been discovered? He craned his neck, leaning as far forward and to one side as he dared; but by a perverse fate the older man moved also, his shoulder effectually concealing the rest of the message.

Storm cursed him softly beneath his breath, still maneuvering desperately to read the lines so tantalizingly withheld from him. Confound the old dotard! If he would shift that paper only a bit to one side, hold it a matter of a few inches higher, the whole article could be read, for he sat so near that even the small type would be plainly legible to Storm's sharp eyes.

While he writhed impotently the unconscious reader turned the page, and in the flirt of the paper Storm caught a fleeting glimpse of the last word on the headline. It looked like "Found," but he dared not trust the evidence of that swift glance. He felt an almost uncontrollable impulse to stride across to the other man and tear the paper from his hands; but the reader must have lost the thread of the article in which he was engrossed, for even as Storm struggled with his maddened impatience he turned back, raising the paper so that the whole upper part was in plain view.

"Horton's Body Found."

His instinct had been right, after all! Storm's heart hammered in his chest, and for a second time his vision blurred, only to clear the next instant; and he read without effort through to the end of the brief news item. It told only what he of all men already knew, what he had wished the world to learn.

The older man folded his paper, yawned, and departed, and Storm called for his check and strolled out of the hotel with a serenly detached air; but although the night was warm he shivered as if a sudden chill had swept over him. That phase of the investigation was over; now the search would begin in earnest for the black bag.

Suddenly he recalled Millard's conviction about the telephone message which Chief Nairn had received in their presence and the added reservation in the latter's manner when he bade them goodbye. Millard must have been right; that message was a report of the finding of the body!

As he journeyed homeward he felt a sense of relief that the suspense was over. Horton was no longer lying out there — but what did Horton matter? He was dead and that was an end of it. How easily his skull had caved in beneath the force of that single blow! How easily the whole thing had been accomplished!

But was the money really safe in his apartment now that the search would narrow down to the bag and its contents? Would it not be wiser if he were to hire a safe-deposit box somewhere under an assumed name—? But even as the thought came he negatived it. Wise or not, he realized that he could not know a moment's rest with the money for which he had risked so much out of his immediate possession. He would wait until the bag was discovered and the news of it had been forgotten and then slip unostentatiously away. This might come at any day; he must be prepared.

Thank heaven he had mentioned his proposed trip to George long before Horton crossed his path once more! Now his suddenly announced decision would call forth no surprise from that devoted friend, and George could be depended upon in the depths of his innocence to explain the situation to any curious acquaintances.

"Poor old Norman!" he would say, shaking his head sadly. "Went all to pieces over the loss of his wife. Health gave out completely, you know; couldn't eat, couldn't sleep, racked with nerves! Sea voyage is the best thing for him, and he'll come back a new man."

Storm laughed at his own conceit, but by morning his resolve had strengthened and definite plans began to form themselves in his mind. When he was safely away—in Japan, perhaps,—he would change some of the banknotes at a foreign branch of one of the banking houses and send back a draft to old Foulkes to take up that mortgage on the Greenlea house with Langhorne; he could get a far better price for the property unencumbered.

Still later he could write to old George and deputize him to sell it. George would be pained, of course, but what did that matter? He could explain that he meant to extend his trip and could never, in any event, bring himself to a return to Greenlea. He could tell George also to dispose of what personal belongings still remained of Leila's among her friends there and to sell the house as it stood.

The morning papers threw no further light on the subject of Horton's murder, yet Storm knew that no stone would be left unturned in the search for the bag, and he felt that its discovery might be imminent. A week or two at most after that took place and the whole affair would vanish from the public mind.

He would be prepared to sail at once, but in cutting absolutely adrift from the old life he meant in no sense to become a pariah. When he was satiated with travel he would settle down in some Continental city and enjoy life untrammeled by memories.

That night he took stock of his own belongings. He had left the details of his removal from Greenlea in George's hands, and the latter had made a free selection. When Storm had weeded them out from Potter's effects he looked at the conglomeration in despair. He meant to travel light, taking only his fresh mourning attire with him, which could be discarded readily enough as soon as he was away from his circle of condoling friends; and his old clothes could be given to Homachi.

But George had added a collection of junk which could not be so easily disposed of without opening even that credulous individual's eyes to the real state of Storm's mind. His glance swept in exasperation over the room; that reading lamp, for instance, his favorite edition of Balzac, the antique clock, the bronze desk set! George's infernal sentiment must have directed his choice, for these had all been gifts from Leila; they couldn't very well be given or thrown away!

The impulse came to Storm to tumble them all into an old trunk and ship them back to Greenlea, and his mood demanded instant action. He might as well get them out of the way now and have done with it! There would be plenty to do in the days ahead, and at least he would have the cursed things out of his sight.

Whistling cheerily he took off his coat, dragged the trunk out from the storeroom and opened it. He had scarcely started upon his task, however, when there came an insistent double ring at the bell.

George, again! Storm sat down deliberately and swore. But it would not do to offend him, and the time would be so short...

He rose and opened the door to disclose George, beaming, his arms filled with awkwardly held paper bags and bundles. As he moved, one of them crashed down upon the mat and a thin line of white liquid meandered from it.

"Ouch! There goes the cream, I am afraid!" George's smile faded, and he gazed ruefully down at the mess. "I thought we might make a rarebit, and I stopped—"

"Well, never mind! Come in. There is more cream in the ice chest." Storm pulled his guest unceremoniously within and closed the door. "Homachi can clean the mat in the morning. Here, I'll take all that stuff to the kitchen."

"Just finished a rubber of bridge over at the Abbott's and as I hadn't seen you in two days—" George explained to the empty air. "Why, what the—!"

His ejaculation reached Storm in the kitchen and the latter returned to find his guest staring in surprise from the opened trunk to the disordered room.

"I'm packing up some stuff to send back to Greenlea," Storm explained briefly. "All those things Leila gave me, you know; I can't stand seeing them around me any longer."

"I'm sorry. I thought they would make it more homelike for you here," George said simply, in honest contrition. "I might have known you wouldn't want them about just yet, to remind you—Here, let me help pack them."

Storm masked a smile. Old George was almost too easy!

"All right, then, if you want to," he acquiesced. "Take off your coat and we'll pitch in. There is a pile of old newspapers on the pantry shelf—"

George trotted obediently off and returned with the papers.

"I say, wasn't that a fierce thing about poor Jack Horton!" he exclaimed. "You saw it in the papers, of course? He was found murdered—"

"I know!" Storm interrupted hastily. "Mind what you are doing with that clock!—Yes, it was very sad, of course, but a chap in his line of work takes chances, and I suppose he took one too many."

"It doesn't seem possible! Poor old Jack!" George's tone trembled with real feeling. "It is odd that we should have been talking about him only two nights ago; I don't think we've even mentioned his name before in years. And at that very time he was lying dead out there on the Drive, and no one knew! It's horrible! Why, we passed twice right within a few feet of the spot!"

"That's so, we did," Storm said slowly.

"Did you see the latest editions of the papers tonight?" George pursued, and then not waiting for the other to reply, he went on: "That young girl who was in love with him—Big Jim Saulsbury's daughter—gave an interview to the reporters in which she said she would never rest until his murderers were discovered and convicted. Big Jim is backing her up, too. He came on here to New York, and although he refuses to talk for publication it is understood that he has hired the best private detectives in the country to supplement the authorities. By Jingo, I hope they get them!"

"Do they think some gang were out after him?" Storm asked.

"They don't seem to think anything!" George waxed indignant. "I tell you, things are in a pretty state in this town when a chap can be decoyed off a train, robbed of a hundred thousand dollars and murdered in cold blood! Where were the police, I should like to know?"

Storm smiled.

"We had a little talk about crime not so long ago, if you remember," he observed. "You didn't quite agree with me when I suggested that a person could commit any sort of crime and get away with it if he used his brains, but this looks like a case in point, eh?"

Suddenly he caught his breath. It had occurred to him that George's glance had fallen idly upon the sheets of newspaper with which they were packing the articles into the trunk, and remembrance came to him. They were using the outer sheets only from the top of the pile on the pantry shelf; the inner sheets of those papers were wrapped about Horton's pistol in the bag! Had George noted anything unusual? His manner certainly did not show it, and he was packing with a preoccupation which boded ill for the safe arrival of the fragile lamp at Greenlea.

To test him, Storm repeated:

"It looks as if the fellow was going to get away with it in this case, at any rate."

"They've only just started," George replied significantly, adding as he eyed the half-filled trunk: "We should have put those books on the bottom, but never mind now. Does this desk set go in, too?"

"Yes." Storm breathed more easily, but his vaunted foresight had received a shock. Why hadn't he destroyed those confounded outer sheets of the newspaper?

The thought brought a swift reminder to him. Why not get rid now of the cap which Horton had worn on that fateful walk? There was room in the trunk...

He dashed to the closet.

"Wait a minute, George. When you packed up my things to move in town you brought along a lot of old clothes that I shan't have any use for in a dog's age. Might as well ship some of them back to Greenlea now and have done with it."

"Sure!" responded George equably. "Bring them along."

Storm returned, his arms filled with a miscellaneous collection of coats and headgear. Among the latter was a certain cap of thin dark blue cloth, and as he saw it disappear into the trunk he heaved a sigh of relief. That, too, was gone! He turned to his companion.

"Oh, did I tell you that I saw Horton's girl yesterday; this Miss Saulsbury?"

"Where?" George demanded, staring.

"At Police Headquarters. A friend of Millard showed us around."

Storm told in detail of the scene at the Bureau of Missing Persons, and George listened with deep interest.

"Mighty loyal of that girl to stand up for poor Jack when the whole world was ready to condemn him as an absconder, wasn't it?" he commented, as Millard had done. "Even I— well, it did look pretty black against him, didn't it? They'll get his murderers, sure!"

"So Millard thinks. He is crazy about the work of the Department since he has been given a glimpse behind the scenes, and he swears they can't fail." Storm laughed. "In fact, we have a little wager on about it, and you are to hold the stakes. He is coming up to dinner next Tuesday night."

"Well, for an old friend of Jack, you've taken a queer stand, it seems to me," George said slowly. "Anybody would think you didn't want to see his murderers punished!"

"Not at all!" Storm retorted coolly: "There is nothing personal in this; it is a purely abstract question. Millard believes in the infallibility of the Department, and I don't. What have they done so far? Horton was last seen alive in Poughkeepsie on Wednesday afternoon; he is murdered in New York some time that night, and his body is not even discovered until Friday afternoon. This is Saturday night, and what progress has been made in the case? Exactly none! They don't know how Horton came to be out there on the Drive, who killed him or where the money is!"

"They've found the bag it was in, anyway."

"What?" Storm stared at him as though he could scarely believe he had heard aright.

"Uh-huh. The last edition of all the papers is playing it up big. The bag with poor old Jack's hat and a pistol and a lot of old newspapers inside was discovered in the parcel-checking room of the Grand Central Station." George paused and added: "Isn't that marvelous police work for you? They must have doped it out that because he disappeared presumably from the terminal the bag would be found somewhere around there, and by Jingo, it was! Think of conceiving the idea of searching the parcel room and then tell me a fellow can get away with anything in this town when such minds as those are on the job after him! Wonderful work, I call it! When they find out who checked that bag there, they've got Jack Horton's murderer!"

XX

MARKED!

They finished packing the trunk, made and devoured the rarebit, and still George lingered. His mind had been jarred from its placid routine by the tragic death of their former classmate, and he dwelt upon the reminiscences which were an added torture to Storm's perturbed mental state.

The bag had been discovered, but did the porter remember checking it? Did he remember the face of the man who had given it into his charge? That was a paramount question. He had not noticed that the papers he brought home with him were not the final edition, and now it was too late to procure one even if he could get rid of George. He felt that he could not wait till morning; he must know I Dare he ask his companion for particulars? Surely it would be only natural for him to show as much casual interest as that in the mystery surrounding an old friend's death!

"What do you think about the case yourself?" he queried at last, abruptly cutting off the flow of reminiscence. "What is your theory as to how Jack came to his death?"

"Well," George helped himself to a cigar. "He may not have been killed on the Drive, you know. His body may have been brought there by automobile and thrown over the wall, and a high-powered car travels fast; the murder may have taken place miles away. I'm going down and have a look at old Jack tomorrow if they will let me—I have a theory about the whole thing that I would like to try out for my own satisfaction."

"And what is that?" Storm inquired with a jarring note of sarcasm in his tones.

"Oh, I don't pretend to be any amateur detective," George returned mildly. "But I knew old Jack! They're all taking it for granted that he wasn't killed in New York because he had no business to be here; at least, he was supposed to have gone right on through. Now, his character may have steadied down and grown more dependable with the years—it must have, since he has been so uniformly trusted in such responsible positions—but you can't change a person's natural propensities, and Jack was always keen for a good time. Understand, I'm not casting any aspersions on him; I don't say he would have taken a chance of trouble with that money in his care, but what if he didn't think he was taking chances? What if he ran into some people he knew and trusted as he would himself, was persuaded to stop over and then taken unawares?"

"But what grounds are there for such a supposition?" The sarcasm had gone from Storm's tones and they were muffled and oddly constrained. "Didn't the papers speak of a struggle? That doesn't look as if Horton were caught off guard by people he might have been chumming with."

"That's why I want to see the body," responded George. "It could have been banged about and the clothes torn by that fall over the wall and down that steep, rocky incline."

"Of course," Storm commented; "but ordinary footpads could have set upon him from behind—"

"Ordinary footpads would not have known the contents of that bag," objected the other. "Now, if he really boarded that train alive in broad daylight, he must have left it willingly, and therefore he must have done so at the terminal in New York, for no amount of persuasion or coercion would have made him get off at an intermediate station with that bag in his possession."

"And since the bag was found at the terminal, you think he was murdered there?" Storm laughed shortly.

"No, but I do think he was murdered somewhere within the city limits; you couldn't get a dead or drugged or resisting man off a train in broad daylight without attracting attention, and as a matter of fact the autopsy shows that Jack wasn't drugged. He may have met some old pal on the train or in the station and decided to wait over for an hour or so in town before continuing on his journey, and it must have been someone he knew well. If he left Poughkeepsie on that four-something train, he must have reached New York in time for dinner, and it has been established that he wasn't killed until around midnight. It seems to me that if the police would look up what friends of his were in New York that night, they might learn something to their advantage."

"You are getting to be quite an analyst, George; I should never have suspected it." Storm yawned openly and tossed away his cigarette. "What about the bag? You said that when they found the man who checked it they would have Horton's murderer. It has been established, then, that a man did check it? They have a description of him, perhaps?"

He waited breathlessly for the answer, but George merely shrugged.

"No. It was checked some time on Thursday; that's all they know. The hat and pistol were in it, wadded out with newspapers, but not another scrap of evidence." George rose. "Guess I'll be getting on downtown. If I can get Abbott's car tomorrow afternoon, do you want to run out somewhere for dinner? You're not looking up to the mark lately, old man; too much brooding and sticking around by yourself. The air will do you good."

Storm assented absently, and after he had shown his visitor out he sprung the light in the bathroom and examined his face in the mirror. It bore a grayish, unhealthy pallor, and there were lines about his mouth which certainly had not been there a month before. His eyes, too: there was a look in them which Storm himself did not care to meet, and for the first time he noted a faint touch of gray in the dark hair at his temples. He shrugged and turned away.

Ah, well, a few days now and he would be on his way to new fields. A few gray hairs: what did they matter? It was this ceaseless strain of being on guard, the constant rankling torture of memory! Let him once start afresh, with the past behind him, and he would soon regain his own old snap and vigor.

Since that memorable Wednesday evening his rooms had become as hateful to him as the house at Greenlea. Horton had only passed a few hours there, yet he had left a vivid impression behind him as disturbing as the effect of Leila's influence in the home. Every time Storm entered the livingroom he seemed to see Horton's figure seated in that heavy armchair, his legs stretched out luxuriously, and the smoke curling up from his cigar. The empty walls echoed with his loud, self-satisfied voice, his coarse, good-natured laugh.

Storm felt that the end must come soon; he must get away, come what might, from these surroundings.

The next day when he and George were bowling along the Long Island roads in Abbott's car, he broached the subject.

"Do you remember that I said some time ago I would like to chuck the trust company job and get away somewhere for a time? I've just about made up my mind to do it."

"Don't be a fool, Norman!" George advised with the roughness of sudden feeling in his tones. "I know you are dragging your anchor just now, but you'll come up in the wind all right. We all get over things in time; we have to. You would never get such a position as you have with the Mammoth Trust, and you haven't the temperament to start out for yourself."

"I'm not dependant on that position, as it happens," Storm remarked coldly, but his pulses leaped at the inward significance of the statement. What was fifteen thousand a year in a treadmill of precedent and prejudice to a hundred and twelve thousand and the world before him?

"I know you are not, but the remains of your father's estate won't last you long." George spoke with dogged patience. "You are not the sort to tie yourself down later to an inferior position where you would feel galled and embittered by the driving methods of the average commercial concern. You've got it pretty easy there, Norman, with the Mammoth people."

"I don't care! I have enough for myself if I never do another stroke of work and I have no one else to consider. I want to be my own master! I want to be free!"

The cry was wrung from him in an unguarded upward surge of exasperation, but George shook his head.

"We are none of us that, ever," he said slowly. "We think that we can fly from our memories, but we can't old man. It is only from within us that resignation comes, and peace, and finally, if we are strong and patient enough, something that passes for happiness."

"How do you know all this?" Storm demanded. "Where did you get your philosophy?"

"From sticking it out." George stared straight ahead of him, and his tone was a trifle grim. "Don't think you are the only one who has had to make the best of things and go on; I tell you, you can get used to anything in time."

"I don't propose to!" Storm cried recklessly. "I've had enough of this, I tell you; I've got to get away!—Not permanently, you understand, but for a good long trip."

He added the latter as a sense of caution returned to him, and George retorted:

"What at the end of it? You've got luxurious habits; there is no sense in blinking the truth. After you've wandered around the world lonelier than you are now and spent all your capital, you'll come home to find your position gone and nothing in store for you. You've been through the worst of it; stick it out now and try to work all the harder."

"I tell you I've come to the end!" Storm cried desperately. "I don't mean to be violent, old man, but I've got to have a change or I shall go mad! I thought if I left Green- lea and moved into town things would adjust themselves, that I should feel better; but I don't. I haven't the least intention of beggaring myself as you seem to think; why, I shan't be away more than a few months at most, and I have other things in view for my return. I've been sticking too long at the trust company, practically rusting. I need fresh interests, a new impetus. This whole damned town stifles me!"

"Then why not ask for a month's vacation and come upstate on a fishing trip with me?" George asked after a moment. "Abbott can look after my affairs, and it isn't too late for the trout. You used to be fond of fishing—"

Storm moved impatiently in his seat.

"I don't want to do any thing I'm used to!" he declared. "I want complete change, new scenes, everything! Can't you understand?"

"I think I can." George kept his eyes carefully trained ahead, and he seemed to be choosing his words with unusual deliberation. "But you can't fight anything, you can't forget anything, by running away from it, Norman."

"I'm not running away!" The denial came hotly from the other's lips, and he eyed his companion in swift, furtive alarm. "I'm worn out and my nerves are gone; that is all there is to it! You are so confoundedly phlegmatic, George, that you could keep on in the same old rut if the heavens fell! This isn't a wild impulse; I've had it in mind ever since—since Leila left me. Don't be surprised if you hear of my pulling up stakes any day."

George had no more to say, but Storm felt uneasily that his announcement had not been received quite as he had hoped it would be. To his own mind his proposed trip seemed natural enough on the face of it, but it was evident that to his conservative friend the deliberate relinquishment of a life-long sinecure was not justified by his mere desire for a change of scene. George was not proving as easy to handle, after all, as he had anticipated; and if he thought the proposed departure strange, how would the rest of their world look upon it?

But what did it matter what any of them thought? Leila's death had been declared accidental, and that incident was closed forever, while no possible link remained to connect him with the murder of Horton. Storm told himself angrily that this utterly unwarranted apprehension showed the state his nerves were in. He must get away!

That night, obsessed with the idea, he looked up sailing dates. This was the tenth of June; if he left New York on the following Saturday, the sixteenth, he could journey by rail across the continent, allow a day or two in which to look about San Francisco and catch the *Chika/matzu* from that port for Yokohama. It would be a simple matter to make his way from there to the China coast when Japan palled, and from there to India, to Egypt...

Six days more! He could possess his soul in patience for that brief period, and it would be none too long to enable him to put his affairs in final order. The investigation into Horton's death and the disappearance of the money had reached the point which he had anticipated; now it would remain at a standstill until finally dropped for lack of further evidence. As far as he personally was concerned, the affair was over.

With his decision made and the date of departure fixed in his mind, all nervous misgivings fell from him, and the news of the two succeeding days contained nothing to reawaken any disquietude.

The police were noncommittal, but it was evident that they had nothing to offer in response to the clamor of the press for a report of progress in the case. The private detectives working at the behest of 'Big Jim' Saulsbury's daughter and those of the Mid-Eastern Corporation were assiduously following chimerical clues. The investigation appeared to be indeed at a standstill, and Storm's spirits soared.

He even anticipated with a certain sly amusement the dinner on Tuesday evening when the wager with Millard was to be ratified in George's presence. Those two wiseacres, with their convention-bound souls and orthodox respect for the majesty of the law, should dine calmly within arm's length of the money the disappearance of which they would so solemnly discuss! How he would draw them out, listen to their fatuous exposition of their theories and laugh in his sleeve at them both!

Homachi was eager to exhibit his culinary ability, and master and man planned a perfectly appointed little repast, the former with a nice discrimination as to wines. His guest must be in a mellow, receptive mood, for he meant to take this occasion to announce his imminent departure definitely; he could depend on Millard to spread the news about Greenlea, and the attitude in which he received it would indicate the spirit in which he would disseminate it.

George was the first to appear on the scene, and his good-natured face wore a little, worried frown as he shook hands.

"I heard downtown today that you had closed out your account at the bank, Norman!" he began. "You are not actually preparing to go away, are you?"

"I told you on Sunday," Storm reminded him grimly.

"I know, but I—I really hoped you would think better of it." George shook his head. "I can't stand by without a remonstrance and see my best friend throw his whole future away on a mere restless whim. You know you are fixed for life with the Mammoth people, and no man in his senses would turn his back on an assured and ample income to gratify such a suddenly aroused desire for travel. What is it, Norman? What is on your mind?"

"What do you mean?" Storm's eyes narrowed and his voice was ominously calm. "What should be on my mind, George?"

"I don't know! Hang it, I wish I did!" the other retorted. "It just isn't reasonable, that's all. I don't want to—to touch on anything that will add to your sorrow, Norman, but I can't help feeling that there is something more in this than just an attempt to forget your grief over Leila's death. A man might naturally hanker for new scenes, but he wouldn't sacrifice his whole future for a few months' change. Tell me what is at the bottom of this crazy move of yours, won't you? I know you think I'm just a stodgy old fool, but maybe I can help."

His tone was pleading, his affectionate concern so evident, that Storm felt a twinge of compunction even as his annoyance at the other's persistence arose.

"Your attitude is not very flattering, George," he responded coldly. "You talk as though I were an hereditary pensioner of the Mammoth Trust, as though I would not be worth my salt in any other capacity. I do not owe you or any one else an explanation of my conduct—"

"Norman I" George's face flushed with pain and mortification, and he half rose from the chair.

"Sit down, old man. I know you mean this in pure friendship, but I'm not in the mood for advice." Storm controlled himself with an effort and went on carefully. "The fact is that even if I did not contemplate this trip I should sever my connection with the trust company. There you have it straight. I'm not getting the right deal there, and I mean to branch out for myself; I should have done so long ago, but I did not want to take a chance on Leila's account. You will forgive me if I do not discuss my future plans with you at the moment. They are not sufficiently matured, and incidentally I mean to travel for a few months. That is the whole thing in a nutshell."

"I am sorry," George said stiffly. "I didn't mean to butt in. I shall miss you."

The constrained tone, the wounded expression in his faithful, faded eyes only fanned his host's dull anger; but the entrance of Millard, pompous and radiating a spirit of selfsatisfied elation, brought an end to the situation.

"Aha! How are you both?" the newcomer asked breezily. "Had to finesse to get off this evening; bridge party on at the house and a devil of a row over it, but it was worth it, I assure you! Great old diggings you have here, Storm! How is the real estate game, Holworthy?

The latter responded while Storm went out to the pantry to perform certain functions with a cocktail shaker. When he returned he found that the irrepressible Millard had already plunged into the subject of the wager.

"Really, you know, in the interests of law and order you should drink to my victory, Storm!" the latter declared jovially.

"By all means!" Storm smiled. "For the good of the commonwealth as well as to avenge the memory of the man I knew at college, I hope that Horton's murderers will be brought to justice; but as a mere matter of personal opinion, backed by fifty dollars, I do not believe that the authorities are equal to the task."

Millard drank with a consciously superior air and then produced his wallet.

"Here's my fifty to declare that they are!" he said.

"The murderers *and* the money?" Storm laughed.

"*And* the money!" retorted his guest.

"I say, I don't like this transaction a little bit, at least as far as my part in it is concerned," George objected. "Holding the stakes on a bet of this sort seems scarcely decent, to me. Jack Horton was my friend."

Jokingly they overruled his scruples and went in to dinner ; but from time to time Storm found himself eying Millard askance. The latter bore himself with an air of ill-concealed mystery which augmented his natural self-importance, and his knowing smile was irritating to a degree. More than once as the meal progressed he seemed on the point of volunteering a statement, but each time he checked himself, though Storm plied him assiduously with the contents of the cob-webbed bottles.

Storm himself drank more than was his wont, but his brain remained clear and became if anything more coolly, keenly critical. It was evident that Millard had something which he was eager to impart, but an unusual caution weighed upon him. Was it merely a theory of his own concerning the murder, or had he really succeeded in learning anything at Headquarters which had been withheld from the public despite the taunts of the press?

After the wager had been settled, Millard had sedulously avoided all reference to the crime, and Storm's efforts to reopen the subject met with no response from him. At length the latter desisted and allowed the conversation to drift to other topics, although he kept his guests' glasses constantly filled.

George left his almost untouched, and his face grew graver as Millard's became more flushed. Storm knew that he was brooding in his dull, ruminative fashion over the situation which Millard's entrance had interrupted, and as the meal drew to a close he decided to make his announcement and have it over with.

"I am especially glad to have you two good friends here with me tonight—" he began.

"Hear! Hear!" Millard interjected.

"No; this is no speech, but it is probably the last occasion on which we three shall meet for some time," Storm pursued. "I'm leaving town in a few days — making quite an extended trip, in fact, — and I doubt if I shall be back much before it is time for George to hand me your fifty dollars, Millard."

"Going away!" Millard exclaimed blankly. "Where, old chap? What's the idea?"

"I'm not very well; nerves gone to pieces. I need a long sea voyage to buck me up, the doctor says, and I'm planning a trip to the East," Storm explained. "When I come back I am thinking of going into something new. The Mammoth Trust is all very well, but it doesn't offer a wide enough scope for the future. I am out after something big, but I want a rest first, and change."

Millard nodded solemnly.

"Best thing for you," he said. "Change, and all that, and then strike out for yourself. Dry rot in most of those old, conservative institutions. Hope you'll come back to Greenlea in time for the election of the club officers in the Fall. Here's luck, but don't count on that fifty of mine! If you knew what I do, you'd kiss your own goodbye!"

As he spoke he knocked the ash from the cigar which he had just lighted and a few flecks fell upon his host's knee. Storm brushed them off with a quick gesture of loathing. Ashes! God, could there be something prophetic in Millard's words?

He leaned forward in his chair.

"Look here, what have you got up your sleeve?" he demanded. "The bet goes as it lays, but I hope you haven't been letting them jolly you at Headquarters into believing that you are coming out an easy winner. They always pretend secret progress when they are stalled on a case, and they are at a deadlock now."

"Deadlock, nothing!" Millard crowed, his caution forgotten at the jibe. "That's what the chaps who did for Horton are thinking right now, but just wait till they try to pass one of those bills from the wad they stole!"

"Why?" Storm was not conscious that he had spoken, that he was clutching the table edge in a grip that embedded his nails in the cloth.

"Why? Because their numbers have been flashed all over the United States; the Chief of Police in every big city has been warned to be on the lookout for them, and long before the scoundrels can reach another country, provided they sue- ceed in getting out of this one, the news will have preceded them!" Millard waved his pudgy hands excitedly. "You didn't suppose they would give the bills out to Horton at the trust company without jotting down the numbers in case of error or accident, did you? It really wasn't sporting of me to bet on a sure thing; but do you think now that your man has a chance of getting away with the money?"

"Millard, you're going to win!" It was George who spoke, and firm conviction rang in his tones.

"Win? Hah!" Millard sat back in his chair. "The minute one of those bills makes its appearance, the man who offers it will be held for murder!"

XXI

THE UNCONSIDERED TRIFLE

Baffled fury that was half despair swept over Storm at Millard's words, but he controlled himself by a mighty effort. More vital than at any moment in the past was his need now of quick, coherent thought, and he forced himself to rise above the crushing blow. The bills were numbered and traceable! He should have thought of that! But the gold! The gold!

His throat was dry and parched, but he dared not lift his glass lest the shaking of his hand betray him. He swallowed and forced a laugh, but it sounded strained and unnatural in his own ears.

"Is that the big secret?" He was mortally afraid that his voice would crack, but it was evident that so far the others had noted nothing amiss; and emboldened he went on: "Good Lord, Millard, the criminals may be plain thugs, but are your friends at Headquarters such utter fools as to think they wouldn't realize the bills were numbered? They won't take any chances on them, you may be sure of that. It was the gold they were after! No attempt was made to check up on that, was there? I mean, it wasn't a fresh coinage or anything of that sort, with some mark that could be traced?"

Ages seemed to pass before Millard slowly shook his head, crestfallen that his news had been so tamely received.

"No," he admitted. "But there isn't such a lot of gold in circulation, you know. Anyone trying to get rid of it in large quantities will be open to suspicion. Besides, there hasn't been a line in the papers about the bills being spotted, and you can't credit gangsters and highway robbers with the intelligence you or I would have. It is ten to one those bills will show up before long."

Storm drew a deep breath and in a quick gesture raised his glass and drained it. How much of that hoard for which he had risked all was in the now useless banknotes and how much in precious gold? His whole future hung on the answer. He had counted it so carefully when he stored it away! Why couldn't he remember?

He opened his lips to voice the query, but George forestalled him.

"I have maintained from the very beginning that Jack Horton was not assaulted by mere gangsters or thugs," he remarked. "I don't believe there was any struggle; I told Norman so. The condition of the body as the papers described it could have been due to its having been flung over the wall; all except the single blow on the back of the head which caused death, of course. I tried to see the body at the undertaker's on Sunday, just to satisfy myself on that point, but it had already been shipped. I tell you, I think poor old Jack was taken unawares by that one foul blow when he thought he was safe among friends; or with one supposed friend, for that matter. It would have taken only one man to commit the crime, if Jack trusted him sufficiently to place himself in his hands."

Millard had been listening with all his ears, and now he brought his hand down on the table with a blow which made the glasses tinkle.

"By Jove, I believe you've got it!" he exclaimed. "It's hard to see how a man constantly on guard as he was could have been spirited off the train from Poughkeepsie against his will, and he wasn't killed until hours later. Now if he had met a friend—I must really suggest that at Head quarters!"

"Another cigar?" The urbane host, quite his old self again, smiled as he leaned across the table. "Try some of that 1812 brandy, Millard; you'll appreciate it. Old George here has been full of theories since Horton's murder, but I am afraid they are not practicable, and you won't find much sympathy for amateur efforts at Headquarters. I think myself that the body was brought there in a machine from the Lord knows what distance and thrown over the wall, but beyond that who can tell?"

"Well, there is something in support of that theory." Millard bristled again with an assumption of his former importance. "Just between ourselves, it is known that a machine came tearing down the Drive at a little after one o'clock that night going to beat the devil and it must have passed that spot. The occupants were yelling and carrying on, and the policeman who tried to hold them up at One Hundred and Tenth Street thought they were just a bunch of drunks out on a joy ride. I don't mind telling you they've been scouring the city for that machine ever since."

Storm gazed into his liqueur glass with inscrutable eyes. He remembered that car and its roisterous crew. It had passed just before... He roused himself to hear George's dogged, mildly insistent tones.

"It isn't logical to suppose that people on such an errand would draw attention to themselves. I don't mean that Jack walked deliberately at that time of night to the spot where he was found murdered, but—"

"It is possible that he may have done just that." Millard paused to sniff the bouquet of his brandy with the air of a connoisseur and added: "The policeman on the beat reported that two men passed him going north on the Drive toward that identical spot at approximately the hour of the murder. They were walking briskly and talking together in a casual sort of way, and he did not notice them particularly; but from what description he was able to give, one of them might have been Horton.—I say, old chap, you *have* done it! That cognac is worth its weight in gold!"

The stem of Storm's glass had snapped between his fingers. That policeman! Thank the fates they had not passed him beneath the street lamp! In spite of himself his mind had been diverted from thought of the money by Millard's revelations; but the latter's final word recalled it, and as he dropped the broken fragments of glass upon a plate he murmured:

"Habit of mine. These are Potter's glasses, too! All this is highly interesting, but it won't lead anywhere. The authorities will do well to keep their efforts centered on the recovery of that money. By the way, how much of it was in bills and how much in gold?"

"Only about ten thousand in gold, I believe," Millard responded carelessly. "The more ignorant of the miners for whose wages the money was intended demand gold, you know; they hoard it away and take no stock in paper certificates, but they are in the minority. Roughly speaking, a hundred thousand of it was in greenbacks."

A hundred thousand of his capital swept away at a word! Storm could have flung himself upon that smiling, self satisfied wretch across the table in bitter rage and disappointment! A hundred thousand; only a paltry ten thousand left, little more than enough to get him out of the country! What next would the cursed fates have in store for him?

Then a swift thought made his blood run cold. He should have remembered that the bills would be spotted, of course; that was the one flaw in his reasoning. The fact remained that he had not done so, however. What if he had not gotten Millard here tonight and loosened his tongue? If he had not been so providentially forewarned, all the structure he had so carefully built up might have fallen about him and carried him to ruin beneath it at his first attempt to make use of his newly acquired wealth!

"I wonder if it could have been Jack Horton and another man whom the policeman saw?" George cogitated. "That couple walking, I mean? If it were, it would bear out my theory. Of course, we don't know who Horton's intimates were of late years, nor what he could have been doing up in this part of the city so long after he should have been on his way; but it is not impossible, as you say. The policeman doesn't remember hearing anything a little later? A cry or anything of that sort? Why on earth didn't he follow them? Two men on that lonely stretch of drive at such an hour! He might have known there would be foul play—!"

"My dear George!" Storm laughed, but his hand shook as he refilled Millard's glass so that a drop or two of the pale golden liquid fell on the cloth. "Don't try to endow the Department with supernatural powers of divination! You and I have taken many a midnight stroll on the Drive since I took over Potter's rooms here. Would you have had a policeman dog our footsteps to see that we didn't murder each other? It is inconceivable that it could have been Jack Horton; remember that his bag, with the hat and pistol inside, were found in the Grand Central Station. If he had been killed out there where he was found it would have been far simpler for his murderers to have left them there with the body and just made away with the money."

To this George found no answer, but Millard smiled a trifle crookedly as he set down his glass, and a knowing leer spread over his flushed countenance.

"Something more was found in the bag besides the hat and pistol!" he observed. "This isn't supposed to be known, but I've got inside dope on it straight from Headquarters. Lot of old newspapers were wadded around the pistol. You might say there would be nothing in that, but there was something funny about those newspapers; the outside sheet was missing from every one of them!"

Storm drew a deep breath that was almost a sob and a great fear gripped him. Only three nights before when they were packing the trunk to be sent back to Greenlea, they had used the outer sheets of those same newspapers, and the old doubt returned to him. Had George noticed? He had said nothing, and his manner as Storm recalled it conveyed no intimation that his thoughts had been even momentarily distracted from the discussion then under way. Storm stole a furtive glance at him, but George seemed not to have heard. He was playing idly with the cigar-lighter, and his face wore a frown of labored concentration.

If it were only possible to silence Millard! But the latter continued with evident relish:

"And why was it missing? Because those papers weren't bought haphazard at a news-stand; they'd been delivered from day to day by a regular vendor, and the outer sheets had been removed because they bore the name of the person to whom they had been consigned." Millard produced a small notebook from his pocket and ruffled its pages importantly. "Look here! I jotted down the dates of those papers: May twenty-eighth, thirtieth, thirty-first, and June first, third and fourth, of this year, too! Not so old, eh? They come down to within a day or two of the murder!

I guess that's bad evidence! Those newspapers had been delivered to the person who packed that bag, old chap, or he wouldn't have been so infernally careful, and he is one of those who murdered Horton!"

"You cannot trace parts of newspapers if they have no distinguishing mark on them!" Storm said hastily, casting about in desperation for a change of theme. "Your friends at Headquarters are remarkably painstaking, but have they considered the possibility that Horton may have stopped over in New York to see this girl in whom he was interested, and been waylaid?"

"There's not a chance of that." Millard shook his head. "She has told all she knows, and it has been proven that he never went near her; never even communicated with her, although so many hours elapsed between the time his train reached the city and the murder. Oh, it's a poser, all right, but they'll solve it. I'll win my wager yet, old chap."

He cast a wavering and reluctant eye upon the clock and rose.

"You're not going yet?" Storm asked mechanically. "Have another smoke—?"

"Must be getting on if I'm going to catch the midnight, and if I don't there'll be the deuce to pay!" Millard's tone was frankly regretful. "Wish I could stay and make a night of it, dear boy, but you know how it is! You know how I'm situated! It's been some evening, though, hasn't it? I envy you, Storm; such rooms, such a cook, and call your soul your own!"

"Yet I am anxious to start on my trip," Storm remarked. "I want to get away—"

"I know, dear old boy! Memories!" Millard heaved a lugubrious sigh. "I don't blame you, but we'll all look forward to having you with us again. I'll look in on you before you start, of course.—Coming my way, Holworthy?"

"Eh?" George glanced up with a start, as if suddenly aroused, his near-sighted eyes blinking. But Storm intervened.

"Oh, George will stop for another smoke and a chat. It is early for him yet, you know; he's a bachelor!"

He fairly hustled his departing guest into his coat in fear lest George should insist upon accompanying him. They must not leave together, presenting an opportunity for Millard to expatiate on his theme of the newspapers! Dense as he was, few things escaped George. He might have only subconsciously noted the trivial episode of the other night; but would he remember it later? Storm felt the moisture start suddenly upon his forehead, and the smoke-wreathed air seemed dense and choking.

"Yes, I—I'll stay a little while," George said absently. "You don't know that policeman's number, do you, Millard? The one who passed those two men on the Drive?"

"No, but I fancy you'll find him out there almost any night about the same time." Millard paused at the door. "Run out to Greenlea and dine with us soon, Holworthy; I suppose it is no good asking you, Storm? Well, thanks for a top-hole evening and don't forget our wager!"

The door closed behind him at last, and Storm turned to face his remaining guest with the cold fear still clutching at his heart.

"Beastly bore, Millard," he commented, lighting a cigarette with a critical eye on the hand that held the match. God, how it trembled! Had George seen? "That is a rotten way for a host to talk, I know, but he gets on a fellow's nerves with his everlasting chatter. I made the wager with him to shut him up, but it had the opposite effect. Personally, I don't believe he knows anything more of what is being done in the case than is given out to the press; they certainly wouldn't take a he-gossip of his stamp into their confidence at Headquarters. He made all that stuff up just to create an impression."

George shook his head slowly.

"I don't know. He must be right about the numbered bills. I thought of that myself and wondered why the papers didn't make a point of it. The men, too, on the Drive; I would like to have a talk with that policeman."

"Are you going to turn detective, too?" Storm's laugh grated unpleasantly on his own ears.

"No, but I believe if the authorities followed that lead they would be on their way to the truth," George responded gravely. "I can't help feeling that I'm right about poor old Jack. He would never have taken his hand off his number if he had not been absolutely sure of his company."

"It seems to me that you are a little over-confident of the character of a man you haven't seen in twenty years!" Storm sneered, his equanimity partially restored. It was evident that George suspected nothing. "How do you know what he might have done, what impulses may have guided him?"

"A man's whole nature doesn't change, even in a generation," the other observed. "I studied him at college as I did the rest of the crowd, and subsequent events have proved that my judgment in any of them wasn't far wrong. Moreover, the testimony of this Saulsbury girl, of his employers and everyone who was associated with him in these later years bears out my estimate of him. Jack was done in at a single blow by someone he knew and trusted, and I say it is a damned shame and outrage!"

"Well, don't get excited about it," his host advised coolly. "It won't help the poor chap now, you know. I take more stock myself in that story of the motor car on the Drive than the possibility of one of the two pedestrians having been Jack."

"The fact that the bag was found at the terminal, of which you reminded me, would have no more bearing on the theory that his body was brought there than that he had walked to the spot where he was murdered," George contended tenaciously.'
"Odd about those papers which were stuffed into the bag, wasn't it? About the outside sheets being missing, I mean. They were for the twenty-eighth, thirtieth and thirty-first of May, and the first, third and fourth of June, he said; didn't he? I wish I had thought to ask him what newspapers they were. It presents a rather nice little problem."

Storm's breath fluttered in his throat, but he contrived to reply with an assumption of carelessness.

"Oh, that's nothing! Newspapers cannot be traced. That was just a mere detail."

George had heard, after all, but the incident of the previous Saturday night had utterly escaped him! In the wave of relief which swept over him Storm felt ironically that he had never before appreciated the virtue of his old friend's density. But for his slow wit and lack of imagination the man sitting there smoking so placidly before him might have been his accuser!

"Mere details left unguarded are what show up many a criminal," George remarked sententiously. "The unconsidered trifles are what turn the scale of evidence against an intelligent man more often than a big error in judgment."

Storm writhed inwardly, but the mask of half-contemptuous amusement still veiled his face.

"It doesn't take much intelligence to hit a man over the head!" he observed. "You're talking through your hat, George. If they succeed in landing the murderers, which I very much doubt, you'll find your theory knocked to smithereens. Horton may have left the train in company with a crowd he trusted, all right, but remember he has led a rough sort of life for years in mining camps and collieries, and his associates are bound to have been men of a coarse, elemental stamp. They have probably laid for him for weeks, planned this ahead and made their get-away before the body was even discovered."

"Well,"—George rose with a touch of weariness in his manner—"I must get home. Time will tell, but I've a feeling that poor old Jack's murder will be avenged. I was sorry to hear that you have planned an immediate departure. You won't reconsider and try a fishing trip with me first? It might buck you up and give you a fresh outlook on things."

Storm shook his head.

"Thanks, old man, but I've got to get away from everything and everyone, even myself. I can't bring her back, and I can't forget while there is anything about to remind me of the old life."

"I suppose you are right," George admitted slowly. "I am afraid you will regret it, though, from a monetary standpoint. Look in on me tomorrow at the office if you get time, Norman. Good night."

After he had gone Storm shot the bolt in the door and dashing into his bedroom pushed aside the panel which concealed the safe. He must see for himself if it were true that all but a mere fraction of his money would be forever useless to him.

Homachi had departed hours before, the shades were drawn and in his solitude Storm spread the packets of bills out upon the bed and counted them feverishly. It was true! A hundred thousand dollars which would have meant years of ease and luxurious travel had been transformed by the magic of a few words into mere worthless scraps of green paper!

The numbers upon them seemed to dance diabolically before him, and wild thoughts of the possibility of erasing them flashed through his mind, but he realized the futility of such a hope. He knew nothing of the use of acids or chemicals in such a procedure, and to take anyone into his confidence was unthinkable even had he known where or how to find a man for the task.

Then a quick revulsion of feeling came, and his mercurial spirits rebounded. The money those bills represented was not lost to him forever! In spite of Millard's boast that their numbers were known, there would be plenty of places in far-away corners of the globe where they would be accepted without question. As long as they were genuine, the money changers of Japan and Egypt and even the cosmopolitan continental centers would not look for the numbers upon them, and he had more than sufficient gold to get him out of the country and to some haven where he might safely begin to turn this paper into coin of the realm.

Had his fortune been in gold it would have been impossible, through its sheer weight, for him to have transported even a quarter of it. The greenbacks in any event were far safer. No bag for him! He could fasten those packets beneath his coat over his heart where he could feel them with each beat!

He laughed aloud at Millard's cocksure statement. He would show them all!

George's attitude worried him, however. The former had all the obstinacy of the man of few ideas, and Storm knew that he would cling to his theory of Horton's death through any amount of argument and ridicule. The fact that that theory was dangerously near the truth—was, in so far as it went, the truth itself—did not tend to allay his anxiety. If once the merest inkling of the real identity of the murderer came to George, it would mean the end. That coincidence of the newspapers would have been sufficient to arouse his suspicion if he had noticed the fact of the missing parts the other night. It was sheer luck that he had not done so; but would that luck hold in other respects?

Storm lay for long hours staring into the darkness and grappled with the new problem which confronted him. Dense as he was, George had felt that there was something deeper than mere grief back of Storm's determination to leave the country. Suppose, after he had gone, George's eyes were opened to the truth? Storm well knew that no corner of the globe could hide him from the authorities and the agents of the Mid-Eastern, and George had a queer, old-fashioned sense of justice. If he suspected, he would speak! Perhaps it would be as well to defer his departure and stick to George until the affair had completely blown over; but Great Heavens, what a bore!

He was not yet free! The bonds which held him were invisible, intangible, yet he felt their pressure and writhed beneath it. God! Would he ever succeed in breaking them? Must he be forever a prisoner in these chains of his own forging?

XXII

AT THE CLUB

On the following day, to George's surprise and gratification Storm appeared at his office at noon and dragged him unceremoniously off for lunch. In the course of their long friendship he had been almost invariably the one to seek out his more brilliant companion, and he was touched at this evidence of a need of him.

"I must say you look pretty bad, Norman," he began with tactless solicitude. "And you were as nervous as a woman last night; I could see it. You are not taking care of yourself—"

"I don't sleep well," Storm interrupted shortly. "I wanted to talk things over with you. I've been thinking about that trip I proposed taking—"

"Yes?" George urged eagerly as he paused.

"Well, I don't know but what you are right if I can only pull myself together somehow." Storm weighed each word with care. "You cannot appreciate what I have been through in the last month or you would realize how desperately I want to get away from all reminders of my—my grief; but if I can fight it without cutting myself adrift and losing my connection with the trust company, it would be foolish to sacrifice such a sinecure, especially when I have nothing else absolutely definite in view."

He could invent that 'something else' easily enough, he reflected as he watched George's glowing face, when the moment came for departure. Meanwhile, he had decided to play safe; it would not be long! As the words formed in his mind he shuddered involuntarily; that had been Jack Horton's expression! He had boasted of playing safe in the very hour of his death!

"Of course it would! I knew you would come to your senses, old man!" George cried warmly. "I do realize what you must have suffered, but the only way to forget is to fight it. You—you can count on me, you know!"

Storm nodded.

"I am sure of that." He paused and added: "About that little fishing trip you suggested; do you think you could get away?"

"Surest thing you know! I'm feeling seedy myself, and it will do us both good. Shall we ask Millard to join us?"

"Heavens, no! He is an infernal nuisance!" Storm exclaimed hastily. Through the long night hours he had planned his trip for the express purpose of keeping George and his inconvenient theories away from the too loquacious disseminator of news from Headquarters. "I only want you, George. How soon do you think you can get away?"

In secret distaste he watched the other's puppy-like wriggle of affectionate gratification at this mark of favor. What a fool he had been to fear him! Yet there might still be a chance for George to suspect, and if he did he would not rest until he had ferreted out the truth.

"Let's see; this is Wednesday," George responded. "I ought to be able to make it by the first of next week. I'll talk to Abbott about it this afternoon and let you know later. Say, why don't you meet me at the Club?"

Storm made a quick gesture of rejection.

"I haven't been there since—"

"I know, and that's just why it will do you good," George urged. "You've got to take the plunge some time, you know. There is no good in isolating yourself and brooding, as you have been doing. Most of the fellows are away now for the hot weather; you won't find half a dozen there before dinner."

"We-ell," Storm conceded. The ubiquitous Millard would not be present, at any rate, nor would anyone else who had the slightest interest in the murder of an obscure paymaster; and now that the suggestion had been made he felt a vague desire to see the old club once more. "I'll meet you there at half-past five."

The papers were still devoting much front-page space to the murder and robbery, but it was concerned principally with the activities of the detectives employed by Miss Saulsbury and those of the Mid-Eastern Corporation. The Police Department was reported as making progress, but its nature was not disclosed; and Storm smiled to himself as he read. No mention was made of the two men seen walking on the Drive, but the incident of the motor car was prominently exploited, and the generally accepted theory seemed to be that the body had been brought from some undetermined distance and flung over the wall.

All reference to the bag and its contents when found at the terminal had been permitted to drop, and he looked in vain for any suggestion that the numbers of the bills were known.

When he reached the club that afternoon he found that George had not yet arrived; but a tall, lanky figure arose with outstretched hand from the window seat.

"Hello, old fellow! Glad to see you back! We've been asking about you."

"Thanks, Griffiths. I've not been away," Storm replied briefly. "Just haven't felt sociable, that's all."

"I know. We heard of course. Very sad! We all felt for you."

The lawyer, who was noted for his eloquence in court, halted now in a constrained fashion, and Storm replied quietly. "I'm sure of that. Everyone has been very good, but this is the sort of thing one has to bear alone. I am thinking of getting away shortly for a trip—"

"There was another matter, too, of which I was sorry to learn," Griffiths interrupted him. "You were badly hit in the Mertens-Du Chainat swindle, weren't you?"

"I?" Storm's surprise at the question was unfeigned, and his eyes shifted beneath the other's level gaze. "Indeed, no! Where did you hear that?"

"From a rather direct source," the lawyer responded slowly. "In fact, from a private examination of some papers belonging to the pseudo Du Chainat which were unearthed after his departure. A client of mine happens to have been among his victims, and I was in a conference of attorneys who were permitted to make an examination of the effects which Du Chainat overlooked or had no time to destroy. Among them was a list of his victims, together with the amount he had obtained from each; a methodical scoundrel, wasn't he? He had you down for sixty thousand, and as all the other items on the list were verified by the victims themselves I naturally concluded that his plans had gone through in your case. Sorry if I have made a stupid mistake."

"Not stupid!" Storm smiled frigidly. "Natural enough, under the circumstances. I met the fellow and he put his proposition up to me; I didn't bite, but I let him down so easily that probably he considered me one of his prospects. To tell you the truth he interested me as a type, but I wasn't fool enough to fall for his game."

"I am glad for your own sake." There still remained that dry note of mental reservation in the lawyer's tone. "He victimized some of the most astute business men in the country.—Hello, Holworthy!"

Storm turned as if stung. George was coming forward from the door with a preternaturally grave expression upon his wide, ingenuous face. How long had he been standing there? Confound his pussy-footing ways! How much had he heard? Storm was inwardly seething with rage at Griffith's interference in his affairs as well as at George's inopportune arrival, but he forced himself to greet the newcomer equably, striving to learn from his manner if the conversation had reached his ears.

"I was late because Abbott kept me going over some details at the office," the latter explained quietly. "He thinks I can get away all right by Monday. Suppose instead of the Beaverkill we try the north woods? The bass ought to be running well up there—"

"So that's the trip you meant, eh?" Griffiths interrupted. "Gad, wish I could join you! I'd like to get a breath of the big woods in the silence and peace of it after the eternal court wrangles of this last term, but there isn't a chance for me. I envy you two fellows!"

Two more members, a banker and the editor of one of the big dailies, joined them, refreshments were ordered, and to Storm's relief the talk drifted off on general topics; but he studied George furtively. If he had heard, would he accept Storm's denial that he had been victimized by Du Chain- at? The lawyer had evidently remained skeptical, but he was not as conversant with Storm's affairs and financial position as was George. If the latter believed that his friend had been hard hit, would he not naturally wonder where he had obtained the money for the long overseas trip he contemplated, and wondering, blunder upon the truth?

A half hour passed, the little group broke up and Storm and his companion were on the point of departure when a hearty, good-humored voice boomed from the doorway and an elderly man with a bluff military swagger bore down upon them.

"Great Guns, Storm, but it's good to see you here again! I wrote you—you got my letter?—when I heard of your loss. Terrible thing, terrible! Damn fine little lady—"

He paused, clearing his throat and clapping Storm resoundingly on the shoulder.

"Thanks, Colonel; yes, I received your letter," the latter responded. "Meant to reply to it, but George here can tell you that I've been rather unsettled—"

"Heard you had moved to town and taken somebody's rooms up on the Drive," Colonel Walker interupted. "We've needed you here for a fourth at bridge; had to take on Paine, and he's rotten—"

"I like that!" the editor retorted indignantly. "Who revoked twice in one evening—?"

"That was because we were playing for low stakes. I'm never on my mettle unless the game is away over my head." The Colonel laughed and added: "Saw you the other night, Storm, and tried to hail you but you got away in the crowd. I wanted to drag you off to a stag house party up in Westchester. Let's see; that was last Wednesday night, over by the Grand Central Station—"

"You must have been mistaken!" Storm interrupted hastily. He could feel George's eyes upon him, and this fresh turn of affairs left him aghast.

"No, I'm not," Colonel Walker insisted bluntly. "It was Wednesday night, I remember, just around dinner time, for it was raining like blazes and you were dodging along under your umbrella—"

"Oh, yes!" Storm parried desperately. "I recall it now, but I didn't see you, old chap. I was on my way to my tobacconist's. By the way, that was a wonderful brand of cigarettes you used to get from Turkey before the war. I've been trying to remember the name—"

The colonel's laugh boomed out in good humored derision.

"Much good it would do you now! They aren't made any more; in fact I doubt if that grade of tobacco is grown over there since the world turned upside down! I've found something new, however; try one of these."

He passed around a cigarette case and the hoped-for diversion was created, but Storm's heart felt like lead within him and he dared not meet George's eyes. He tried to think collectedly, but the very weight of his own guilt prevented him from viewing the case sanely from an unbiassed attitude. Here, within the hour, the last links in the chain of circumstantial evidence had been forged against him in George's eyes had the latter but the sense to grasp the full significance of what he had learned. The reported loss of his capital, his presence at the terminal at the time of Horton's supposed arrival, George's own theory that Horton had been a victim of someone he knew and trusted, the proximity of the place where the body was found to Storm's rooms, the testimony of the policeman as to the two pedestrians, the coincidence of the newspapers in Horton's bag supplying the missing parts of those in Storm's possession; why, the thing was patent on the face of it!

Only George's ignorance concerning the newspapers, his blind faith in his friend and the improbability of his grasping so monstrous a solution stood between Storm and certain exposure. But was it an improbability? Was George even now putting the facts together and waiting to strike?

Storm sat back in silence, puffing his cigarette and leaving the burden of conversation to the others. He heard the Colonel's deep bass, Griffiths' keen, incisive tones and George's measured, phlegmatic voice with no change in its unemotional timbre, but they came to him as from a distance. Did George know? The thought held him as in a vice and he longed for yet dreaded the moment when they should be alone together, which he felt must reveal the truth.

At length George rose somewhat heavily and turned to his friend.

"Shall we be getting on, Norman? Unless you would prefer to dine here, of course—"

"No." Storm, too, got out of his chair. "We've a lot of things to settle about our trip."

They took leave of their friends and left the club, and still George's manner remained, to the other man's over- analytical state of mind, significantly grave and reticent. He could endure the suspense no longer, and a spirit of bravado entered into him.

"That did me good, rather; to get to the club and see some of the old fellows again," Storm declared mendaciously. "What are you silent about, old man?"

"Nothing; I've been thinking," George responded. "All your fishing gear is down at Greenlea, isn't it? Can you write to MacWhirter and get it here by Monday?"

Storm gave a furtive sidelong glance at him, but George was plodding along with an inscrutable countenance.

"I can run down overnight and pick out what I need," Storm asserted shortly. "We can make out a list tonight. Suppose we stop at the Blenheim Grill here for a bite and then go on up to my rooms?"

George accepted without comment, and they were soon ensconced at a table as far as possible from the blatant orchestra, in a corner half screened by palms. As Storm studied the menu he glanced up to find his companion's eyes fixed upon him in troubled, questioning scrutiny, and he flung the card aside.

"What is it?" he demanded savagely. As well to have it over here and now! He could endure the suspense no longer. "There's been something wrong with you ever since we left the club. For heaven's sake get it off your chest!"

"Well," George responded slowly. "I couldn't help hearing what Griffiths said as I came in, and to tell you the truth, old man, I am rather hurt at your lack of confidence in me."

Storm unconsciously braced himself. It was coming!

"You mean about the Du Chainat affair?" he blustered. "That meddlesome old fool knows nothing about my business! I call it infernal cheek, his attempting to say the man ever victimized me! There's not a word of truth in it."

"I read of the swindle in the newspapers, and I remember that I was the one to tell you of the Du Chainat exposure; I showed the article to you myself." George spoke more to himself than to the other man, as though correlating his thoughts aloud. "I recall that you seemed interested about it, even excited, but you never mentioned the fact that you knew the man, much less that he had tried to take you in on his schemes. It wasn't like you, Norman; you've told me everything, ever since we were boys, and I am wondering where I could have failed you."

An injured, plaintive note had crept into his patient voice, and in a sudden access of hope Storm seized upon his opportunity.

"You haven't failed me, dear old George! It was my accuresd pride, as usual. I wouldn't admit it to Griffiths for worlds, but I did pretty nearly fall for that fellow's bunk! When you showed me that the whole thing was a swindle I was aghast at my narrow escape, and I made up my mind I wouldn't give you the chance to preach at me again about reckless investments. If I had told you how nearly I came to letting Du Chainat hoodwink me you would have been as worried as a maiden aunt about any future venture I might want to make, and I didn't care to have you know what an ass I had been!" His tone was a perfect simulation of shamefaced confidence. "Millard might have told you that I knew the pseudo Du Chainat. He introduced me to him himself, and if it hadn't been for Mrs Millard, who holds the purse strings, the old boy would have been one of Du Chainat's victims. He was strong for the scheme, but for once I had a gleam of sense and held out."

George shook his head.

"I'm sorry if I have seemed to preach at you," he said. "Your money is your own, of course, to do with as you please, and you are a man grown, but you have always been to me the impulsive, reckless boy I knew at college—"

"Whom you helped out of many a scrape!" Storm put in quickly. "You don't think I have ever forgotten, do you, old man? It wasn't lack of confidence, but fear of 'I told you so' that prevented me from telling you what I knew personally of Du Chainat. Griffiths was all wrong in that, however. Du Chainat may have put me down for a boob, but I never dropped a cent in his scheme."

"I'm glad to hear it," George remarked earnestly, but to Storm's apprehensive ear there was the same hint of skepticism in his voice that the lawyer's had evinced, and he burst out recklessly:

"Look here, you don't think I am holding out on you now, do you? You don't think I was such a fool? If I had put all my capital in Du Chainat's hands, and he had taken it to the bottom of the sea with him, where on earth would I have gotten the money for this long trip I proposed taking or investment in a new concern when I got back?"

He could have bitten his tongue out the instant the words had left his lips. What a consummate fool to open the way for suspicion to enter George's mind, if it were not there already! But while he sat inwardly cursing himself for his mad indiscretion, the other's face cleared as if by magic.

"Of course, Norman! I have been worrying a little for the last hour, but I might have known you hadn't gone into the scheme, for it would have pretty well cleaned you out, wouldn't it? Now that you are going to stay on at the trust company " he broke off and added: "I'm sure that you are! Our fishing trip will buck you up wonderfully, and you'll come back in fine form!"

"I hope so." Storm breathed freely. The danger point was past! But he must cinch it in the other's mind... "I've still got my capital, you know; what there is left of it from that copper gamble two years ago."

"Well, nothing is sure but death and taxes, you must remember. Even the Mammoth Trust might go under, so don't regard your fifty thousand as velvet and take some wild flyer with it, without consulting Foulkes or me." George checked himself with a sheepish grin. "There I go preaching again! I vow I won't any more.—Say! That waiter has been hovering about for the last twenty minutes. What are we going to have?"

Dinner ordered, the conversation turned upon their forthcoming expedition, and as the meal progressed all of Storm's wonted self-confidence returned to him in full measure. These vague fears about old George and his suspicions were nothing but the chimera of exhausted nerves, and he was a fool to permit them to give him a moment's disquietude. Millard and his damned wager had worked upon him, but Millard was an ass! The very way that he had fallen for Du Chainat proved—Storm caught himself up in his chain of reasoning with a grimace of ironic disgust. He, too, had fallen for Du Chainat, and harder even than had Millard. Gad, was he getting so that he believed his own lies?

At any rate, the result of the wager was a foregone conclusion. He could not fail to carry on successfully to the end now; his plans had been laid too well! Not one single setback had occurred and no one, nothing could touch him. He could endure old George's unadulterated company for a week or so, and the sojourn in the woods would steady his nerves and give him time to plan cool-headedly for the future.

By the time they returned, the Horton investigation would have slumped to a mere nominal affair, and soon thereafter he might announce his adherence to his original plan, to which George could then have no opposition to offer since his own suggestion would have failed of its object. Everything would work out smoothly, perfectly; the greatest stunt of the age would go through without a hitch; and it was all due to his foresight, his genius for detail! There was nothing he could not accomplish in the future, no one living who was his master; and the best of it all was that no one suspected his greatness! Not a living soul with whom he came in contact realized that he was other than a pleasant enough fellow, a gentleman born and bred but without much business head or executive ability; a tame, futile sort of person, who would never set the Thames on fire. God, it was the biggest joke perpetrated on the community since time began! It was almost too good to keep!

But as they left the grill and made their way to his rooms, in the midst of his exultation there came to him another dampening thought. Had George noticed the coincidence of his having been near the Grand Central Station at the very hour of Horton's supposed arrival, as revealed by Colonel Walker's unlucky chance remark? Storm dared not draw his attention to the coincidence itself if it had escaped him, yet a perverse instinct drove him on to ascertain if he had noted the significance of the date mentioned.

"Old Walker is putting on flesh again since demobilization took place," he began tentatively. "I hear he has been hitting it up quite a little lately."

"He is a pretty good fellow," George replied tolerantly. "Likes to swagger and make out that he's a regular devil, but there is no real harm in him.—Say, we'd better get some new G. lines, and if I were you I'd look over that four-and- a- half-ounce rod of yours."

"That's all right." Storm returned insistently to his point. "I wonder who was giving the stag house-party up in Westchester for which the Colonel was bound when he hailed me? Odd that I should not have heard him, for he bellows like a bull."

"Oh, well, in a crowd—" George's tone was absent and he broke off to announce with vigor. "I'll tell you one thing; *if you* expect any luck you had better get a Montreal or two. The pet Parmachini Belle of yours would make any bass in the lake give you a laugh!"

Another dangerous chance eliminated!—Danger? Storm chuckled with amusement at the thought. To test old George further was like taking milk from a blind kitten! Only a miracle could harm him now and the age of miracles was past. He was invincible, indeed!

"Ashes be damned!"

XXIII

THE SCOURGE OF MEMORY

The next morning as Storm was on the point of starting for his office Homachi ushered in a visitor. He was a sturdy, well-built man with sandy hair and a lean, lantern-jawed face, and as he advanced and stood fumbling with his cap only a slight limp and sag of one hip betrayed the artificial limb which replaced the one he had left in France.

"Well, MacWhirter," Storm began cordially, and then his tone sharpened. "There isn't anything wrong at Green-lea?"

"No, sir." The erstwhile gardener shifted uneasily. "Everything is right as can be. Since you left me there as caretaker there's been nothing for me to do; not even a stray dog to be warned off the place."

"Then sit down, man, and tell me what brings you here." There was a trace of impatience now in Storm's voice. Another reminder of Greenlea and what had happened there!

"Well, sir, it's just that; I've not enough to do." MacWhirter eased himself down gingerly upon the edge of a chair. "I'm not earning what you pay me and I'm well fit—"

He flushed, glancing down at his curiously stiffened leg, and Storm said hastily:

"Of course you are! You're in every way as efficient as you were before the war. I put you in charge because you are a responsible man and I trusted you. All I want is to have the place guarded and looked after during my absence."

"I know, sir. Eve kept the flowers up, though you told me not to bother, because it's a rare fine garden to go to waste and because the mistress took such pride in it, begging your pardon, sir. I've never forgot her kindness in keeping my place open for me and sending me word at the hospital that no matter how bad I was hurt I was to come back." The man's honest eyes misted and his voice grew unsteady, but he controlled it respectfully after a moment's pause. "If I felt that the place or you, sir, actually needed me I'd stay on, but—"

"You want to leave, eh?" Storm interrupted shortly. "Well, you must please yourself, MacWhirter. You are getting a head gardener's wages now."

"Yes, Mr Storm, and I'm not earning it, though I'm as able to as any man alive. If I keep on being just a caretaker, folks'll think I'm not fit for anything else. I'm a farseeing man, and I've got to look out for the future." The shrewd, kindly Scotch eyes narrowed and then swiftly darkened as he added in a lowered tone, "It isn't only that, sir; it's main lonesome out there now."

"In Greenlea, with all the neighbors about?"

"Not Greenlea; I mean the place itself. There's something about it since—since it has been closed up that fair gives me the creeps, sir! Something uncanny, like! I—I'd rather not stay on, sir."

There was a note of superstitious awe in the man's tones which awoke an unexpected answering chord in Storm, and his anger rose swiftly to combat it.

"You're a fool, Mac Whirter!" He exclaimed roughly. "There's nothing wrong with the place. However, as you. say, I don't really need you there; the night watchman at the country club can look after things for me. I hope for your own sake that you have another position in view—?"

"They'll take me on as assistant ground keeper at the club, sir." MacWhirter's tone was abashed. "Please don't think I'm ungrateful—"

Storm waved that aside.

"It will be mean less wages." He watched the man closely.

"Yes, sir. But I—" MacWhirter's eyes fell. "I'd rather take it, sir, if you don't mind."

Storm shrugged.

"It is all the same to me, MacWhirter. Let me see; your month is up—?"

"Tomorrow, sir." There was unconcealed eagerness in the man's tone. "Of course, if you were thinking of getting another caretaker, I could wait—"

"I shan't." Storm spoke with sudden decision. "I'm going away on a long trip myself, and I have closed out my bank account, but I'll pay you off now in cash. Put the place in good order and mail me the keys tomorrow."

"I've brought them with me, sir." MacWhirter rose, placed a bunch of keys upon the table and gravely accepted the money. "Thank you, sir. You'll find the place in perfect order and the garden doing brave and fine if you run out before you go away. I appreciate what you've done for me, Mr Storm, and I wouldn't speak of leaving but for the lonesomeness and my being of no real use."

Storm cut the man's protestations short and got rid of him with a curtness but poorly masked. His manner more than his words had conjured up a picture of the silent, deserted house standing amid the bright flowers like a corpse decked for the funeral which made Storm's senses recoil as before a vision of something sinister and full of dread.

For the life of him he could not put from his mind the swiftly recurring memory of that sleeping garden on the night when he had cast the handful of ashes out upon it and then drawn the curtains that the coming moon might not peer through at what lay within. Had those ashes of his first crime bred a fatal growth there among the flowers? Had a phoenix risen from them to cry the deed in tones audible only to MacWhirter's susceptible Celtic ear?

In vain he cursed himself for a superstitious fool. Of course the place was lonesome, but thank God! he was rid of the man and his silly whims and fancies! No caretaker was needed there, anyway, and in the fall he would cable George to sell it for him. Every closed, deserted house in the country bore an aspect which the ignorant would term 'uncanny', but there could be nothing real, nothing tangible in the sensations which had driven MacWhirter away; no lingering influence of that night's event could remain to manifest itself to those who might come within its aura.

He would like to have asked MacWhirter to explain himself, had not common sense forbade. He felt an inordinate curiosity as to the latter's sensations, and a sort of dread fascination settled itself upon him, a desire to see for himself if that house at Greenlea retained the power to thrill or unnerve him.

Then with a supreme effort he cast aside the spell which had held him in thrall. What utter rot such superstitions were in these materialistic days! MacWhirter was lonely, and he had made use of the first excuse which came handy to get out of an uncongenial job. No ghosts walked save those which lived in memory, and Storm would soon be free from them forever! But he must go soon! Such a mood as this could not have fastened upon him had he not been near the breaking point; not now, when everything had gone so splendidly, when with consummate skill and daring he had attained all his aims, overcome all obstacles, turned the very weapons of fate into tools to serve his own ends!

He told himself defiantly that everything was before him, but he was deucedly tired, that was all. He would rest thoroughly in the woods, recoup his nerves and then start upon the real adventure. Meanwhile, for the sake of his continued sanity he must put all morbid thoughts of MacWhirter's nonsense and of Greenlea from his mind.

Yet when he presented himself before Nicholas Langhorne in the latter's sanctum at a little before noon his haggard face was sufficient excuse for his errand.

"I wanted to know if it would be convenient for me to turn my work over to someone else for the next week or two, Mr Langhorne," he began. "I'm not feeling quite up to the mark; thought if I got away for a time—"

"My dear Storm, I was going to suggest it to you myself." Langhorne waved him to a chair. "I've noticed that you were looking badly, and it is natural enough under the circumstances. You really should have taken a good rest at the time—er, a month ago. Arrange for as long a vacation as you need to put yourself in shape again. Sherwood or Bell or any of the minor officials can take over your work."

Storm flushed in resentment at the unconscious imputation. So that was how his services were regarded by this pompous old idiot! That was how he was appreciated!

"Thank you," he said stiffly, adding in swift irony: "If you can possibly get along without me I should like to leave town almost immediately."

Langhorne nodded blandly.

"Just turn over your books to Sherwood tomorrow morning and don't give another thought to business until you return. Where have you planned to go, my boy?"

The note of personal interest was as unusual as the paternal address, but Storm still glowered.

"Up in the north woods, I think, for some bass fishing. I shall not be gone longer than about ten days." He rose. "I'm glad you can spare me for I feel about all in."

"Fishing!" Langhorne mused. "There is a lot of malaria in those woods, Storm, and the discomforts of camp are abominable, to say nothing of the indigestible cooking provided by the average guide. Now, if you will take my advice, you will pick out some nice, quiet country club with a good green and play your eighteen holes every day. There is nothing like golf to set a man up; gentleman's game, steadies the nerve, clears the eye, fills the lungs with good fresh air and not too strenuous. Golf—"

"I've played it," Storm interrupted quietly, but the cold fury which possessed him trembled in his tones. "I prefer fishing and I want to rough it for a time. I won't detain you any longer, Mr Langhorne. My books are in perfect order and can be turned over tomorrow."

He withdrew, inwardly seething. Great God, must everyone he encountered remind him? That driver, with the smudge of blood and the long golden hair clinging to it, rose again before him as it had so many times before, and in the privacy of his own office once more he buried his face in his hands to ward off the vision. When, in heaven's name, would he be free from them all?

At least, his dismal treading of the eternal mill here had ceased forever. When he turned over his books to Sherwood on the morrow and locked his desk, he knew that he would never reopen it. When he returned from the fishing trip it would be easy to plead further ill-health until the moment came to send in his resignation. This phase of existence was over.

He raised his head and looked about at the small but luxuriously appointed office, grown familiar through more than fifteen years of occupancy; revoltingly familiar, he told himself bitterly. He loathed it all! How had the smug, complacent years slipped by without arousing rebellion in his soul before this? He had been a mere cog in the machine No! Not even that!—a useless appendage, tolerated because of his father! And all the time, how little these daily associates of his had known of the real man, of his possibilities, his subsequent achievements!

He had fooled them, deceived them all, gotten away with two stupendous crimes under their very noses, by gad, and not one of them had an inkling of the truth!

A tap upon the ground glass door interrupted his selflaudation, and Millard entered.

"Hello, Storm. Came to see if you would run out and have a bite of lunch with me," he began. "Glad you've reconsidered your decision to take that long trip. Holworthy told me the news. Deucedly hot today, isn't it?"

"Holworthy?" Storm repeated in unguarded annoyance. What perverse fate had brought those two together?

"Yes," Millard replied to the unvoiced query. "When he 'phoned to me this morning I asked him out to Greenlea, but he said he couldn't come; had to work late at the office with Abbott putting him in touch with his details for the next fortnight because you and he—Holworthy, I mean—were going off fishing together. Delighted to hear it, old chap; only I wish I could join you, but you know how I am tied up at home. It will do you a lot more good than months of poking around by yourself thousands of miles from home."

He chattered on, but Storm scarcely heard. What had George telephoned to him about? The Horton case had not even been mentioned between them on the previous night, but Storm knew well the tenacity of George's grasp of an opinion or theory. Had he been sufficiently interested to try to probe Millard for further news? But what news could there be?

This time he voiced the thought aloud.

"How about our wager, Millard? Still think you are going to win?"

"I wish I were as sure of eternal salvation!" the other retorted stoutly. "Of course I'll win, Storm; that man and the money will be found!"

"So it is 'that' man now, eh?" Storm watched him narrowly. "Your friends at Headquarters have given up the idea of a gang, then? They think it was a one-man job?"

"Well, no, not exactly." Millard wriggled uncomfortably in the chair in which he had seated himself, uninvited. "I haven't learned anything further from that source, but Holworthy's theory the other night sounded mighty feasible to me. It is a lot more likely that Horton met some close friend .and went off quietly to make a night of it than that he trusted himself with that bag in his possession to a crowd; and he couldn't very well have been kidnapped. Holworthy is getting to be as much of a bug on the case as I am. Said his one regret in leaving town was that he would not be able to keep in touch with it. He told me when he called me up to ask about the papers—"

"What papers?" Storm interrupted.

"Why, those that were found wadded around the pistol in the bag," explained the other. "He wanted to know what the names of them were and I told him they were all 'Daily Bulletins' of May twenty-eigth, thirtieth—"

"Oh, for the Lord's sake Millard, don't go over all that again I" Storm cried in uncontrollable exasperation.

Millard snickered.

"That's what Holworthy said, or words to that effect. He had the dates all down pat." Then his face grew grave. "You may laugh at it if you like, but I think it is a very important clue and one that is apt to be a big factor in the solution of the case."

"If you are basing your hopes of winning the money on a wad of unmarked sheets of newspapers, I'll get it from Holworthy and spend it for you now." Storm laughed a trifle grimly. "You two are a couple of nuts over this thing! I hope Holworthy will leave his theories behind him when he hits the woods trail with me!"

Millard took the hint and rose.

"You'll see!" he declared. "How about lunch?"

Storm shook his head.

"Sorry. Like to, old man, but I'm turning my books over to an associate tomorrow and I'm up to my ears in work. By the way, I've dismissed my gardener, MacWhirter, who has been looking after the house out at Greenlea. It really doesn't require a caretaker, you know, and he has got a job as assistant ground keeper at the club."

"He is a very good man," Millard observed. "He kept your garden in wonderful shape in the old days. How proud your poor wife was of her flowers!—Well, I'll run on. Hope I shall see you again before you start on your trip, but if I don't, I wish you the best of luck!"

"And you, with your wager," Storm called after him. "Remember, the money *and* the man, Millard!"

When the door had closed he sprang from his chair. Leila and her flowers! Would no one let him forget? On a sudden impulse he had told Millard a modified version of MacWhirter's defection in order to silence any idle gossip which might spring up at the club and in so doing he had brought that tactless reminder down about his own ears.

He could see her now in a soft cotton frock standing out under a towering old lilac bush, its top just burgeoning in clusters of misty lavender, the sun glinting down between the branches on her golden hair. When she was warm it used to curl in little moist tendrils about her forehead and the nape of her slender, white neck, and it felt like spun silk between one's fingers...

Storm struck his forehead sharply with his clenched fist. What was the matter with him today? Why couldn't he control his treacherous, wandering thoughts? This last unnerving vision had been Millard's fault, curse him! Well, he was through with Millard, just as he was through with Langhorne and all the crew here and at the club! They were out of his path from this moment on! Only George remained to be tolerated a while longer for discretion's sake—

Then the thought recurred to him of George's telephoned query to Millard. What on earth did he care about the papers that were found in the bag? Horton had been a mere acquaintance of his of years gone by; why should he take such a profound interest in the murder?

Could old George have begun to suspect the truth after all? During the long evening in his rooms on the previous night nothing had been discussed save the proposed fishing trip, and at its end they had not definitely decided where to go; but George had seemed full of plans and as carefree and eager as a boy for the anticipated outing. Could this have been all a blind?

He remembered, too, how George had evaded comment on Colonel Walker's disclosure. Storm had concluded then that the whole thing had gone miles over George's head; but what if it had struck home? What if he were mulling the affair over in secret in his slow, plodding mind, correlating the facts he had learned, fitting them in with his theory?

But the most important link of all, the keystone upon which any structure of circumstantial evidence against Storm could have been built in the other's thoughts, was the one thing which had assuredly escaped his notice: the fact that the newspapers with which they had packed the trunk had been incomplete, and the significance of the dates. Amid the turmoil of Storm's own brain that loomed as a clear conviction beyond all doubt, and once more his fears subsided and confidence was reborn.

George had expounded his theory as far as it went, and it pointed merely to some unknown friend of Horton's, some presumable associate of his later years. Pah! Let George play upon that string until it broke; let him spend the rest of the summer trying to ferret out Horton's immediate past and round up the latter's acquaintances, if he had become such a "bug" about the case as Millard had asserted! Let them both work themselves into a fine frenzy over the missing sheets of the "Bulletin," memorize the dates, hang about Headquarters, make asses of themselves generally!

Once and for all, he was done with weak misgivings and unwarranted fears! They would never learn the truth; no one would ever know it. It was locked in the breast of the one man in the world who had the genius to conceive such a brilliant, sublimely simple coup, the courage to carry it out and the patience and strategy to await the assured outcome. What had he to do with these lesser minds and their quibbling and straw-splitting?

A bit of current slang came whimsically to his mind, and Storm smiled as he slammed down his desk and reached for his hat. He had put this stunt over; now let them all come!

XXIV

IF GEORGE KNEW

After a hasty and solitary lunch Storm returned to his office, and forcing all other thoughts aside he devoted himself throughout the long afternoon to getting his books and files in order to hand over to Sherwood the next day. He had always been as methodical as a machine in the affairs of the trust company, and his task itself was not difficult, although he found it no easy matter to concentrate, and his head ached dully.

The first real heat of the summer had come in a blaze of tropic intensity which seemed to rise in blasting waves from the baking streets, and as Storm worked he felt a strange lassitude creeping over him. What if he were to be ill? That was one consideration which had not occurred to him, and, stifling as he was, a chill seemed to strike at the core of his being. Illness might mean delirium, and in delirium men babbled of the most secret, hidden things! He imagined himself lying inert and helpless, the guard of consciousness loosed from his tongue, his disordered brain stealing back over the forbidden hours of the past; and in fancy he could hear the words which should spell his doom issuing from his fevered lips.

It must not come to pass! By sheer force of will alone he must not permit himself to fall ill, at least until he had left the city and all who knew him forever behind; until he was in a strange land, where his very language would not be understood!

Bright spots were dancing before his eyes, and the pain in his head had increased; but by a supreme effort he flung off the lethargy which had settled upon him and completed his task. The building was almost deserted when he made his way out at last; the rush hour had started, and he turned disgustedly from the swarms of wilted, wearied toilers who blocked the entrance to elevated staircases and subways. Thank God that tomorrow would be his last day of all this!

Sunset had brought no relief, and the reeking asphalt seemed to melt and sink beneath his feet as he dragged himself over to the Square for a taxi. Was it only the heat that was affecting him so strangely or could it be really illness after all? Would Homachi find him in the morning muttering and raving at the two shadowy figures which delirium would bring to stand at his bedside? Would strange doctors come to listen and wonder and finally summon the police?

Shuddering with horror at the vision, Storm climbed into the first open taxi that he saw and giving his Riverside Drive address, sank back against the cushions with closed eyes. He felt that never in his life had he so wanted human companionship, not even on that night when he had encountered Jack Horton in the rain; yet he dared not summon anyone. George would drop his affairs with Abbott and come, of course, but George was the last person in the world whom he would want near if he were not to be in full possession of his faculties. There was no one he could trust; he stood alone! In health and strength, with the guard of reticence about him, he could walk among men, but at the first weakening, the first inkling of the truth all mankind would be upon him like a pack of wolves, tearing him down!

As the taxi turned into the Drive at length a breath of cooler air blew up from the river, and when they reached the door of his apartment house Storm felt more at ease, although his head still throbbed and a weight seemed dragging at his limbs.

His rooms, as he let himself in with his latchkey, were dim and cool and inviting, and with a shiver of distaste at the thought of food he threw himself across the bed and almost at once fell into a heavy, troubled sleep.

When he awoke the moonlight was flooding the room, casting vague, fantastic shadows in the corners and grouping them about the head of his bed. Storm sat up, bewildered. His throat felt drawn and parched, his head ached splittingly and a vague but insistent craving assailed him.

Then he remembered and got weakly to his feet. He had had no dinner, nothing since that hasty, unappetizing noonday meal. He groped his way to the light switch in the living-room and turning it on, blinked dazedly at the clock. It was after midnight! He must have lain for many hours in that exhausted sleep as if drugged.

But he felt better, at any rate; the lassitude was gone and his head was clearer, even though it ached. He would be all right in the morning...

Foraging about, he found bread and cheese in the pantry and milk and fruit in the ice chest and upon these he made a simple but satisfying meal.

It was cooler; there was no doubt about it. A freshening breeze was sweeping up from the river and blowing in the curtains at the living-room windows.

Storm decided impulsively upon a stroll before turning in again. He had not indulged in one of his nocturnal walks since that momentous one with Jack Horton the week before; but he need not bring that back too vividly by venturing in the same direction, and his throbbing head demanded the fresh night air. Why should he think of Horton now? Last week was past and dead, as dead as last month, as this whole, wretched, nerve-racking time would be a year from now when he would be far away, and all of this forgotten!

Yet when he reached the path he found his feet insensibly turning toward the incline beyond the viaduct, around that turn where the ground sloped so sharply down from the wall. With returning strength the impulse came to test himself, to see if he had sufficient nerve to stroll past that spot where in the darkness he had struck that single, sure blow. Why not? Surely no suspicion could attach to him for that! It was public property, the path was free to all and there would be nothing strange about a midnight stroll after the terrific heat of the day should anyone chance to cross his path.

Could he do it? Could he bring himself to walk slowly, steadily up that incline, to pass without faltering that place against the wall where Horton's body had crumpled; to go on without a backward glance into the shadows that would lurk behind? Surely no other man in the world would dare such a supreme test of his fortitude, his strength! Could he see it through?

Storm threw back his shoulders and with measured, determined tread started upon the path. The moon was sinking behind a cloud, the breeze blew in sharper, angrier gusts and the stir in the treetops had become a sibilant, whispering chorus. It might be that a storm was brewing, but it would not come until long after he was safe at home again, and he was rather glad that the moon's eerie light was fading; it had a tricky way of bringing unfamiliar angles into sharp relief, casting weird shadows to creep after one, filling one with a senseless desire to walk faster, to glance behind...

Here was where they had walked when Horton boasted so about his girl! What a complacent, self-satisfied creature he had been! Common, too; how a few years of roughing it brought out the bourgeois streak in a man! Everything about him had grated, repelled; his swagger, his laugh, the animal-like gusto with which he ate and drank and smoked. What a boor!

Yonder was the street lamp and here the place where Storm himself had halted ostensibly to light a cigarette, but in reality to wait until the approaching figure of the policeman should have advanced into the surrounding shadows. There was no policeman tonight; no living thing seemed to be abroad save himself, and the path ahead looked all at once lonely and foreboding.

It rose sharply now; he had reached the foot of the incline. This was where Horton had first suggested going back, and he had argued for the sight of the river steamer when she came around the turn. Horton had been descanting on his future with the Mid-Eastern people; his future, which had come to an end there ahead where the wall sloped! He had been so sure of himself!

But surely the wind was rising! These summer showers came up with amazing suddenness; perhaps it would be as well—?

No! Storm shook himself angrily and plodded doggedly on. He would make no weak excuses to himself, pander to no womanish impulse to evade. This was a moral test and he would see it through!

It was just here that the automobile had appeared, roaring and careening down the road. What fools the authorities were to make such a point of its wild progress! Even old George, dense as he was, had seen the improbability of its connection with that night's event.

There was the turn in the path just ahead, where the shadows lay thickest. Storm could feel the moisture gathering beneath the band of his hat, and it seemed to him that an ever-increasing weight was attached to his feet, dragging them back. The whisper in the trees had changed to a rising moan, and the swaying branches threw clutching shadows out across the path.

Here was the spot, at last! Here was where he had suggested that Horton look to see if the steamer were coming, where he himself had stepped back, rasping a dead match against his cigarette case that the other might hear and not wonder why his companion loitered; where he had gripped that heavy cane part way down its length, where he had raised it—A-ah!

A sharp, hissing gasp escaped from Storm's lips, to be caught up and carried away on a gust of wind, and he halted, staring at the figure which had seemed to rise from nowhere to confront him.

Then for a fleeting instant a rift in the cloud wrack sent a streak of pale moonlight shimmering down, and by its glow Storm saw the familiar blue uniform of a policeman.

"Good-evening, Officer." Was that his own voice, that casually cordial drawl?

" 'Evening, sir." The other's tone was civil enough, but was not his glance a trifle too keen, too questioning?

"Looks as though we were going to have a storm."

"It does that, sir."

What was the fellow waiting for? Why didn't he go on about his business? Storm felt that he himself could not move. He seemed held to the spot as by invisible chains. Why was the policeman eying him so strangely?

"I've walked further than I meant, myself, but I guess I'll get home before it starts." He forced a laugh. "Couldn't sleep and came out for a stroll and then remembered about that murder last week; thought I'd have a look at the spot, but I can't seem to find it from the newspaper description. It happened somewhere about here, didn't it, Officer?"

"*Just* here, sir. You're standing on the very spot now," the policeman responded with emphasis. "See that place on the wall there by the bush? That's where they figure the body was thrown over. As for the murder itself: well, it's not come out yet where that was done, but 'twas just down from here that the body was found."

"Indeed! Are you sure?" Storm assumed an unconsciously clever imitation of Millard's eager curiosity.

"I ought to be, sir! I've pointed it out enough of times since." There was a touch of weariness in the official's tones. "What with them operatives from the private agency, and the coal company's men, to say nothing of the nuts and cranks—"

He paused significantly and Storm took up the cue.

"I'm coming back here in the daytime; I've a theory of my own about this case!" he announced confidentially. "Let me see; I'll know the spot by that clump of trees and the bench. You know, Officer—"

"Excuse *me*, sir!" the policeman interrupted in utter boredom. "I've got to be getting on down my beat."

"I'll walk on with you," proposed Storm equably. "I live down the Drive a bit and it is too dark for me to poke around up here now."

The other accepted his companionship with resignation, and they started down the path while Storm inwardly congratulated himself upon the skill with which he had handled the situation. It was unique, unheard-of! That he, the murderer, should encounter an officer of the law on the very scene of his crime, successfully foster the belief that he was a harmless crank and presently slip through that official's fingers! Oh, it was colossal!

"I've read every word the papers have printed about this affair," he went on, still in that guileless, confidential tone. "I can't conceive why the body wasn't found before."

"Reason enough!" the officer asserted with warmth. "There's no path down there, nothing but a steep slope of shale and bushes between the wall and the railroad tracks, and no one's ever along there but a track walker now and then. There's a dump and two docks near, but the road leads down from under the Drive at the viaduct. If it hadn't been for them boys playing around, the body mightn't have been found till Christmas, and no blame to the Department!"

Every nerve in Storm's body shook with the tension, and he could feel the sweat starting from his pores; but they had left that spot behind and every slow, swinging step took them further from it. He had no intention of permitting the policeman to note the street near which he lived; a few blocks further on and he would take leave of him and cut across the Drive. A few blocks—but he must play up, he must not drop his role for an instant.

"I don't think that automobile that the papers make so much of had anything to do with it, do you, Officer?" he asked in a loquacious tone, adding: "A friend of mine has a friend at Headquarters who told him that two men were seen walking together on the Drive here only a little before the time when the murder was supposed to have been committed, and one of them—"

"Say!" the other interrupted disgustedly. "Some guy at Headquarters must have a mighty big mouth! You're the second that's been after me about that!"

"After you!" Storm repeated.

"Sure. I'm the one seen them," the policeman retorted. "And what of it? I've had no orders since I've been on the Force to interfere with two respectable-appearing gentlemen walking along cold sober and peaceable, and minding their own business, just as you come to be out here tonight yourself, sir! They'd no more to do with the murder than you had! Of course, when the body was found I had to report them, but that would have been the end of it if some guy down there hadn't been shooting his mouth off!"

"But if you are the officer who passed them," Storm insisted, "my friend says he was told that your description of one of them fitted the dead man—"

"As it would fit any big, well-built fellow you met in the dark!" the policeman snorted contemptuously. "Besides, as far as I made out from a passing look at him he was wearing a cap of some kind. There was none found anywhere near the dead man, and his own hat was hid away in that bag down at the Grand Central Station. If that boob at Headquarters—"

"But the other man who was with him—?" Storm steadied his voice carefully. "Did you get a good look at him, Officer? What was he like?"

"Look here, what are you after, anyway?" the policeman demanded in exasperation. "What's it to you? I'm not here on my beat to be answering questions and I had enough last night with that little fat guy pestering me for an hour! I've nothing to say, sir! Go to the friend of your friend at Headquarters and get what you can out of him!"

'Last night—little fat guy'! The words struck Storm with the force of a blow, and he recalled that the officer had complained only a few minutes before: 'You're the second that has been after me'! Who could that other have been? Not Millard, surely! He voiced the doubt aloud:

"It couldn't have been my friend who bothered you about it last night, Officer. He's getting stout, but he is not short."

"Well, this guy was, and with a big bald spot on top, too, as I saw when he took off his hat to wipe his forehead under the lamp there! He kept squinting at me with his nearsighted eyes and jotting down what I said in a little book till I felt as if I was up before the Board!" The officer's tone had grown slightly mollified. "You'll excuse me for being short with you, sir, but this thing happening on my beat and all has made me fair sick. I've not eyes on the back of my head nor yet the kind that can see in the dark, and I can't be in two places at once! You'd think to hear some of the knocks I've had right in my own platoon that I'd been asleep on the job!"

'Bald—nearsighted— —!' George! The questioner had been George Holworthy!

"I don't know how you could be expected to see a dead man being brought to that spot on the hill up there and dumped over the wall if you were down—well, here, say," Storm remarked consolingly, but his tone was absent. He must get away from his companion at once; he must be alone to think.

"Great Scott, I've passed my street and I believe—yes, it's beginning to rain! Good night, Officer! I'm glad of this little talk—"

"Don't mention it, sir!" The other's words had been balm to his sore spirit, and the policeman beamed. "Good night, sir!"

Storm crossed the Drive, and despite the rain which came pattering down in a quickening shower he turned north again to make good his statement. At the end of the block he halted beneath a jutting cornice and waited until he calculated that the policeman must be a safe distance away, then retraced his steps and hurried on down the Drive to his own rooms, heedless of the torrent which drenched him.

So Millard was right! George had become a 'bug' about the Horton case! Storm recalled that at the dinner on Tuesday, when Millard told of the encounter on the Drive with the two men which the policeman had reported, George had announced that he would like to talk with the officer. Millard said he could be found on his beat at about the same time on any night, and George had evidently taken him at his word. He must have hunted up the policeman immediately after leaving Storm's rooms on the previous night. What could have put the impulse into his head? For a wonder, the murder had not even been mentioned between the two during the entire evening.

Why had he not announced his intention? Storm could not conceive of deliberate reticence on the part of old George I No, he couldn't have planned it; he probably ran into the policeman by accident after he left the house, and remembering the incident which Millard had described he must have plied him with questions until the good-natured official writhed.

Yet he had jotted down the replies in a little book, and in the morning he had called up Millard for further information as to the name of newspapers found in Horton's bag. He could not have an inkling of the truth, of course. It must be as Storm had concluded that morning; that George, still adhering to his theory of the murder having been a one-man job, was seeking to confirm it in his own mind before trying to locate some recent associate or crony of Horton's who might have been with him on that night.

He would never reach the true solution, of course, but it was just as well, all things considered, that he was to be dragged away on that fishing trip and compelled to drop his self-imposed rôle of investigator until the police themselves relegated the case to the shelf.

Storm had removed his dripping garments, and arrayed himself in his pajamas, and as he turned off the light and went to bed a thought came which made him smile grimly in the darkness.

He had done it twice, and gotten away with it. He could do it a third time! If George knew, if George betrayed the least sign of being on the right track, then he, too, must be eliminated!

Up there in the woods alone Storm could sound him, could analyze every word and inflection and look; there would be no habitation near, no one within sight or hearing for days. If murder could be so simply, successfully accomplished here in the heart of the city, what mere child's play it would be up in there in the wilderness!

He chuckled aloud, unconscious that he was giving audible voice to his reflections:

"One thing is sure; nothing must interfere with that trip! *I've got to go fishing with George!*"

XXV

THE FINAL TEST

When Storm arose in the morning his head still ached in a dull, insistent way; but his energy had returned, and the thought which had been his last before sleep had crystallized into a definite decision. He must study George's every move during that fishing trip, probe him on every point of the case, weigh with a clear, unprejudiced mind every slightest possibility of his learning the truth and then act as his final judgment dictated.

The midnight shower had cooled the air, and Storm reached his office early, determined to conclude the formalities there in as short order as possible. He found Sherwood awaiting him, and they put in a busy morning over the transfer of the books and files. He listened in a sort of grim apathy to the kindly expressions of good-wishes for the pleasure and benefit which his vacation might bring to him, took leave of his associates, shook the flabby hand of Nicholas Langhorne and made his escape.

At last! He was through! Through forever with the dull grind, the hypocritical sympathy of his colleagues, the maddening patronage of that pompous old millionaire, who hadn't one-tenth of the brains, the genius that was his! How little they had known him through all those years; how little they suspected that this brief vacation would be extended for a lifetime, that he had shaken the sanctimonious dust of that most aristocratic institution from his feet forever!

He had laid his plans in that long hour before sleep came to him, and now he hurried to the nearest telegraph office, sent off several despatches and then called up George.

"Say!" that individual expostulated over the wire. "How on earth are we going to start on Monday if you don't make up your mind where you want to go? I expected to hear from you all day yesterday—"

"That's all right; I've fixed it!" Storm responded. "Come up to my rooms tonight. I'll have Homachi give us a little dinner and we can talk over the final arrangements then."

"Did you get those bass flies?" demanded George.

"No. I will, this afternoon."

"Well, have you sent word out to MacWhirter to have your fishing gear brought in? How about your clothes? Will he know what to pack?" George's tone was filled with an anxious solicitude that was almost ludicrously maternal. "You needn't bother about mourning up there, you know; you'll want the oldest clothes you've got, and your hip boots, and don't forget about that rod—"

"I know, I—I'll attend to it," stammered Storm. "Come up about seven, will you?"

He rang off, his mind in a quandary. George had known nothing of MacWhirter's defection, but his words had reminded the other that the house at Greenlea was locked up and there was no one to pack up his fishing gear unless he went out and did it for himself. He could not send Homachi, who would not know where to find anything, and the thought of telephoning to one of the neighbors of the Green- lea colony and enlisting their aid was out of the question; they, male or female, would like nothing better than a chance to go through the house unmolested and pry into every detail of the home which had been so tragically broken up.

He must go himself; that was plain. He thought of MacWhirter's manner on the previous day and shivered involuntarily; then the episode of the night recurred to him and he smiled. He had tested himself and in the test had encountered the unforseen, but it had not daunted him. His strength, his nerve, his ingenuity had been equal to the situation, would be equal to any exigency of the future! What was there now in all the world for him to fear?

He would go back to Greenlea, and George should go with him! They would spend the night there, and then whatever ghosts of memory the old house held for him would be laid forever.

His decision made, he stopped at a sporting goods shop, purchased the flies, lines and a new reel, and then returned to his rooms to await the replies to his telegrams of the morning.

Here a new difficulty confronted him. The money! Those packets of greenbacks and tiny roulades of gold which he had taken life itself to gain! He could not go away for a week or more and leave them reposing there in that flimsy safe! There were duplicates of it in every apartment in the house. It was even conceivable that Potter himself might have missed something of value and thinking that he had left it in the safe, return unexpectedly and open it. There might be a fire! Any of a hundred possibilities could happen which would betray his secret to the world.

Yet it was out of the question for him to take it with him. He could not carry it about him, for in the enforced intimacy of camp life he would be unable to conceal it from George; and he well knew that the latter would rummage at will in every article of hand-baggage. Moreover, the packets of bills were too bulky, and the ten thousand dollars in gold alone must weigh approximately forty pounds

But where could he secrete it during his absence?

Storm sat with his head upon his hands, wrestling with the problem. The fishing trip could not be given up now. He must go with George, must try him out and then if he were likely to prove a menace, must destroy him. But the money! There was no hiding place in the world where it would be safe...

Then the solution burst full grown into being; and he sprang from his chair.

Greenlea! There was a place in the cellar of the house where the concrete floor had been removed to lay some pipes and had never been replaced. Sand and soft loam filled the space, and it would be easy enough to bury a tin despatch box there. Several such boxes were in the attic, he knew, and packed carefully in one of them the bills and gold would be safe from discovery for the brief time he would be away.

But if George accompanied him, how could he——? Bah! He had nothing now to fear from George or anyone! He could pack the money into a bag and carry it down under George's very nose and he would suspect nothing! It would take nerve, of course, but was he not master of himself, invincible?

He would keep the bag close beside him throughout the night, and in the morning, at the last moment, he would contrive an excuse to remain behind George. There would be so much to do in town that the latter would be compelled to take an early train back, and after his departure it would not be the work of half an hour to stuff the money into the despatch box and bury it in that open space in the cellar. The thing was as good as done now!

Sending Homachi out to purchase supplies for the dinner, Storm waited only until the door had closed after him, and then, rushing to the storeroom, he dragged out a huge, battered old valise. Into this he transferred the money, packing it carefully between layers of old clothing, lest the cylinders of gold become unrolled and clink together. When it was all safely stowed away he filled the top of the valise with discarded linen and closing it, lifted it experimentally from the floor.

Its weight seemed prodigious, and he was badly out of condition, he knew. Would his flabby muscles stand the strain of carrying it? Storm set his lips resolutely. He must force himself to do it; there was no other way. He had whipped his faltering strength into obeying his will before, and his will was. absolutely supreme!

When George arrived promptly at seven he found his host in a more genial mood than he had exhibited for weeks, with a hint of eager anticipation in his manner which recalled the old, high-spirited Norman of days long gone.

"You look better already!" George beamed at him. "Where are we going, anyway? You said over the 'phone that you'd fixed it, but I don't—"

Storm gathered up a sheaf of telegrams from the desk and seizing his guest by the arm dragged him off to the dining-room.

"Come on and let us have dinner. We can talk while we eat; we haven't any too much time."

"Time!" repeated George. "We're not going anywhere this evening!"

"Aren't we?" Storm laughed. "Homachi has a chicken casserole for us tonight and some new asparagus with a sauce which he fondly believes to be Hollandaise. I hope you are good and hungry; I know I am."

"But what's all this mystery?" George demanded, after Homachi had served them. "Who are all those telegrams from? I hope you haven't gone and arranged some long trip, Norman. You know we can't stay away for more than a week, and we'll get mighty little fishing if we spend most of the time on the cars!"

George was a poor traveler and knew it. Storm smiled.

"Do you remember that old hunting lodge up on Silver Run where we camped when we went fishing one year a good while ago? I happen to know that it has been unoccupied for several seasons, and I wired to the owners to borrow it. Pierre, my old guide, lives only about twenty miles away, at Three Forks Carry, and I sent a telegram to him to go and get it ready for us. Here are the replies." Storm produced two of the messages and handed them across the table. "The others were to fellows whose camps I thought we might use if the lodge wasn't available, but they are all occupied."

"It sounds good," George said slowly as he passed the telegrams back. "But did you arrange for this Pierre to stay and look out for us? You know you are not much on roughing it, and I—I'm getting confoundedly fat!"

"Lazy dub!" Storm jeered. Then his tone grew pleading, although he could feel his face flushing, in spite of himself, beneath the other's candid, inquiring gaze. "That's just it! We don't want Pierre, or anyone. That was the trouble with all those places you suggested; they were too civilized, too popular. I don't want to go and live at a club or farmhouse and whip up a stream where you are likely to meet a dozen other fishermen in a day! I don't even want to have a guide fussing around; I want to be just alone with you. I thought if we could get away absolutely by ourselves and tramp and fish and do our own bit of cooking and sleep out in the open on the ground if we felt like it, that it would be immense!"

He paused, waiting with keen anxiety for the reply. Would George rise to the bait?

"You've caught any number of fish, but did you ever clean 'em?" the other asked doubtfully at length. "You know you hate cold water, and the last time we went to the Reel and Rifle Club you kicked like a steer because the beds were so hard—"

"Oh, if you want modem plumbing and silver platters, don't come; that's all!" Storm interrupted in well simulated disgust. He had detected the signs of yielding in George's manner and knew that the way was clear. "I tell you I really want to go back to primitive things. I'm sick of the world and everything in it!

I wish I had stuck to my original plan and thrown over everything here and gone out to the East—"

"All right!" George exclaimed hurriedly. "I was only thinking of you. I would like it first rate, and this Pierre of yours says that the bass are running fine! Only, if you come back with sciatica from this open air sleeping stunt, don't blame me! I shall take a hammock!"

"Good old sport! I was sure you would see it my way. We'll have the time of our lives!" Storm touched the bell. "Homachi, bring our coffee in a hurry, will you, and whatever else you have? We've got to be off!"

"Off where?" George betrayed symptoms of anxiety. "I thought we were going to pack!"

"Pack what?" demanded Storm coolly. "I haven't a blessed thing here, old man."

"Norman! I told you—!" George paused. "And tomorrow is Saturday."

"I know, but I forgot to tell you; there is nobody out at Greenlea." Storm chose his words carefully. "MacWhirter came in yesterday and told me that he had been offered another position with bigger money immediately, and as his month was up I was forced to let him go."

"There's gratitude for you!" George snorted indignantly. "And all your stuff down there—"

"I never thought of that until you mentioned it over the telephone today." Storm sighed, watching his friend furtively. "I'll have to go myself, of course. I will not have time tomorrow, and if I appeared in Greenlea on Sunday you know how the crowd would all come trooping in to see me and condole with me all over again. It would drive me mad! There is only tonight, George, and the thought of spending it alone in that house—I thought perhaps you would come down with me and see it through—"

"Of course I will!" George said warmly. "I wouldn't think of having you down there all alone in that empty place in your state! What train can we get? I haven't anything with me—"

"We can catch the nine o'clock if we start soon. We will find everything that we may need for the night down there." Storm's face was inscrutable. "I'm taking down an old valise with some things in it that I want to leave there; stuff I forgot to put in that trunk we sent down last week. If you have finished your coffee, I'll ring for a taxi."

When the car came Homachi stood ready to take his employer's bag out to it, but Storm waved him aside.

"I'll carry it myself," he said.

"It looks deucedly heavy," George remarked, eying the valise critically as they passed out of the entrance. "What's in it anyway?"

"Just some old clothes, some account books and a—a packet of letters that I brought up with me myself." Storm deposited the bag carefully on the floor of the taxi between his feet and then sank back with his face in the shadow. "I thought I might like to look them over but I—I can't, just yet."

George's hand gripped his shoulder for a minute in silent sympathy, and Storm suppressed a smile. What a sentimental, gullible fool! One reference to Leila, however vague, and he became the conventional mourner at once. He was really too easy!

When they reached the station Storm left the other to pay the taxi and holding his valise so that his arm would not betray the strain upon it too obviously, went ahead through the gates.

There was no one on the train whom they knew, and during the brief ride out to Greenlea they discussed the fishing trip in desultory fashion. George was evidently apprehensive of the effect upon his friend's spirits of this return to old scenes saddened with tragic memories, but Storm himself felt no depression.

The money was there at his feet! The money to take him away from all this forever! When he cabled George later to sell the house, let *him* come out here and weep over the relics if he felt like it! This was just another final test of his own nerve, that was all, and he defied the house or its memories to break him down. The past was dead, and this was just a visit to its grave, nothing more.

They found a jitney at the Greenlea station, and this time George stooped for the valise, but Storm forestalled him.

"No, thanks, old man. I don't mind carrying it."

"But you are tired. Let me—"

"For heaven's sake go on!" Storm exclaimed irritably. "I want to carry it myself, I tell you!"

Once in the jitney, however, he essayed swiftly to efface the effect of the outburst.

"Don't mind me, George; I'm not quite myself. It is a little trying, you know, to come out here again, but I didn't mean to act like a spoiled kid over such a trifle."

"That's all right, Norman; you're tired." George's tone was affectionately magnanimous. "Go to bed tonight as soon as you feel sleepy and I'll finish the packing. I know every inch of the house and just what you will need to take with you."

Nothing more was said until they drove up before the veranda. Everything was dark and abysmally silent, and the vines had grown in a tangled riot over the steps. Storm stumbled with his precious burden and almost fell, but he caught himself in time, shaking with sudden fear. God, if he had dropped that old valise and it had split asunder scattering the gold and banknotes in the darkness!

XXVI

THE KEY

By Jove, old man, I forgot that I have had the gas fA and electricity turned off!" Storm's voice echoed back eerily, mockingly, from the silent rooms to where George had halted on the threshold. "The water is on still, though, thank the Lord! and the telephone, too. We'll need that in the morning to 'phone for a car to take us to the station, for we both forgot to tell that jitney driver to come back for us. — I know where there are a lot of candles upstairs. You wait here and I'll get them."

George stood obediently by the open door and heard Storm's fumbling footsteps pass up the stair. Then they died away into silence. The jitney had chugged off down the road, and only the sound of the night breeze rustling the vines on the veranda came to him. Unimaginative as he was, the house was so filled for him with memories of his friend's wife that it seemed to him a gentle presence slept there, waiting only for light and the sound of their voices to call it into being. He could not have spoken aloud at that moment to save his life, so profoundly stirred was he; and he wondered at Storm's fortitude. It was only a bluff, of course, a brave attempt to hide his breaking heart, and George felt a swift, strong wave of compassionate admiration for his friend. Poor old Norman!

Presently he heard him moving about overhead, and at last a light appeared, dim and wavering, at the head of the stairs. Other lights sprang up and then Storm descended.

"I've left four burning up there; got to go back and get the rods and bags and stuff," he announced. George noticed that he had left the heavy valise upstairs. "Here! You hold this and we'll light more and stick them around."

"Not all over the place!" George objected. "Get all your things together in one room and we'll pack there."

"All right. The library, then." Storm made for the door, his candle held aloft over his head, and paused. "Hello I MacWhirter had that trunk I sent down dumped in here!— Never mind, it won't be in our way."

George had moved about the room, lighting candles and placing them in every available receptacle with a fine disregard of the dropping wax; and now he turned to his companion.

"Where is your old camp outfit?" he asked.

"Oh, Pierre will have all the blankets and pots and pans and things of that sort," replied Storm carelessly. "We will take our supplies from town. All we need from here are clothes and fishing gear and the bags to pack them in. The clothes are in the closets upstairs and the rest of the stuff in the attic."

"Well, let us assemble it all here first and then sort it out," suggested George. "If I once get it all together you can go to bed whenever you like and I'll finish the job. You look about all in."

Storm shook his head, but he realized the truth of his friend's words. The continued strain of the past days had been terrific, and the effort to nerve himself for this final test of his own strength and endurance had proved greater than he knew. The pain in his head, which had throbbed ceaselessly for two days, was gone, but he felt a sense of mental and physical fatigue which was akin to exhaustion.

The test had proved to be no test, after all. This dark, silent, dismantled house had seemed utterly strange to him from the moment when the first echoes of his voice had died away. Even the familiar furniture was distorted and unreal in the flickering flames of the candles. Daylight perhaps would bring poignant memories, but tonight he was too tired. It did not seem that he and Leila had ever lived there, and the events of that hideous night were like a dream. The only real, vital thing in all that house to him was that valise beneath his bed upstairs. If ghosts stalked in the morning he would have but to fix his mind on that and they would vanish!

"If you are too tired I can get the stuff together myself." George's patient voice broke in upon his musing, and he roused himself with a start.

"No. Come along. It won't take long."

Together they made several trips, and soon a heterogeneous collection of clothes, boots, bags, baskets and fishing paraphernalia overflowed from the couch and chairs into great heaps upon the floor.

"Oh, Lord!" groaned Storm. "What an infernal mess! We'll never get it straightened out, George!"

The other made no response. He was running a practised eye over the conglomeration, and at length he glanced up.

"Where is that four-and-a-half-ounce rod?" he demanded.

"Isn't it there? We must have overlooked it." Storm rose wearily from the top of the trunk where he had perched himself. "It wasn't with the others, so I may have quite a search for it, worse luck!"

"Let me—" George offered, but Storm shook his head.

"No. I want to be sure I didn't leave any candles burning up there, anyway."

While Storm was gone George made a swift inventory. In his own mind he believed privately that his impulsive companion would tire in a few days of the discomforts of camping without a guide and would himself suggest going to the nearest club. That would be the Reel and Rifle, George reflected, and there was a passable nine-hole course there. Storm would want his golf sticks along, but where were they? Surely they had not been taken to town...

Then he closed his eyes and his face contorted in a spasm of swift pain. The last time he had seen those golf sticks they were lying across the table in the den while Leila's body, mercifully composed on the couch after the coroner's visit, lay awaiting the last sad offices.

They were there still in all probability, and George decided to get them himself before Storm returned. It would be needless cruelty to suggest that his friend enter that room again.

Taking a candle, he made his way down the hall. The den door was closed but not locked, and he threw it open and stepped reverentially across the threshold.

The room was in order, but it had not been dismantled as had the others; and although a thin film of dust lay everywhere, it seemed, curiously enough, more cosy, giving out the atmosphere of having been more lately occupied than the rest of the house. Could that be because the presence of the woman who had died there seemed still to linger?

George's faded eyes blurred and the candle shook in his hand, but he advanced to the table. There lay the golf sticks just as he had supposed; and gathering them up he left the den, closing the door behind him, and as he entered the other's eyes traveled to his burden, and a sound very like an oath escaped his lips.

"Where did you get those?" he demanded roughly.

"I—I thought we might run over to the Reel and Rifle and you would need them," George stammered. "You ought to take it up once more, Norman."

Storm threw his hands out with an uncontrollable gesture of horror.

"I shall never play again!" he cried hoarsely. "Take those sticks away out of my sight!"

With a pained, bewildered expression George turned obediently and deposited his burden with a clatter in the corner of the hall. He did not quite understand his old friend these days, and seemed to be forever offending when he meant only to be kind and thoughtful. Of course Storm and Leila had played golf together always, but they had gone on fishing trips together, too, and Storm did not appear to mind the prospect of that. Why should golf hold such particularly poignant memories for him?

Storm meanwhile was fighting hard to regain the mastery over himself that the unexpected sight of those wretched golf sticks had for a moment overthrown. Curse that meddlesome fool! Why had he taken it upon himself to suggest that damned game, above everything else, and how had he dared to get those sticks without even asking!

But the fire of rage died out within him as quickly as it had arisen. Let old George think what he pleased; it didn't matter. He was too tired to dissemble, and besides it would not be worth the effort. George would put it down as just one of his moods, that was all.

Then another thought came to him, and he moved swiftly to the table and opened the drawer. His pistol lay within, and as he picked it up a grim smile twisted the corners of his mouth. It was quite improbable, of course, but there was just a chance that he might find use for it on that fishing trip!

"What are you doing with that?" George demanded from the doorway, much as Storm had spoken the moment before.

The latter laughed jerkily.

"It's not loaded! I was looking to see if it was all right, for we'll take it with us, of course." He threw it carelessly to the couch and reached in the drawer once more. "Here is a box of cartridges. Put them in, too, old man."

"I don't see what you want it for!" George grumbled anxiously. "If two men can't protect themselves against anything they met in those woods without a gun—"

"Silver Run isn't the Beaver Kill, you know!" Storm retorted in a significant tone as he reached into his hip pocket and produced a silver mounted flask. "I'm confoundedly tired; think I'll take a bracer.—Have one?"

George shook his head and Storm drank deeply, then replaced the flask in his pocket with a sigh.

"About that pistol, though. I really prefer to take it along."

"All right." George acquiesced somewhat dubiously. "I never did any hunting, and I am not crazy about having firearms lying around; but if you'll be careful of it and see that it doesn't go off—"

"We won't even load it until we get to the lodge." Storm yawned and sweeping a pile of old corduroys off the nearest chair, sank into it. "Give me those lines and reels and I'll sort them out."

George complied, and for a time they worked in silence while the candles burned low and a fat, furry moth or two thumped against the window pane. Storm took another long drink, but his languor increased, his hands moved more slowly among the tangled lines and at length dropped inertly to his knees. George glanced up to find the other's head fallen forward upon his breast and his eyes closed.

"Norman! Norman, old fellow!"

Storm's head came up with a jerk, and he blinked in the flickering light.

"I—I must have dozed off," he mumbled. "It's funny, but I don't think I ever felt so tired in my life."

"Then go to bed, do! You are worn out, and sleep is just what you need," urged George.

"And leave you with all this to do alone?"

"It won't be as bad as it looks. When I finish picking out what we'll need I can get it stowed away in the bags in no time."

Storm hesitated, and once more a slang phrase came whimsically to his mind. Well, "let George do it," if he wanted to take it upon himself. He was intoxicatingly sleepy, in a spirit of utter relaxation such as he had not known for many weary days. Oh, for one night untroubled by rankling, corroding thoughts and yet more hideous dreams! He felt that he could sleep at last, and nothing else mattered. No harm could come.

"All right, I think I will go to bed, then, if you don't mind." He dragged himself to his feet. "Your old room is all ready, George; the front guest one. Just turn in whenever you are ready, but be sure to put out the candles."

"I will, old man." George nodded from the floor where he sat sprawled, a fat bag braced between his knees. "If you want anything, just call. Good night, and try to get a good rest."

"Good night," Storm responded, and taking up a candle he left the library and went slowly up the stairs.

God! how tired he was! His own bed looked soft and inviting, and he took a pair of old pajamas from a drawer and disrobed as quickly as his fumbling fingers could perform their task, tumbling the contents of his pockets out in a heap on the corner of the bureau. Then he flung himself into the bed and blew out the candle.

Ghosts? Bah! Nothing could trouble him now, and nothing could harm him in the future, for the means was there, within reach of his hand, to carry him far beyond the reach of memories.

With a last waking effort he stretched his arms down and pulled the valise half out from under the bed, where his hand could rest upon it. It was good to feel that bulge beneath the leather! Money was real, all else was but the chimera of one's thought. There was no yesterday, only tomorrow... His reflections dulled, dissolved in chaos, and he slept.

Below in the library George had replenished the candles and returned to his task. He was tired, too, and this return to the old house had depressed him, but he was glad to have relieved Norman of the packing, glad the poor old fellow was going to get one night's tranquil rest.

The fishing gear took the longest to sort and stow away, but when that was finished he turned to the boots and clothing with a relieved mind. A half hour more and he would be through.

The pistol and cartridges he laid gingerly upon the table. They must go in last, and Norman should carry that bag himself. George wished that he would not take it, for in his nervous state he might peg away at some other fishermen by mistake, and there would be the devil to pay! No thought of thwarting his old friend crossed his mind, however; if Norman wanted twenty pistols with him he should have them, if only he returned from this expedition more like his old self!

His task was completed at length, and with a sigh of satisfaction George started to close the last bag when a sudden thought struck him. He had packed everything but headgear. Norman must have some old caps lying around somewhere; old golf caps would be just the thing. He hadn't seen any when they poked about in the closets upstairs. They must be in Norman's rooms in town.

Then his gaze fell upon the trunk. Why, the caps were in there, of course! He had helped to pack them himself only a week ago. Norman must have the key to it on his ring, and it would be a pity to disturb him now; still, George felt that it would be better not to leave it till the morning. In his methodical, bachelor existence he liked to finish a thing once he had started it.

But perhaps he could get the key-ring and open the trunk without disturbing old Norman! If he walked very softly the other need not awaken, and he could give him back his keys in the morning.

George took up a candle, and shielding its flame carefully with his hand he started up the stairs, tiptoeing with exaggerated care. Once a loose board creaked beneath his feet and he paused, as apprehensive as though he were bent upon committing a burglary.

From the stillness above came a long-drawn, reassuring snore, and relieved he plodded on again until he reached the top.

Storm's door was closed, but he turned the handle noiselessly and opening it inch by inch, peered within. Storm was fast asleep, his jaw drooping and upon his relaxed face the hint of an expression which George had never seen before. He looked almost as if he were smiling; smiling at something that was not pleasant to see.

Then George's eyes softened as they traveled down the outflung arm to the inert hand resting against the valise. Poor old Norman! Even in sleep he cared for her, he reached out to touch the receptacle in which were her letters, all that remained to him of her! No one else could realize how much he had cared, he was so self-contained, but George knew!

He glanced somewhat doubtfully at the clothes tumbled upon a chair. Would the key-ring be there in one of the pockets? Somehow, he didn't quite like the idea of going through them. His eyes traveled to the bureau and rested upon the little heap of coins and a watch and other small objects, and he tiptoed over to examine them. There lay the key-ring!

He picked it up and, turning, gave one last look at the sleeper. At that moment Storm's face twitched and the hand against the valise flexed, then slowly relaxed again. Still thinking of her!

George tiptoed out the door and closed it noiselessly behind him.

XXVII

IN THE LIBRARY

George returned to the library, and sorting the smaller keys from the others on the ring he tried them one after the other in the lock of the trunk. He was beginning to despair when at length one fitted, and snapping down the hasps he threw back the lid.

They could not have packed very well, he and Norman, or else the expressmen had been unusually rough in handling the trunk. Its contents had been flung about in wild disorder, and George thought ruefully of the delicate clock and the glass inkwell of the desk set.

He picked out the caps and a mackinaw which might come in handy, and was on the point of closing the trunk when he hesitated. It might be as well to see if that clock were damaged or not; it had been Leila's gift and George knew how much Norman thought of it.

He lifted the other garments out and then the books, revealing the remaining articles wrapped loosely in newspaper. He felt about among them until he found the clock, and as he took it up the paper fell from it and partially opened as it dropped to the floor.

The clock looked all right; its works might be damaged, but at least it was not smashed!

With a sigh of thankfulness George stooped to pick up the paper, when the printed line upon the top margin caught his eye.

"Daily Bulletin, June Ist."

That was an odd coincidence! His thoughts strayed back to the notes he had taken from Millard's disclosures in the Horton case. How many thousands of those newspapers were scattered throughout the city and its environs! Somewhere, someone had put a copy identical with this to its sinister use. Poor Horton!

These were only the outside sheets, too! That was funny! The inside ones must be about another package in the trunk, of course. On a sudden impulse George picked up the desk blotter and unwrapped it. Its covering proved to be the outer double page of the 'Daily Bulletin' for May 28th! Another of the corresponding dates to those on the papers in Horton's bag!

By jingo, there was something queer about this! Without consciously following his bewildered train of thought any farther, George took each package one by one from the trunk and unwrapped it carefully, laying the papers in a neat pile. When he had finished and the trunk was empty he took the newspapers to the table, and spreading them out with trembling hands he sorted them.

Four were complete copies of the 'Bulletin' for June sixth, seventh, eighth, and ninth; the remainder were the outside pages of that paper for—he caught his breath sharply as he examined them—for *May twenty-eigth, thirtieth,* and *thirty-first, June first, third,* and *fourth!* And on each of them was scrawled a rough circle with Storm's apartment number, *"One-A",* within it!

No other scrap of newspaper was visible anywhere, and George knew they had left none about in that living-room in town when they finished packing. Where could the inside pages be?—He must be mistaken in the dates of those papers found in Horton's bag! His memory had failed him!

IN THE LIBRARY

With shaking fingers he tore the notebook from his pocket and read the entry, his eyes fairly starting from his head. No, there had been no mistake! The dates were identical!

This was the most extraordinary, unheard-of coincidence in all the world! But even as his slow-moving mind strove to grasp it, the conviction came that it *could* not be a coincidence! One newspaper, maybe, or two, but not six and only six with the inner sheets gone; *the same six* whose outer pages were missing from those in Horton's bag!

As the monstrous, almost unbelievable fact was borne in upon him, George started back from the table, both hands clutching at the meager hair on his temples. He must be going mad! His mind, usually slow and groping, raced back over the events of the past few days, seizing upon events scarcely considered then but now standing out in awful confirmation.

On Wednesday afternoon at the club Colonel Walker had told of meeting Storm near the Grand Central Station on Wednesday of the previous week around dinner time; the day and hour at which the train Horton took from Poughkeepsie arrived! Storm had tried to deny it, but when Walker added that it was raining as additional proof of the day, Storm hurriedly admitted an errand to his tobacconist's. *Why had he denied it at first?*

Then, too, when George arrived at the club he heard Griffiths commiserating with Storm over having been swindled by Du Chainat, and Storm indignantly denying that, too. He remembered the conversation later at dinner in the grill-room, when he had taxed Storm with concealing his acquaintance with the swindler from him. Storm said that he had not told him of it because he was ashamed to admit that Du Chainat had almost duped him. *Almost?* Had Storm *not* been fleeced, he would not have concealed his acquaintance with the swindler! His egotism would have made him boast of his escape at the moment of the furore over the Du Chainat exposure!

Griffiths had said that Storm was down in the swindler's list for sixty thousand; that would have meant every cent and more than George knew Storm possessed in the world! From whence, if he had indeed lost that, had come the money for this long foreign trip so suddenly decided upon without apparent reason?

George recalled his own theory of Horton's death: that he had met someone he knew well and trusted absolutely, and placing himself utterly in the supposed friend's hands, had been done to death without warning.

It could not have been Norman Storm! Not that old friend of twenty years, sleeping so peacefully upstairs! George tried to thrust the thought from him in an agony of unspeakable horror, but it remained and would not be exorcised.

Suppose by sheer accident or stroke of fate Horton and Storm had met near the station and the latter had taken Horton to his rooms? His rooms, which were so near the place on the Drive where the body was afterward found! Suppose Horton had told of the huge amount in cash that he carried, exhibited it, perhaps, and the sight proved too great a temptation for Storm, already half-crazed with the loss of the last of his fortune?

George could not conceive of the man he had loved as a brother deliberately planning a cold-blooded murder, but every known fact fitted in with this hideous supposition. Storm could not have killed Horton in his own rooms and conveyed the body to the place where it was found, but if he could have induced Horton to accompany him there on some pretext—

Then the testimony of the policeman whom he himself had met and questioned on Wednesday evening recurred to George's mind, and he commenced to pace the floor in short, nervous steps as though to get away from the fearful thought that hounded him.

The policeman's description of the heavier set of the two pedestrians whom he had passed on the night of the murder might have fitted Horton—according to the newspaper report on the body—or any of a million other men, perhaps. But his account of the taller man—! George picked up his notebook from the floor where it had fallen from his paralyzed fingers in the shock of the verification of his discovery and read the description again:—"Tall, thin, with a smooth-shaved face and small hands—I saw that much when he put a match to his cigarette. He was dressed all in dark clothes; black, maybe."

George closed the notebook and put it back slowly into his pocket. Tall, thin, smooth-shaven, in mourning, with the inevitable cigarette! It was Storm to the life! His heart, all the accumulating affection of years cried out against the justice of that verdict. A tall, thin man dressed in dark clothes; were there not thousands in the city? But that methodical, inexorable brain of George's had gone back swiftly to the night after that on which the murder must have taken place, when he and Storm had motored out in Abbott's car up the road for dinner.

They passed twice by the very spot where Horton's body must still have been lying, and on the first occasion—God! how it had all come back I—Storm had leaned forward, staring, then uttered a sharp exclamation and sank back in his seat; George had had to speak to him twice before he answered. *He knew then what lay beyond that wall!*

The visit to the Police Headquarters, the wager with Millard: all that had been sheer bravado. But what horrible manner of man was this whom he had thought he knew so well! With what outward calm he had received Millard's revelations at that dinner on Tuesday night! The fact that the newspapers stuffed in Horton's bag—from which he had thought to remove all clues by taking off these outer sheets with the apartment number on them—had been made special note of must have been a shock to him, and also the news that the bills were marked and a warning had been sent out for them. But perhaps he had already discounted that, perhaps he was depending on the ten thousand in gold to get him out of the country.

But why should he go? His salary at the trust company each year was that amount and half again as much. Unless he were quite mad he would not have dreamed of throwing up such a position and committing murder for a comparatively paltry sum in order to gratify a sudden whim for a few months of travel in the East.

George's heart rebounded in a sudden leap of loyalty, and he sought eagerly for evidence in rebuttal. That desperately tired, harassed man who was his friend; that man whose presence was so near, who even now was sleeping the sleep of utter exhaustion upstairs was not guilty of this fearful thing! Storm would certainly have been mad to commit a crime; but Storm was certainly not mad! He was nervous and worn out and grief-stricken, but he was unquestionably sane. By what ruse could he have gotten Horton's pistol from him? How separated him from the bag in his charge and how and why become possessed of his hat?

These were but trivial details and immaterial to the mass of circumstantial evidence, George realized, and his heart sank once more. Storm could easily have persuaded Horton to leave the bag and pistol there in his own rooms while they went for a short midnight stroll. But what of the hat—?

The policeman's testimony again! He had said that the stocky, heavy-built man wore a cap of some sort! George's eyes traveled shrinkingly to those he had taken from the trunk. No cap had been found near the body. Perhaps—perhaps it was one of these, here in this room!

If events had really occurred as he was mentally evolving them, the bag, together with the hat and pistol, would be all the evidence of the crime except the money itself which remained in Storm's hands; and he could very readily have been the one to check the bag with the other articles inside at the terminal the next morning as the easiest method of disposing of them. But what had he done with the money? Where was it now?

George dropped limply into a chair, his mind struggling with the problem. It did not matter so much at the moment what had become of the money as why Storm had done this fearful thing.

For he must have done it! Here was the evidence of the outer sheets of the newspapers, with the apartment number scrawled upon them to corroborate the police theory as to why they had been removed; and every fact, known and surmised, bore out the hideous truth!

Why had he killed Horton? The obvious reason, of course, was the possession of the money, but although his capital must have been swept away if he had really been duped by the swindler, he had still his comfortable income in a lifelong sinecure. Only desperate men kill, but why was Storm desperate? To get away?

Surely that mere impulse would not have been strong enough to force him to murder! What had he to get away from? Only grief-stricken memories of his dead wife, and other men lived down such sorrow. Grief alone could not drive a man from his assured place in the world to become a wanderer in strange lands, a self-exiled pariah! Nothing but the consciousness of guilt could do that, and the fear of retributive justice; but Storm had been guiltless of anything then. George could well imagine his desire to flee the country after Horton was found with his head crushed in—

So, too, had Leila died! George sprang from his chair with both clenched fists raised above his head. She, too, had been found with her head crushed, as though by the blow of some heavy, blunt instrument!

But, no! No! He was going crazy! Poor Leila had suffered an attack of *petit mal*, she had fallen and struck her head on that rounded brass knob of the fender! *But had she?* Storm had told him that Dr Carr had advanced that theory, but George recalled in a sickening wave of horror that the doctor himself had unconsciously contradicted that statement when he was called hurriedly to attend Storm on the night after the funeral; after the visit of the Brewsters with their confession, when Storm had broken down for the first time.

Carr had said then that it was Storm who suggested the accidental cause of Leila's death, but George had been too worried and upset to note the discrepancy at the time.

It could not be! It was too vile, too impossible! He was letting his mind run away with him! What cause could Storm have had to kill the thing he loved best in all the world? Leila had been a perfect wife, their happiness was unalloyed. Men only did such a fearful thing in a fit of jealous rage or madness, and Leila had been the last woman in the world —

Then the Brewster's visit recurred to him once more, and Leila's little white lie which he himself had called forth. And then, without warning, that almost forgotten scene of the morning on the down-town street, before the entrance to the Leicester Building to which he had been a wholly inadvertent witness flashed before his mental vision as though thrown upon a screen, and the whole truth was revealed.

George cowered back aghast as from the mouth of a yawning abyss, but he could not deny what his inmost soul confirmed.

Storm could not have learned of her birthday surprise for him. His face as George had seen it from across the street had revealed utter stupefaction at seeing his wife issue from the Leicester Building. Then that same evening on the veranda when Leila denied having been in town for weeks and told that palpable falsehood about lunch at the Ferndale Inn: what murderous demon must have entered his breast with the jealous conviction that his wife was deceiving him! George knew his pride, his swift, uncontrollable passion; the thought must have been like a white-hot iron searing his brain!

But who could he have imagined had supplanted him? The answer came even as the question formed itself in his mind. Brewster! Richard Brewster had called on Leila the following night to ask about his own wife's affair. Could Storm have returned early and in secret and found him there? Brewster's office was in the Leicester Building, too; George had called there on him more than once. Why, the thing was as clear as day!

Storm and Leila must have had a fearful scene in the den after Brewster's departure, and the culmination must have come with that swift, awful blow which laid her dead at her husband's feet! But with what weapon had that blow been struck?

George closed his eyes, shuddering, and visualized the room which was as familiar to him as his own. It contained nothing which could have been put effectively to such a foul use. Even the poker had been removed from the fireplace when it had been banked with ferns for the spring.

Horton might have been killed—and probably was—by the blow from a heavy cane, but there was none in the den

The golf sticks! They had been lying there across the den table where he had found them tonight. Storm's oath when George had brought them here to the library a few hours ago, his gesture of horror and repulsion, his cry to take them out of his sight, that he should never play again—how comprehensible it all was now!

All but overcome with the horror of the thought, George went silently out into the hall, gathered up the sticks and returned to the library. As he did so a bestial, raucous snore drifted down from above, and for a minute the very soul of him shook with the longing to rush up the stairs and destroy with his bare hands the vile thing which lay there. The years of friendship were gone wholly now, blotted by his hideous knowledge of the truth. The Norman Storm whom he had known had vanished; indeed, had never existed. In his stead this dissembling creature with a murderer's black heart had walked among men, free until this hour!

Trembling, George laid the sticks one by one across the couch and examined them. No mid-iron could have struck that blow; it would have crashed through the temple and left a frightful, gaping, ragged wound. It must have been something round and smooth, not unlike the brass knob on the fender, since the doctor and coroner had both been easily deceived. Not the putter nor the brassie nor the cleek,—the driver! George picked it up and carried it close to one of the candles. Could it be that he really saw a faint tinge of brown upon its hardwood knob?

He laid it aside with a sigh and started once more his restless pacing up and down, as his thoughts returned to the events immediately following Leila's death, from the moment when he himself had been summoned to the house.

No wonder Storm had collapsed in the presence of Richard and Julie Brewster. They had all unconsciously revealed to him his wife's innocence of the sin for which he had taken her life. It had been not grief alone, but remorse which struck him down! What credulous fools they had all been not to have seen the truth!

A confirming memory came to him of Storm's manner when he awakened from his drugged sleep on the following morning. How anxious he had been to know what he had said during his unconsciousness! That was an effort to learn if he had betrayed himself. How they had all played into his hands!

No wonder, too, that later, after George had returned to town, when he telephoned to Storm that Potter's rooms were to be vacant, he had required little urging to escape from the scene of his unspeakable crime! No wonder that he had said it was "hell" at Greenlea!

The consciousness of the undeserved fate which he had *visited upon the woman who at the altar had placed her life in his keeping must have driven him all but mad!

And yet how quickly his conscience, if he had ever possessed one, had died in the quick fire of his egotism at the ease with which he had evaded justice! George recalled his wild talk about crime; how a man could do anything and get away with it if he only had brains enough. His remorse had been swallowed up by his malevolent, distorted pride of achievement.

How easy it was now to trace the subsequent steps! The constantly reiterated condolences of his acquaintances on every hand must have driven him to frenzy; and then had come the chance of miraculous wealth through Du Chainat, for Griffiths must have been right. A lawyer of his brains and reputation would not have referred to it unless he had seen the virtual proof, and George remembered the skepticism with which he had received Storm's hasty denial.

Storm had staked his all on the chance, and lost! Then, hounded by guilty memories and desperate, he had encountered Horton, and the rest was explained.

But the money! Where could it be? Having risked so much for it, he would scarcely be likely to leave it out of his immediate possession, and a bag full of money—

The valise upstairs! The obviously heavy valise which he would not permit George to touch, which no one else must carry but himself!—Leila's letters? George's lip curled in bitter self-scorn. How credulous he had been!

Storm must have intended to secrete the money here about the house somewhere until their return from the fishing trip and then make his getaway. But why had he so suddenly changed his mind and evinced willingness to go on the trip at all? Was it to get out of sight and still keep in touch with the progress of the investigation until it had ceased through lack of further evidence to engage the activities of the police?

Or was it to get George himself away? Storm knew his theory; George cursed himself for his stupidity, his blindness! He had descanted at length upon his idea of the murder, and Storm, realizing how dangerously near the truth it was, may have planned to keep him out of mischief until the case was dropped.

But was that all he had planned? George stood still, stunned with the thought which came to him. Storm had killed two people and gotten away with it; why not a third? Why not George himself, if he suspected that George was likely to come upon the truth? The red trilogy!

That selection of a deserted lodge hidden miles away in the heart of the wilderness far from the beaten paths for their headquarters during the fishing trip; the determination to be absolutely alone with George, without even the services of a guide; the insistence upon taking the pistol along—!

George eyed the thing with horror and loathing as it lay in the top of the open bag. Then he walked grimly over to it, and picking it up together with the box of cartridges he took it to the table and loaded it with awkward, unaccustomed hands.

There was no doubt in his mind as to the course he must pursue; there had been no question of it, from the first moment when conviction came to him that Storm had killed Horton. Now, at the thought of Leila, a passionate regret that his part was not to be a more active one filled his soul, but it brought no hesitation.

Laying the pistol down he crossed to the door, and as he closed it softly that harsh, stertorous snore came down the stairs once more, and again that primitive instinct to destroy laid hold upon George; but he shook it off resolutely and returned to the desk. Yet with his hand upon the receiver of the telephone he paused.

Dare he speak? That man lying there upstairs in brutish unconsciousness was surely the vilest thing that lived! Yet dare he speak and throw out into the world the knowledge of this fearful thing?

Slowly, determinedly, George lifted the receiver.

XXVIII

JUST A MOMENT PLEASE

George slipped into the bedroom, and drawing a chair close to the sleeper he bent forward and uttered one word which cleaved the silence like a clarion call.

"Leila!"

"Ah-h!" The answering cry of stark terror echoed back from the night as Storm started up, convulsed, in his bed. "Take her away! Take her—George! My God, don't look at me like that!"

He cowered, trying to cover his face with his shaking hands, but the other's eyes held him.

"You killed her with—this!" George suddenly produced the driver, and Storm shrank away in horror.

"No, no! For God's sake, George!"

"You killed Jack Horton!" The inexorable voice went on. "His money is here in this valise at my feet. You would have killed me, too, up there in the woods, but I beat you to it!"

Great beads of sweat glistened upon Storm's brow and rolled like tears down his gray, pinched face as he made a terrified, ineffectual attempt to deny; but the other cut him short.

"I've got you, you can't get away, and they're coming for you, do you understand? They're on their way!—Sure, smoke if you want to!"

The hunted eyes had turned instinctively toward the cigarettes on the stand, and Storm lighted one feebly. Its tip glowed crimson, then dulled as the surface became filmed with ashes.

George smiled grimly as a swift memory came to him.

"You owe Millard fifty dollars!"

A dull, sodden look came over Storm's face, and his body slumped as though slowly disintegrating before the other's eyes. As he fell back the scream of an approaching siren cut the stillness, and the ashes from the cigarette fell in a soft, crumbling mass upon his breast.

THE END

Assembling the greatest detectives all together

Covering the full range and history of detective fiction.
From Zadig, *The Moonstone*, and Dupin through Sherlock Holmes, Loveday Brooke, Montague Egg, Lord Peter Wimsey, *The Thinking Machine*, Father Brown down to Solar Pons.

For more details and a full list of titles:
visit https://www.hachetteindia.com/home/yellowbacks

WELCOME BACK TO THE GOLDEN AGE